ASIF

Diamond Books by Jodi Thomas

NORTHERN STAR
THE TENDER TEXAN
PRAIRIE SONG
CHERISH THE DREAM
THE TEXAN AND THE LADY

THE TEXAN AND THE LADY

JODI THOMAS

DIAMOND BOOKS, NEW YORK

This book is a Diamond original edition,
and has never been previously published.

THE TEXAN AND THE LADY

A Diamond Book / published by arrangement with the author

PRINTING HISTORY
Diamond edition/January 1994

ISBN: 1-55773-970-6

Diamond Books are published by The Berkley Publishing
Group, 200 Madison Avenue, New York, NY 10016.
DIAMOND and the "D" design
are trademarks belonging to Charter Communications, Inc.

PRINTED IN THE UNITED STATES OF AMERICA

10 9 8 7 6 5 4 3 2 1

To my sister
Dean Price Paxton
who, after college and a career,
found her adventure in raising a houseful of boys

Chapter
One

Iowa, 1880

Jennie Munday straightened the pleats on her service-able navy blue dress. Without looking in the mirror, she covered her ebony hair with her old felt hat and lowered the thin veil over her face. "I'm leaving," she whispered to the orderly little room. "I'm going to find out if there's more beyond this town than the edge of the trees. I'm going to discover if there's anything more for me than being an old maid."

Lifting a tattered carpetbag in one hand, she picked up a train ticket with the other and took one last look at the room that had been hers all her life. "If I stay here, all I'll ever be is poor Jennie, oldest daughter of Reverend Munday. Poor Jennie who never had a fellow. Poor Jennie who never had her own life. I want to see the West and meet the men who are taming it."

For twenty of her twenty-eight years she'd taken care

of her younger brothers and sisters during her mother's "weak spells." Now the others were all grown and married. Only she remained at home because everyone thought it proper that she should.

"I may get lost out west, but I'm going," she whispered as loud as she dared. With one final consideration, she removed from her bag the Bible her father insisted she read each night and switched it for a stack of dime novels she kept hidden under her bed. "I want to find a hero worth loving."

Jennie stepped into the hall and tiptoed past her parents' room to the kitchen. Collecting the small lunch she'd packed for the trip, she hurried onto the back porch. Icy rain drizzled in the darkness, collecting in large enough drops to make noise tumbling off the roof. First light wouldn't be for hours, and by then she'd be moving west. Come morning, no one in Iowa would have any idea where Jennie Munday had gone.

She reached for an old barn lantern with her free hand. All she had to do was turn at the red ribbon tied to a fence post down the road and she'd find her way to the depot.

Half an hour later she set the lantern down on the edge of the platform without bothering to blow out the light. As she moved toward the train, the tiny flicker of fire seemed to wave good-bye.

Maybe someone would find the lantern and think she'd walked off somewhere near the train station and lost her way. After all, they'd remind themselves, poor Jennie can't tell her right from her left, much less directions. They'd never guess she'd taken a train. Not Jennie. She'd never been more than a few miles from her home.

"All aboard!"

Jennie looked around, wondering who else the conductor was yelling at, as she was the only person standing on the platform. She'd purchased a ticket to Kansas City without giving her name and doubted the night agent knew her on sight. By dawn she'd have changed trains and be traveling on a Harvey Employee train pass. No one would be able to trace her progress.

Climbing the metal steps, Jennie forced herself not to look back at the shadows of a town that had always been her home but had never welcomed her. She moved through the passenger car noticing only a few people who, like herself, were too poor to afford anything but a third-class ticket and who would spend the night sitting up.

A few men in mercantile suits were playing cards near the front of the car, seemingly reluctant to allow anyone to catch them asleep. A woman in a wine-red coat was curled up alone on the last bench with her face tucked low into her collar. Several couples cuddled together trying to keep warm and comfortable in each other's arms.

Jennie took an empty bench and forced her heart to stop pounding. She'd made it this far; now all she needed was some sleep before she had to switch trains in Kansas City.

But sleep was as elusive as a comfortable sitting position on the bench. She couldn't ignore the laughter from the card game in the back or the steady snores of those few who managed to doze.

When she disembarked in Kansas City, every muscle ached, but there was no time to complain or anyone to hear. She checked her watch and hurried to the platform where a train was already loading for Florence.

A man in railroad blue was sitting behind a portable table at the top of the platform steps. "Harvey employees to the left, all others to the right."

Jennie hesitated a moment then moved toward the line containing almost all young ladies. When she passed the desk she said, "I'm an employee." Jennie fished in her bag for the letter she'd been mailed instructing her to report January 3, 1880.

The man handed her a ticket stamped "Employee" across the top. "Wait with the others, miss." He glanced up and raised one eyebrow as though doubting her honesty, then shrugged as if reminding himself he wasn't paid to think.

Jennie smiled down at the ticket. Freedom felt wonderful in her hand. Moving out of the way, she noticed that the woman who'd been alone on the train from Iowa was now in the employee line as well. Her face was still deep into the collar of her wine-red coat.

Jennie looked over the heads of the other women on the platform. Not only was she taller than most of them, she was also older. They chatted excitedly amid the train's smoke while she silently watched, counting the minutes until she could head farther west.

"Harvey employees!" a middle-aged conductor yelled. "Have your tickets ready."

The crowd of people pushed forward as the conductor continued, "Welcome to the Atchison, Topeka, and Santa Fe." He tipped his hat to the ladies. "I thought the Harvey girls in Topeka were the prettiest I'd ever seen, but you ladies rival them. Mr. Harvey's going to single-handedly settle the West, if he keeps shipping such fine womenfolk into the frontier."

The other girls giggled and chattered in a nonstop fashion, but Jennie remained quiet. She'd answered the ad to go west, not to stand on a platform and be flirted with by a middle-aged conductor. Fred Harvey might consider himself a self-appointed civilizer, but Jennie wanted to see the land before civilization succeeded.

Skirts rustled as everyone moved toward the doors of the train. One by one they climbed the metal steps. Jennie waited her turn, her mind whispering, *I'm never going back home. I'll starve or let the Indians get me before I run back to a life crammed full of nothingness.*

She moved with the flow of bodies onto the train and down the narrow aisle until she found an unoccupied bench. People talked and shouted all around her, but she looked no one in the eyes. There would be time to meet the other employees later; now was her first day of freedom. A gulf of silence must divide her two lives so her past couldn't accidentally spill into her future.

Looking out the window, Jennie smiled. She might not be the youngest or the prettiest woman ever hired to be a Harvey girl, but she'd be the best. She'd heard Mr. Harvey expected his waitresses to be spotless in dress and very proper. Well, if she'd been nothing else in her life Jennie Munday, oldest daughter of Reverend Matthias Munday, had been spotless and proper.

Men began moving boxes into the aisle as the conductor shouted, "Sorry for the inconvenience, folks, but we don't trust this china in the baggage car!" The conductor grinned as though he were the only one on the train who understood what fine china Fred Harvey always used in his restaurants. "Get your tickets ready. I'll be back to check them as soon as we're on our way."

Jennie's head jerked backward against the seat as the train moved forward. Buildings from a city she'd never seen before slipped past her window like raindrops sliding sideways on the cold glass. She'd done it! She'd broken away.

Forcing her fingers to relax around the handle of her bag, Jennie lowered it toward the space under her seat. She shoved hard, yet the bag wouldn't slide beneath her feet. She tried again, forcing action into tired muscles, then leaned over and looked under the bench.

There, curled into a ball of rags, huddled a tiny person looking back at her. Huge blue eyes sparkled with tears inside the dirtiest face Jennie had ever seen. The child shoved hair the color of dried mud away from a tear-streaked face and looked directly at her.

"Please," a tiny voice begged. "Don't tell 'em I'm here."

Jennie bolted upright. She looked around, thinking half the car must be watching, but no one seemed even slightly interested in her or her discovery. They were all talking among themselves. She didn't hesitate in her decision. Extending a Christian hand outweighed any knowledge that she would be cheating the railroad out of a fare. Jennie had never followed her father's belief that a sin was a sin. "Lord," she prayed beneath her breath as she had a hundred other times, "I'll explain my actions when I get to Heaven."

She set her bag down in the seat beside her and moved her skirts to completely cover the child at her feet. Apparently she wasn't the only one running away, and from the looks of the stowaway, the boy could be no worse off where he was going than where he'd been.

The train picked up speed, and everyone around her settled into small groups. Everyone except Jennie. She'd never been much of a joiner. Her family had made sure there'd never been enough time for parties or teas for their Jennie. After all, someone needed to stay home.

Jennie closed her eyes, thinking that when she got to Florence, Kansas, she'd probably be too busy to talk.

Harvey girls were expected to work ten-hour days, six or seven days a week. But the work didn't frighten her. She'd worked hard all her life, and the loneliness of being out in some little train station in the middle of nowhere seemed almost exciting after the life she'd led.

By now her parents would be awake wondering where their breakfast was. At least one of her sisters would have stopped by to leave her children, while she did some shopping or had tea. It was always so handy to leave them with Jennie. She never seemed to mind, even if the house was already full with other nieces and nephews.

A smile brushed Jennie's lips. Well, today, she minded. Today, she wouldn't be there. *Today,* she'd live a tiny part of the adventures she'd always read about in her hidden novels.

"Pardon me, ma'am?" A low voice shattered Jennie's thoughts. "Mind if I take this seat?"

Glancing up, she stared at one of the tallest men she'd ever seen. His sandy hair almost brushed the top of the car as he removed a wide-brimmed hat and regarded her with tired eyes that seemed banked in anger.

Jennie looked around, hoping there'd be another seat where she could direct him, but every bench was already occupied. Without smiling, she lifted her bag and set it in her lap. "Of course, you may."

The stranger raised his rifle to the rack above their heads and adjusted a long Colt pistol strapped to his leg so he could fold into the seat. His knees bumped the bench in front of them, and Jennie realized this man would probably be far more comfortable on a horse than in this train.

"You with this herd of Harvey folks?"

"Yes." Jennie tried to guess what type of man felt the need to travel so well armed. Though clean, his clothes were not quite the cut of a gentleman's. "I'm going to be a Harvey girl."

Surprise arched his eyebrows, and she felt her muscles tighten in response. Jennie could do nothing about her plain features, and though near the top, she was within the age range the ad had requested, so he might as well stop looking so surprised.

Suddenly, she wanted to test her new wings and strike back. "Are you hoping for employment? I understand there are still a few dishwasher jobs open."

A smile touched his full lips but wasn't mirrored in his tired eyes. "No." He moved slightly, trying to make more leg room in front of him. "I'm just passing through to Texas. Left my horse in Florence. Soon as I get back to God's country, I don't ever plan on leaving the state again."

He pulled a thin cheroot from his pocket and rolled it slowly between his long fingers. "That is, if I still have a job when I get back."

Jennie didn't really want to talk to him. He made her nervous, sitting so close they almost touched. She couldn't remember ever being this near a man who wasn't kin to her. "You're a cow man?" Her words came out a bit too loud in an effort to prove she wasn't nervous. She'd read in her books about the romantic cattle drives from Texas to Dodge City, Kansas.

"No." He paid more attention to his match than he did her statement. "I'm a federal marshal. Or at least I am until those damn Yankees in Washington make up their minds to fire me."

"Did you do something wrong?"

He struck the match. "Just wasted too much lead,

that's all." He touched the light to his cigar. "Problem was they kept having to dig it out of outlaws."

As smoke filled the air between them, Jennie had trouble making sense of what he said. He couldn't be a hero marshal like the ones she'd read about. He wasn't dashing enough. A real hero's clothes wouldn't need pressing, and his boots would be polished, not scuffed. As far as she could tell, the only thing polished about the man beside her was his worn Colt. And judging from what he said, the guns had been used too often to collect dust. "I really wish you wouldn't smoke," she whispered without being aware she spoke the words aloud.

He studied her through the haze for a long minute before slowly lowering the cigar to the floor and crushing it with his boot. "Certainly, ma'am."

"It's *miss*. Miss Jennie Munday," Jennie answered, raising her chin slightly. "And thank you. I realize this is going to be a long journey, but I think you'd be wise to smoke on the platform between the cars and not in this crowded compartment."

She turned slightly to see if her lecture had made him aware he was in the presence of a lady and not the type of woman he was probably accustomed to in Texas. But, to her amazement, his eyes had closed in sleep.

Jennie fought the urge to elbow him hard. How dare he sleep when she was in the middle of setting him in his place? To add to her insult, he folded his arms over his chest and slumped farther into the seat.

She sat up straighter, afraid if she moved even an inch she'd touch this rude stranger. She tried to appreciate the country passing by, or consider the child hiding beneath her, but all she could think about was the man's slow rhythmic breathing. When he awakened, she'd give him another lecture about politeness.

"Ticket, miss."

Jennie jumped at the conductor's words, then quickly handed the man her employee pass. "Aren't you going to wake him?" She pointed a slender finger at the sleeping man at her side.

"No, miss." The conductor shook his head. "That's Austin McCormick. I wouldn't want to startle him. Value my life more than that. I'll check his ticket later, when it's safer."

Jennie tried not to look disappointed that the inconsiderate man wouldn't be disturbed. But now at least she knew the marshal's name. *Austin McCormick.* He might frighten the conductor, but no one would ever bully her into a corner again.

Trying to relax, she let the morning slide by with the countryside. By noon, her body ached from holding herself upright and trying not to accidentally brush Mr. McCormick. When the train finally pulled to a stop, he moved, coming awake like a wild animal, all at once and with every muscle alert.

"Twenty-minute stop!" someone yelled from the back of the train. "Food shack to your right, saloon to your left."

Everyone hurried to disembark. The marshal stood and stretched long powerful muscles. He glanced at her as she pulled her lunch from her bag. "If I were you, lady, I'd stretch my legs while I had the chance."

"I'm perfectly comfortable," Jennie lied. She hadn't forgotten the child beneath her seat and had no intention of leaving and taking the chance that someone else might discover the stowaway.

The marshal crammed his hat low over his forehead and nodded. "Suit yourself."

Jennie watched him disappear before holding half her

sandwich beneath the seat. "Would you like some?" she whispered.

A thin, dirty hand hesitantly reached forward and took the sandwich.

Jennie put the lunch bag at her feet and looked around to make sure the car was empty. Only the tiny woman in the wine-red coat remained. The dark wool almost covered her nearly colorless hair and face. She looked sound asleep on the last bench. Jennie could see a few people from her window picnicking beneath leafless trees several yards away. The cool fresh air looked inviting, but she couldn't leave the child alone.

She looked in both directions then leaned down until she could see the child's face. "What's your name?"

"My momma called me True," the stowaway mumbled between mouthfuls.

"And your father? What did he call you?"

"Never had no father. Momma died last year. Ain't never had no name but True."

The muscles around Jennie's heart tightened. "True is a nice name." She offered the child the other half of her sandwich. "In fact, I think it may be about the best name I've ever heard."

The child became silent for several minutes then finally whispered back, "Why didn't you turn me in, lady? All you'd've had to do was tell the conductor."

The question was so honest it had to be answered directly. "Maybe because I'm running also." Jennie looked out the window at all the people talking and laughing. All the world seemed to come in groups, except her. Somehow she'd been left out. If life were a dance, she not only didn't have a partner, she hadn't even been invited. "Maybe," Jennie whispered more to herself than to the boy, "I, too, have no place to go except away."

A thin hand reached from beneath the seat and touched Jennie's gloved fingers. "Thanks," True whispered before pulling back into safety. "I owe you, lady."

Jennie stared at the dirt on her always spotless glove. For once, the stain didn't matter. The child had touched her as no one else ever had. She hadn't been just convenient to lean on; she'd been genuinely needed.

"True," Jennie whispered. "You can trust me."

Jennie thought she heard a sniffle from beneath the seat and tried not to think of how the child was probably wiping a dirty nose with an even dirtier sleeve cuff.

"I have to, lady," the child answered. "You're all I got right about now."

Chapter Two

*M*ind if I sit with you for the next leg of this trip?"
A woman's voice forced Delta Criswell to raise her
head from the warm wool. She pulled her wine-colored
coat close around her aching shoulder as the woman
continued, "I was sitting up front before we stopped
for lunch, but I thought it might be a little less smoky
toward the back."

Delta forced the pain from her mind and tried to bring
the woman before her into focus. She was tall, six feet
or more, and her long, rust-colored braid of hair was as
thick as a man's forearm. The word pretty would never
be joined to her name, but she had a beauty about her
that was ageless.

"I guess you're like all of us in this car. You're
heading to Florence to work at the Harvey House."

The woman moved into the seat beside Delta, seeming
to pay little notice to Delta's silence.

"I'm Audrey Gates from Flatwater, Missouri. Had to travel all night to hook up with this train."

The stranger paused as if waiting for Delta to comment, then continued, "Flatwater's not much of a town really. Just a little place along the river. In fact, from time to time most of the place is under the Big Muddy rather than next to it."

As Delta looked puzzled, Audrey laughed. "I guess no one outside of Flatwater has laughed at that in years."

When Delta didn't make a sound, Audrey changed the subject without taking any offense. "I noticed you didn't get off the train at the stop. Can't say I blame you. I heard the men say all they had in the saloon was rifle whiskey."

Tilting her head, Delta looked questioningly at the woman.

Audrey giggled. "Haven't you ever heard of rifle whiskey? They say the bartender has to take a man's guns away from him before serving a round, or a fellow's likely to shoot himself when the whiskey hits his throat."

Delta managed a smile as Audrey continued, "Course, we won't have anything like that where we're going. I'm so excited about this job, my nerves are full of fleas. Part of me wants to jump right out and run to Florence, but I've been on one train or another for so long I'm not sure my legs would work." She glanced out the window. "You know, I think I could probably make better time than this train. Once we're moving, it's fine, but seems like we don't finish gathering speed from the last stop before we start slowing for the next one."

Attempting to keep her eyes open, Delta smiled wanly at Audrey. Delta had spent all night and most of this morning huddled in the last seat trying to keep warm and awake enough to watch in case anyone passed through the car looking for her.

"I guess I'm like everyone else." The woman straightened her red braid as though it had only one proper place on her shoulder. "I want to go out west somewhere and find a handsome man to marry. Well, hell! I don't care if he's all that easy on the eyes as long as he's big enough to lift me off the ground when he hugs me. The only eligible men in my hometown were the town drunk and my four brothers, so it was either answer the Harvey ad for a pastry cook or mark 'old maid' by my name in the church record."

The woman's constant chatter caused the pain in Delta's head almost to rival the pain from the knife wound in her shoulder. Delta cuddled against the cool window.

"Not that I haven't tried other occupations." Audrey folded her arms. "My parents are firm believers that a young lady should test her wings. I tried being a schoolmarm for a year before I figured out I hated kids, then I went to nursing school. Nursing wasn't bad except for the blood. I did get tired of that after a spell. Dear Lord, you wouldn't believe how much folks tend to bleed! I can still smell it now."

Audrey smiled at Delta. "Course, I didn't tell the Harvey people I'd been a teacher. I heard they don't like to hire teachers. Too set in their ways most of them."

Finally, Delta could hear the woman no more. She leaned against the window and welcomed the quiet river of unconsciousness that flowed over her as Audrey's voice faded.

The river ran swift with memories in Delta's mind. All the sadness and loneliness washed across the years of her life in dark waves. Delta couldn't remember ever

feeling like a child. Even her first recollections were of
trying to take care of her mother. There never seemed
to be enough food for the table or wood for the fire, but
somehow Mildred Criswell had always found the pen-
nies needed for the dark bottles she called her medicine.
Delta's visions of her father were always gray and fuzzy.
He was no more than a tired, broken man who shuffled in
after working in the mines, his back permanently bent,
his face always stained with coal dust. They'd finally
moved back to her mother's parents' farm, hoping to
stop his cough, but the cough continued, as did the
poverty.

"Wake up, miss." A voice floated over the river of
dreams to Delta's mind. "I can't hold you much longer.
Please, wake up."

Delta opened her eyes and saw the redheaded woman's face only inches from her own.

"You need a doctor, honey," Audrey whispered.
"There's blood all over your coat sleeve."

"No!" Delta didn't want to draw any attention to
herself. "I'll be fine. I have some more bandages in
my bag. I only need to wrap it again. Please don't alert
the conductor. He might put me off the train."

Audrey studied her closely for a long moment, then
whispered, "Can you walk?"

Delta nodded slowly, mistrusting any quick offer of
help. There was goodness in the woman's eyes, but Delta
had seen goodness turn cold more than once.

"Well, let's go freshen up." Audrey stood and pulled
her up with little more effort than a child would use to
carry a doll at her side. "If it's just bandaging, I can do
that with flying colors. Now, if you had locked bowels or
some such, we'd be in a heap of trouble 'cause I skipped
that lecture in school. Figured it'd be something I'd face

if the time ever come. Some things it don't do any good worrying about in advance."

Before Delta could argue, they were moving down the aisle and out the door. Audrey was stronger than Delta figured any two men would probably be. By the time they reached their destination, she was leaning on the redhead heavily.

While the self-appointed angel of mercy helped Delta off with her coat and set to work, she never stopped talking. She washed the wound and commented, "The cut's not deep, but we probably need to have it seen about when we stop. A slip of a girl like yourself don't have any extra blood to lose."

Delta looked into honest brown eyes. "I'd rather no one knew about this, Audrey." She decided to try honesty herself. "You see, there's someone following me, and if we reported a wound, he might find me."

Audrey put her fists on her hips. "You're not wanted for a crime, are you? If you are, I heard a man near the front say he was a federal marshal."

"No." Delta smiled, thinking if her stepfather or his son ever crossed her gunsights, she would be. "There is no need to bother the marshal."

"Then I'll say nothing. And don't you worry, honey. When we get to the Harvey House, you'll be safe as a babe in her mother's arms. I'll keep an eye out for trouble, and there ain't many men who can get past me."

"Thanks." Delta offered her hand. "I'm Delta . . . ah . . . Smith, from nowhere in particular."

Audrey shook her hand. "Glad to meet you, Delta . . . ah . . . Smith. But you can't be from nowhere. That makes folks too inquisitive. I tell you what, you can be from Flatwater, Missouri, too. Now that I think of it, you grew up not a mile down the road from me. By the time we get to Florence, Kansas, I'll tell you everything that's happened in Flatwater for twenty years. Living there might not have been so wonderful, but it's a nice place to be from."

Delta cradled her arm and agreed. Somehow the nightmares of her life didn't flow as close to her mind with Audrey by her side. She'd never been offered friendship so readily, but something about the woman was so solid and good. Delta felt as if she'd finally met the very friend she'd been looking for all her life.

As the two women stepped onto the platform between the cars, gunfire suddenly shattered the rhythmic rattle of the train. Men on horseback galloped alongside the track shouting and shooting in the air.

Audrey shoved Delta inside and pushed her low in their seat. "Hell's bells and buttermilk!" she shouted. "We're goin' to be robbed!"

Then, for the first time since Delta had met her, Audrey Gates had nothing else to say.

Chapter Three

The clatter of the train's wheels blended with the low rumble of horses' hooves, rivaling the iron machine's speed. Women screamed and ducked for cover while the few men on the train scrambled for the best defensive positions from which to fire. The whistle blew a long cry and was answered by gunfire.

Men on horseback galloped close to the windows, waving rifles as Jennie had always imagined a war party of Indians would brandish their spears just before the kill. She'd been told to stay down, but fascination ran with fear through her veins. Never in her life had she seen such excitement.

"Fire back at them!" she shouted at the marshal who shared her bench seat.

Austin McCormick leaned against her shoulder for a closer look at the riders, showing little more interest than a bachelor who looks at a baby.

Jennie shoved him away, prodding him with her finger,

tapping hard against his chest. "Do something! They're
trying to stop the train."

Though Austin still appeared only mildly interested
in the men outside the window, the woman beside him
had finally drawn his full attention. "How about I break
your finger if you poke it in my ribs again, lady?"

If looks could have killed, Jennie Munday would have
had the marshal staked and burned in a blink of her green
eyes. She hadn't left home to be shot by robbers her
first day out. "I'm not standing by and letting innocent
people be attacked. Give me that gun! I'll do something
myself." She grabbed for the Colt at his side. "Those
things couldn't be very hard to operate if you can handle one."

Suddenly, Austin came alive. Before her fingers closed
around the handle of his gun, he'd jerked her arms and
twirled her in the seat until her back was flat against
his chest. "Never lay hands on a man's sidearm!" he
whispered with deadly calm. "Call it a matter of pride,
but a man's gun is his alone."

Jennie struggled, thinking she'd like to wound more
than the man's pride. Between clenched teeth she
answered, "Then do something or we'll all be killed."

The marshal didn't ease his hold on her. His grip was
so tight, she could feel his heart pounding between her
shoulder blades, and the slow rise and fall of his chest
moved her a fraction with each breath. Suddenly, fear
won the race in Jennie's mind. A fear that had nothing
to do with train robbers. A fear unlike any she'd ever
known in her quiet, calm, dull life in Iowa. She realized
this man would be deadly to cross and probably just as
dangerous to care for. Yet a tiny part of her longed for
the warmth of a man's body against her in a caress and
not in anger.

The marshal shifted slightly so that his words came close to her ear. "If you'll take a minute to notice, Miss Munday, you'll see they're firing in the air. My guess is the worst we've got here is a robbery by a handful of greenhorns, and with any luck no one will get killed." He paused and slowed his words even more, as if she were a child who needed time to digest each sentence. "If they were trying to kill us, they'd be shooting at the train not at the clouds; and, as crowded as this car is, someone would already be dead."

Jennie felt his words warm the side of her face. His breath brushed lightly against the lace of her high collar. The faint smell of cigars and leather blended with the hint of whiskey, reminding her of how totally different this man was from any she'd ever met.

"I'll not stand by and be robbed." She tried to pull an inch away, but his grip was iron. "I'll not let them have my life, or even my bag without a fight. It's all I have to my name." She tried to hold herself stiff, but she could feel his warmth against her back. Her heart pounded louder than the thunder of horses outside, and for the first time in her life she felt she had touched adventure. She could feel it, see it, smell it in the air. Adventure all wrapped up in fear and noise and panic around her . . . and in the man beside her. Adventure better than any dime novel could ever have painted.

Austin chuckled suddenly. "I doubt there's much of interest in your bag to a train robber. More likely, they'll take only jewelry and money. Maybe a payroll riding in the mail car."

He relaxed his grip on her arms and slid strong fingers along her sleeves to rest at her waist. "If I let you go, will you promise not to try and shoot anyone?"

"Excluding you?"

Austin laughed again. "Tell you what. If I promise not to let anyone bother your bag, or the child you keep hidden beneath your skirts, will you promise not to shoot me? Then we both might get through this robbery alive."

Fire danced up her neck and onto her cheeks. A million words came to her mind, but none seemed to form in her throat. She nodded and twisted in his arms until she could see his eyes. Something dark and bottomless flickered in his stare, a flash of summer gold inside the brown depths. Perhaps a look of passion sparkled there, as she'd seen only when men looked at other women. She was too much a novice at the games men and women played to read the look.

"How did you know about the child?"

"I'm a man who makes a habit of knowing what's around me. The kid's been wiggling for an hour."

"You won't tell anyone?" The train was braking to a stop, but Jennie couldn't take her gaze off the man only a breath away. Her need to protect True suddenly outweighed the threat of robbery. The marshal was right—except for her novels, she had nothing of value in her bag. But the child, that was another matter.

Austin didn't answer, but only held her to him as though his arms could stop any harm from reaching her. In the glint of his eyes, she saw it then, the last glimpse of a knight long ago buried by life's hardness. The armor might be tarnished from battles fought, but the metal was still solid and pure.

"I won't tell anyone." His words were low, rusty from the few times he'd used total honesty in his speech. "Your child is safe."

All the dreams lonely little Jennie had ever dreamed came true. She looked into the eyes of a real hero, and for a moment, she believed what she heard.

Then she remembered that dreams are never real and heroes exist only in the pages of the books. His words were somehow a trick, a deception to lure her into a belief in him that might not hold true. Well, Jennie Munday wasn't some moonstruck schoolgirl! She was a woman long past marrying age and long past falling for a washed-out marshal's tricks.

She straightened, pushing him away with her thoughts more than with her body. "I'm sure the child will appreciate your silence."

Austin's eyes narrowed to slits. "And you?"

Jennie raised her chin. "The child isn't mine but . . ."

"Don't bother to lie." His words were steel as he turned toward the gunmen outside. He hadn't even noticed they'd stopped, but now his trained gaze took in the number of robbers and every detail about them.

"I've never lied in my life, Marshal McCormick." She could feel the muscles along her spine tighten. How dare he think the child beneath the seat was hers! How dare he call her a liar!

"I noticed how open and forward you were with introductions when I sat down." The spinster beside him drew Austin's attention as though the robbers were no more than flies compared to the tiger by his side.

"The child was there when I took the seat."

"I wasn't born yesterday, lady. You've been guarding that youngun like a mother hen this whole trip."

"I'm surprise you noticed, Marshal. You were so busy sleeping and drinking your lunch. I've had to sit next to a snoring drunk, and you dare mention a harmless child wiggling beneath the seat."

Both ignored the noise outside as armed men filed into the car, frightening the other passengers into silence.

Few things bothered Austin more than parents who

didn't take care of their children. Memories mingled with anger as he raised his voice. "It's not any of my concern, but the little one couldn't be too comfortable down there huddling on the cold floor."

Jennie wasn't about to apologize for something she had no control over. In fact, she had been concerned about the child's comfort as well, but knew she didn't have enough money to buy another ticket. She stood and yelled, "I'm telling you, the child is not mine!"

He unfolded from the seat and looked down at her. "And I'm telling you, you're about as sorry an excuse for a mother as I've run across . . ."

The leader of the gang of robbers jabbed the butt of his rifle hard into Austin's side. But as the masked man cleared his throat to order the loud couple back into their seats, Austin swung around and slammed his forearm into the bothersome intruder's face.

In one bone-shattering second, all hell broke loose. The man who'd interrupted Austin and Jennie's argument fell backward into a cluster of women huddled together in fright. His rifle fired wildly, shattering the windows above Jennie's head. He dropped the weapon and grabbed his nose, jerking the bandanna mask from his face to try and stop the gush of blood.

Austin completely ignored the man he'd harmed. He grabbed Jennie and dropped to the floor between the seats. In less time than it took her to blink, the marshal pulled his Colt and fired at another masked robber blocking the car's entrance. The gun dropped from the robber's hand as he fell backward out of the car, his shoulder splattered in crimson.

Suddenly everyone in the compartment seemed to move at once. A redheaded woman in the last bench rose like a warring Amazon and attacked the unlucky bandit left guarding the back exit. She grabbed a hatbox from the rack and swung it at him. He fought her off as he tried to raise his gun and aim.

But the tiny woman Jennie had noticed sleeping on the back bench cocooned in a wine-colored coat suddenly came alive to defend her friend.

"Get down, Audrey!" the tiny woman shouted as she pulled a Patterson pocket pistol from her coat. "Drop that gun, mister, or you're a dead man!" The little gun shook in her hands while she tried to aim.

As her petite partner stepped forward, the other woman hit the floor none too gently. "Go ahead and shoot him, Delta!" the redhead yelled.

When the cold metal barrel pushed against his forehead, fear widened the robber's eyes. He dropped his gun and raised his arms in slow motion, surrendering to a woman half his size.

Near the front of the car Marshal McCormick lifted the leader to his feet. The outlaw still held his fist to his nose, fighting to stop the blood gushing over his unruly mustache. Austin jammed a gun into the man's ribs and shoved the bandit toward the front of the car. "Tell your friends it's over, partner, or your lungs will be having new holes to breath through."

The robber's eyes glinted graveyard cold. "You wouldn't shoot me in front of the women."

Austin twisted the man so he could see the back of the car, where a small blonde held a pistol on another gang member. "Hell, if I don't, *she* will."

Both men looked around the car. All of the once-frightened passengers were angry. The petrified young ladies who'd screamed in fear when the bandit fell against them now inspected their blood-spattered traveling dresses and stormed with revenge. It looked as if any one of the passengers would gladly have served as hangman at a moment's notice.

"See a friendly face?" Austin asked.

The man turned toward the door and yelled, "Frank, let the engineer go! We're done for. It's over."

"Tell all your men to come out with their hands high," Austin ordered as he shoved the man forward.

The command was followed. Robbers, little older than boys, stepped from the train.

The conductor and several other men moved slowly in front of them to collect weapons.

Austin turned to Jennie as he reached the exit. "I'm not through talking to you, lady." His eyes were still stormy.

It frightened her to know that catching the robbers had been little more than a day's work for him. She was the cause of his angry stare.

Jennie could sense everyone on the train watching her. "Well, I'm through talking to you, Marshal McCormick." She lifted her chin, irritated by his words and the way he'd made her feel. "Did you find it necessary to shatter that poor man's nose for interrupting our discussion, or were you actually trying to do your duty?"

Austin's eyebrows shot up in disbelief. "You're the one who wanted to shoot them, remember? Besides, we weren't having a discussion, lady. We were having an argument. I'm mighty sorry the train robbery got in the way, but as soon as I get these men tied up and doctored, I'll be back to finish what you started."

"I have no intention of talking with you further, Marshal."

"Good!" Austin pushed his prisoner forward. " 'Cause all you need to do is listen. I plan on doing all the talking."

Chapter
Four

*L*end me a hand. This girl's been shot!" the redheaded woman in the back screamed above the train's long whistle.

Jennie twisted in her seat as everyone between her and the back of the train jumped to offer aid.

"Quiet, Audrey," the petite blonde beside the shouting woman insisted as folks moved closer. "It's nothing. Only a scratch."

Someone in the crowd shouted, "Look, there's blood all over her coat!"

Another yelled, "We oughta string them fellas up!"

Jennie raised one eyebrow at the marshal, who was about to take his place on their shared bench. She didn't give him time to sit down. "Don't you think you'd better investigate?" How could he be so calm, when the girl was wounded? Jennie wondered if folks often had to explain the marshal's duty to him or if he'd simply lost his senses this trip. She decided the man could have driven a temperance leader to drink. He had the oddest habit of getting riled over nothing and looking at the shocking with indifferent eyes.

She'd hoped to be at the final stop before he made it back to his place beside her, so she wouldn't have to answer any questions about the child beneath her seat. Her luck had held to within a few miles of Florence, Kansas. The train was already slowing for the last bend when he stormed into the car. His gaze never wavered from her face, leaving no doubt that he planned to finish their argument.

Now, while everyone in the car was talking about the wounded girl, Austin McCormick turned his dark gaze toward Jennie. "I don't remember anyone dying and leaving me in charge of this train, lady. Why is it every time something happens, you nominate me to do something about it?"

"But you're a federal marshal!"

"On leave, lady. Hell, when I pick up my orders in Florence, I may be going back to punching cows in Texas. Meeting a few more women like yourself would sure make those lonely drives seem more appealing. You've taken up trying to run my life faster than a babe takes to a mother's milk."

Jennie didn't try to hide the impatience in her voice. "We have to do something to help if that woman's been shot. I'm not surprised someone was hurt with as many bullets as there were flying through this car. We have to at least stop any bleeding until we can get her to a doctor."

Austin opened his mouth to argue, then closed it in frustration, realizing that the spinster beside him was right, much as he hated to admit it. "Not we, lady, me. Why don't you try to stay out of this one? You caused enough problems during the robbery." He turned and stepped into the aisle.

"Me!" Jennie fought the urge to take a swing at his back. For a half cent, she'd have given him the dressing down he deserved, but right now she had to consider the advantage of having him as far away from her as possible. So she remained silent as he moved down the aisle toward the wounded girl.

Jennie watched him disappear into the crowd of people who'd surrounded the last few benches at the back of the car. "Now!" She grabbed hold of the child's hand and pulled True from under the seat. "We've got to get you off before anyone sees you."

True's tiny hand held on tightly, surprising Jennie with its strength. They moved along the aisle toward the front entrance. The passengers were too busy trying to see who'd been shot, or packing up preparing to leave the train, to pay them any notice.

Jennie was on the platform between cars even before the train stopped. She could see the conductor leaning out several cars down, but chances were he'd be too preoccupied with the robbers to notice True slipping off before anyone else.

"As soon as the train stops, jump and run hide among the boxes." Jennie looked down at the child, wishing she could clean off a few pounds of grit from True's face.

"I can take care of myself, ma'am," True whispered, but didn't lighten the hold on Jennie's hand.

Jennie smiled into the bravest eyes she'd ever seen. "I know you can, True. I was kind of hoping you'd take care of me. You see, this is the first time I've ever been away from home, and Florence, Kansas, looks like the end of the world. I'm not sure I can make it on my own."

True stood an inch taller. "Well, why didn't you say so, ma'am? I'd be mighty glad to teach you."

"You're not afraid?" Jennie saw the unshed tears in the child's eyes. True was such a tiny thing to be out in the world alone.

"No, ma'am," True answered. "I got a guardian angel looking after me. My ma said she'd point one in my direction just as soon as she got to Heaven."

Jennie wanted to say that the angel must be taking his time finding True, but she didn't trust her own voice not to break. She studied the stacks of boxes along the platform, looking for a place for True to hide. Finally, she found an opening in the supplies.

"Do you think you could run when the train stops and crawl in between those crates and stay there until I can come back for you?"

True nodded, following Jennie's gaze.

Kneeling, Jennie whispered, "Could you give me a hug to help me not be so afraid until I see you again? It may take me until after dark before I can get back to you."

Thin arms no wider than a yearling willow circled Jennie's neck. "I'll wait," True whispered. "I'll wait until you come for me even if it takes all night. But don't worry none about me, ma'am. I'll be waiting just to see if I can help you."

Suddenly Jennie forgot about the layered dirt on True's face. She hugged the child tightly and kissed the dirty cheek as she'd always longed to do with a child of her own. "Go," Jennie whispered, pulling away. "And may the angel protect you."

True quickly jumped from the train and disappeared into the wall of boxes. Jennie stood, feeling suddenly cold and very alone. She couldn't help but wonder if True could take better care of them both than she could, for the past hour had frightened her more than she'd ever allow anyone to know.

For a moment she watched, making sure True wasn't seen. But all attention was drawn to the other end of the car, where Marshal McCormick carried the wounded woman off the train. Jennie could hear several conversations at once. Some repeated the injured girl's name, Delta Smith. Others assured friends the injury had probably only been a flesh wound, nothing more. Jennie was thankful that the woman's injury was no more serious and that Delta Smith had gotten the bothersome marshal out of her way.

Jennie could never remember being affected so strongly by a person. She thought for a moment she'd seen a hero's spirit in his eyes; but, thanks to her dime novels, she knew what a true hero should be. And to her way of thinking, Marshal Austin McCormick had a long way to go.

As he carried the girl into the depot at Florence, he looked tall and powerful, but there was no human softness in him. No touch of tenderness blended with the steel it took to be a real hero. He was doing a job, nothing more.

Jennie moved along with the crowd of other Harvey employees from the station toward a huge hotel to the south of the depot. Everyone talked and laughed, advancing like a swarm of bees upon a new hive, but she didn't even look up for several steps. Her thoughts were on a child hidden between boxes. A child who had somehow stolen her heart.

When she finally looked up, Jennie could hardly believe the sight before her. The first full-service Harvey

House loomed ahead, a massive place designed not only to feed travelers, but put them up for the night. The hotel had been built in a wooded area and was bigger than she'd guessed. Twin fountains banked the entrance to the two-story building, adding a touch of Fred Harvey's England in this small Kansas town.

A man in a red cap stepped onto the porch and sounded a golden gong to silence the crowds. "Welcome!" he shouted. "Welcome, ladies and gentlemen, to Clifton House. You'll all be shown your rooms later, and tomorrow you'll become Harvey employees, but this evening we invite you to be our guests for dinner at the finest restaurant west of the Mississippi."

Jennie expected to see a mass rush to the dining hall and eating counters after the poor food they'd had along the trip, but everyone hesitated. Maybe it was the size of the place, or maybe it was the first time most of these people had been treated like guests in a fine home. A reverence settled over the future employees. The men held the doors for the women. Girls who'd never been treated with the respect accorded a lady back home suddenly straightened their hats and squared their shoulders in pride.

The men were all something more than farmers and workers now. They were Harvey employees. The women were more than chambermaids and seamstresses. They were Harvey girls and as such must be polite and proper. After all, Fred Harvey wasn't only bringing fine food to the West, he was bringing civilization.

Something else blended among the crowd. A feeling of family, an invisible bond that forms between people who work together to be the best they can be.

As Jennie entered the foyer, she couldn't deny the feeling of coming home. The wood was polished and warm, the glass crystal clean. The Clifton House was a grand queen opening her arms to new subjects.

The smell of roasted chickens and baked cinnamon apples blended with the aroma of fresh bread, making Jennie reluctant to breathe out. The hotel was warm on this cold January night, warm with steamed heat as well as friendliness. The sounds of dinnertime floated like a healing prayer across her tired, hungry body.

A plump woman of about fifty stood at the counter just outside the dining room. She took down each person's name as he or she passed. Jennie could see the people moving by her to register, but she remained frozen, afraid her dream would shatter at any moment and she'd be back in her parents' home with nothing but sameness to look forward to. She was afraid someone would stop her and tell her to go back home because she didn't belong here.

When the hall had cleared, the older woman looked up at Jennie, her quiet smile genuine, her water-colored eyes understanding. "I'm Mrs. Gray, the head waitress. May I have your name, miss, and the names of those you'd like to room with? We'll try to have your room ready by the time you finish eating."

"Jennie Munday," Jennie whispered, suspecting that this woman didn't even notice her age or height, but looked straight into her soul.

"And the two women you'd like to share a room with?"

Jennie glanced around and realized everyone else had already molded into small groups. By not taking the time to meet anyone on the train, she had now left herself out of getting a roommate.

"I'm . . ." Jennie didn't want to use the word alone again as long as she lived. She'd always been alone.

Even with her brothers and sisters, she'd always been treated as an outsider. Suddenly the wounded girl and her friend came to mind. Since they were the only two who'd stayed at the train station with the marshal, they must need a third to fill their room. "I'm rooming with a girl who was injured during the train robbery, Delta Smith."

The older woman nodded. She'd already heard bits and pieces of the story. As a good waitress, she'd learned years ago to put the pieces together in her mind without taking the time to ask questions. "And the third girl?" she asked.

"Audrey." Jennie remembered hearing the tall red-head's name. "I'm afraid I don't know her last name. She stayed behind with Delta."

"Audrey will be fine. I'm sure we'll find out later. Now, you go on in and make yourself comfortable while I get everything ready."

Jennie hadn't eaten all day, but the thought of True waiting alone down by the depot made her force the hunger pains aside. "Do you think I might help with preparing the room? Then, when Delta gets here, we can put her straight to bed. She's lost a great deal of blood."

Mrs. Gray nodded slowly. "Of course. I'll send a meal up for three." She looked at Jennie with a direct honesty. "That was very thoughtful. You'll be an asset to Clifton House, Miss Munday."

"I hope to be." Jennie followed the old woman up the stairs, feeling a slight twinge of guilt for lying. "As soon as the room's ready, I'd like to run back down to the station and check on Delta."

"Of course." Mrs. Gray opened the first door. "This room's a little larger than the others. I think you and your friends will be most comfortable in here."

Jennie held her smile as Mrs. Gray directed girls to make up the three beds immediately.

While the girls worked, Jennie moved to the tall window. She watched the evening shadows fall across the depot a hundred yards away.

She'd be safe here at the Clifton House, maybe as safe as she'd always been in her parents' home. But safety weighed lightly against her need to help True. To do so, she had to get back to the depot and somehow avoid Marshal Austin McCormick.

Chapter Five

The pale light of a winter sunset reflected through the windows of the depot and danced in beams of dust around the ticket office. One of the railroad employees had stoked the Franklin stove and stacked blankets atop a bench for Delta to lie on. Nothing seems more silent than a depot after the last train leaves, and that night's quiet was broken only by the marshal's pacing as they waited.

Austin pulled on his gunbelt more out of habit than the need to relieve his hips of the weight of his Colt Peacemaker. "Doctor'll be here in a minute, miss," he said to the redheaded woman guarding the patient, then nodded at the slight blonde cuddled amid the blankets. She didn't seem in any great pain, but Austin had learned from years of handling wounded that the injury's seriousness and the amount of complaining were not always related.

"Thank you, Marshal," answered the tall woman. "In all the commotion, after the robbery attempt, I didn't show my upbringing and properly introduce myself. Name's Audrey Gates of the Flatwater, Missouri, Gates."

Austin couldn't hide his smile. He always wondered about folks who introduced themselves by their heritage. She was a fine-looking woman, though. Not the type to be courted with flowers and pretty words. More the sort some farmer would marry to help with the chores and rear a half dozen children. He admired this Audrey Gates, though, for her bold beauty and her loyalty to her friend. Loyalty was one trait he'd found in short supply among the few women he'd known, almost as rare as honesty.

His smile was all the encouragement Audrey needed to continue, "And this poor victim is my dearest friend, Delta Smith. She grew up not more than three miles from me, but I was several rows ahead of her in school."

"Rows?" Austin questioned.

"We may have only had one room, but we had eight rows. Every year a student moved over one, except of course my second brother, Ben, who must have liked the third row so much he stayed there for three years. He probably never would have advanced, only others kept complaining about having trouble seeing around him."

Delta smiled, seeming to forget her pain. "I remember that," she said shyly.

Austin didn't miss the way Audrey turned and nodded toward the younger woman as though showing approval for such a small comment.

A porter brought in a bowl of water and an armful of towels. "Doc says to clean the wound and he'll be here as soon as he can drink enough coffee to sober up."

"Well, Hell's bells!" Audrey said the words like an oath. "I swear, Delta, we've been dropped off at the end of the world. First the train robbery and now only one doctor and he's a drunkard."

"No, miss, Florence ain't the end of the world, but I think you can see it from here. It's just over the Oklahoma Territory and into Texas." The porter giggled like a stuttering hiccupper. When he noticed the frown on Austin's face he elected to change the subject. "Most folks about these parts think the doc does his best work drunk."

Helping Delta remove her coat, Audrey said, "Well, I've had some training in medicine, and if he doesn't do a fine job by my friend, he'll be dancing to a six count."

"A six count?" Austin didn't understand, but he had to admire this woman's spirit. He'd seen chiefs who didn't protect their whole tribe as carefully as Audrey protected her friend.

Audrey studied him a moment before answering, "You sure you didn't sit too long on the same row yourself, Marshal? How about counting the bullets in that Colt you're so fond of patting and maybe you can figure out the dance."

Laughter exploded from Austin before he could stop himself. It had been a long time since anyone, man or woman, had questioned his intelligence. First, Jennie on the train and now this redhead. He figured he'd better get out of this town as fast as possible, while he still had enough self-respect left not to drool.

Audrey didn't pay any attention to his revelry as she unbuttoned the top few buttons of Delta's blouse and pulled blood-soaked bandages away from the injury.

Austin swallowed his laughter the moment he saw the wound. It was over two inches long and in the shape of a V. Blood still oozed from the deep gash, but no redness festered around the wound promising infection. "But I thought . . ."

Glancing up at him, Audrey's eyes narrowed. "You'd best leave," she demanded. "I can clean the blood while we're watching for the doc."

Austin raised his finger and started to put her in her place. He might be a road-weary lawman and it might be dusk, but he'd be three days cold before he couldn't tell the difference between a gunshot hole and a knife wound. Plus, if this little lady had been shot on the train, she couldn't possibly have had time to dress the injury. Those bloodstained bandages had been wrapped by someone who knew what they were doing, not just stuffed over the wound until the train stopped.

Before he spoke, he turned to Delta, wondering what lie these two women were trying to pull on not only him, but the whole town. The petite blonde's pale blue eyes stared at him with such fear, Austin forgot what he was going to say. He'd seen fear in eyes before. Fear of the law, fear of the truth, fear of death. But never this kind of bone-crushing terror. She looked at him as if he might do worse than send her to hell and back for lying about being shot during the robbery.

"The bleeding is slowing up some. I might be able to close the wound with a tight wrap." Audrey broke the barrier of silence that seemed as thick as mortar between him and the women. "Wish there was something you could do to hurry that doc, Marshal."

Austin moved toward the door. He had to break Delta's stare. He doubted he could help with the doctor, but he had to wash his mind clear of what he'd seen in her eyes. Her look made him believe there was something uglier than death in this world and she'd already experienced it in full measure.

He stepped out into the cool night and took a deep breath. "Lord," he whispered, "if that child wants to claim a knife wound is a bullet hole, I'll not add to her pain by arguing."

Moving into the shadows of the train station, he leaned against the cold brick and closed his eyes. He took a deep breath and tried to relax muscles that had been knotted since he'd heard the first shot fired during the robbery.

He stared at the lights flickering from town and had the feeling he was alone on earth. Stepping farther into the darkness, he tried remembering when the years of loneliness had first started. He'd ridden the same road long enough to know that he'd never share life with another, but he was still young enough to remember how it felt to dream. Sometimes, he longed to have another person to talk things out with, to sleep beside, to believe in forever with. But each year on the trail hardened him, driving him further from his dream.

His life had always balanced on a plane of right and wrong. But somewhere during the long fight, he'd turned and lost his footing. He was still fighting for the same thing, but some days he wondered if it mattered to anyone but himself which side won the battle. He was a warrior who fought alone against an army. A warrior without anything or anyone to return to when the battle was fought.

His solitude was both his protection and his private jail. He'd built it brick by brick. A defense against the pain from his job. In his line of work a man couldn't afford to care. The isolation protected him against all feelings.

When had he stopped being a man and become only a marshal? Even on the train Jennie Munday had only been talking to a silver star and not a man.

A smile widened his lips slightly as he thought how he'd like her to see him as a man. She might not be the most beautiful woman he'd ever met, but she had a fire in those green eyes that would be worth a dance or two. "It'll never happen, McCormick," he said to himself. "Not in this lifetime."

"What won't happen?" Jennie's voice startled him into a year's aging.

He opened his eyes and saw his thoughts take shape. She stood three feet from him, her hands on her hips and the same fire in her eyes. Her frame was still as straight and unyielding as ever, her hair as black as midnight and her voice cold as stone. Austin couldn't stop his fists from clenching. The hunger to touch her twisted like a dull pain in his gut. It wasn't a need to cherish or dominate, but a longing to prove to himself that such a woman lived and breathed, a desire to know how a woman like her would feel pressed against his heart. A need to end his solitude, if only for the length of one dream.

Jennie seemed unaware of his struggle as she moved a step nearer. "Shouldn't you be in the station helping that poor girl who was shot instead of lurking in the shadows talking to yourself?"

Her words were like a cold blast over his senses. Like water turning to ice, he hardened from the outside in. He wondered, if he shot her right now, whether he could convince everyone that he thought her a robber in the darkness? He knew he could never do such a thing, but the idea was more than appealing. He admired her strength as much as he hated her manner. "I was just waiting for the doctor."

Jennie's slender body swayed with impatience. "Well, Marshal, don't you think you could do that more effectively waiting on the side of the building that faces town? I've never been good at direction, but it doesn't take a genius to see the lights of Florence. I doubt the doctor is going to materialize out of these boxes of supplies."

This woman was starting to get on his nerves. It wasn't because of her orders as much as her bothersome habit of being right. Austin stopped trying to defend himself and stepped onto safer ground. "I'm not finished talking with you about that child."

"You've said that before."

"What happened to the little fellow?"

Jennie didn't blink. "What child? I don't remember seeing one on the train."

"Now, don't try that with me, lady. I—"

The sound of a horse galloping fast drew Austin's attention. He took a step forward, still keeping in the shadows, until he knew who approached from town.

A man rode to a halt at the end of the loading dock and dismounted. As he neared the light, Austin could see he was much older than he appeared while in the saddle.

When Austin glanced back toward Jennie, she was gone. He knew she was still near. He could almost feel her watching him, but he didn't have time to look for her. With his luck, she'd be showing up any minute to give him more orders.

"Marshal!" the old man yelled as he wiped his face with a wrinkled bandanna.

Austin swore under his breath as he turned back to the man. If he ever saw Jennie again, he planned on hanging onto her until he'd had his say.

"I'm over here." Austin tried to think of his job and not her green eyes. "You the doc?"

"Nope." The man spit into the blackness behind him. "Name's Moses Mason. I'm the barkeep over at Salty's place."

Austin started toward the door of the depot, already dreading what else the man had to say.

Moses sidestepped behind him much like a child would follow a rattler's trail. "I was the one elected to come tell you the doc ain't in no shape to ride, much less do any business. He scalded his tongue on the coffee we was pouring down him and had to treat himself with whiskey. The cure worked; he ain't in no more pain. Fact is he's hardly breathing, near as we can tell, so you can forget about him doing any healing."

Austin mumbled an oath. "Then we'll have to do the best we can. Gunshot wounds can't wait until he sobers up." Or knife wounds, he thought to himself.

Moses continued to sidestep around the marshal even though the tall man was no longer moving. "I heard tell once that vinegar mixed with frog blood will take any poison out from a black-powder wound."

As Austin reached for the handle, Audrey pulled the depot door open. She took one look at the two men and widened her stance, blocking the doorway. "Don't know where you think you're going, men, but from what I just heard it's plain to me that you two would be about as much help as the tongue-fried drunk of a doc. I wouldn't let you near Delta with cures like you just described."

She stared at the men as if trying to figure out why God wasted his time making such creatures.

Jennie stepped from the shadows and joined Audrey. "I couldn't agree more. If you'll let me, I'd like to help you with Delta." The shadow of a child slipped behind Jennie's skirts and into the warm depot with only the slight lift of Austin's eyebrow to indicate anyone noticed.

"I'm Jennie Munday," Jennie nodded to Audrey. "Roll up your sleeves, we're going to see what you and I can do about this gunshot wound. I'm not sure I can be of any help, but there's no use asking these two for advice."

The redhead smiled. "Nice to meet you, Jennie Munday, and thanks for offering, but I think I've done about all we can do. I gave up waiting several minutes ago. She's still bleeding, but as long as we keep any fever down, she shouldn't have any problem. The poor girl could use some food. I'm guessing she hasn't eaten in more than three days."

"I've had a room at the Clifton House readied, and the house mother is sending up dinner for the three of us."

"Three?" Audrey glanced at True hiding behind the door.

"Three," Jennie answered slowly, protecting the child with a gentle hand on the tiny shoulder. "I plan to help you sit up with Delta tonight."

Audrey took the second lie she'd heard today as easily as she'd received the first. If Delta wanted to be wounded by a gunshot instead of stabbed and Jennie counted a little short, then so be it. Details never bothered Audrey overly.

While Audrey gave instructions to the men about loading Delta and her luggage, Jennie walked to Delta's side. The blonde had lost a great deal of blood from a body that looked little better than half-starved.

"Audrey?" she whispered without opening her eyes.

Jennie took the girl's hand, trying to reassure her. She saw no point in introducing herself. There would be time enough for that later.

"Audrey," Delta whispered again, her voice weak with pain. "There's a deed in my bag. Take it out and hide it. We'll both be dead if my family finds it!"

"But . . ."

Delta's voice was a soft cry. "Hide the deed or we'll all die."

Jennie stared at the woman, not believing what she'd heard. A thousand questions came to mind, but Delta's words seemed to have drained the last ounce of energy from her. She almost melted into the blankets, as pale as the cold winter moon outside.

Silently Jennie's gaze moved to True's dark blue-eyed stare. No disbelief flickered in the child's eyes. He had seen the underbelly of the world and knew Delta's words could be true. Without hesitation he slipped a tiny hand into Delta's small bag and pulled out a folded paper.

"Is this the deed?" True held the paper up to Jennie.

Jennie nodded, staring as though the very paper were somehow evil and could do her harm.

"I'll hide it, miss," True whispered. "I'll hide it so it will never hurt you or Delta."

Chapter
Six

When Jennie awoke, snow had dusted the world white. Thin eyelet lace curtains did little to keep out morning light through the tall six-foot windows on either side of her small bed. She looked around and smiled slowly, thankful yesterday hadn't been a dream. She wasn't back home, but in the new Harvey House. She was out west, living her adventure.

The room was painted white, with dark walnut wood framing the windows and door. Three beds lined the wall opposite the entrance. A washstand and wardrobe flanked the door, leaving only enough room for a tiny dressing table to be crammed into one corner.

Jennie crawled from her bed, enjoying the warmth of the wood floor thanks to their location over the kitchen. Moving as silently as she could, she crossed the room and opened the wardrobe. There, cuddled inside the closet, True still lay fast asleep. The little boy had eaten until they'd thought he'd explode and now seemed to be hibernating. He looked warm, banked by the dark rose-wood cabinet and the bed of feather pillows Audrey had somehow found down the hall. His hands and face had been scrubbed, revealing the face of an angel beneath all the mud. They'd have to work on the rest of him when there was time. Cleaning True wouldn't be an easy project. His hair was matted in rootlike hunks, and his clothes looked as if he'd lived several seasons in them without taking them off.

Jennie carefully closed the wardrobe door all but an inch as they'd agreed upon the night before. She knew she and Audrey couldn't hide the child forever, but maybe for a few days.

"Morning." Delta yawned and rose to one elbow. Her voice was stronger, but her eyes were still filled with pain. "Did you sleep well?"

Hurrying to her bedside, Jennie answered, "Wonderfully. Better than I've slept in my whole life. But how are you this morning?"

"I'm much better," Delta admitted. A hint of color touched her porcelain cheeks as she smiled. "The noise from the hotel was almost like a clock ticking to put me to sleep. I feel safe here."

Jennie had never felt threatened when she slept. Unhappy sometimes, or lonely, but never unsafe. "I felt like there was something worth waking up for today," she whispered more to herself than Delta. How many mornings had she lain awake just before dawn, already knowing everything that would happen to her in the day about to be born?

"It's nice here, isn't it?" Delta looked directly at Jennie, and both women knew that what made this place right had little to do with the warm room and clean sheets.

"Are you in much pain?" Jennie touched Delta's forehead, testing for fever. With one touch, she knew the color in her cheeks was due to fever. She was healing, just as Audrey had predicted she would as soon as they got a good meal into her, but she still had a way to travel before she'd be well. No new blood stained the bandage Audrey had put on just before they'd retired. That was one good sign at least.

"I'm weak, but alive." Delta looked around as if really looking at the room for the first time. "Where's Audrey?"

As though she'd heard her name from the hallway, Audrey bumped her way into the room. She carried a huge tray of hot coffee and homemade cinnamon rolls. "I was wondering when you two sleepyheads would be awake." She sat the tray down on her bed. "I've been downstairs for two hours helping the pastry cook get ready for the first train. She leaves next week to marry some farmer. After seeing the way she beats the life out of yeast dough, I'd say there's one farmer in for a disappointment or two."

Audrey popped a piece of roll into her mouth and mumbled to Jennie, "You'd better get dressed. There's a marshal been drinking coffee in the dining room for an hour waiting for you. He didn't look in any too good a mood. Didn't even smile when he tasted one of my rolls, and if that don't sweeten a man, nothing will."

Jennie didn't seem in any hurry as she poured herself a cup of coffee and moved to the dressing table. "I know what he wants and there's nothing to say. He thinks I'm True's mother." While she spoke, Audrey poured True half a cup to allow time for the hot liquid to cool for the child.

Raising an eyebrow, Audrey asked, "Are you?"

Jennie shook her head. "No, I found him under my seat like I said last night, but the marshal doesn't believe me."

"Well, True can't be more than five or six years old, so we're not turning him over to the marshal to go live in one of those child work farms. They'd half starve him." Audrey added half a measure of milk to True's cup as she noticed the child crawl from the wardrobe.

Winking at Jennie, Audrey acted as though she paid no notice of tiny hands reaching for a roll. Jennie sipped her cup silently and Audrey poured Delta a share.

Delta took the cup Audrey offered. "Audrey's right. If we turned True over to the authorities, there's no telling what would happen. These are hard times, and no one's going to be willing to take on another mouth to feed."

"No one but us." Audrey nodded once to Jennie. "How about we all three agree to raise True? Surely we can do it at least until he gets too big to sleep in the wardrobe. Besides, from the looks of the men in the dining room, it won't be long until one of us gets married and can set True up in a real home."

"I didn't come to marry," Jennie objected. She could almost hear her family laughing all the way from Iowa at the very thought of their Jennie marrying.

Both women looked at her in disbelief. Delta added, "I didn't come to marry either. But can we keep True a secret if we live here?"

"Maybe." Audrey downed another roll. "I've seen a few little boys working around here. Maybe once we clean him up and cut his hair, Mrs. Gray will agree to find a place for him."

True took another roll from the plate. "I don't need no one to take care of me. I'm doing fine all by myself. I only stayed around here last night because you three looked like you could use some help."

Audrey seemed to agree completely. "Thank you, True. How about you just stay around here and help me eat the leftover food? It would be a shame to throw out the fried chicken we're going to have for lunch."

"It sure would," True mumbled between bites. "I guess I could stay awhile. But don't start thinking I need mothering. I can make it fine alone."

Jennie tried to hide her giggle as she scrubbed her face. "Well, I'd better go take care of the marshal before he decides to come looking for True." She studied herself in the mirror for a moment. No one had reminded her in over twenty-four hours how plain she was, and she wasn't about to remind herself.

Thirty minutes later Jennie passed the marshal's table for the third time with a hot pot of coffee. "Would you like another refill?"

"I'd like a minute to talk to you about a few things." The marshal's none-too-sunny mood had darkened a little with each of the ten cups of coffee he'd already had.

"I'm sorry." Jennie's words were so sweet no one in the room could have guessed she was lying. "I'm working right now. I know you'll be wanting to get on the road to Texas, so I'll just say good-bye and I hope to see you when you pass this way again sometime."

Austin had had all the coffee and stalling he was going to take. He stood, fully intending to have his say with Jennie, even if he had to do it in front of everyone at the Harvey House. But before he could get his throat cleared, an old woman stepped between him and Jennie. She was no more than five feet tall, but with her arms folded, he could tell she thought herself as impenetrable as a union fort.

"That's him, Sheriff." She pointed at Austin as if he'd massacred half of Texas and now planned to do the same to Kansas. "That's the man who's been bothering one of my new girls all morning."

To Austin's amazement, an old man wearing a tarnished badge moved beside the little lady as if he thought himself to be some help to her. "Now, you don't want to cause Mrs. Gray any trouble, do you, son?" The fellow took a toothpick out of his mouth and pointed it at Austin as though it were a weapon. The old sheriff's mustache curled at the tips, making him seem as if he were smiling, while the stubble across his chin made him seem more the town drunk than a lawman.

"No one's called me son in years, Sheriff." Austin whispered the words between clenched teeth. He could never remember using force against anyone so old, but there might be a first time hatching real soon.

The old sheriff put his arm on Austin's shoulder. "Well, son, why don't we go outside and you can properly introduce yourself to me?"

Austin didn't budge. Suddenly all the stubbornness accumulated over his entire life grounded him to the floor like railroad spikes through his feet. "I'm Marshal Austin McCormick, and I'd like to talk to this lady about an incident on the train yesterday without interference." He relaxed a little, thinking that he'd given just enough information to get these two aging pillars out of his way.

The old man laughed with a sudden snort and slapped him on the back. "Well, it's good to meet you, son. I've been waiting for you to show up to claim your horse for three days."

When Austin raised an eyebrow, the sheriff continued. "I've got your orders from the home office in Washington." The old man smiled so big whiskers pointed out in every direction. He lowered his voice as though not wanting all the room to hear official business. "I'm happy to tell you, you've been reassigned here for the time being."

"What!" Austin forgot all about Jennie and the lecture he'd planned to give her on being a better parent. He'd just been ordered to spend time in hell, and the old guy acted like it was a promotion.

"I'm Jim Morris, sheriff, justice of the peace, and part-time blacksmith in these parts. If you need your horse shod, your daughter married, or your drunk brother-in-law thrown in jail, just ask me. Most folks just call me Spider." The sheriff slapped Austin on the back again. "I'm happier than a single piglet at dinnertime to have you here in Florence."

Austin marched toward the door. "There must be some mistake!" He had to straighten out his future before he dealt with Jennie. As he passed her, he raised a finger. "I'm—"

"I know," Jennie interrupted and handed him his hat. "You're not finished talking to me yet." Her smile left no doubt she knew she'd won yet another round.

Austin fought the urge to grab her and rattle the grin off her face. He stormed out of Clifton House and was halfway to town before he realized he had no idea where the sheriff's office was located. When he turned around, he noticed Spider Morris strolling along behind him. Though the man was not tall, his legs were long, probably the origin of his nickname.

Waiting for the sheriff to catch up, Austin yelled, "Do you think we can wire headquarters and get this straightened out? There has to be some mistake. I'm due back in Texas in a week. I can't waste my time in a little town like this."

Morris shook his head. "I already checked. They posted you here."

"But why me?" Austin couldn't see the logic. "I've been on the trail for ten years. They've got men to handle trouble with train robbers, and this town's already got you for a sheriff."

The old man moved even with Austin and shifted his toothpick from one side of his mouth to the other before speaking. "Maybe they figure the storm that's headed our way needs two men. It's nothing to do with that train robbery you were involved in yesterday. However, that is how the trouble all started six years ago."

"If it's been six years, the trail's a little cold by now." Austin matched Morris's steps.

"Oh, we caught those bandits. Sent six men to the federal prison for robbing a train. It was one well-planned robbery out of many they'd pulled, and one hell of a night till we caught them. Before dawn the day after the robbery, several men and one woman were dead. The leader of the gang swore he'd come back and burn the town down."

"Every man I've ever helped convict made such a promise," Austin added.

"Yeah, but this one is named Buck Lawton, and I got word three days ago that he and his men broke out of jail. He's got some country to cross, but my guess is after he's rounded up his old gang, he'll be paying us a visit."

"You really think he's heading this way?" Austin asked.

"I'd stake my badge on it." Morris slowed his pace. "But I'm not willing to risk everyone in this town, so for the first time I wired for help. By the time Lawton rounds up his gang, he'll have twenty or more men, so I asked for several federal lawmen. The home office said all I'd need was you."

Spider smiled as he studied Austin. "I figure you must be one hell of a lawman."

Austin laughed. "I don't know whether to be flattered or question if they think they've found a way to retire me permanently. This isn't my kind of assignment, sitting around waiting for trouble to show up."

The sheriff grinned and winked at the same time, making his face resemble a raisin. "Maybe the federal office figures you could learn a few things from me while we're waiting."

"How so, old man?"

"I've been a lawman for near thirty years and never killed a man yet."

Austin hardly saw that as a recommendation. He'd run into quite a number of men in the past few years he considered would do the world a favor by being six feet under. "What makes you so sure they'll come? If this Buck Lawton is smart, he'll be halfway to California by now."

"He's coming. Besides promising to kill the men who caught him, Lawton buried the loot from the last robbery somewhere around here." Spider Morris shoved his hands in his pockets. "We got big trouble coming, son. I been watching the signs like a farmer watches the clouds, and the storm's already on the horizon.

"I can feel it in the air. Folks around these parts are getting jumpy, pulling out guns every time they see a shadow. They're libel to shoot one another before Lawton and his men ever ride into town. Don't you think we could work together to make sure none of the town folks, including that lady of yours over at the Harvey House, gets hurt?"

Austin stepped up on the wooden porch of a building. He dodged the swinging board branded "Office and Jail." "She's not my lady," he mumbled, trying to push Jennie from his mind as he concentrated on the problem. Though he knew he'd never stay here long, he might take the time to help this old man. Hell, if Buck Lawton's men hit this town, he'd put his money on Audrey and Jennie handling them before this old spider of a man. The sheriff wasn't even wearing a gun.

But Austin didn't like the idea of trouble visiting the women at Clifton House. Oh, they were strong, he reckoned, but he didn't want to see any of them hurt. Maybe he'd stay awhile. "You got a place for me to bunk?"

Spider Morris walked across the porch and opened a door. "This here's my office and the jail, but we haven't had any need for it in years. There's a bed in the back, or you can probably get a room over at the boardinghouse."

"Thanks. This will do fine." Austin resigned himself. He fought down a sudden smile. The only good thing about this assignment was he'd be seeing Jennie Munday again. Just once he'd like to see a fire that wasn't anger in those eyes.

He glanced around the office, not missing his saddle and gear stacked on a bed in the back room. He took a second look at the sheriff. "You already knew I'd stay."

Morris scratched his whiskers. "I knew it the minute I saw you carry that woman off the train. You're not a man who runs from trouble."

"And you're sure trouble's coming?" Austin asked.

Spider laughed. "Son, you were already courting a handful of trouble when I found you. I didn't miss the

way that waitress looked at you. Buck's gang may try
to kill you, but that little lady will steal your heart."

"Not likely, old man." Austin lifted his saddle from
the bed. "I haven't got one. Gave it up years ago when
I pinned on this badge."

Austin could hear Spider Morris chuckling as he
walked out of the office and closed the door.

Chapter
Seven

*J*ennie worked harder than she'd ever worked in her life. By the time the evening train departed, her legs were so numb they no longer hurt. She'd assisted with serving lunch, then been assigned her own tables at dinner. When she wasn't cleaning or setting tables, she polished the silver or dried the china. And never, ever, was a Harvey girl allowed to look tired or out of order. In one day she'd gone through three aprons. Every time the others had taken a break, she'd hurried upstairs and checked on Delta and True. Just before the gong sounded announcing the last seating of people for dinner, she'd looked in to find Audrey about to cut True's hair and bathe him. She wished she could have stayed to see what a fine boy he'd be all clean.

As she removed the last bundle of linen from the tables, Jennie smiled. It felt good to have worked so hard. She'd watched folks tired and exhausted from

the train ride come through the door and leave thirty
minutes later smiling and well fed. Jennie slipped her
hand into her pocket and felt the coins her customers
had left. *I'll start a savings for True's education,* she
thought. *Someday he'll be a great lawyer or doctor.*

Mrs. Gray crossed through the room checking to
ensure everything was in order. "You did a wonderful
job today, Jennie." She had a way of making everyone feel valued. Even when she'd corrected Jennie
for serving from the wrong side, she'd done so only
once before slipping a string around Jennie's right
wrist.

Touching the string, Jennie answered, "Thank you."
Her brothers and sisters would have made a long round
of jokes about it, just as they had the red ribbons she
tied on the posts so she could find her way to town,
even though it was only a short distance away.

"Why don't you take the linen out back to the wash
house and call it a night?" Mrs. Gray was already moving away. "Be sure and tell Audrey we'll need her in
the kitchen at four in the morning."

Nodding, Jennie lifted the bundle of linen. "Good
night, Mrs. Gray."

"Good night." Mrs. Gray allowed her shoulders to
lower slightly as she slowly climbed the stairs.

Jennie marveled at how the woman could have an
ounce of fat on her body, for she was in constant motion.
Whenever something hadn't been done properly, she was
there to straighten things out. When one man refused to
wear his coat, she was beside him, softly telling him it
was the policy at all Harvey Houses. She didn't order
him to either put on his coat or leave, she only asked if
he'd be dining with them or would rather have his meal
boxed.

Jennie walked toward the laundry house several yards behind the hotel. She could make the trip in the dark; she'd made it many times already today. The cold air felt good on her warm skin, and the sky was more dusty blue than black. The Kansas sun had melted away all trace of the early morning snowfall, but the slight north wind promised more.

As she turned to walk back to the house, she saw a lone man standing by the back steps. For a moment, alarm shook the exhaustion from her, then she realized the too-tall outline could be no one else but the marshal.

Taking a deep breath, Jennie decided now was as good a time as any to face him. It shouldn't take her more than a few minutes to make plain how she felt about him. She couldn't go the rest of her life avoiding him. Besides, he couldn't prove there was a child. Not without climbing the stairs to the girls' wing, and Mrs. Gray would have him tarred and feathered before he was halfway up the steps.

"Evening, Marshal." Jennie nodded as she passed.

"Miss Munday." Austin touched the brim of his hat. "I was wondering if you might have the time to talk to me now."

"I'm not sure Mrs. Gray would approve of us talking out back like this. She has very strict rules." Jennie took the first step up the stairs. She waited, holding her breath for him to argue, but he didn't. She took the second step.

"Walk with me, Jennie." Austin's voice was so low she wasn't sure she understood what he said.

"What?"

"I said walk with me." He pushed his hat back as if aggravated he had to ask twice. "I'd like to talk with you awhile."

Closing her eyes, Jennie tried to make herself believe what she'd heard. How many times had she dreamed of hearing a man say such words to her? She'd told herself she'd probably never hear a man say "I love you," or tell her how pretty she was, but sometimes she prayed for someone just to want to talk with her. How many thousands of times had she hoped some man would ask her as she left church to stroll the few hundred yards to her house? And how many times—every time—had she walked alone?

Jennie turned around, unwilling to throw away her one chance. It didn't matter that the night was cold or that it was late. Now she could say she'd been asked. "I'll walk with you only down to the depot and back. It wouldn't be proper anywhere else."

Austin nodded as if her words made sense to him and offered his hand. When his fingers accepted the weight of her hand, he realized he should have taken off his gloves. He wanted to feel the touch of this woman. He wanted to know that someone who seemed so strong and determined could be real and not just a silhouette of what he thought he saw.

Jennie felt the soft warmth of leather as well as the strength beneath. "Marshal McCormick, I ask only one favor tonight. Could we not argue? I'm afraid I haven't the energy."

Austin moved her hand to the bend in his arm. "Agreed. I've done my share of fighting for one day also."

They walked in silence along the dark path to the front of the hotel. When Jennie's shoe slipped slightly, Austin's fingers tightened over her hand. Protecting. Guiding.

Several yards away from the front fountains of Clifton House, he spoke. "I'm not much good at just talking."

"I noticed." Jennie laughed. "But to tell the truth, neither am I."

Austin nodded as they passed the shadowy outlines of other couples bracing the chilly night for a few moments. "How's Delta doing?" he asked when they were once again alone.

"Very weak." Jennie relaxed a little. "Once we got a few pounds of food into her, she looked better. Audrey told Mrs. Gray she'll need at least two weeks of total bed rest before she tries even getting dressed. But she did sit up for a while this afternoon."

"And the boy. Is he with you?" His question was so casual, Jennie didn't react at once.

"What boy?" She tried to pull her hand from his arm, but his fingers trapped hers.

"The boy who rode halfway across Kansas under your seat." Austin stopped walking and faced her. The light was too dim to see her eyes, but he didn't have to see the look in those green depths to know she'd lied.

"I don't know what you're talking about, Marshal." Jennie forced her voice to be calm as another couple passed only a few yards away.

Austin took a deep breath. "Look, I don't want to hurt the boy, just make sure he's somewhere safe." Austin could tell by the way she still tugged, trying to free her hand, that she didn't believe him.

Suddenly, he admired her very deeply. Anyone who looked at her could tell she was a fine woman, unaccustomed to lying. Hell, she probably carried a Bible everywhere with her. But she was willing to lie to protect a child. A child she claimed wasn't even hers. A barrier cracked around his heart that he'd held tightly in place since his brother died years ago.

"I need to know . . ." His words were more to himself than her. "Because I remember how it felt to be out in the world at that age. I know how cruel people can be when they think of you as no more than a maggot." He was no longer looking at her, but into the darkness, into his past. "I know how hard it is to tell good folks from the bad when they're all twice your height. You'd be surprised how often a handout comes with strings. If the child's not yours, I want to know that he's all right."

"You were alone at True's age?"

"No." Austin looked away from her into the shadows. "I had a brother a year older. At least we had each other until he died just before the war."

"Was he all that was left of your family?"

"Yes." His answer was emotionless now as he pulled himself back to the present.

Jennie's fingers tightened slowly over his arm. "I'm sorry," she whispered.

Austin didn't look at her. "I didn't tell you to hear how sorry you were. I told you so you'd understand why I need to know if the boy is all right. If he's not with you, I plan to look for him and keep looking until I find him. I don't think I can sleep tonight unless I know he's at least warm and safe."

Jennie moved closer to Austin. Somehow in the darkness she could see the lonely little boy in the shadow of the man. "True's warm and safe," she whispered. "And the handout has no strings tied to it."

The marshal nodded once. "I'm glad." He pulled his hat low so that even in the faint light only blackness covered his face. "Could we make a deal, Jennie? I'll ask no more questions, if you'll promise to let me know if the boy needs anything."

Jennie smiled. She could see the knight's armor shining again beneath the hard crust of this lawman. "Deal."

Austin suddenly seemed nervous. "We best get back." He turned toward the hotel.

"Yes," Jennie answered. "It's getting cold." She couldn't help but feel a little sad. Now that the marshal had said what he needed to say, her one-and-only stroll with a man was over.

Austin stopped and lifted her hand from his arm. He pulled off his jacket and wrapped it over her shoulders. "I'm sorry." His voice tumbled over the words. "I should have noticed you didn't have on a coat."

Jennie stared at him in disbelief. Never had a man been so kind to her. She warmed, not from the feel of leather, but from his action.

They walked in silence all the way to the back door of the hotel. He could have taken her in the main entrance, but they both seemed to agree silently to say good night in the shadows.

When she took the first step, she turned, trying to think of what to say. She didn't want to leave him, but there seemed no more words.

Finally breaking the silence, he said, "I enjoyed the walk." He shoved his hands into his back pockets. "I don't suppose you'd want to walk with me again sometime?"

"Why?" Jennie asked. She was old enough to know things were usually not as simple as they seemed.

Austin removed his hat. "I guess I'd like to talk to you some more."

Jennie couldn't hold the giggle. "Oh." They'd spent most of the walk in silence.

Austin shifted from one foot to the other. Damn if this woman didn't have a way of crawling under his skin and tying up his nerves. "I'm probably not the kind of man who usually asked you out back home."

"No," Jennie answered. She assumed the marshal wasn't asking because he was interested in her. There had to be another reason. Maybe he wanted to find out more about True, or maybe he'd seen Delta's wound and knew, as she had with one look, that it hadn't been caused by a gunshot.

Jennie had to know the truth. She wasn't some young girl who wanted to dream of what a man might think. She moved closer. With her feet on the first step, she was almost at eye level with him. "If we go walking again, Marshal McCormick, what would be the purpose?"

She was so close he could feel her breath brush the collar of his shirt. She smelled of soap and cinnamon and woman. He couldn't remember how long it had been since he'd stood this close to a desirable woman. "Jennie . . . ," he whispered and saw the question in her emerald eyes. "Jennie."

All his life he'd acted with logic, but she was drowning his senses like hundred-year-old moonshine. Before he let reason rule him, Austin pulled her into his arms and lowered his mouth over hers.

His kiss was hard and demanding, the only way he'd ever known. Before he touched her, he hadn't really thought much about how she'd feel in his arms, but now he knew—she felt perfect. He realized he'd wanted to kiss her from the moment he'd seen her sitting alone on the train so proper and untouchable. Her back might be overstarched, but her lips were made for kissing . . . full, warm and inviting.

His hands circled her slender waist and lifted her off the step as he continued. She felt so good pressed against him. Austin fought the urge to pull the ribbon from her hair and see how far her ebony mane would tumble. Her lips were soft and yielding beneath his mouth, yet every muscle in her body remained flexed.

As he traced the outline of her bottom lip with his tongue, he wondered how long it would take the fire he was kindling to move through her body. She would be paradise to hold when she melted with passion. She'd be the kind of woman to make every dream he'd ever had come alive.

"Relax, Jennie," he whispered against her cheek. "Kiss me back."

"I'm waiting for you to stop."

Austin pulled an inch away and looked down at her. "You're not enjoying this?" He didn't think of himself as much of a ladies' man, but the few women he'd kissed hadn't complained. Jennie looked at him with repulsion, as if she were watching a wolf spider crawling across her bare toes.

He set her back on her feet and fought to keep anger from exploding in his words. "Why didn't you push me away if my kiss was so unpleasant?" The light from the kitchen reflected in her eyes and showed curiosity, but no passion, and her cold look wounded him dearly. "Hell, Jennie, I thought you were just standing there waiting to be kissed. Now you look at me like I did something terrible by taking you up on your offer."

"I've never been kissed before." Her voice shook slightly, but her eyes stared hard at him.

"I find that hard to believe. If ever I've met a woman with a mouth meant to be tasted, it's you, Jennie." He didn't know why she was lying, but he hated her for it. "You must come from a town long on idiots and short on passion, or you're lying to me again. I'm afraid I'll have to believe you're lying."

She didn't want to explain why she'd never been kissed. She wanted kindness, not a cross-examination. Since he was the only man who'd ever tried, she tended to believe *he* was the shortsighted one, not every other man in the world.

"What made you think you had a right to kiss me, Marshal? I don't understand. Have I done or said anything that made you think I would welcome such an advance?" She tried to pull away from his grip. "I'd like to know so that I can be careful not to repeat the behavior."

Austin lowered his hands from around her waist. "No, ma'am. I guess I was out of line. Would you like to slap me, or shall I slap myself, Miss Munday?" In truth he felt like a fool. Her words had already hit him harder than her hand ever could. The passion he thought he'd seen banked in those emerald eyes was false. Jennie apparently had no more warmth in her than a tumbleweed in January. Oh, she'd tasted good, all right, but Austin decided it would be a cold day in hell before he came back for another sampling.

"Good night," he blurted, suddenly in a hurry to be out of her sight.

"Good night." Jennie turned and climbed the stairs. She made it all the way to the landing before tears started falling.

"My family would have been proud of me," she whispered. "I showed no emotion." Fighting down the sobs, she straightened. "Then why do I feel so empty inside?" she wondered. "Why couldn't I have kissed him back?"

"Jennie!" someone shouted from the back staircase landing. "Jennie, is that you?"

"Yes." Jennie forgot her troubles and ran toward the sound of Audrey's voice. "Is something wrong? Is Delta worse?"

"No," Audrey answered as Jennie reached the top of the stairs. "It's True."

"Did Mrs. Gray find him? Is he sick?"

"No." Audrey pulled Jennie into their room. "I cut his hair and went down the hall to get the water for his bath. When I came back, he was gone."

"But where?"

"I don't know. It's been hours and I've looked everywhere."

Jennie pulled the marshal's jacket tighter around her shoulders. "We have to find the boy."

Audrey shook her head. "I've seen kids like him before. They know how to take care of themselves. If he doesn't want us to find him, we might as well not waste the energy looking."

"But . . ."

"But I've already been to town and back looking and it's too late to walk the road again."

Jennie knew Audrey was right. "He'll come back." She tried to make herself believe her words.

"Of course," Audrey agreed. "He'll be back when he gets hungry."

Chapter
Eight

As he walked the back alleys of Florence, Austin cursed himself for kissing Jennie good night. He'd told Sheriff Morris that he'd make a late check of the town. From the way he was feeling, he figured he'd have time to circle the little settlement ten times before his anger settled down enough for him even to trust himself around anything but a grizzly bear.

She was driving him mad, he decided as he crossed soundlessly between two buildings. He almost wished Buck Lawton and his gang would show up tonight. He'd take all twenty of them on single-handedly if it would help put her out of his mind. She had such a soft-sounding name. Jennie. The kind of name men made up songs about out on the trail, to settle the herd. But her name didn't match the way she made him feel, be it anger or need. She was the first woman who'd made his solitary life seem more a curse than a blessing.

She'd gotten more upset that he didn't believe her lie

about never being kissed than she had about him actually kissing her. Did she think him simpleminded? No woman who looked like she did, with hair of midnight and eyes the color of evergreen, could have reached full growth without men fighting over her.

How many times had he told himself he'd never care for a woman who lied, and as near as he could tell it was a universal trait of the gender.

Austin circled the depot and headed back toward town, trying not even to look in the direction of the Harvey House. Paying little notice of the leaves blowing across the road or the crackle of winter sounding behind him, he moved through the night.

He wasn't about to care for her, he thought. Not if she were the last woman west of the Mississippi. Not if she came to him and begged him to forgive her for lying. Miss Jennie Munday could wait until she was old and gray before he'd bother to kiss her again.

"Evenin', McCormick," Spider Morris whispered as they passed the lights of the Harvey House.

Austin jerked so violently he almost tripped. "Where'd you come from!"

Morris laughed away Austin's question. "I've been walking in your tracks a spell now. Hell, if I'd have had a mind to, I could have tattooed the stars and bars on your back for all the notice you've paid."

"I knew you were there."

Spider waved his defense away and pulled an ancient pipe from his pocket. "Sure you did, son. You were just interested in my heritage when you almost fell over your feet there. Tell me, how'd you live so long in Texas without getting bushwacked?"

Austin knew the old man well enough to realize that he might as well take the ribbing quietly or he'd never hear the end of it. "I guess I got more on my mind than usual."

Spider Morris sucked on his pipe stem while he cradled his rifle in his arms. "I feel the same. I don't know what it is, but I can almost taste trouble in the air."

Austin thought of reminding Morris that any taste was probably coming from the wool and tobacco in his pocket, but he knew what the old man meant. After a while a lawman developed a sense for danger. For no reason at all, he'd tighten his muscles and walk a bit softer. Austin couldn't remember how many times the feeling had passed over him strong enough to make him check the bullets in his Colt, or untie the leather holding his rifle in place on his saddle.

Spider lit his pipe. "It was a night almost like this one six years ago when Buck Lawton and his gang robbed the train. The six-fifteen out of Kansas City was late that night. Some gamblers from Dodge had been up to the city for a high-stakes card game. Talk was the game had run all day and all that night when they decided to move the table down to Dodge. The gamblers boarded the train planning to make it to Wichita by dark."

When Morris seemed more interested in smoking his pipe than continuing, Austin asked, "And the train was robbed near here?"

Morris nodded as he smoked. "I think Buck planned to rob it anyway for the strongbox, but the quarter million in table stakes the gamblers carried made it all that much sweeter a pie."

"But from what I've seen of gamblers, they don't part with their stakes that easily."

"That's what Buck found out. By the time the firing stopped, half of Lawton's men were dead and most of the gamblers. Buck never made it back to the car carrying the strongbox, but he did get the gambling money. Afterwards none would say just how much money was on the table, and we never even found the carpetbag the robbers stuffed the money into."

Austin was interested, but not in any treasure hunt for lost millions. Stories about hidden gold and lost mines were the fabric of legends worn only by fools. "So why Buck's hatred for Florence?"

"That's what puzzled me some." Spider Morris dusted his ashes on the road and tried refilling his pipe. "Oh, we hunted him down, but he wasn't hard to catch with a bullet in his leg and another wedged in his cheekbone. He seemed to take it real personal when we sentenced him to life."

Austin laughed. "Puzzles me, too. After all, you only sent him to jail for the rest of his days. Why should he be mad?"

Morris rubbed his week-old beard, rearranging whiskers in every direction. "No, it wasn't that. It was like he hated not just the folks who caught and tried him, but the whole town. I could see it in his eyes. He'll never lose that kind of hate until Florence is in ashes."

"But why?"

The old sheriff shrugged. "When we caught him, one of the posse said he was with a woman dressed in black traveling clothes. In the fighting she disappeared. Some say she took the money; others say she broke Buck's heart by not even showing up at the trial. There was even talk that she was wounded when she ran."

"Maybe we'll find out if he returns," Austin said.

"When he returns," Morris corrected. "He'll be back, and when he comes, we'd better be ready for him. I got a feeling all hell is gonna break out in this town."

A movement in the shadows beside the dry goods

store made both men stop in midstep. Austin silently eased his Colt from leather. He motioned for the sheriff to wait while he moved in closer. Morris raised his rifle with polished skill, showing that his dislike for guns hadn't corroded his instinct.

Slowly Austin removed the first box. "Might as well come out now and save me the trouble of moving all this trash."

Spider laughed. "You're going to be real sorry you said that if there's a skunk behind there."

"Any critter would have had sense enough to be real still or run before now. Whoever, or whatever, is in this trash is courting a bullet." He knocked another box free from the pile, and it rattled across the alley.

A minute hung in silence. Austin raised his hand to remove the next box, but something moved near his feet. He stepped back as a tiny child crawled from the trash. The same child he'd glimpsed on the train, only slightly cleaner now and with short hair.

"I ain't no critter." True stood tall. "Name's True, and I weren't bothering nobody. Can't a body get some sleep without having the law knocking the door down?"

Austin allowed no emotion to show in his face. "Not much of a door."

"Ain't much of a house, but it was this or sleeping at the Harvey House, where they seem to think bathing is healthy for a body. Henry told me I'd be safe enough here. Guess he didn't know about you two."

"Henry?" Austin looked around for someone. "Who's Henry?"

"He's this boy I met yesterday." True watched both lawmen carefully. "Can't say if he's a friend yet. I already had to beat him up once today."

Morris couldn't resist joining in the conversation. Old

men and children seemed natural allies. "If you don't mind me asking, True, why'd you have to beat up this poor fellow Henry?"

True pulled on oversized pants. " 'Cause he made fun of me not knowing how old I am. He says he's eight, but I'm littler so I must be five or six. I sat on him and kept hitting him in the face until he said I could be eight, too."

Morris tried to hide his laughter. "And where is this friend, Henry?"

"He's got a home he has to go to when it gets dark."

Austin didn't miss the longing in True's voice. He watched the child closely as he asked, "But you have Jennie Munday and the Harvey House."

True shrugged. "When they ain't trying to scrub me raw. I keep telling them it ain't healthy to take your long johns off till spring. I ain't bathing while it's winter, and that's a fact."

"But you'd be warm and well fed there. Surely a bath would be worth that." Austin squatted down to the child's level.

"I'm fine on my own. Once my belly's full I can make it for days between meals. As for warm, I don't figure on taking advice from a man who doesn't even wear a coat out on a winter night."

Austin glanced down, just noticing he'd left his coat with Jennie.

Morris started to say something, but Austin cut him off. "So True's your name," he said to the boy.

True nodded once without volunteering any other information.

"Well, I'm not fond of children, but there's an extra bed over in the back room of the jail. You're welcome to sleep there tonight."

With a fist almost black with dirt, True shoved hair from his deep blue eyes. "Well, I ain't partial to marshals. Even if I didn't have another place to sleep, I'm not sure I could bed down in the same room with one."

Austin's face didn't alter. He understood the game True was playing. "If you've another place, what are you doing out here? It might snow by morning. There's a stove in the jail's office."

True stared at him as though talking to a wooden Indian. "I wasn't sleeping here for the night. I was just resting until those women get bathing off their minds. Then I'll go back and be warm and snug until next Saturday night."

"Plan on disappearing every Saturday night?"

If the child had been his height, Austin would have walked softer around True, for the anger in those blue eyes was unsettling. "I figure my plans is my own business, Marshal; but I'll tell you one thing, I don't plan on keeping you informed of my whereabouts."

Austin finally couldn't hide his smile. He was starting to like this dust rag of a kid. "You don't like me very much do you, True?"

"I don't know," True answered honestly. "I didn't like the way you yelled at Miss Jennie on the train, but you were real careful carrying Miss Delta off when she was hurt."

Austin shoved his hat back. "Tell you what, True, until you decide if I'm a good guy or a bad one, why don't you give me a chance? I could use some help over at the office every day that you can find the time."

"Maybe," True answered. "You pay?"

"Two bits a day."

Austin could see the child adding up the money. "I might, Marshal. I may need some traveling money. From the way you two were talking when you woke me, this may be a town to be leaving from."

"Well, until you do, I'll depend on your help." Austin extended his hand for the child to shake.

True hesitated. Tiny fingers rested in Austin's palm for only a blink in time. "I'll be there," True said.

"One other question," Austin added. "Is Jennie Munday your mother?"

True's eyes hardened again as if seeing a trap. If the answer was yes, Austin would know Jennie had lied to him. If it was no, he'd know True had no home.

"Does it matter?" True asked. "Can I still have the job one way or the other?"

"One way or the other," Austin answered.

Smiling suddenly, True darted around Austin. From the darkness, he heard True yell, "Well, I guess it doesn't matter how I answer. I'll take your two bits a day, Marshal, but you can keep your questions to yourself."

"True!" Austin shouted, but only silence answered. Silence, then Spider Morris's laughter.

Chapter
Nine

*H*aven't seen your marshal this morning," Audrey mumbled as she sampled her fresh-baked roll. "Fact is, I haven't seen him but that first morning in the week we've been here. You figure he left for Texas while we weren't watching the road, or maybe he's made up of mostly shadow like our True?"

Jennie pinned her apron on without looking up. "First, he's not my marshal, and second, when have either of us had time to watch the road even if we cared?"

Audrey's laughter filled the quiet predawn kitchen. "Oh, he could be yours, honey. He could be. I saw the way he looked at you. Beneath all that anger burns a mighty big fire."

"I don't think so," Jennie lied. She'd sent his jacket with True to the jail without even a note.

"Trust me." Audrey dusted her hands free of flour and poured herself a cup of coffee. "I've seen that kind of fire before in a man. It may come out as anger or rage or heaven knows what, but it's going to boil into passion when the flame gets hot enough."

Jennie laughed. She'd never heard such nonsense, but it was fun to dream of such a possibility. She'd found herself looking for him every evening, but he hadn't come to take her walking again.

"Not that I'm an expert on men," Audrey admitted. "But, I've felt the warmth a few times. Trouble was I've never found a fellow I figure to be man enough to handle the wanton woman I'd become if I ever allowed myself to fall in love."

Touching her lips, Jennie remembered Austin's kiss as Audrey continued talking about the perfect man. Jennie guessed Austin would be man enough for her, but she feared she'd probably disappoint him greatly. She didn't know if she'd be woman enough to make any man happy, much less one as strong-minded as Austin McCormick. He'd need one of those women she'd read about in her novels. Women full of strength and fight. Women who could survive all alone on the frontier.

"Yes sir," Audrey continued, "give me a man who can set my heart afire. One who'll stay put in one place and love me. I want a man who plans on being buried next to me on land our great-grandchildren will still own."

"Mind if I wash up?" A man's voice startled Audrey from her ramblings as cold air and sunlight filled the room.

Both women turned to face the back door. There, shadowing the doorway, stood a mountain of muscle and tanned flesh. The huge man took a step forward, almost brushing the frame on both sides. The kitchen light danced in his chestnut hair and warm hazel eyes. "I didn't mean to frighten you, ladies." He hesitated, then slowly removed his hand from where he'd been holding his wadded up shirt near his throat. A crimson stain marred the cloth and splattered across his tan skin.

Neither girl seemed capable of speech, so he continued, "Name's Wiley Radclift. I was just delivering beef and cut my neck on one of the hooks. It's not deep. Just need to wash off the blood. I promise I won't bleed all over your kitchen."

Jennie motioned the man in and handed him a clean towel. She stared at his boots, forcing herself to take deep breaths and forget the blood.

When he accepted the towel, she noticed his hands were huge. The kind of hands that could rock a baby in one palm, or crush a man's jaw with one fist. But there was nothing frightening about the stranger. A gentleness lumbered in his hesitant steps and low voice rich with a Southern accent.

While he dabbed at the wound, Jennie pumped fresh water in a pan for him to wash. As he stood beside her, she was once more aware of his brawn. His height probably missed by a few inches being as tall as the marshal, but he must have been twice the weight, and not an ounce of it was fat.

"Thank you," he said almost shyly. He wet the towel and began washing the cut near his throat.

As he worked, Jennie glanced at Audrey. The tall redhead was standing with dough in both hands and her mouth wider than a day-old bird at feeding time.

"Audrey!" Jennie scolded, wondering where the "I've lit a few fires" woman had gone. "Put down the dough and help. I'll pour this poor man a cup of coffee. Maybe we could spare one of your wonderful apple rolls if he lives through your doctoring."

The man turned to face Audrey. His shoulders looked oak solid. He made no attempt to cover himself, or boast under her careful examination, but merely waited until her gaze returned to his face. "Thank you, ma'am, but I need to get back to the farm. It looks like a norther is fixin' to blow in."

Audrey finally found her voice. "You'll do no such thing." She dropped the dough and wiped her hands on her apron. "I've had some nurse's training, and unlike Jennie, the sight of a little blood doesn't make the air seem thin to me. Allow me to doctor that while you, at least, have a cup of coffee. A few minutes won't make any difference and it might keep the infection down."

She smiled bigger than the Rockies as she passed Jennie. "I can at least tend to you till you get home to your *wife*."

The stranger accepted the coffee Jennie offered without allowing his gaze to leave Audrey. "I haven't got a wife."

Jennie fought down a giggle as she watched Audrey straighten slightly, shoving out her chest and pulling in her stomach. "Well then, we'll fix the wound properly, and before you leave, I'll pack you up some of my rolls."

"But I'm fine," the man tried to argue.

"Of course you are." Audrey wasn't looking at his cut when she said the words.

When Audrey began dabbing salve on the stranger's already bloodless cut, Jennie knew it was time for her to leave. She opened her mouth to excuse herself, but realized neither of them would miss her if she disappeared in a cloud of smoke. Slipping from the room, she decided Audrey just might have met a man big enough to sweep her off her feet.

The rest of the day passed in one endless job after another. Jennie teased Audrey about her giant every

time she passed the kitchen, but other than that the day
brooded dark and rainy. By nightfall the rain had formed
into a full-grown storm and the road outside Clifton
House looked like a chocolate-colored river. Everyone
seemed to feel the downpour, as if the water had soaked
into their skin and weighed them down. At sunset folks
dragged themselves off to bed.

While Audrey went downstairs to line up all her ingre-
dients for the morning baking, Jennie ate her dinner
upstairs with Delta and True. They'd covered the windows with blankets, but the room still seemed cold and
damp. Delta had dressed today, then slipped back into
bed exhausted. True woke her in mid-afternoon to hand
her a telegram that had been delivered, addressed to
Delta Smith. Since then something had been bothering
Delta, something worse than a fever. If Jennie were
betting, she'd have put money down that it had to do
with the deed Delta had told them to hide the first night
they'd come.

Jennie decided to broach the subject as they finished
their dessert. "Delta, are you feeling all right today? Is
it the pain in your shoulder or something else bothering
you?"

Steel-blue eyes stared up at Jennie. The fear was back
in Delta's eyes.

"If it's about the deed, True and I hid it that first
night in the train depot. Don't worry, no one will find
it."

Delta closed her eyes as if in prayer. "I thought I'd
told Audrey, but it doesn't matter as long as he'll never
find the deed even when he finds me. And he will
find me."

"Who?" Jennie hated seeing the way Delta trembled
with fear even more than she had with fever.

"I owe you an explanation." Delta moved her untouched dessert aside.

"You owe me nothing." Jennie knew she'd stand beside Delta without ever knowing more.

"The deed is to land that's been in my family for generations. The man who married my mother a few years ago thinks it belongs to him, but it's still mine. He'd kill me if he thought he'd get the land."

"Is he the one who stabbed you?" Jennie asked.

"No." Delta looked over to make sure True was fast asleep. "That was his son, Ward. He held a knife at my throat because I told him he was never touching me again. When I fought, the blade twisted and went into my shoulder. All the bleeding made him angry. He told me to go clean the blood off then come back so he could finish with me or he'd kill my mother. I went into my bedroom, wrapped the cut as best I could and dressed. I stuffed the deed into my bag and climbed out the window."

"Did your mother get away?"

"No. I don't know what happened to her. When I left, I could hear Ward yelling at her for raising such a fool of a daughter." Delta didn't try to stop a tear from rolling down her cheek. "My mother was the one who told him he could have me as long as he brought her more whiskey. She didn't care what he did as long as I was up and walking in time to fix breakfast. She says that's just the way it is when a girl reaches full growth in a house full of men."

Jennie moved around the table and put her arm over Delta's shoulder. The pain was so great inside Delta, she could almost feel it against her palm. "I don't know what to say. I'm so sorry." Jennie wished she could do something, anything, to help. Delta was speaking of an evil so ugly she didn't even want to face it, but Jennie couldn't and wouldn't let Delta down. "Don't worry, he'll never find you."

Delta cried softly. "Yes, Ward will, and he'll kill me. He told me that first I'd learn to do what he wanted; then after the first year, I could start making some of his drinking friends happy. Ward said it would save him money and wouldn't hurt me none.

"I'm so afraid I can't even breathe sometimes when I think about what he has planned. Now, since he's had to track me down, he'll figure I'm not worth keeping alive. I thought I was lucky last week. A friend who worked at the depot helped me get a ticket and told me about the Harvey House openings.

"I wired her that I was safe. This morning she wired back that my stepbrother boarded the train heading west last night. He tried to get her to tell him where I'd gone. Luckily, she's got several brothers to protect her from his threats. But he saw the Harvey House bulletin posted, and she said he ripped it off the wall when she tried to hide the announcement from him. It's only a matter of time before he finds me. I shouldn't have taken the deed. I should have let them have the land. Maybe he'd have been satisfied."

"Don't worry, you're safe here."

"No, he'll stop at every Harvey House until he finds me, and then he'll make me pay for the trouble I've caused him!" Delta cried. "Before Ward kills me, he'll make me wish I was dead."

"He won't find you." Jennie tried to make her voice sound sure. "Even if Ward does show up in town, we'll think of some way to protect you. I promise." She'd never used a gun, but she could learn. Her father only kept one old rifle, which he used to kill varmints trying to get the chickens. This Ward sounded like the worst varmint she'd ever heard about. Jennie had no doubt that if he ever showed his face at the Harvey House, she'd shoot him dead, providing she could load Delta's pocket pistol.

Delta leaned back, too weak even to keep her eyes open. "He may be on the last train tonight. He'll kill us all to get the deed."

"Don't worry about us." Jennie laughed, wishing she believed her own words. "We can take care of ourselves. Besides, the last train won't be coming in because of the storm, so you can rest easy until morning, then we'll figure out a plan."

Delta relaxed in sleep, curled up beside True while Jennie cleared the dishes. Jennie couldn't help but smile at the small woman next to True. She looked more like another child than a woman fully grown. The wound in her heart would take far longer to heal than the knife wound, but each day she'd grow stronger now that the fever had cooled.

Jennie watched them sleeping as she thought of how needed she felt here. Despite the hard work, her days were filled with a sense of belonging.

Slipping Delta's small gun into her pocket, she decided she could at least hit this Ward with it if he appeared. She'd talk to Audrey, and together they'd find a solution to Delta's problem. They'd managed to hide True in this big hotel; surely they could hide Delta somewhere in the West where her stepbrother would never find her.

When Audrey entered and began preparing for bed, Jennie took the tray downstairs, allowing her a few moments of privacy. There would be plenty of time to talk in the morning.

As Jennie entered the kitchen, she breathed deeply of the wonderful smells. The aroma of dinner—roasted pork and fresh bread—blended with the lingering memory of a dozen apple pies that had been baked only hours before. Banked for the night, the fire's low glow still filled the room with golden light. All the pots and pans were scrubbed and hung and every dish put away and ready for the morning. The two late-shift cooks shared the last of the coffee before calling it a night.

Jennie washed her dishes while making small talk about the rain. As she turned to put away the tray, she heard the long sound of a train whistle above the thunder. "Is there another train in tonight?"

The cook shook his head. "No, miss. Not unless the six-thirty is running way behind. We figured it was canceled." He stood and moved closer to the door, listening. After a pause, he continued. "By sundown the tracks were starting to flood on that last bend just before the station. The wires have been down for over an hour because of the storm, so who knows? Maybe another train is trying to make it . . ."

What sounded like a roll of thunder rattled every dish in the kitchen and shook the floor. Jennie glanced from one cook to the other, then dropped the tray she'd been drying and ran toward the front of the hotel. She could hear the hard sound of metal slamming against metal somewhere outside in the drizzle. A scream echoed in the night, sounding more like a hundred voices than an engine's brakes.

People were everywhere. Jennie was swept along with others out the front door and onto the huge porch. It was raining so hard the lights of town were only soft splotches.

"What is it?" she yelled above the shouting.

For a moment no one knew, yet everyone seemed to know something terrible had just happened. Jennie could feel the hysteria in the damp, icy air around her. She stared into the soupy rain, trying to make sense out of the flickers of light near the depot. The lights were like fireflies leaving the depot and moving into the blackness beyond.

Finally, in what seemed slow motion, one of the lights approached the house. Everyone grew silent as they watched a lone man materialize out of the night. "Help!" he shouted. "The train's derailed at the bend." He pushed through the rain until he reached the bottom step. "They're hurt! Dear God, there are so many hurt!"

He fell on the first step of the hotel. "Please hurry. I think some may be trapped."

Jennie heard herself draw in a breath to scream, but her ears were so full of others' cries she couldn't find her voice to add to the noise. People moved in circles wanting to help but not knowing what to do. Some ran for their overcoats, others grabbed lanterns and headed for the barn, but most just stood around in panic.

One clear voice shouted above the crowd. "Everyone, stop!"

To Jennie's surprise, all the people froze in midstep, and Mrs. Gray's voice continued. "We'll be of no help panicking like a bunch of chickens." Like a general, she took her place on the third step of the stairs. "We don't know how many are hurt, but we've got to be ready. Amos, ride to town and get all the help you can. All you other men need to don your coats and hitch up the wagons. Any women who aren't squeamish go also. The rest of you help me. We'll need coffee, blankets and towels ready for when they get here. Before the first wounded arrive, I want this place ready to serve as a field hospital."

As Jennie ran up the stairs, Mrs. Gray ordered the dining room turned into a makeshift ward. Suddenly Jennie had no doubt where the little lady had received her training. Girls, still in their nightgowns, rolled blankets and pushed tables together. Women, who an hour before were so tired they could barely climb the stairs to bed, ran full speed to ready the hotel.

Jennie hurried through the open bedroom door to grab her coat. "Did you hear, Audrey?"

"Yes." Audrey was already stuffing her hair into a hat. "I'm going down to the wreck. I've got to help." She stomped down the steps with Jennie right behind her. "I'm not staying behind and making coffee when folks down there are hurt."

"But one of us has to stay here!" Jennie shouted at Audrey, knowing no one would bother to listen to their conversation in the panic. "Delta got a telegram today. Her stepbrother is on his way, and she's not strong enough to fight him."

They'd reached the porch. Audrey suddenly turned to face Jennie. "He'll kill her!" She didn't shout, yet the words seemed to ring between them both.

"I know." Jennie fought back the tears. No one who'd seen Delta's fear could doubt such a fact.

Audrey stepped into the rain. "I have to help those people."

"I know," Jennie answered.

"You best stay here and be ready if he comes. Delta told me one day that he was barrel-chested and as hairless as a boiled onion. If such a man opens our bedroom door, shoot him."

"I've never . . ."

"Don't matter. Shooting a man ain't something most folks need to practice." Audrey looked off into the night. "I'll be back as soon as I can."

"Be careful!" Jennie shouted above the storm.

"I was raised with mud deeper than this during any drought in Flatwater," Audrey answered as she took a lantern. "See you later."

Jennie tried to watch Audrey, but the rain curtained everything. She stood on the porch feeling useless. She wanted to go to the wreck; but Audrey was right, someone had to stay and protect Delta.

"Pardon me, Jennie!" a voice shouted as a tiny hand tugged on her skirt. She turned to see True at her side. "What if he's wearing a hat?"

"What?"

True leaned closer. "What if that stepbrother is wearing a hat and we can't tell if he's bald?"

Holding the child tightly, she answered, "I think we'll know him. We have to do our best to protect Delta. He may not even be on the train, but we have to be prepared."

True looked up. "I can help. My ma taught me how to load and fire a gun."

Jennie thought a moment about handing the child Delta's gun but decided against it. "Here's our plan. I'll stand on the porch and watch for him. You go upstairs and take care of Delta. If I see him, I'll come running right up and we'll lock ourselves in until Audrey or the marshal gets back."

True nodded. "I'll wait with Delta. No matter what, I won't leave her alone."

"Thanks." Jennie hugged the child. "I don't plan on allowing a single person in this house tonight without checking them out. With us on guard, Delta will be safe."

True pulled away and vanished as the first wagon from the wreck pulled up to the porch. Without hesitation Jennie stepped into the rain and held her arms wide to help.

Wagon after wagon rolled to the porch, each one filled with people, cold, crying, hurt. Jennie helped them down, softly welcoming them, trying to convince them they were safe. As she worked, she carefully watched for a man with a barrel chest and no hair. He'd be traveling alone, and she had the feeling she'd be able to see the evil in his eyes and know who he was even before he took his hat off.

Some folks hugged her tightly as they cried on her shoulder and bled on her clothes. She held them, offering them all her strength as she led them into the foyer. Slowly she realized that when people were hurt, no matter what age, they wanted someone to hold them.

People continued to come until the house was filled. The injured the worst were put in bedrooms upstairs; others were made as comfortable as possible downstairs. One by one the people drained all energy from Jennie, yet she returned again and again to the porch to wait for the next load. She said a little prayer of thanks each time the wagon contained no man matching the description Delta had given Audrey.

Finally, no more came, yet still she waited. She tried not to notice the icy wind or the steady drizzle. Her clothes had been wet so long her shoulders ached from the weight. She'd seen Austin McCormick several times riding on horseback beside the wagons, but he hadn't spoken to her; he'd only touched his hat in salute. Somehow the knowledge that he was near made her less afraid.

"Jennie." Mrs. Gray stood at the doorway. "Come inside and get warm. There are no more wagons. Everyone has been cared for."

"No," Jennie whispered without turning around. "Audrey and the marshal are still out there. They'd have come in if everyone was found." No matter how cold she was, she wouldn't leave her post until she knew Delta would be safe for the night. And Delta wouldn't be safe until Jennie had seen everyone who was on the train.

Mrs. Gray nodded and returned to the house packed with wounded passengers. "I don't know where we'll put any more injured if they do come."

Chapter
Ten

*J*ennie watched the shadows, waiting for Marshal McCormick and Audrey to return. Finally, after what seemed like hours, she saw Austin moving toward her. He plowed slowly through the mud leading his horse. As he neared, Jennie saw Audrey balanced atop the animal. She held a small woman in her arms as a mother cradles her child.

When the marshal was a foot from the steps, men ran from the barn to assist. He handed them the reins and turned to accept the injured woman from Audrey.

"Careful," Audrey ordered. "We've hurt her enough pulling her from the train."

"We had to pull her out. We couldn't just leave her there to die in the rain. No telling how many bodies we'll find come morning." The marshal's voice sounded exhausted and worried.

As he moved onto the porch, his gaze met Jennie's.

"She's hurt bad," he said. "She needs a bed."

"There are no more." Jennie forced herself to look down at the woman. Her face was covered in mud and blood. "We filled even the last bedroll half an hour ago." Jennie turned back to Austin, but he was waiting for directions.

"Take her to our room. She can have my bed," Jennie answered. "I'll sleep on the stairs."

Blood dripped onto Austin's coat as he carried the injured woman up the stairs to Audrey and Jennie's room. She seemed so small, reminding him a great deal of the other woman he'd carried to the same room only a week before. But he feared this woman was far more gravely injured than Delta had been, and from what he could tell, she must have been traveling alone, for no one looked for her at the wreck. If he hadn't seen her hand, she might still be under the pile of steel and boxes.

"She's far worse than the others," Audrey admitted, opening the bedroom door for Austin. "I don't know if there's much we can do to help her." She glanced in the room at True. "Get some towels, True. Jennie and I'll clean her up."

They could hear Jennie's deep intake of breath. "I . . ."

Audrey looked at her friend. "You'll help," she said, simply willing Jennie to be strong enough to do what must be done.

Jennie closed her eyes. "I'll try." She hadn't signed on to be a nurse, but it seemed as if she'd seen more blood this past week than she'd seen in her lifetime.

As Austin stepped past the women and into the room, he saw Delta asleep on one of the beds, her back turned to him.

"Quiet," Jennie whispered. "Delta needs rest."

The marshal placed the patient on the nearest empty bed without making a sound. Blood dribbled from the woman's mouth, and her face was covered in mud. Austin forced himself not to look too closely, for he knew he was looking at death.

Audrey began to undress the patient. "Best go down and get yourself a cup of coffee, Marshal. I'll let you know how she is as soon as I do all I can. If the doc's sober, send him up, but I'll not have him in this room smelling of spirits."

"Send True down with any news." Austin knew the boy was listening just outside the door to every word they said. In the past week True had shadowed him most nights when he'd made his rounds.

"I'll do that." Audrey smiled silently, thanking the marshal for knowing about True yet holding his tongue.

Austin slapped his wet hat against his leg and moved to the door. "Don't forget to put a bandage on that leg of yours."

Looking down at the long, thin cut on her calf, Audrey pronounced, "It's no more than a scratch, but don't you worry. I'll get to it in time."

Austin moved away knowing he'd have to attend to his horse before he settled down to coffee. As he shoved through the crowd along the hallway, he admitted to himself that he admired the redhead more every time he saw her. She was a strong woman, but he doubted even her will could pull the injured girl away from death's door.

Crossing through the rain to the barn, he found, to his surprise, the men talking of Jennie Munday.

"You should have seen her helping folks down from the wagon like they were all her family," one said.

"Yeah, far as I know she was the only one of us who

didn't go in for coffee," another added. "She wouldn't even quit until Audrey got back. Guess she knew if her friend was still out there, then it wasn't over."

Another said, "I don't think there was a person who came through that door tonight that she didn't comfort. I saw her put her arm around man and woman alike while she calmed them. Even gave up her bed, I hear."

Austin listened as he rubbed his horse down. He'd thought Audrey a hero, but what Jennie had done was no small thing. She'd been on his mind all week, and the feel of her in his arms had been dancing through his dreams every night. He needed to talk with Jennie worse than he figured he'd ever needed anyone's company. Maybe all he wanted was what she'd given everyone tonight—a welcome.

Ten minutes later, when he stepped in the dining room, Mrs. Gray, the resident dictator, confronted him before he could even reach the bottom of the stairs.

"You planning to stay a while, Marshal?"

Austin tossed his hat and damp duster on a hook and nodded. He could see from the movement in the room that this was not a place to have a quiet cup of coffee. There were people everywhere and not a single chair vacant.

"Well, we've got folks to see after and the hungry to feed. Since most of my girls are busy nursing, I know you won't mind helping us out."

Austin raised his eyebrow. If the lady tries to lasso an apron on him, she'd find she was out of luck.

Mrs. Gray smiled as if she'd read his mind. "All I need you to do is take this pot of coffee over to the lunch counter where the men are drying out. We always ask folks if they want coffee, tea or milk. If they say coffee, pour them a cup. If they say tea or milk, ask one of the girls to help them."

Austin nodded. "Sounds simple enough." If anyone else in the world had asked him, he would have turned her down; but Mrs. Gray had a way about her that made even someone twice her size not want to argue.

He wrapped his fingers around the warm handle of the huge kitchen coffeepot and moved to the counter. "I assume you want coffee," he said with a scowl to the first person sitting at the counter.

No one argued with Austin as he moved down the counter pouring cup after cup of the hot liquid. No one dared order anything else except what the marshal served.

An hour later Austin stood on the porch with the last cup of hot coffee in his hand. He watched the rain. His clothes were still damp, but he was too tired even to feel the cold. As soon as he heard about the woman upstairs, he planned to head back to his room behind the jail. He wished he'd had time to talk to Jennie. The lady seemed to have a moment for everyone except him, and he wasn't about to admit he needed her, even if he could feel an ache to touch her go all the way to his soul.

"Marshal," a voice whispered behind him.

Austin turned and looked down at True. "Yes, son."

"Audrey said they got the woman all bandaged up and she's resting." True moved closer. "But she was hoping you could check on Jennie."

"Is she hurt?"

"No, sir. Audrey says some women ain't meant to see all that much innards at once. Jennie helped her do the doctoring, but then she ran out of the room."

The marshal started to move toward the door, but a tiny hand shoved Austin's hat and duster at him. "Jennie ain't upstairs," True said. "I followed her down the back steps. She's out in the wash house."

Austin bolted off the porch and started around the house. "I'll find her," he called back.

"When you do, tell her not to worry about Delta," True yelled. "I'm watching over her."

Austin moved through the blackness toward the wash house. For a moment he couldn't find her in the pale light coming from the main house, but he could hear her softly crying. As his eyes adjusted he saw Jennie standing over a washtub rubbing something white up and down the washboard.

"Jennie," he said as he moved forward.

She stopped suddenly as though she'd been caught doing something wrong.

"Jennie, don't be frightened."

She looked up but didn't seem to recognize him. Even in the shadows he could see the tears streaming down her cheeks.

"Jennie, I'm here." He wanted to hold her, but he wasn't sure he wouldn't frighten her more if he moved too fast.

"Austin," she whispered. "I can't get the blood out of my apron. I can't get the blood out, and you know how we have to have spotless aprons." She started rubbing the cloth back and forth along the scrub board.

Austin pulled the apron from her fingers. "We'll get you a new one tomorrow. Right now you need sleep. It's been a long night."

"I can't go back to my room. I'm afraid someone is going to die in there tonight. I can smell death in the air, feel it clammy next to my skin."

He pulled her against him. "Jennie," he whispered over and over as he stroked her hair. "Everything's going to be all right." She hadn't had any sleep in almost twenty-four hours. He'd seen seasoned soldiers crumble with less than she'd had to endure tonight.

"Jennie, I've got to get you warm and dry or you'll be sick. It's freezing out here and you're dripping wet. You need to go in."

She tried to pull away. "There's no room inside. People are sleeping shoulder to shoulder on the floor. I've nowhere to go."

"I know a place." He draped his damp duster over her shoulders and lifted her in his arms, then stepped back out into the rain. She held to him tightly as he walked around the hotel and up the road leading to town.

Her crying stopped, but her hold around his neck didn't, as they reached the first buildings. In an hour it would be morning, but now everyone in town was asleep. Austin turned down the alley and within minutes had kicked open the back door of the jail.

"This isn't much, but at least you can get dry and warm up before I take you back. You need some hot coffee in you before you have to face that crowd at the hotel again."

"I'm fine now, honest. I don't know why . . ."

He could feel her back straighten. She was pulling away from him even though her body hadn't moved. He shook his head. "It's all right. I figure everyone, man or woman, has got a right to crumble now and then."

"Thank you for being there to pick up the pieces." Jennie smiled, very much aware that he was still holding her.

"Oh," he laughed as he lowered her legs to the floor. For a moment she still clung to him. With his rough hands, he pushed the wet hair away from her face and fought the urge to kiss her. If ever there was a woman who looked like she needed kissing, it was this one, but he'd promised himself she'd be the one to make the next move.

He forced himself to pull away as he removed his duster from her shoulders. "I'll light the stove and boil some coffee. Why don't you pull off that wet dress? You can wrap up in a blanket from one of the cells. It may be dusty, but at least it will be dry."

Jennie nodded and moved into the shadows. Being careful to keep his back turned, Austin could still hear her moving around. He heard wet clothes hit the floor as he reached for a light and decided he was getting plenty warm without the stove. Another garment plopped on the wood, and he fought the urge to turn around as he shoved logs into a still-warm Franklin stove.

"When's the last time there was a prisoner in this place?" Jennie whispered from close behind him.

Austin turned and almost dropped the pot of coffee. Lord, but she looked beautiful standing there wrapped in an old blanket. Her hair waved in wet curls to her waist. He could see the white straps of her undergarments where one of her shoulders lifted above the blanket.

Her cheeks glowed with warmth as she noticed where he was staring. She shifted the blanket slightly, trying to cover herself, but only succeeded in revealing more of her legs. "I'm sorry," she mumbled. "The quilt isn't quite long enough. Maybe you should only save shorter women in the future."

Austin glanced at her slender legs, bare from the knee down. He sloshed the coffee onto the stove as he set the pot down and hurried to a back room. "I can fix that," he yelled over his shoulder in a voice that sounded like it should have belonged to someone half his age. He returned with one of his flannel shirts. "If you'll allow me." He held it open for her.

Jennie turned her back to him and slid the blanket to her waist. While she tied it, he watched the lamplight dance off the silky paleness of her back.

When she stepped into the shirt, his arms wrapped around her with the material. She lifted her arms to pull her hair free of the collar. His large hands slid down her sides, pressing the soft flannel against her cold skin with a gentle force.

"Thank you," she whispered without stepping away. Slowly, a fraction of an inch at a time, he pulled her against his chest. She could feel the warmth of his body through their clothes. Warming her from inside. His breath moved softly against her neck as his hands slid around her waist and drew her solidly against him.

"Do you want me to move away?" His voice was so low it could have been a thought that passed between them.

"No," Jennie answered and felt his arms tighten slightly.

"I don't want to be out of line again, but damned if you aren't the hardest woman I've ever come across to keep my hands off."

Jennie loved the way he felt, so solid and strong against her back. "I'm sorry about that night. You weren't out of line; I was." She brushed her hair against his chin.

"No." He rolled his face into the damp curls beside her forehead, drowning in the scent of her hair. "I shouldn't have thought just because you walked with me that you'd welcome my advances."

He moved his hand to her damp hair and pulled the ebony strands away from her throat. Gently, very gently, he pressed his mouth along the cool softness of her neck.

The steady pounding of her pulse welcomed him.

Jennie couldn't stop the sigh that escaped. "I didn't mind the kiss," she whispered. His lips advanced across her skin, firmer this time. When she sucked in her breath suddenly, she felt his arm tighten just below her breasts. She needed to feel him close to her tonight more than she'd ever needed anything. It didn't matter if he believed in her, she believed in him.

"Why didn't you kiss me back, Jennie?" he asked, his lips moving against her throat.

Jennie leaned her head on his shoulder, allowing him more freedom.

She could feel his words near her ear. "Don't tell me it was because you didn't want to be kissed." He spread his hand wide at her waist, loving the way she moved in pleasure to the rhythm of his touch. "I know that would be a lie."

"I didn't think." She stopped as his fingers twisted the shirt, pulling it tight over her chest. How could she tell him that she didn't think he really wanted to kiss her? She'd already tried to tell him no one had ever kissed her before, and he hadn't believed her. She didn't want to start an argument; she only wanted to feel him next to her.

His lips were liquid fire as they trailed down her skin. "If I ask you to kiss me again, will you?" she whispered as she felt herself stepping off predictability and into the unknown.

He turned her slowly to face him. "Are you asking?"

Jennie raised her arms around his neck and leaned against him. "I'm asking." She giggled softly. "Anything to get you to stop talking."

Austin didn't wait for a second invitation. He lowered his mouth over hers and kissed her with the longing that had been building inside him. When she was proper, she could be a cold northern blast, but now, like this in his arms, she was a fire he'd let consume him before he'd pull away an inch.

Chapter
Eleven

*J*ennie lowered her eyelids and smiled as Austin's lips touched hers. His kiss was soft, almost hesitant this time, not hard and impersonal as it had been a week ago.

She was unsure what she should do, so she moved her fingers across his shoulders and into his hair. His sandy-colored hair was brown with dampness from the rain and softer than she would have guessed as it drifted between her fingers.

"Damn," he whispered against her mouth. "You taste as good as you look."

Jennie pulled his head closer and pressed her lips harder against his. No one had ever told her she was good-looking, and she somehow wanted to believe it was true, if only for tonight. The fire popped with damp wood. Shadows danced on the bare walls around them. The air smelled heavy with rain, but Jennie closed her eyes and believed in enchantment and knights . . . and magic.

Their kiss lingered long and tender, allowing a feeling of belonging to gently encircle them, caressing them both, fulfilling a need nestled deep inside each of their hearts since childhood.

Austin finally raised his head an inch and studied her closely. "Did you mean it the other night about never being kissed before?" He held her hesitantly as if afraid she might dart from his arms.

"Yes," she whispered, loving the way her lips touched his with her words. She moved a fraction closer, silently telling him she had no plans of leaving the circle of his arms.

"One man asked my father for permission to call on me, but Father told him I didn't have time. If I'd have known kissing could be so pleasurable, I might have made the time."

Austin laughed softly against her cheek. "Damned if I don't want to believe you." He kissed her lightly several times. "I'd have had a slightly more forceful talk with your father, if I'd have been the man coming to call."

Picturing the confrontation, Jennie laughed.

Jennie looked closely at the man holding her, wishing he'd been in her world earlier. When he wasn't frowning, he looked younger, maybe not more than a year or two older than her. He'd seemed so hard before she'd have guessed him well into his thirties; but now, with his hair across his forehead and his eyes bright with fire, he could have been no more than in his late twenties.

"How long have you been fighting?" She didn't need to say the outlaws, or Indians. She had a feeling Austin had been fighting all his life. Absently, she brushed the worry lines along his forehead.

"I lied about my age and joined the Union army at fourteen." He played with a curl of ebony hair resting on her shoulder. "My brother, Pete, and I were more interested in three square meals a day than the war. He was only a year older than me, but he never saw his sixteenth birthday. I stayed in the army after he died because there was nowhere else to go."

He continued talking as his hands lightly caressed her shoulders. "By the time my company moved out of New Orleans in '68, I was shaving regularly and ready to fight, so I signed up for the frontier and went to Texas. When the Indians settled down, I became a federal marshal. I can't remember a time when a gun wasn't strapped on my hip, or I stayed in one place long enough to watch the seasons change."

Jennie didn't have to ask to know there had been very little softness in his life. She saw it in the way he looked at the world, as if always waiting for the worst to happen. She felt it in the gentle way he touched her, as though fearing any moment she might shatter like fine bone china in his rough hands.

"Do you think we could talk later, Jennie?" He moved his finger slowly down the front of her shirt to the first button. "I'd like to kiss you again, if you've no objection. I'm not sure how long I can stand here looking at you dressed like you are and not hold you."

"But what if we're not doing it right?" Jennie smiled, feeling beautiful. More beautiful than she'd felt every day of her life combined. "If you've little experience and I've none, no telling the mistakes we're making."

"Then we'll have to practice until we get it right." He tugged at the curl he'd been holding and then lowered his head as his arms pulled her against him once more.

He captured her lips before she had time to protest. His mouth was more insistent this time, more demanding of giving, as well as taking, pleasure. She answered his need by moving closer, allowing her curves to mold against him.

When she leaned into him, Austin could feel his heart trying to break through his ribs, and there didn't seem to be enough air in the room to fill his lungs. A woman had never stepped so willingly, so innocently, into his embrace. He'd made a point of keeping folks at arm's length, but Jennie was having no trouble tumbling every fence he'd ever put up.

Her body shifted slightly, setting every nerve of his alive with pleasure. There was a heaven of pure joy in holding this woman, unlike he'd even known existed in more than dreams.

His hands moved from her back to her sides. The longing to touch her was a need within him as great as survival. With a gentle pressure he slid his fingers up her body until the palms of his hands rested just under her arms. He could feel her rib cage rise and fall with each breath. When he moved slightly, the fullness of her breasts strained against his open palms.

Jennie gasped for air as his hands moved against her. The warmth of his touch passed through the flannel and into the softness of her breasts. Her bottom lip trembled against his mouth, silently begging him not to stop.

No touch had ever been so bold, rocking longing from its hiding place. She opened her kiss to his in a silent cry of joy as his hands brushed over her pointed mounds.

Slowly, his fingers moved to her waist and back again, applying a fraction more pressure with each pass along the swell of her breasts.

When she cried against his lips in pleasure, his tongue entered her mouth, changing the kiss from play to passion. The storm within him began to rage far stronger than any outside. He could feel lightning sparking through his mind and thunder rumbling in great quakes from his heart.

He loved the taste of her. She was wonder and magic, all sugarcoated in longing. His brain felt as if he must be suffering from sunstroke. His hands ached to move completely over her skin, just as every muscle in his body longed for the feel of her beneath him. But he forced himself to move slowly, unwilling to risk frightening her away. He'd never hesitated in his life. It was the one trait that had most kept him alive in dangerous situations, but he hesitated now.

Forcing his hands to leave her sides, he laced his fists into her long hair, pulling her head back slightly. He could never take this woman, even if she were willing. He'd only lead her gently into lovemaking, for he wasn't sure the passion she brought wouldn't consume him in its fire if he moved too quickly.

The blanket around her waist tumbled to the floor and she leaned closer into him, pressing against the center of his desire.

He was going mad an inch at a time, and she seemed determined to push him the last few paces into Heaven. "Jennie," he whispered as his lips moved from her mouth to the silk of her neck. "Dear God, Jennie!"

Jennie looked up at the lamplight dancing off the cobwebs in the rafters and laughed. "If you haven't got kissing right," her hands couldn't keep from moving across his chest, feeling the warmth of solid muscle, "I don't think I could endure any improvements you plan to make when you finish learning."

"There is more," Austin whispered as he tasted her ear, "far more I'd like to give you."

She wanted to ask him—no, beg him—for lessons, but his mouth returned to claim hers. As her body warmed from within, she felt his large, rough hand slide over the flannel covering her hip and onto the bare skin of her leg. His fingers spread wide, branding his warmth into her flesh with a loving caress.

Suddenly Jennie had to feel his flesh against her hand. She pushed his shirt aside and lay her fingers over his heart. The muscles were strong, but she could still feel the pounding of his heart beneath her touch. When she moved her hand slightly, his kiss deepened and she sensed the power she had over this strong man.

His embrace was warm and loving and filled with a need she didn't quite understand. But she was learning and loving the lesson.

If he'd told her she could fly, she would have believed him; but the creaking of a door shattered the moment and brought her feelings crashing to reality.

Austin's head jerked up, and one hand pulled her behind him as the other reached for his weapon. His stance widened, preparing for battle, and Jennie felt his body turn to stone in front of her.

"Morning, son," Spider Morris mumbled as he pulled off his wet hat and slapped it against his knee. He would have been completely blind to miss the scene he'd interrupted. Jennie stood behind Austin clothed in nothing but a man's shirt, while Austin braced like a warrior ready to defend his lady.

"Hell of a wreck last night." Morris moved to his desk without seeming to see anything out of place. "I thought I'd get a dry pipe and head on over to the Harvey House and see how many injured we have." He replaced his hat low over his head. " 'Spect I'll be seeing you over there later, since there's nothing going on around here."

Austin didn't answer.

Morris opened the door and disappeared into the rain without a backward glance.

Jennie grabbed the blanket and pulled it tightly around her. "Do you think it possible he didn't notice us?"

Austin ran his fingers through his hair. "I've worked with him for a week, and there's not much he misses. He noticed us, but if anyone ever asked, I'd bet a month's pay the old man swears he didn't see a thing."

"Really!" Jennie could imagine how such a scandal like this would spread over her hometown.

"We weren't breaking any law, so I guess he figures it was none of his business." Austin watched her closely. "Unless he thought I might be forcing myself on a lady who didn't welcome my advances."

Jennie laughed and moved into the shadows, collecting her drying clothes as she walked. "More likely it was the other way around, Marshal."

Austin fought the urge to follow her into the darkness. "No regrets?"

"One." Jennie's voice came from somewhere in the blackness of a cell.

"What's that?" Austin stiffened. The moments preceding her answer ticked by one eternity after another.

"We got interrupted before the lesson was over." She walked into the warm glow of the lamplight, her clothes still wet and clinging to her slender frame. "Though I found the learning very interesting."

His frown spread into a smile across his tanned face. He watched her as she walked up to him unafraid and buttoned his shirt. The casual touch made him want to hold her once more, but he was afraid if he touched her now, he would frighten her with his need for her. "I'd like to see you again. I've never met a woman like you before. All proper on the outside and fire on the inside.

I've never wanted to hold anyone so much."

Jennie could feel the heat climbing up her body as if he still touched her. "I'd like that," she whispered. "I'm a little afraid . . . afraid I'm dreaming."

"Well, if you are, we're both having the same dream."

He didn't say another word as he wrapped his duster around her. He held her hand tightly as they hurried through the predawn blackness to the Harvey House.

When they reached the edge of the trees, he pulled her suddenly against him. The rain pounded above them, but neither felt the cold. They held to each other as if to life. Now their touch was no longer filled with passion, but longing. Then, as suddenly as he'd hugged her, he moved again, placing his arm around her shoulder and pulling her across the river of mud toward the lights.

"If you ever need me, just walk out the front of the hotel. From there you can see the light of the jail. It's the first building in town. We usually keep a lantern on till late, in case anyone needs us."

"And if I should need you one night?"

"I'll be waiting," Austin promised.

He didn't let his grip around her slacken until they reached the back door of the hotel. When she stepped inside, she felt his arm leave her. Before she could turn around, he disappeared into the rain, but the memory of his kiss warmed her as she climbed the back stairs to her room. It was very late, but people were still moving around, tending to those in pain.

When she opened the door, Audrey and Delta's crying shattered her thoughts.

"What is it?" Jennie ran to the foot of the bed both women sat beside. "Is True hurt?"

Audrey looked up and wiped her nose with the corner of her robe. "No, True's fine. Crawled under the bed about an hour ago and fell asleep."

Jennie glanced at her bed. All the air in her lungs seemed to rush out at once. The blond-haired woman Austin had pulled from the train wreck slept quietly in Jennie's bed. Too quietly!

"Is she . . ." Jennie couldn't finish as she knelt beside Audrey.

Audrey nodded. "About thirty minutes ago. I did all I could, but she never even opened her eyes." Audrey started crying again, and Delta joined in.

Finally Audrey handed Jennie a stack of letters tied up in a blue ribbon. "We thought we'd look through her carpetbag and see if we could find her name. Something isn't right when a woman dies without anyone even knowing her name."

Jennie looked down at the letters addressed to a Mary Elizabeth O'Brian as Audrey continued. "Those tell the whole story. This poor girl has no family back east. She answered one of those ads men place in the personals and traveled all this way to marry a man she doesn't even know, an old widower by the name of Colton Barkley."

Jennie found herself fighting back her own tears. She hadn't even spoken to the woman, but it seemed so wrong that she'd die just as she was about to marry and have a family.

"She must have had a pretty bad life back east," Audrey continued. "Look at her clothes, they're little more than rags. But she didn't have to answer that ad to get away. I've heard stories about what a hard time some of these mail-order brides have. They come all this way to be little more than slaves to a man too ugly to find a decent wife."

Delta patted Audrey's hand. "Maybe the widower isn't as bad as we think. He did offer to let her stay one

month before the wedding. One of the letters says he'll
buy her a ticket to anywhere she wants if she decides
not to marry him. Now, that doesn't sound like someone
who just wants a slave."

Audrey blew her nose again and nodded. "Too bad
someone doesn't make you that offer. We could get
you so far away from here with a free train ticket your
stepbrother would never find you."

Jennie moved to the window, tapping the letters against
her palm. She stared out the pane, too deep in thought to
see anything. The woman had died, forfeiting a chance
for freedom Delta would have done anything to have.
If Delta's stepbrother hadn't been on the train last night,
he'd be on one soon. Then Delta might be the one sleeping
forever. "I know exactly what we're going to do," she
whispered first to herself, then to the others. "Do the
letters say the widower has ever met Mary Elizabeth,
or exchanged pictures?"

"No," Audrey said. "In fact he said he was sorry that
she didn't have a picture to send him, but it didn't really
matter to him what she looked like. That didn't seem to
be a factor in making the offer of marriage."

Jennie smiled at Delta. "Then you can take the widower up on his offer."

"But I can't take her ticket." Delta shook her head.
"I can't act like I'm going to marry some old man then
change my mind just for a free ticket. He'll know I'm
not her. All we have is his letters. We don't know what
she wrote to him."

Audrey straightened, pushing all grief aside as easily
as an old maid folds her wedding dress up with her
dreams. "Mary Elizabeth isn't going to use the ticket,
and the widower can afford it or he wouldn't have
offered. Look at it as a business deal. You'll give him

a month's worth of work for his money."

Jennie joined in. "After a few days on his farm, you'll be good as new. And you can say you're memory is a little foggy after the wreck. After all, you did get hit in the head."

"I did?"

Audrey agreed. "Yes, you did."

"But . . ." Delta's light blue eyes filled with doubt.

"No buts about it," Audrey answered. "Jennie's got a great idea. You're almost the same height, near as I can tell, and you're both blond-haired. The widower's never seen her, so you could be her."

"But . . ." Delta shook her head. "What if she wasn't blue-eyed?"

"We could look at her eyes," Jennie answered in a room stagnant with sudden silence.

"Not me," Delta whispered.

"Not me," Audrey echoed.

Jennie moved to the edge of the bed but couldn't seem to make her hand touch the stranger's face. She'd seen dead folks before . . . but she couldn't bring herself to disturb the poor girl. Finally she turned to Delta. "We'll let her sleep," Jennie whispered, "and pray she had blue eyes."

"But what if she didn't and she wrote it in one of her letters? I can't very well claim the train wreck changed my eye color."

Audrey placed her hand on Delta's shoulder. "Then you'll do what all women do when confronted with such a problem. You'll shrug your shoulders, smile sweetly and say, 'I lied.' Then look at him like it's his problem, and most men somehow think it is."

"But what about the body?" Delta whispered as if the dead girl might overhear them.

They all three looked at one another, then Jennie whispered, "It's really sad, but Delta Smith took a fever and died tonight."

"What!" Audrey's eyebrows rose almost to her hairline.

Jennie's expression didn't change. "We thought she was getting better, but she must have been bleeding inside from injuries suffered during the train robbery."

Audrey looked doubtful. "From a week ago?"

Jennie's mask never altered. "From a week ago."

Delta closed her eyes and raised her face to the ceiling. When she opened them, cold steel blue looked at first Jennie, then Audrey. "Delta Smith died tonight, poor girl. You'll hold her belongings should her family come looking, won't you?"

"Of course." Jennie nodded.

"And the deed." Delta looked straight at Jennie. "The deed will never be found."

"Never," Jennie agreed. "In fact I've never heard of such a thing."

Chapter
Twelve

*T*hough the rain stopped a little after dawn, the day never brightened beyond dreary. Audrey went down to tell Mrs. Gray the sad news about the death of Delta Smith. The old woman had only seen Delta a few times, so there was a good chance that Jennie's plan would work.

While Audrey told her tale, Jennie helped Delta into Mary Elizabeth's faded clothes and wrapped a bandage around her forehead and neck. Thanks to Jennie's hat and the bandages, most of Delta's face was covered. Even someone who'd known the girl all her life would have to look twice to recognize her now.

"All you have to do is stay out of sight until the widower comes." Jennie examined her work. "Some of the men were saying it may be two days before they get the wreck cleaned up enough for another train to arrive. If your stepbrother is on it, you'll be long gone."

"Or long buried," Delta added. She was busy handling each of Mary Elizabeth's belongings, trying to become familiar enough with the few personal objects the woman had so that she could think of them as her own. "I know what we're doing is the only way out; and if poor Mary could tell us, she'd probably say 'go ahead,' but I'm not sure I can use all her personals. Somehow taking her name and future doesn't seem as bad as using her brush and comb."

"You have to," Jennie answered as she stuffed Delta's own personal items into a small trunk. "If your stepbrother comes looking for you and sees the grave, but your things are not all here, he'll know something is wrong."

"I feel like I'll have nothing of me to hang on to when I leave this room." Delta closed her fingers around air. "Could I at least take my Paterson pistol? It was my mother's. I feel somehow less afraid with it in my pocket."

"No, I don't think it would be for the best." Jennie could understand, but she had to think logically. "The deed will be missing. That's enough. If anything else is, your stepbrother, Ward, might get suspicious."

"You're right," Delta admitted, shoving the last of Mary Elizabeth's belongings back into what was now her bag. "He might even decide to make it hard for you and Audrey, thinking you stole something from the trunk."

Audrey opened the door, as always lugging a tray of coffee. She set down the tray, blended True a cup of half coffee, half milk, then turned to the women to tell her news. "Everyone in town's been in this morning to dry out. Some want to help, but most just want to visit about the wreck. They've found a few bodies, but according to the conductor's count, there's still three men missing."

"Missing?" Jennie tried not to let Delta see how worried she felt.

Audrey nodded. "They may be dead, or wandered off toward town last night in the rain. Who knows, the conductor could have miscounted. Trying to count folks in this place is like counting flies buzzing a watermelon."

Jennie couldn't help but smile. "So what else is going on downstairs?"

"Since no trains will be arriving until they get the tracks clear, Mrs. Gray says the coffee's free to the locals," Audrey said. "I don't think one of those three men could be your stepbrother, but we need to get you out as soon as possible just in case."

"Agreed," Jennie added.

Audrey poured herself a serving and continued, "While I was telling her about poor Delta's death, we spotted the undertaker downing his third cup. He said unless the rain starts up again, the funeral can be held this afternoon." Glancing at the dead girl, Audrey added, "She looks so different."

Jennie straightened with pride. "I put her in Delta's new uniform. After all, if we're burying a Harvey Girl, she should look like one." Tending the injured might be hard for her, but dressing the dead was something every preacher's daughter became accustomed to.

"It's fitting she should be buried in new clothes. Poor thing didn't have a stitch in her bag that wasn't worn bare." Audrey studied the body and nodded. "No one will see anything but the uniform."

"That's what I hoped." Jennie moved out from in front of Delta. "How do you think Mary Elizabeth looks?"

Audrey smiled. "Mighty good. What I can see of her."

"Exactly," Jennie answered.

"Do you think anyone will remember her from the train wreck?"

Jennie shook her head. "Besides us, I doubt anyone took a second look at her last night, except maybe Marshal McCormick. All we've got to do is keep Delta out of sight until the widower comes. She can spend a month resting on his farm, then she's free."

True downed the cup of half coffee and half milk. "I know a place she can hide till it's time to go. Henry and me found it the other night."

All three women looked at the child as True explained. "When this hotel was built, they must have added on at different times because there's a gap between the center wing and the left of the hotel. It's like one long hallway to nowhere."

"Big enough for Delta—I mean, Mary Elizabeth?" Jennie knelt to True's level. The child rarely spoke, and when True did, the stories were a mixture of half lies that only a child would believe. True was like a little mouse, moving soundlessly around the hotel, disappearing for long periods, then reappearing at mealtimes. In the week they'd been here, the huge building had become a playground for True. Thanks to the number of people, even if True were seen in the hallways, everyone assumed he was one of the local boys used as runners.

True's deep blue eyes lit up with pleasure. "Plenty of room for even Audrey to stand up in, and it runs from the back of the hotel to the front. I don't know where the front opens up or if it does, but the back passage is behind the water storage for this floor."

"Well, let's go." Delta carefully nestled her arm into a sling. "I need to get out of here before the undertaker comes for my body."

True slipped a hand into Delta's. "I'll show you, Miss Mary Elizabeth." The child's eyes danced with delight at the game the three women were playing.

Delta glanced at Jennie. "What will you do if anyone comes looking for Mary Elizabeth?"

Jennie dusted her apron, as if showing little interest in the question. "She's downstairs having breakfast with the rest of the train wreck victims, I would guess. Wasn't hurt near as bad as everyone thought. Most of that blood must have been someone else's splattered on her."

"That's a possibility," Audrey agreed. "Head wounds do tend to bleed a great deal, though. You might try looking for Mary Elizabeth downstairs in the crowd. Like my Granny Gates used to say, 'There's enough poor souls down there to encourage a tent preacher to lengthen his invocation.' "

Delta smiled down at True. "Let's go. When I walk out that door, I'm Mary Elizabeth O'Brian."

An hour later the undertaker and Sheriff Morris toted a coffin up to Jennie and Audrey's room. Jennie stood alone in the hallway and listened as they nailed the box shut. She closed her eyes and thought of all the dull, endless days she'd lived at home. There had been nights back then in which, if she lay very still in bed, she'd have sworn she heard the nails of her own coffin being hammered. But no longer; now she felt alive.

"Jennie!" Audrey yelled.

Jennie moved to the railing at the top of the stairs.

"Mrs. Gray said we could have the rest of the day off." Audrey hurried up the steps with two shawls over her arm.

She wrapped one around her head, and Jennie wrapped the other around hers. When Morris and the undertaker carried the coffin out, the girls followed a few feet behind crying softly. Jennie was thankful for the cold wind as they moved outside. She could pull the shawl close around her face. She wasn't sure she could look the old sheriff in the eyes after the way he'd seen her dressed before dawn. Also, if he were as observant as Austin claimed, he might see the lack of grief in her face.

The funeral was simple. With no regular minister in town, Sheriff Morris read a few words over the body and said a prayer. Jennie and Audrey watched the casket being lowered into the shallow grave, feeling relieved that the first part of their plan had worked.

Jennie lifted a handful of wet dirt and dropped it atop the wood. The earth would hide their secret, forever keeping Delta safe.

An hour later, in the dining room, they were not so sure the second part of the plan would work. Jennie and Audrey had just finished having a late lunch when they both turned to stone at the sound of a low voice talking with Mrs. Gray in the lobby.

"I'm Colton Barkley, and I'm here to pick up a Mary Elizabeth O'Brian. I believe she was on the train last night, but no one seems to know where she is now."

Before Jennie could stand for a look at the widower, Marshal McCormick stepped between her and the man. "She was injured," Jennie heard the marshal say. "But I'm sure she received fine nursing."

Audrey reached across the table and touched Jennie's arm. "Now, settle down. If we're going to get through this, we've got to go slow and easy, like we're too upset about our poor Delta to be worried about some stranger named Mary Elizabeth."

Jennie agreed and slowly lifted her fork, forcing herself to continue eating. Her gaze never left her plate until she heard Austin's voice behind her.

"Pardon me, ladies." His hand lightly touched Jennie's back. The touch went unnoticed to everyone except her. She could feel the warmth of his hand through the layers of fabric. His slight touch reminded her of what had been between them and offered a promise of what would be.

"I understand it's been a hard day for you both. I would have liked to come to the burial, but couldn't." He removed his hat and crushed the brim in one large hand. "I know Miss Delta was a friend."

Audrey sniffed. "Thank you for your kindness, Marshal, but it was God's will Delta passed on, and ours is not the place to question."

Jennie almost caught herself saying, *Don't question, please don't question.*

The man beside the marshal moved impatiently. "Marshal." His voice was winter hard and low with anger.

Austin raised his hat as if just remembering the man shadowing him. "Yes, Mr. Barkley. I'm aware you're in a hurry to make sure your fiancée is all right, but these are the women who took care of her."

Jennie looked up into the blackest eyes she'd ever seen. Colton Barkley had obviously been a week or more away from a razor and, judging from the amount of dust on him, at least three days on the trail. But the dirt and stubble hadn't watered down his hawklike stare, which looked as if it had been brewing more than one lifetime in a batter of mistrust and hate.

There was a hard handsomeness about him Jennie found more frightening than appealing. His lean body hinted of a strength beneath his muddy clothes. Colton Barkley was a thunderstorm in the flesh. His hair was charcoal, his skin weathered hard and his stance alarmingly rigid. But most surprising about this man who seemed to rattle the china with his unvoiced anger was the fact that he was young. He might be a widower, but he was not out of his twenties. It seemed unbelievable that someone could grow so cold and bitter in so few years. Jennie couldn't help but wonder if he'd frightened his first wife to death.

Standing, she tried to keep her hand from trembling as she offered it. "I'm Jennie Munday and this is Audrey Gates. We've enjoyed meeting your intended, Mary Elizabeth."

He took her hand only briefly enough to be considered polite. "She's not badly hurt?" His gaze narrowed.

"Oh, no." Audrey stood. "Give her a few weeks and she'll be good as new. But she's been through a terrible shock, Mr. Barkley. I'm sure you'll be wanting to postpone the wedding for a while."

Colton didn't alter his stormy expression as he looked at her. "Could one of you tell her I'm here, or point her out to me? I need to be on my way if I'm to reach my land by sundown."

Both women reacted like schoolchildren at the sound of a bell. They darted for the stairs without saying another word. Neither wanted to stay in Mr. Barkley's presence a moment longer than necessary.

Halfway up, Jennie pulled Audrey to a stop. "Are we making a mistake? That man's stare could scare small children out of a year's growth."

Audrey shook her head. "He does have a powerful amount of anger in him. He looks like he just walked out of hell on a rainy day. But we've made our bed."

"Or Delta's," Jennie added.

"What else can we do now," Audrey started on up the stairs, "tell Delta there's a good-looking young man waiting downstairs but she can't go because he looks angry?"

"But we can't let Delta go with him," Jennie whispered as she fell into step with Audrey. "He's not the type of man I thought he'd be at all from his letters." In fact, he wasn't like any man she'd ever met. "He'll frighten poor Delta. When I looked into those black eyes, I almost jumped out of my skin."

"What are we going to do? Tell everyone she died, too? Make me look awful poor at nursing if all my charges die. Plus, where are we going to produce a body if he wants to take her home and bury her? Somebody's bound to notice if we run down to the cemetery and dig up poor Mary Elizabeth."

Jennie suddenly realized what an insane plan this had been from the start. She'd thought the widower would be old. All he'd talked about in his letters was his land and living alone. "We just can't allow Delta to go with the man."

"What man?" Delta crawled from behind the water storage.

"Colton Barkley is downstairs," Audrey announced.

Delta looked from Jennie to Audrey. "Is he very old and ugly?"

"No," Jennie answered. "He isn't old." She couldn't bring herself to say that he was handsome.

Delta dusted off her clothes. "I'm going with him. I don't care if he's ugly as the devil's twin. I've no other road to follow."

"But," Jennie shook her head, "he looks so cold and hard. He looks like he's made of coal."

Delta didn't seem the least deterred. "I've been around weak men all my life. He can be no worse. This is my one chance and I'm taking it. No matter how hard he is, in one month I'll be on a train to California or somewhere and never have to think of him again."

Jennie looked as if she were about to argue, but Delta added, "I'll be fine. One of the things I buried with Delta Smith this morning was all my indecision. The way I look at it, if the Lord gave me this chance, I'm not throwing it away. Not even if the widower turns out to be younger and made of stone."

The others followed Delta toward the back staircase. "Now, remember," she fretted, making sure her bandages were in place around her face, "I'm Mary Elizabeth and you two hardly know me, so don't make a scene when I leave." She leaned low and hugged True. "Take care of them, True," she whispered. "I'll send word where I am if you ever need me. And keep practicing your reading on Jennie's novels until you know all the words."

True's short brown hair covered his blue eyes. The child nodded once before running back into the shadows of the hallway. "I'll watch after them," True promised. "Somebody better."

Without another word, all three women descended the stairs.

When they reached the dining room, only the marshal stood where the two men had been. He watched Delta carefully, as if sensing more than knowing that something was out of place.

"Morning, miss." He removed his hat and leaned down slightly, trying to see her face. "I never figured you'd be up and about this morning."

Audrey didn't allow Delta time to answer. "She's very weak, Marshal. Where is Barkley?"

"Colton said he rented a wagon. It seems he wasn't expecting you for another week and was moving cattle to winter grass when he heard you were here." Austin paused as if waiting for an explanation while Jennie and

Audrey flanked the injured girl as though she might fall at any moment. When no one said anything, he continued, "He's pulling the wagon around back, miss. He thought it would be less steps for you."

Jennie maneuvered between Austin and the girl. "I thought he looked a little muddy for a bridegroom," she said, stalling the marshal a moment.

Delta took the opportunity. Without meeting the marshal's eyes, she turned and passed through the door to the kitchen. Everyone followed as she moved across the kitchen and out onto the back porch without a word to the marshal.

"She's still not feeling well." Jennie tried to stay between the marshal and Delta.

Before Delta reached the end of the porch, Colton was on the first step coming up. "Mary Elizabeth?"

Delta's gaze met the man she'd agreed to spend the next month with. "Yes." Her voice was so soft it seemed to hang in the humid air. There was no turning back now. With the single word, she'd switched identities and forever altered her fate.

"Are you able to travel?" He took another step toward her, offering no apology for his dress or the condition of the rented wagon. "Or do I need to book you a room here?"

"I'd like to go on to your place, Colton," Delta answered. "After hearing all about it in your letters, I'd like to see the land myself."

She couldn't have said something more right. Colton's hard face altered slightly into a brief smile. "I'll drive careful, Mary Elizabeth."

Without waiting or asking for approval, he lifted Delta up and carried her to the wagon. When he placed her onto the wagon bench, her hat tumbled off into the mud.

She cried out and reached for it, but he quickly scooped up the muddy felt remains and tossed it in the buckboard. "Forget it, it's ruined." Colton's voice seemed harsh, but his intent was not. "I'll pick you up another when I get supplies. Along with whatever else you need."

Delta didn't answer, but Jennie could see a tear rolling down her cheek. Jennie guessed Delta had never in her life been asked what she might need.

Colton moved around the wagon and climbed in beside her. "We'll be at the ranch in a few hours." He slapped the team into action without even looking back to say good-bye.

Jennie fought the urge to run after them and beg Delta not to go, but Audrey's fingers at her elbow reminded her that this might be Delta's only chance. She'd be killed if her family found her. At least now she might only be ignored for a month.

When the women turned to go back into the hotel, Marshal McCormick blocked the way. "We need to talk," he ordered.

Both girls looked at each other before staring at him blankly.

Austin frowned, knowing they were not going to make it easy on him. "I'd like some answers."

"To any particular question?" Jennie remarked, trying not to smile. "Or shall we just throw them out in general?"

Audrey raised her hand to the marshal's head. "Did you hurt yourself last night? Maybe a head wound? You don't look like you slept well. Maybe you should get some rest."

Austin shoved her hand away. "Stop this nonsense, ladies. You may have fooled everyone else, but the girl who just climbed into that wagon was not the girl I pulled from the train last night."

Jennie couldn't look him in the eyes. She wanted to tell him the truth, but Delta's life might balance on her silence.

"Of course she was," Audrey snapped. "What do you think, we went upstairs and brought down the wrong Mary Elizabeth O'Brian?"

"I'm not sure what to think," Austin admitted. A moment ago he would have sworn the woman leaving with Barkley was Delta, but Audrey seemed so convinced he was making no sense. He looked from Jennie to Audrey. "You two are up to something."

"Nonsense." Audrey acted as if she were insulted by such a suggestion.

"I'm telling you that's not the girl I pulled from the train. If I were putting clues together, I'd swear that was Delta Smith—though you two did a very good job of bandaging her face where not even her own mother would recognize her."

"I can't believe you'd suggest such a thing. What would be the point?" Audrey was now doing a great job of acting insulted.

"I've got more sense than to be fooled by a few bandages." He looked at Jennie, silently demanding she tell the truth.

Audrey grabbed Jennie by the arm and moved around the marshal. "My Granny Gates was right," she whispered loud enough for Austin to hear. "Some jackasses are bound and determined they have horse sense."

The girls disappeared into the house, slamming the door behind them.

Jennie didn't see the marshal until well after dark. She took her turn waiting tables for the few folks wanting a late supper.

When Marshal McCormick entered the dining room, she couldn't make herself stop watching him. He moved to a back table and folded his length into a chair. Jennie could almost feel his hands touching her as he studied her from across the room. She remembered the way he'd kissed, and her body warmed to the memory. Looking at him now, it was hard for her to believe his eyes had turned liquid with desire only hours before.

Moving to his table, Jennie filled his cup while he waited in silence. "I'll only ask one time," he said as quietly as if they were making polite conversation. "Don't lie to me, Jennie. I could never care for a woman I couldn't trust."

Jennie sat the pot down and looked directly at him. His eyes were warm with a need that frightened her. This was a man who valued honesty above all else. A man whose love would be true if he ever offered it.

"Who was the woman who climbed on that wagon this afternoon with Colton?" His gaze locked on her, demanding she tell him the truth. "Was it Delta Smith or Mary Elizabeth O'Brian?"

Jennie lifted her chin slightly. If she lied, she'd lose the one man who'd ever thought she was pretty. The one man who'd ever kissed her. He was like the heroes she'd read about in her novels, strong and tender at the same time. But he demanded one thing of the woman he cared for—honesty.

Yet she had to protect Delta. If he knew whose body was buried in the grave, he'd have to tell the truth if the family came looking. He might be a hero always honest and true, but the best Jennie could hope for was to be a true friend. "Mary Elizabeth O'Brian climbed into that wagon. We buried Delta Smith."

"Are you sure?" She could see his tired stare fill with anger as her words pushed them apart. He didn't believe her. She could read it in his stance, but he wanted to hear the lie one more time.

"I'm sure," she promised. "Audrey and I will both swear to it."

Austin stood and tossed two bits on the table. "Then I'll be saying good-bye, Jennie."

"Good night," she whispered as she watched him walk out the door without even glancing back. "Good-bye, my hero."

Chapter
Thirteen

Delta watched Colton Barkley storm up the steps and go into the colorful mercantile. He hadn't said a word to her since they'd left the hotel, only driven into town with a frown molded as if permanently on his handsome face. But his temper didn't seem aimed at her. Near as she could tell, he hadn't even looked in her direction—not even when he climbed down and went inside.

She sat very still on the bench and watched the people pass along the wooden walk in front of the stores. With only one main street in the town, most folks had seen her with Colton Barkley, and now that he'd gone indoors, they seemed to be taking the opportunity for a closer look at her.

As group after group drifted within a few feet of the wagon, Delta grew more nervous. No one spoke to her, and their sidelong glances grew bolder the longer she waited. She felt like screaming, "Don't look at me!"

but she'd only draw more attention to herself. The folks circled, unsmiling, like vultures waiting for her death before moving in. She thought of climbing down and going into the mercantile, but didn't trust her own strength. Also, from what she'd seen of Colton, he was little more friendly than the town folks.

They reminded her of what her mother called "the good folks" in every town she'd lived in. They were all dressed in "Sunday, go to meeting" clothes, but there was no kindness in their manner. They expected a large measure of politeness from those they thought their lessers, but offered no kindness in return. Delta looked down at her hands and wished as she had a hundred times before that she could be invisible to "the good folks."

"Sorry to keep you waiting." Colton startled her as he stepped to the back of the wagon. "Had a few more things to get than I planned on." There was no apology in his tone, only low, controlled anger somewhere deep below the surface.

She didn't miss how boldly he looked at "the good folks" or how quickly they turned away. They didn't look down their noses at him. They didn't look at Colton Barkley at all. Maybe he'd found the way to hold up his head and be invisible to them.

Delta didn't say anything as Colton and a man who looked to be the proprietor of the store loaded several boxes in the back of the wagon.

The people who'd passed so close only moments before widened the boundary. They were far more cautious with their stares now that Colton stood near her.

The man who'd help load the supplies walked to Delta's side. His girth matched his height, and his smile reflected the amount of money spent and nothing more.

"Name's Luther, miss." He extended his hand. "Mr. Barkley tells me you're a friend newly arrived from back east. Welcome to Florence. I'm mighty sorry to hear about you being in the train wreck."

"Thank you." Delta couldn't help but like the man despite his soft hands. He reminded her of a shopkeeper when she'd been a child who'd always slipped her a candy stick whether she had money or not.

When the middle-aged man smiled, his eyes disappeared into wrinkles. "I tried to get everything Mr. Barkley said you lost in the wreck, but it may take a few days. I'll send the goods out to the ranch when they come in."

Looking over Luther's head to Colton, Delta noticed he was busy tying the supplies down and didn't look up. "Thank you," she said to Luther, but her words were meant for Colton.

"Oh, no problem," Luther answered. "If he forgot something, you just send me a note by the ranch cook and I'll see you get it."

Delta was saved from answering by Colton climbing into the wagon. He handed her a box and half saluted the shopkeeper. "Thanks for your help, Luther, but we best be on our way." He slapped the horses into action with a nod to the store owner while he totally ignored everyone else on the street.

Watching the people look away, Delta couldn't help but smile as most of the folks pretended they hadn't noticed the couple moving down the middle of the street.

She followed Colton's example and waved at Luther, noticing that the town folks were already converging on the mercantile.

"Aren't you going to look in the box?" Colton's voice was a low rumble.

Delta had been afraid to. After all, he hadn't said it was for her.

Slowly, as if testing uncharted waters, she opened the box. There, resting in a cloud of thin white paper, was a wool hat of dark winter green. As she lifted it gently, she saw a matching scarf beneath the hat. She knew she was suppose to say thank you, but all she could do was softly brush the knit of one of the finest hats she'd ever seen.

"I know it's probably not what you would have liked, but Luther said women with light blond hair look good in green."

Delta couldn't believe such a hat belonged to her. She'd seen women wearing hats and scarves to match, but she'd never thought she'd have something so fine on her head.

Colton moved the reins to one hand and reached behind him. "I thought I'd buy another blanket. I need it at the ranch, and you can wrap up in it on the way home. Soon as the sun lowers, it gets cold out here this time of year." He handed her the colorful blanket. "I noticed you didn't have a coat or cape beyond that traveling jacket so I ordered material."

"I appreciate it," she whispered, wondering how a man who looked cold as a winter storm could be so thoughtful. "And thanks, but you didn't have to. I can make it just fine."

"Like I told Luther, the railroad hasn't found your trunk, and you had to borrow a few things from the Harvey girls."

Delta smoothed the worn material of Mary Elizabeth's best dress and silently agreed to Colton's lie. Part of her wanted to tell him not to spend any more money on her for she wasn't the bride he'd sent for. But another part of her wanted to crawl into the wagon bed and look in all the boxes. She could never remember owning anything someone else hadn't worn first.

Slowly, as if enjoying every second of her time, she placed the hat on her head and wrapped the scarf around her neck. Since she didn't have a mirror, she closed her eyes and pretended with all her heart that she was somebody.

Colton pulled the wagon onto the muddy road, seeming totally absorbed in driving. As the holes in the road tossed them one way and the other on the narrow bench, he placed his hand behind her back, steadying her and providing a brace.

At first she remained stiff in the seat, trying to fight the tossing of the wagon. Slowly, inch by inch, she relaxed against his arm and was surprised how much more comfortable she was.

Eventually the road turned onto one less traveled and smoother, but he didn't withdraw his support and she didn't move away. She cuddled into the blanket and felt herself relax. Somehow this man's formal politeness made her feel safe.

In a low voice, he spoke as if to himself. "I figure there's a few things we need to say to one another."

"All right," she answered. "If you wish."

He drove the team for several more minutes in silence, and she decided he'd had second thoughts. When his words came, they were slow. "How bad are you hurt? No one told me."

"My shoulder's bruised and cut," she answered. "Also, I bumped my head. I don't think I need the bandages as much as my nurses thought I did."

When he glanced at her, she pulled away, afraid he might see something about her that told him she wasn't Mary Elizabeth.

Colton cleared his throat and stared back at the road. "Your hair's lighter than I thought it would be. You said in one of your letters it was yellow. But it's so light it's almost white."

Delta pulled away a little more. What else had Mary Elizabeth written that might hurt the plan to fool him? "I'm sorry," she whispered, more because she couldn't think of anything else to say than because she regretted what she'd done.

"I don't mind," he answered. "You told me so little, I didn't really have a picture of you."

Delta let out a long held breath. "I guess I was afraid you'd be disappointed. Are you?" She bit her tongue. *Why had she asked? What did it matter?*

Colton looked at her for the first time. "No," he finally said. "I'm not disappointed. In truth, your looks are not important. That's why I never asked. Your willingness to come out here was all that mattered."

Now it was Delta's turn to look at him. He had a strong, handsome face despite his dark mood. She found it impossible to believe such a man would have to order a wife by mail. "But why?" she asked.

Colton stared at the road as if into the past. "Mary Elizabeth, I'm not an easy man to live with. My land has always been more important to me than anything or anyone. Since my wife died six years ago, I've been alone except for the folks who work for me, and they'll tell you soon enough I'm overloaded with a temper and shy on patience."

She was so still, he thought she might jump from the wagon if he reached for her.

"But," he continued, "I swear I'll never touch you unless you want it; so there's no reason to be afraid of me. You've no need to jump when I step within a foot of you."

"I'm not afraid." Delta steadied herself as if ready for battle. She would not live another day of her life in fear of any man. "I'll stay a month, providing you don't try to hurt me. That's the only promise I make, Mr. Barkley. One month."

"Agreed." He looked at her closely. "Whoever turned you against men did a grand job, but I hadn't expected you'd come without a few ghosts haunting you. After all, I have my share."

He slowly pulled a small derringer from his vest pocket and held it out to her. "Tell you what, if it makes you feel safer, you can shoot me if I ever break my word. There's only two shots in it, but I guess they'll do the job if need be."

She accepted the pistol. She'd missed the comfort her little gun had brought her. "Don't worry," she whispered, "I will."

"Fair enough," he said. "You'll have to learn that I'm a man of my word. Until you do, the gun is yours."

Delta moved the weapon beneath the blanket. *A man of his word.* She almost repeated the sentence aloud. As if such a thing existed outside of Jennie's dime novels.

Chapter
Fourteen

"*M*arshal?" True leaned the broom against Austin's desk and faced him. "I've been noticing a suspicious-looking man hanging around. Maybe he's the one you and Sheriff Morris been waiting for. He looks the type of fellow who'd have a grand time burning a whole town to the ground. In fact I'm sure he's that man Buck Lawton, just from the look of him."

Austin took a break from his paperwork and smiled at the boy. In the week True had been showing up to do odd jobs around the jail, the child had managed to have a different story for him every day. True had picked up just enough information from him and Morris to see an outlaw around every corner. And the ragamuffin's imagination was growing wilder by the minute inside the dirt-covered body. "Another suspicious stranger? What does Lawton look like this time?"

True looked offended. "This one's real, I swear. Even

Henry saw him and said he looks evil to the bone."

Austin's smile widened. Since no one but True ever saw Henry, he seemed less than a credible witness, yet Austin played along. "Want to describe this stranger?"

True motioned with tiny hands. "He's a big man, with a big chest. Not fat, just big. But not like a bear because he doesn't have any hair on him. From head down he looks slicker than a cleaned fish from what skin's showin'." True's eyes danced with make-believe. "Maybe he was tortured by wild Indians years ago, and they pulled the hairs out one at a time."

"True!" Austin stopped the child. "Stick to the facts and leave the guessing aside."

True nodded as if giving important testimony. "Yes, sir. Well, Henry and me noticed him a few days after the train wreck. He's been sleeping in one of the stalls over at the livery, but something's wrong. He don't try to get a job or nothin', and he ain't too friendly. Like maybe he was treated real bad the last time he tried to be nice. So bad the niceness in him just up and died."

"What else did you see?" Austin waited patiently. In truth, he loved hearing the child's stories almost as much as True seemed to enjoy making them up.

"Well, for one, he sleeps with the horses, but he don't like them. Henry and me heard him cussing them something awful this morning. Seems to me a man who don't even like horses couldn't be a good person. If I had a horse, I'd feed him ever'day whether I got to eat or not. Henry said he'd do the same."

"But what makes the hairless man an outlaw?" Austin changed the subject back to the stranger before True got carried away with all the things he planned to do if he ever had a horse.

True scratched his dirty brown hair. "Don't you see,

Marshal? A man who had no love for horses wouldn't sleep in the barn. And Henry says the stranger sleeps days and walks around ever' night. Then he goes over to the saloon and gets drunk."

"Doesn't sound like the most outstanding citizen but . . ."

"But if he has money to drink, why don't he stay at the hotel?"

Austin didn't have time to explain to True that poor judgment in a drunkard didn't necessarily mean an outlaw. He just smiled and said, "I'll check the lead out. Tell Henry thanks for the information."

True was satisfied. "I told him you'd want to know what we found. We're keeping our eyes open watching for trouble."

Austin tossed True a quarter. "How about we call it a day? Since there are so many suspicious characters out there, why don't you ride back to the Harvey House with me? I bet they're serving supper by now."

True straightened. "I don't need anyone protecting me, but Henry says there are safety in numbers; so maybe I'll go along with you. Can I ride in front and hold the reins?"

Austin grabbed his hat. "You bet. Then after supper I'll head on over to the livery and check on this big man with no hair while I put up my horse."

"Want Henry and me to come along?" True asked as Austin opened the door. "We could back you up."

Austin crammed his hat low, hoping the child couldn't see the laughter in his eyes. "No, thanks," he answered. "You and Henry best stay inside tonight."

True passed through the door. "I'll tell Henry, but he ain't much for taking orders."

Austin followed, whispering, "He isn't the only one."

* * *

THE LIGHTS FROM the Harvey House had a welcoming glow about them, making Austin homesick for nowhere in particular, just homesick. As he lowered True from his saddle, he heard Jennie calling the boy's name. He hadn't noticed her standing at the end of the porch in the twilight, but now he couldn't take his gaze off her.

One strand of her ebony hair had fought free from her bun during her work and now blew across her face in a lazy curl. She'd removed her white apron and was dressed in black, framed against the moonless sky. She looked up at him with the same longing in her eyes that he felt. He wanted to talk to her, but there was nothing to say. If she wasn't going to be honest, he wasn't going to bend.

True ran past her skirts shouting something about being late for fresh rolls, but Jennie didn't turn away from Austin. For this blinking of time, when the earth was neither in daylight or dark, she seemed more a dream than real, more a making of his longing than a person in the flesh standing so near. He remembered being out on the plains for so long that he thought he'd seen things that weren't there. Now he knew she was only a few feet away, but she might as well have been a mirage.

Without thinking of why, he moved his horse closer until he was at eye level with her. Only the porch railing stood between them. The homesickness he'd felt earlier shone in her eyes also.

Suddenly the emptiness he'd felt all week swept over him. He felt like a man dying of thirst when water was within his grasp.

In one senseless moment he reached for her and pulled her onto his saddle. She raised her hands to hold him, as though she'd been lifted up into his arms a million times. Before anyone noticed, he kicked his horse and disappeared into the deepening shadows among the trees.

Jennie didn't make a sound as he rode out beyond the lights and pulled his horse up. He could hear her breathing and feel the warmth of her body even through their clothes. Even now, with her holding onto his waist, he wasn't sure she was real.

Without a word he twisted Jennie in his arms to face him and kissed her, his lips hard and demanding. He wanted her to feel what she was doing to him with her lies. She had to know how much he wanted her in his arms before he went mad from thinking about her.

She answered his need with her own. Her hands dug into his hair and pulled him closer. The kiss was alive with a passion and fire that had been too long denied.

"I don't care for you!" he blurted as he pressed her against him. "I don't care for you," he repeated as if saying the words could make them true.

He could feel the swell of her breasts against her blouse and the warmth of her leg as it rested over his thigh. While she kissed him, he unbuttoned the first two buttons of her top with hands that seemed clumsy and foreign in even such a simple task.

Jennie leaned away from him, unaware of how white her skin looked in the night. He could see her breasts straining against the top of her camisole as she breathed.

"I've nothing to say to you." She placed her hand lightly on his shoulder. "This is not happening. I must be dreaming. Nothing like this has ever happened to me."

"If we are dreaming, then dream of this," Austin said as he pulled her close and kissed her until he feared he was bruising her lips with his longing.

Her body melted into his arms. Her lips parted in a soft

moan against his mouth. Slowly all the anger he'd felt toward her turned to desire, and his kiss turned gentle.

He couldn't stop his hand from sliding along her throat and brushing the lace against her soft flesh.

"Unbutton your blouse," he whispered into her hair.

"But . . ."

"If this is a dream, let it be a fantasy. Loosen your blouse." His arm at her back held the reins, and he longed for the freedom of both his hands.

Jennie's back stiffened as she pulled away. Without a word she slowly unbuttoned her top to the waistband. Then, with a fist on each side, she pulled the material free until the black of her uniform fell away from her creamy skin.

For a long breath all Austin could do was stare as her chest rose and fell beneath a single layer of white cotton.

She reached up and dropped one strap of her camisole so that the cloth covering her breast dipped dangerously low. "Is this your dream, Austin?"

"It'll do," he answered, longing to touch the flesh she so easily displayed.

Slowly she reached again and dropped the other strap off her shoulder. Now only the rise of her breasts held the cotton in place. "I've thought of you touching me," she whispered so near his ear he could feel the words. "I've wondered if the feel of your hand could have been as wonderful as I remember."

When he moved to raise his fingers, she stopped their progress and returned his hand to her waist. Her action exposed another inch of skin as the camisole slipped lower.

"If we're dreaming, unbutton your shirt," she ordered.

"What?"

"If this is a dream, it's my dream, too." She pulled at the first button of his shirt. "Stop me if you're afraid." Her fingers moved to the next button. "I want to feel your skin." She moved to the next. "Tell me if you're cold."

He'd never felt hotter on a summer day. He knew the air was almost freezing, but the touch of her fingers along his shirt was setting a fire along his flesh.

She moved her hands inside his shirt and ran timid fingers over the dusting of hair there. Her lips moved feather-light across his cheek, as though begging for attention she knew he was more than willing to give.

He could stand her teasing no longer. He pulled her against him and covered her mouth with his. There was no world other than with her, for all else had slipped away.

His kiss lasted so long Jennie felt herself spinning with pleasure. While his lips pleased her, his hand shifted at her waist, straining to move upward. But each time she shoved his hand back in place.

Suddenly he pushed her away. She could see the fire and hunger in his eyes as he looked at her. He raised his hand to touch her breasts, and once more she stopped him.

"You don't care for me," she whispered, "but you want to touch me." She leaned slightly forward, straining the cotton over the heaven he longed for.

Austin slowly lowered his hand, fighting his need. "I'll not touch you if you don't want it."

"I want you to swear to me that your hand will stay at my waist." Jennie was so near, the wonderful smell of her filled his lungs.

"Swear!" she demanded while her fingers lightly shoved his shirt aside.

"I swear," he answered. He didn't know what game she was playing, but he'd allow her to torture him all night. She'd just made him swear to do what he figured to be near impossible.

"Close your eyes," she whispered. "People always close their eyes when they're dreaming." Her tongue lightly tasted the outline of his bottom lip.

Austin did as she wished, even though he wanted to continue to watch the rise and fall of the cotton over her breasts.

"Now, kiss me," she begged softly against his lips. "And promise not to stop until I break the kiss."

He followed her request. As the kiss deepened, she moved closer, pressing her body against his chest.

He felt all logic shatter into passion as he realized her camisole had slipped and her soft flesh was pushing against the wall of his chest.

Her hand covered his at her waist, forcing him to keep his promise while she moved slowly against him. The kiss was endless, as was the pleasure she gave him with her gentle touch. In all the world, in all of time, he'd never been given such a gift.

When finally she broke the kiss and slipped her blouse on, he couldn't find words to tell her how he felt. How could he say thank you for being given a taste of something he'd starve for for the rest of his life. He held her close and rode back to the hotel, stopping well in the shadows.

"Thank you for the dream," she whispered as he lowered her to the ground. "I'll remember it always."

He wanted to tell her that they'd make other dreams, but he knew she was saying good-bye. She might have had a dream tonight, but she wasn't the kind of woman to live her life on dreaming.

He closed his eyes and remembered the way Jennie had felt against him in the shadows. When he looked back, she'd vanished inside and he was in the same place he'd been only minutes before when he'd dropped off True. But somehow in the change between twilight and evening the world had shifted. If he lived to be a hundred, he'd never have a dream as beautiful as Jennie in his arms tonight.

A pleasure so sweet it would rip longing through his heart with every breath he took until his last.

Chapter
Fifteen

Jennie moved through the next week mourning the loss of what might have been with Austin. She pushed herself to work harder and faster, hoping she'd be able to sleep. But each night the memory of the feel of Austin's arms haunted her. The romantic in her wanted him to stop by another night and carry her away, but the realist knew she couldn't weave her future with stolen passion. She relived the night they'd acted out a dream so many times she was unsure where reality blended amid her memories.

Austin didn't seem to share her confusion, for he dropped in for meals as though the Clifton Harvey House were his second home. Since he made no comment or attempt to relive their shared dream, Jennie wondered if she'd been too bold in the shadows. He became so familiar a sight, the other Harvey girls didn't even bother trying to seat him, for they knew he'd be taking a table in Jennie's section.

Every time he walked into the dining room, Jennie could sense his presence, even before she turned around and met his gaze. He made no pretense of being a stranger. While he ordered and ate his meal, he watched her with eyes that seemed to grow darker with anger each day.

Jennie tried to ignore him, but she was drawn to the strong outline of his jaw and the way he moved with assurance and inner strength. Finally, when she could resist no longer, she'd look in his direction, always to find him staring at her. His close scrutiny split her nerves, unraveling the very core of calmness her family had wound around her so tightly for so many years.

She wanted to run to him and beg him to hold her. She longed to feel his lips playfully teasing her mouth. If only she could place her hand over his heart once more and feel the pounding that warmed her blood with desire. Yet all except thoughts were lost to her. He'd made it plain he could never care for a woman who lied, and she could never betray Delta.

One evening, after Audrey had watched in silence for almost a week, she mumbled as Jennie came through the kitchen door, "Honey, you got to do something about that man. He's becoming such a regular they're likely to paint him to match the furniture."

"What can I do?" Jennie set the tray of dishes down and wiped her hands on her apron. "We have nothing more to say to one another."

"Maybe not." Audrey peeked through the crack in the pass-through door between the kitchen and dining hall. "But there may be other things he's needing besides talk. That man looks so unhappy eating his food every night, he's liable to run off business. If there wasn't proof of an empty plate at the end of each meal, I'd swear from his look that he was forcing down dirt."

Jennie laughed. "We could probably serve him sand pies for all the attention he pays. I don't understand. I think he knows I lied about Delta, though he has no proof. He said he could never care for a woman who lied." She pushed damp hair off her forehead. "So why does he come here every night, watching me, but never talking to me?"

"Men are a great puzzle. Sometimes I think the Lord made them the way they are just to keep us women guessing, 'cause there sure isn't a drop of logic in their actions." Audrey flour-dusted the huge wooden bowl she used for making her bread. "Take Wiley, for instance . . ."

"Wiley who?" Jennie raised an eyebrow.

"You know, the farmer who delivers meat twice a week. The one I patched up the other morning."

"Oh." Jennie smiled, remembering the huge man who couldn't stop staring at Audrey. Despite his build, he'd reminded her of a little child passing a store window. He enjoyed the view so much, he should have been charged for looking.

"Well, when Wiley comes in delivering meat," Audrey moved her dough bowl out of the reach of anyone who might accidentally wash it, "if I'm not in the kitchen, the cooks say he hangs around until I appear. He acts all nervous, too, like he was waiting for the Second Coming or something. Then, when I come down, the big oaf doesn't have a thing to say to me."

"Maybe he's waiting for you to offer something more than coffee and conversation," Jennie teased.

Audrey straightened. "Well then why doesn't he come calling some evening? I wouldn't mind taking a walk beneath the moonlight even in the dead of winter. But it's hard to think romantic at dawn-thirty."

Jennie agreed. "Maybe he'll come to the dance next week."

Audrey's smile spoke of possibilities. "And maybe the marshal won't."

AUDREY'S PREDICTION DIDN'T hold. Marshal Austin McCormick was one of the first men to show up at the Harvey House dance. He put his four bits on the table and stepped into the decorated dining area as if he'd had a special invitation. He looked even taller dressed in a black suit and thin string tie. His boots were polished and his sandy hair tamed to almost lay down flat.

Jennie watched him scan the room full of women all dressed in colorful calico prints for the party. She wondered why she'd even gone to the trouble of making her dress. No doubt, just as at the few dances she'd attended at home, she'd spend the entire evening sitting on the edge waiting for someone to ask her to dance. It had been humiliating enough in the past having her family always around encouraging her to go home and stop making a fool of herself. Now Austin would be watching as every other girl danced except her.

"I'm glad you picked the blue print," Audrey whispered as she sat down beside Jennie and sampled one of the tiny cakes she'd made for the party. "It looks good on you."

Jennie tried to smile without saying that this had been the only color that fit her mood. All the other women wore bright calico, reminding her of a wild flower garden, but she'd found hers at the bottom of the stack. A blue on blue calico print. Calico was the only material in abundance besides black, and after wearing black uniforms all day, there wasn't a Harvey girl who would have worn even a black ribbon tonight. Also, the cotton fabric was inexpensive, and no single working woman had money to order a silk or satin from back east.

"Thanks for the compliment." Jennie smiled at Audrey. The brightly colored fabric did little for her friend. With her red hair and warm brown eyes, she was one of the few women who looked very becoming in the black uniform she wore each day. With calico, her coloring seemed to compete with the material. "I'm glad we got the dresses finished. I was getting worried at one point that I'd be selecting from my traveling dress or my uniforms."

Audrey chuckled. "Me, too. Yesterday, I was trying to cook and sew the hem at the same time. I'm surprised someone didn't find a straight pin in their pie."

The band interrupted all conversation by practicing loudly, sounding very much as if they'd all just met, instead of like a group who planned to play the same tune. Men, dressed in their best, continued filing in. Ranchers, farmers, railroad workers. They each stopped to pay, then handed Mrs. Gray their hats as she inspected each man for sobriety. Old Spider Morris stood beside the little lady collecting guns.

The musicians lined one end of the dining hall, while food tables stretched across the other and the women huddled together waiting near the kitchen door.

Audrey shifted nervously. "I'm about to decide to call it a night. I'm not much of a dancer, and there won't be many men tall enough to even ask me."

Jennie's eyes widened. "Why, Audrey Gates, I can't believe you're admitting not knowing how to do something."

Audrey looked guilty. "All right. I lied. I'm a great dancer. My brothers were always looking for someone to practice with. But the other part's true. I find it hard to dance with a man when I can look over his head. I always have the urge to grab him by the ears and pull him up an inch or two while demanding he look at me in the eyes for a change."

"How about that one?" Jennie pointed toward the huge man folding through the door. The farmer's suit was homespun, but well fitted. Unlike most of the men present, he didn't have cotton padding across his shoulders, but rock-hard muscle.

"Wiley!" Audrey's entire face seemed to smile. "He came." She glanced back at Jennie. "Not that I care, of course."

"Of course," Jennie echoed as Mrs. Gray raised her hands to quiet the crowd.

"Welcome, ladies and gentlemen, to the Harvey House's Calico Dance. All men check your weapons at the door, and all ladies make sure you've removed your aprons." Nervous laughter circled the room as she continued. "As is the tradition at our dances, ladies pick your partners for the first come-together, the grand march."

Audrey moved straight toward Wiley Radcliff, leaving Jennie standing alone.

She marched up to within a foot of the huge farmer and raised her hands to dance position. "Well," she said loud enough for half the room to hear, "can you dance the grand march, Mr. Radcliff?"

A slow smile spread across his tan face. "I reckon I could do anything with you in my arms, Miss Gates." His hands moved around her waist, and he pulled her close, his gaze never leaving her eyes.

Several men hooted in laughter, and all at once the room exploded in noise as the women followed Audrey's lead and picked their partners for the first dance.

Jennie watched, laughing at the way the women picked their partners. Some were bold like Audrey, but most simply walked up to stand in front of the man they'd chosen.

"Aren't you going to ask a man to walk the grand march with you?" Marshal McCormick's low voice sounded behind Jennie. "I was hoping you'd offer me the honor."

Whirling, she looked into his smoky brown eyes. "I might, but I didn't think you'd want to dance with me. We seem to have developed a habit of not speaking to one another."

"I don't see that a dance could break up our pattern. We can go back to staring at one another in silence as soon as the music stops."

Jennie could almost taste the tension between them. He was close enough that she could smell the leather and soap about him, but his words blocked any nearness she might feel. "I'm not much of a dancer," she answered.

Austin nodded his understanding. "I guessed if you had trouble telling your right hand from your left, you had the same problem with your feet."

She would have looked down, but his gaze held hers. "I polished my boots, so I might as well take a few spins around the floor if you're agreeable." He took her in his arms. "Don't worry, the way I dance, you'll probably think I don't know my feet apart either."

The music sounded, and suddenly calico whirled around the room. Austin was a better dancer than he'd claimed. His steps were sure and simple, easy for Jennie to follow. After a few false starts, she picked up the rhythm of his movements. He made a habit of pulling her hand slightly when he wanted her to move with her right foot.

They danced three reels before he stopped to allow her to catch her breath. He didn't try to make small talk, and Jennie was grateful. She could have remained in his arms forever, but when she looked in his eyes, she still saw the anger. He'd never forgive her, she decided. As far as he knew, she'd lied to him twice. First about True and now about Delta.

"Excuse me," he whispered and disappeared from her side before Jennie even had time to thank him.

The moment he was gone, men lined up to ask her for the same privilege. At first Jennie thought it must be some mistake. She was nervous as she stepped onto the planked floor with first one then another. However, she soon learned that most of the men couldn't dance even as well as she could, but they all politely asked for another opportunity even after she tramped all over their boots.

Tears came to her eyes when she found herself wishing her brothers and sisters could see her. They'd always made her feel that every man who'd ever asked her to dance had done so as a favor to one of them. Well, there were no Mundays but Jennie here tonight, and men were asking.

After an hour, the band stopped to rest and everyone moved to the food table. Jennie found Audrey in the crowd. "Are you having fun?"

Audrey nodded. "Haven't had to pull a man up by the ears once tonight."

Wiley moved toward them, trying to carry two dainty cups in his huge hands. When he was within a few feet, he handed one to Audrey and politely offered the other to Jennie.

Downing the cider in a single draw, Audrey handed her empty cup to Jennie and addressed Wiley. "I don't suppose you'd be interested in escorting a lady outside for a little fresh air."

Wiley's smile was almost boyishly shy. Then he silently offered her his arm.

Audrey winked at Jennie and wrapped her fingers around his wide forearm. But when she turned toward the door, she hesitated in midstep at the sight before her.

Suddenly everyone in the room seemed to stop talking at once. It was as if someone had called an order for folks to be silent and stare. Jennie turned toward the entrance to see what could have caused such a reaction.

There, standing apart from everyone, was Delta. Her white-blond hair was piled in a halo of curls atop her head. Her face and blue eyes were as pale as ever, but the dress she wore of dark jade made her look like a pearl inside velvet casing.

Jennie couldn't stop the cry that whispered past her lips. For two weeks she'd worried about Delta, wondering how her month was going with Colton Barkley. Audrey had told her a hundred times that she was sure everything was fine, but that hadn't erased the tiny doubt in Jennie's mind.

As Jennie took a step, Audrey's free hand reached out and stopped her. Her face was smiling, but her eyes were not, as she stared at Jennie and said loud enough for everyone around them to hear, "Look, Jennie, it's Mary Elizabeth, the girl from the train wreck. Doesn't she look well?"

Pulling herself in check, Jennie nodded. Several others commented, then were silent once more as a man in black moved behind the lovely young girl.

Colton Barkley might have been dressed in a fine black waistcoat and tailored pants, but he still seemed cold and distant to Jennie, like the north wind. He studied the room, as if waiting for a challenge from someone, then stepped beside Delta.

When no one moved, he offered his arm to Delta with the grace of a polished gentleman and walked toward Mrs. Gray. "I hope it's proper for us to attend." His manner and his words were perfect as he addressed the older lady. "Mary Elizabeth tells me your girls saved her life, and she wanted to come to the first dance and say thank you properly."

Mrs. Gray nodded. "You're more than welcome." The old woman turned to Delta, a warm smile on her lips she reserved only for the house's very special guests. "You're recovering well. I see no sign of the head wound."

"Thank you," Delta whispered. "I'm lucky it was only a few bumps. I don't remember much about the night of the wreck."

"I'm sure that's a blessing," Mrs. Gray answered. "I'll never forget the rain that night."

Delta nodded, her gaze already searching the room for Jennie and Audrey. When she saw them, she lightly touched Colton's sleeve, and he released her hand from where he'd trapped it on his arm.

As Delta glided across the floor like a tiny angel, Jennie couldn't help but notice that Colton's gaze never left her as she moved. He reminded Jennie of a body-guard who took his job very seriously.

Delta's face was void of emotion as she approached. "I've just made a long drive. Could I impose on you two wonderful ladies who patched me up two weeks ago to borrow your room for a few minutes to freshen up?"

Audrey fell into the acting part like a Shakespearean trouper. "Of course you may, my dear. You probably don't remember the way, so we'll be happy to show you." She glanced at Wiley with a touch of regret. "You'll wait for me?"

Wiley's gaze said, *forever,* but his mouth remained mute as they moved away.

Three men watched the women climb the stairs. Marshal McCormick was aware of the other two, but doubted they saw him. He'd been watching Jennie all evening, waiting for the proper time to ask her for another dance. He'd used his time making idle conversation with the other men and trying to figure out just what it was about the woman who drew him more strongly than any streetlight drew a moth.

"Fine-looking woman," the railroad worker leaning against the wall next to Austin mumbled.

"Which one?" Austin answered.

The man laughed. "All of them, I reckon. There ain't a drowner in the litter here at the Harvey House. But I was referring to the little lady who came in with Colton Barkley."

McCormick nodded, wondering if the railroad worker beside him was as stupid as he was blind, not to see that Jennie was by far the most beautiful of the three women reaching the top of the stairs. If she'd just learn to tell the truth, she'd be perfection wrapped in blue.

"Talk is she's going to be Barkley's wife sometime next month."

"That so?" Austin tried to act interested.

"Yeah," the man continued, "he sent away for her all the way from somewhere back east. Wouldn't no woman in this part reel him in if he was the last catch in the river."

Austin wasn't really interested in gossip, but he needed to do something besides look at the stairs until Jennie returned. "Why's that?" he asked, deciding he was getting as bad as True at seeing an outlaw behind every corner.

The man pushed away from the wall and drew closer. Austin could smell the train's oil on his alpaca coat. "Guess you don't know, being new in town and all. Colton Barkley killed his first wife."

"What!"

"Yes, sir. He killed her. Then buried her up on that ranch of his all by himself. Wouldn't even allow her family to come to the funeral. Told them he'd kill them if they set foot on his land even to visit her grave."

"Didn't anyone do anything about the murder?"

The man scratched his head. "Get a look at him with a gun in his hand sometime, mister. He's not the kind of man who takes lightly to being bothered with. Lived here for several years and never tried to make one friend. Folks all knew by the time we got up to the ranch, there wouldn't be no proof of the murder. It'd just be his word against hearsay. He was a respectable man, no trouble-maker or nothin'. I guess ever'one figured what happened between him and his was nobody's business."

Austin studied Colton Barkley as he waited at the foot of the steps. The man moved like a trained killer, slow and deliberate. His body was tightly corded, ready for any fight, and from the bulge beneath his arm, Austin would have bet he was wearing a shoulder holster.

But Austin had been around killers all his life. Wild, senseless ones in the army who loved it like a sport. Cold, heartless ones who stomped out any life that got in their way. Nervous, panicking ones who carried a banner of revenge. Greedy ones who weighed a life against a

dollar. Colton Barkley was none of them. Austin would
stake his badge on that. Not that Barkley wouldn't kill.
Most any man would if the time came and the reason
were strong enough.

No, whatever or whoever had killed Barkley's first
wife had crippled something deep inside of him also.
Austin finally got a handle on what Barkley reminded
him of. A wounded animal, who was growling and
struggling to survive. A man ready to fight anyone or
anything despite the pain he felt inside.

Austin realized one other thing. In a fight he'd rather
have Colton Barkley at his back than any other man in
the room. He wasn't sure why, but he felt it in his gut.
Colton Barkley might have killed his wife, but Austin
would hear the reason before he judged him.

Chapter
Sixteen

*A*udrey closed the door to their room and turned to join in the hug Jennie was already giving Delta.

"Tell us everything," Jennie whispered. "We've been so worried about you."

Delta sat next to a sleepy True and pulled the child close. "I've missed you," she whispered, then her tear-filled eyes looked up to include Audrey and Jennie. "All of you."

"Has Colton Barkley treated you fair?" Audrey asked. "If he hasn't, he'll be kicking the bucket out from under his own gallows before I'm through with him."

Delta laughed. "He treats me fair. In fact, I have no complaints about Colton. He's got a house almost half the size of this hotel, with an older woman who rides over from the next ranch to keep it clean and a cook who sees it as his main mission in life to fatten me up. Except for the first day, I haven't seen very much of Colton. I watch him ride off before dawn every morning, and I fall asleep waiting supper on him at night.

"For a man who sent all the way across the country for a wife, he seems very uninterested in getting to know her. Half the time when we do have a meal together, he doesn't say a word more than what's needed to be polite. I doubt he'll care when I ask to leave in two weeks. It's almost like he's just waiting for me to say the words so he can pack me on my way."

Jennie sat on the bed beside Delta. "He's a strange man, so dark and handsome—and angry. He frightens me a little."

Halfheartedly agreeing, Delta added, "I've been trying to do things to feel like I'm earning my keep around the place. But to tell the truth, I don't think he even notices. Maybe he's sorry he wrote all those letters to Mary Elizabeth, because now it seems like all he wants is to be left alone."

Jennie patted Delta's shoulder. "Two more weeks and you'll be away."

Delta nodded. "That's what I keep telling myself. Living with Colton Barkley is like living with the shadow of a man. He does what's expected, like ordering material for this dress and a cape to match." Delta brushed the soft fabric lightly. "But then he didn't even comment on how I looked tonight."

She paused, forcing back any sadness, and changed the subject. "Has anyone asked about Delta Smith?"

"There was talk of a man who looked like you'd described your brother hanging around town, but he disappeared after Marshal McCormick visited with him."

"Do you think it was Ward?"

"I don't think so," Audrey answered. "True heard the marshal talking to the man, and he didn't have much to say other than he wanted to be left alone. If he'd been interested in you, looks like he would have at least asked after you by name."

"Unless he thought I might have gone to the law about the attack." Delta's eyes widened. "I shouldn't have come tonight. It was too big a risk."

"Nonsense." Audrey patted her on the shoulder. "Who could hurt you at the dance? He's not likely to show up here even if that stranger was your brother. He's long gone by now. Probably miles away. Every day you should feel safer and safer. If Ward hasn't found you by now, he probably wasn't able to track you this far."

Delta steepled her fingers as if in prayer, then looked from Audrey to Jennie. "I'll never forget what you've done for me. You both saved my life two weeks ago."

"You'd have done the same," Jennie said.

"I've come to offer something that might help you." Delta smiled. "I'd like to take True back to the ranch with me for a few days."

"What!" both women said at once.

"I'd take good care of the child, and it would give me something to do. True could play in the sunlight for a change."

Jennie looked at Audrey, reading her face as easily as she knew her own feelings. True would have fun with Delta. It would be good for the boy and as safe as it was here, but even the thought of letting the child go pulled at her heart.

"I don't know," Jennie began. "What would Colton say?"

"I'll ask him if you think it's a good idea." Delta shrugged. "But I can't imagine him saying no. He's not around the house enough to even notice."

True was the only one who moved. "What do the three of you think you're doing thinking you can decide my life? Sometimes I think the angel in charge of sending down guardians must have gone overboard and sent me three. I told you from the first. I'm on my own. I just stay here with you 'cause you might need me."

Delta mimicked True's stance. "I do need you. If you'll come, you'd have a room of your own and miles of land to explore."

True didn't look interested as Delta continued. "The rolls might not be as good as Audrey's, but the cook makes a fine berry pie."

"I got things to do around here," True answered. "The marshal and the sheriff need me."

"But I need you, too. We could explore on the ranch, and I'm sure Colton would let you ride one of his horses."

"Really?"

"Really." Delta had found the key.

True didn't hesitate any longer. "I'll go with you, Mary Elizabeth. I'll sneak down to the wagon during the dance and be waiting when you get ready to drive home," True said, as if the decision had never been any concern of the others. "As long as I'm back in a few days. Henry and me have plans that can't wait much longer than that."

Audrey reluctantly agreed. "You'll make sure True drinks half milk with coffee."

Jennie added, "At least we'll know where True is. I'll tell the marshal. He worries about the child as much as we do."

Delta nodded and stood, then hugged everyone one more time before hurrying downstairs to wait for a chance to talk to Colton.

He was waiting for her at the foot of the stairs, his eyes as black and cold as ever. His dark handsomeness always made Delta pause for a moment to stare. She'd spent many hours wondering if the coldness about him went all the way to his heart. But his hand felt warm as he took hers and they walked slowly into the dining hall. He didn't say a word, but she'd learned not to expect unnecessary conversation with him. The band tuning up for another round was the only sound that passed between them.

As before when they'd entered the dining room that had been cleared to make a dance floor, Delta didn't miss the way folks stopped and stared.

"Do you feel up to dancing, Mary Elizabeth?" He was already leading her onto the dance floor when he finally asked.

"Yes, sir," she whispered, glancing around to witness the way the others watched Colton. Delta couldn't help but smile. She guessed everyone might find Colton Barkley a little frightening with his cold manner and hard voice, but she was drawn to his strength. Never in her life had she been around a strong man. Her father had been broken and weak from the time she could remember, and her stepfather was loud and always bullying.

But Colton never shouted at her or anyone on his ranch as near as she could tell. She'd spent the past two weeks studying the man. His control was stoic, his manner unyielding. He was a private man, and she admired that about him. He offered no excuses and accepted none from others. Colton demanded that any person, including himself, take responsibility square on the shoulders without whimper or compromise. Delta didn't even mind the remoteness he wore like a medal.

When they reached the center of the room, he raised his hand in invitation. As he lead her across the floor with polished skill, his grip was firm around her fingers. The music continued, and Delta felt him relax a fraction, as though his muscles remembered a time he danced for pleasure and not simply because it was expected of him.

When the dance finished, his warm hand slid beneath her arm. They walked in silence toward the line of chairs along one wall.

"Thank you." Delta stared up into his black eyes as he offered her a chair. "I'm afraid I've had very little opportunity to dance in my life."

"You did fine," he answered without smiling. His gaze repeatedly scanned the room, as if watching for trouble. She had the feeling no man would ever catch Colton off guard, not in this lifetime.

"If another asks me . . ." Delta didn't want to have another man touch her. She could relax in Colton's formal embrace, but wasn't sure how she'd react with another.

Colton interrupted. "No man will ask you to dance. You're with me."

"Correction." Marshal McCormick stepped up beside Delta. "I'd like the honor of the next dance, if you have no objections?" Austin knew he was playing with fire, but sometimes a hunter had to poke a hole in a den and just wait and see what came out. If Colton was as hot-headed as everyone seemed to think, better Austin knew now before the little lady left alone with him again.

Delta studied the marshal. She could hardly turn him down, since most everyone in the room knew he had pulled Mary Elizabeth from the train wreck. She glanced at Colton but saw no answer in his dark eyes. He didn't seem to care one way or the other if she danced.

"I'd be delighted, Marshal," Delta answered as she stood.

Austin held her in his arms so carefully she wanted to giggle. He seemed very much afraid of breaking her if he turned too fast.

"How have you been recovering?" he asked, leaning over to talk to her almost like a grown-up would a child.

"Very well." Delta smiled. "I'm not sure I had time to thank you for saving my life."

Austin shook his head. "No thanks needed. Seeing you looking so lovely tonight was thanks enough." Austin hesitated. Whether she admitted to being Delta or not wasn't as pressing as her safety. He slowed his steps so that they didn't quite match the music. "How do you like staying at Colton Barkley's place?"

Delta knew as well as he did that he wasn't asking about the ranch. "I'm being treated with much kindness," she lied. It was more like polite indifference, but no one outside of the ranch needed to know that. Colton's attitude, she thought, must be rubbing off on her, for her guard was up high enough to block out even the tall marshal.

Austin nodded, as though he'd satisfied some law by checking on her. The dance ended before he could ask any more questions. He walked her back to Barkley's side and thanked her for the dance, deciding the railroad worker was out of line to call a man a wife-killer when all he seemed to be was a widower who wanted to keep to himself. Besides, if the truth be known, the little lady he'd just danced with probably had a few secrets in her past as well.

When Delta returned to Colton, she slid her fingers into the bend of his arm without saying a word. For a moment she thought he might pull away, for it was the boldest thing she'd ever done. But he pulled her arm to him, gently pressing her hand between his elbow and rib cage. When she looked up at him, he watched the room as always, but the pressure didn't decrease as he pressed her fingers against his side.

While the evening aged, they enjoyed a few more dances. Except for the marshal, Colton had been right— no one else asked her for the pleasure of a dance. He left her alone at times so that she could visit with the other women, but she noticed he made no effort to talk to anyone in the room. When he disappeared onto the porch, pulling a cheroot from his vest pocket, Delta knew her chance had come to ask him about True.

She followed him out, paying little attention to the stares and whispers.

For a moment she thought he must have left, for only the cold air greeted her in the shadows. She moved silently along the wide veranda, wishing she'd stopped for her wrap before following him.

As she reached the railing, she stood staring out into the clear winter night. Looking closely, she saw the glow of his thin cigar. Finally her eyes grew accustomed to the darkness, and his outline came into focus beneath a tree several yards away. He stood, watching the lights from town flicker in the distance. His body was stiff, not relaxed as though he were enjoying the evening, but hard as if braced against a wind no one else felt.

Delta took a deep breath and headed toward him. The worst he could do was yell at her for following him outside, and she was willing to risk that to have True with her for a few days.

"Colton?" Most men would have been startled, but his body barely moved. He must have known she was there.

He dropped the cigar and turned to face her. "Yes?"

Delta suddenly lost her bravery. He was such a powerful man, and now here in the shadows he seemed frightening. An animal of the darkness in his element. She forced herself to move closer, reminding her shaking body that he'd never harmed her or even hinted that he might.

"I have a favor to ask of you."

He didn't move. She could only see the profile of his face. He seemed made of unyielding stone.

Her hand trembled when she reached out to touch his arm as she had before. She must feel his warmth, know that he was real, before she asked him to take in a child that wasn't even hers.

When her fingers slid along the hard muscle of his upper arm, Colton reacted immediately. She heard the sudden intake of his breath and knew she'd surprised him with her action. She could feel the muscles tighten beneath her touch and was comforted that the shadow had become human.

She'd expected him to move away from even her slight touch, but he remained planted, so close and yet seemingly out of her reach. Without curving her fingers Delta slid her hand to his shoulder. She could feel the power beneath the fabric of his coat . . . If only an ounce of kindness dwelled there as well . . .

"When I was here before, I met a child, an orphan. I'd like to bring him back to the ranch with me. Only for a few days of course." Delta held her breath. She knew just telling anyone about True was dangerous. If he told Mrs. Gray or the sheriff, the child could be taken away. But somehow Delta knew Colton never told anyone anything more than what he must.

"Is this child yours?" His words were bitter winter.

"No," Delta answered, thinking that was a fair question to ask a stranger. Even though she'd spent two weeks in his home, she was still very much a stranger to him.

"Then why do you care?"

Hugging herself more from the coldness of the man beside her than the chilly wind, she answered, "True's all alone. Both parents are dead. When the Harvey girls found him, he looked like he hadn't eaten in days."

"But he's not yours. He belongs to no one." Colton stated the fact.

Delta moved closer, wishing she could see his eyes. She wondered if his thoughts were as cold as his words. Anger fired her reply. "Maybe he belongs to us all. It doesn't matter if I'm his mother; all children need love and care."

He was silent for so long she thought he wasn't going to answer. Turning to face the lights from town, Delta felt the numbness growing around her heart and realized that if he said no tonight, she'd count the hours until she could be out of his sight. She thought about begging or pleading or even crying, but somehow she knew none of those tactics would work on Colton Barkley.

Slowly he removed his jacket and placed it around her. His hands rested on her shoulders so lightly she wasn't sure they were there. "If you wish to have the child with you, I have no objections."

"Thank you." She turned in his arms. "I'll see that he's no trouble."

Delta was so close she could smell the hint of his cigar in the air between them. As before, he made no effort to move away from her. Hesitantly Delta lifted her hand and placed it over his heart. The shirt was cold, but she could feel the warmth just beneath her touch. Somewhere in this stone statue breathed a man. A good man perhaps.

She had to open the door of honesty between them, if only just a crack. She owed him that much. "I know I'm not what you were expecting from my letters." He'd made that obvious by spending almost every waking hour away from the ranch house. "But if there is anything I can do to help you these next couple of weeks until the month is over, then please let me. You've been kind to me and I'd like to repay you."

"There's no need." Again his words were winter ice, but his heart still pounded beneath her fingers.

"Please," she whispered. "I could cook or clean. I can even sew if you need anything."

"No," he insisted. "I have others who attend to those chores."

Delta nodded, feeling guilty that she'd have to take his money for a ticket in two weeks. When Jennie had thought of the plan, Delta had visualized a poor widower whose house would be in shambles, and she'd figured she could feel she'd given him something in return by cleaning and cooking. Delta's fingers lifted from Colton's chest as she stepped away, knowing that it would take far more than the time she had left to be a friend to this man.

When she turned, Colton touched her shoulder lightly, carefully. "There is something," he admitted, "but whether you say yes or no doesn't matter. The child can still come back to the ranch with us."

Delta smiled, happy to be of some help to him. "Name the task, kind sir."

She thought she heard the low beginnings of a chuckle from him. "You're the only person on this earth who would refer to me as such."

"Then they don't see as clearly as I," she retorted, knowing that she'd seen true evil in men and this one before her bore no hint of it. "Name your task." Delta suddenly wanted very much to make his life a little easier.

He took a deep breath before answering. "You know the way you touched me in there, in front of everyone?"

A flush spread across her cheeks. She hadn't meant to embarrass him by her slight display. She'd meant it as only kindness. How could she have guessed such a small touch would have offended him? "I understand," she nodded, "you wish not to be so informal. I'm sorry. I meant no harm . . ." She should have been able to read his disapproval in his cold stance.

"No," Colton interrupted. "I didn't disapprove. No one has touched me like that in years. I wish you to continue both in public and in private."

"But you never . . ."

"Can you do so whether I respond or not?"

"If you wish," Delta replied. Though the request seemed odd, it was a small favor to ask for all he'd done for her. She'd already sensed that he was perhaps frozen beyond all response to any touch. But if he wanted her to play a part, she would do so without question.

"I wish it," Colton answered, turning once more to the lights of town, as though their conversation had been no more than casual comments.

Delta watched him, wondering what made up this strange man and what it must have taken to mold him so tightly. He didn't seem old enough to have lived through all the suffering it would have taken to fire the steel of his frame.

Slowly, without hesitation, she placed her hand in the hollow of his arm. "Are you ready to go inside?"

He nodded and covered her fingers with his own as they walked back toward the party.

"One other thing." He helped her onto the steps. "If you have any other questions or favors, have no reluctance to ask."

"Thank you again, kind sir. I will."

The low chuckle she'd thought she'd heard once before rumbled from him, but he didn't say a word as he led her back inside.

When he closed the door, he glanced once more at the outline of a man who'd been watching the house since they'd arrived. A large man keeping well out of the light.

Chapter

Seventeen

Marshal," True whispered to Austin from outside the window. "Marshal McCormick!" Music and dancers almost drowned out the tiny voice.

Austin turned around and noticed True's dirty little face staring at him with saucer eyes. He backed against the wall beside the window. "Yes, son," he answered.

"Got to talk to you." True disappeared without waiting to see if Austin followed.

Austin glanced around the room, then walked slowly to the door as though he had no more on his mind than a smoke in the cool night air. Everyone seemed too busy dancing or flirting to notice his movements. Even clean-shaven Spider Morris was sitting halfway up the stairs talking with Mrs. Gray like she was newly widowed and he was fresh off a six-month trail drive.

When Austin reached the darkness of the porch, True was beside him. The child made a habit of appearing and disappearing as soundlessly as smoke.

"Marshal, I got a few questions, and they can't wait till morning."

"All right," McCormick answered. "Get on with it, so I can get back to watching every man in the county line up to dance with Jennie."

True leaned close and whispered, "Are you sure that fellow left town?"

"What fellow?"

True swore, using words Austin often used, but getting them out of order. "The fellow who was holed up in the barn. The one without any hair. Pay attention, Marshal! This is important. I ain't got time to keep repeating myself."

Austin smiled down at True. "The big, hairless man. Like I told you, I asked him a few questions and he said he was moving on."

"And he didn't tell you nothin' else?"

"Most men in these parts aren't too friendly with information." Austin leaned against the porch railing. "Course it's not as bad as it is in Texas. Sometimes I've got a feeling everyone in that state's lugging around a secret so huge Texas is the only place large enough to hide it in."

True danced around with impatience. "I ain't asking about other folks. You said the big man was leaving town, and Henry told me he seen him hiding in the trees between here and the depot."

"When?" Austin's muscles tightened, ready for a fight, then he slowed his curiosity as he considered True's past record of telling the truth.

"Tonight," True answered. "He's probably waiting out there planning to rob the whole town while all the men are at this dumb dance. I figure he might not be that Buck Lawton you're looking for, but he could be working for him. Maybe Lawton sent this fellow into town to see just how easy these folks would be to take in a fight."

Austin didn't want to admit that he'd thought the same thing for a moment when he'd first heard about the man sleeping in the livery, but the idea didn't hold water. First, the man in the livery was too much of a lowlife for even a weasel like Lawton to partner up with. Second, if he were just looking the town over, it would have only taken a matter of hours, not days.

"Sheriff Morris said Lawton was reported seen in Missouri." Austin tried to reassure True. "If he's heading this way, he's taking his time. My guess is he's smart enough to stay away from Florence, where we're waiting for him."

"Well, I'll probably miss all the excitement." True sounded disappointed. "But I'm going to have to leave you and Henry to help the sheriff. I got to go with Delta to Colton Barkley's ranch."

"With who?" Austin's question stilled the night air to a corpse's breath.

For the first time since he'd met the child True was perfectly still. "Did I say Delta? I meant Mary Elizabeth. You know how all these women look alike. I get the names mixed up sometimes. I got to go with Mary Elizabeth and Mr. Barkley."

Austin turned toward the child, knowing he'd finally tripped over a way to prove he'd been right about Delta assuming Mary Elizabeth's identity.

"True?" He looked across the porch. "True, I know you're there, so you might as well come close enough for me to see you."

No answer.

"True!"

Austin swore under his breath. The kid was harder to keep up with than a baby cricket. "I'll talk to you when you get back, and you can tell Henry I want to see him in my office also. We've got a few things that—"

"Talking to yourself again, Marshal?" Jennie asked as she moved outside. "Why don't you yell a little louder and maybe the folks in town can hear you?"

Austin swore again before answering. "I was talking to True."

Jennie looked around. "True isn't here."

"I know that!" Austin snapped. "The child is as hard to talk to as his mother."

"We've been through this before. I'm not anyone's mother."

"But the child never strays too far from where you are, and he's as protective of you as I've ever seen a boy be. Add that the two of you both have the same loose grip on the truth, and I can see the family resemblance." He didn't know if he really believed Jennie was True's mother any longer, but he still knew she'd lied to him about Delta, and he wanted so much for her to trust him enough to be honest.

Jennie turned back toward the door. "I didn't come out here to listen to this."

He took a step and blocked her path. "What did you come out here for, Jennie?" He wanted to ask if she'd like to live another dream, but he wasn't sure he wanted to hear her answer.

"I . . ." She tried to step past him, but he was faster. "I thought we could have some peace between us."

Austin knew he should disappear into the night as fast as True had, but he couldn't. Most of his life he'd been happy being alone, but all at once he longed to feel one woman in his arms. Longed for it so deeply he couldn't sleep or concentrate. How could this headstrong, lying woman in this little nothing town make him feel like he'd just jumped off into uncharted waters and better be very careful or he'd drown?

"Is peace what you want between us?" he whispered, as his hands closed over her shoulders. He wanted to hold her so dearly he could feel the ache all the way to his boots. "If we don't want to argue, maybe we shouldn't talk at all."

Jennie jerked free. "I wish you could understand."

"Oh, I understand." He'd known from the beginning that Jennie would never be an only-in-the-shadows kind of lover. That's why it didn't make any sense that she'd lie about Delta.

He suddenly wanted to hurt her a fraction of the amount her lies kept hurting him. "I've got the idea. Barkley's a rich rancher around these parts. The opportunity was too good for Delta to turn down. And True's not your child. The boy just hangs around because of the food." He reached for her again. "Anything else I need to understand before we stop talking?"

Jennie twisted from his arms. "No," she said, hurt that he could think so little of her. "In fact, I don't think I ever need to speak to you again, Marshal McCormick. Good night."

Before Austin could stop her, she vanished through the doorway. He took a step to catch her, then realized how hopeless it would be. Slamming his fist against the railing, he mumbled, "Another trait True and she have in common—vanishing before I finish."

Chapter
Eighteen

*J*ennie opened the back door of the sheriff's office without bothering to knock. "Austin!" she shouted as she stepped inside and closed the door behind her. The air was almost as cold in the office as outside. "McCormick, are you in here?"

Austin came awake all at once. He'd left Jennie two hours before at the Harvey House. As he'd walked home, he wondered if he'd be able to sleep after their argument. She might have vanished from his side, but the touch of her as they'd danced earlier remained in his memory as if it were a tangible presence.

Dear Lord, no woman had ever felt so right in his arms. Part of him wished he had just grabbed her and kissed her when they'd been on the porch. They'd spent the rest of the evening avoiding each other. She might be madder than hell, but a touch of heaven blended in the feel of her.

So he'd returned home more angry at himself than with her. After half an hour and almost half a bottle of whiskey, he'd finally gone to sleep in the back room of the empty jail-house office. It wasn't much for quarters, but he preferred it to the chatty boardinghouse accommodations.

"Stay mad if you like, but let me know if you're here. Time's wasting."

"Jennie?" Austin shook the wash of whiskey from his mind and pulled on his pants. He didn't have to ask; he knew whatever had brought her here this late must be important or she wouldn't have crossed the darkness between the Harvey House and town.

"Last I heard you were never speaking to me again." He fought to keep his words from tumbling out atop one another. "Never's a shorter span of time than it used to be."

She stormed into his little room as a Texas dust devil whirled across open prairie. Moonlight from his window was bright enough to spotlight her in its yellow beams, making her look more dream than real. She still wore her blue calico dress, but she'd tied an apron around her waist. "Stop talking like a fool and get dressed."

Austin fumbled with the buttons on his pants. "How'd you get here?" She looked too beautiful to be flesh and blood before him.

"I walked over, of course. What I have to say can't wait until morning." She pushed a wool shawl away from her head. Shadows made her hair black velvet. "With the moonlight, it's almost bright as day outside." Venturing closer she added, "Austin, you've got to help me."

He ran his fingers through his hair and tried to fit the pieces together. "What's the problem that can't wait?"

A part of him longed to believe that she'd come for his touch.

Jennie paced his tiny room as if looking for the right words somewhere in the dusty shadows.

"Go ahead, tell me." Austin watched her closely, trying to clear his mind of dreams and whiskey enough to deal with her in reality. "There's nothing I can do if I don't know what's got you so upset."

Stopping suddenly, she stared at him. The kind of look that crumpled a man's judgment. Her eyes filled with worry as she spoke. "I just heard Colton Barkley killed his first wife."

Austin smiled and relaxed a little. He'd feared the problem might be far greater than gossip. From the way she looked at him, he'd been ready to promise to ride without hearing the quest.

Jennie saw his face and frowned. She couldn't stop her hand from knotting as thoughts of taking a swing at him came to her mind. "Stop smiling, you vacant-brained lawman. Don't you see, he killed his first wife. What if we just handed him another victim? I've read about his type of villain in books about the West."

"There's a deep crevice between the real world and books, Miss Munday. Who told you Barkley was a killer?" he asked, figuring half the folks at the dance had probably heard the railroad worker's story.

"One of the girls while I was cleaning up. She said a man she danced with told her. It's been years since the murder, but folks around here still talk about it."

Austin tried to look worried. "Did the girl say her dance partner had any proof of such a claim?"

Jennie exploded. "His wife's dead! What more proof do we need? Go arrest him and bring back Del— Mary Elizabeth and True."

"True left with Colton then?"

Exasperation molded on her face with tools of frustration and impatience. She wanted him to act, not question. If he was always so slow at responding to trouble, she guessed most of his outlaws died of old age before they saw a trial. "True rode out with them tonight. We thought it would be all right for a few days. We didn't know we were packing the child off with a killer."

"True mentioned something about going." Austin wished suddenly that the bothersome kid had stayed in town. "Did Colton agree to taking on the extra mouth to feed?"

"Of course, Mary Elizabeth asked him." Jennie lifted Austin's shirt off the room's only chair and offered it to him, hoping to hurry him along. "Now, you've got to ride out to Barkley's ranch and get them before it's too late."

"Already got him tried and sentenced?"

Moving closer, Jennie held out his shirt. "Of course not, but I'm not taking any chances with their lives."

He took the shirt and slowly slipped it on over his shoulders, not bothering to button it. "Doesn't it strike you as a little unusual that a man would agree to take a child along if he's planning the death of his second wife? Seems to me he should at least wait until they're alone after the wedding."

"I don't know. Who knows what goes through the mind of any man?" Jennie turned her face to the windows, not wanting him to see her doubt. She wasn't about to admit it, but his logic was starting to sink in. Colton Barkley would hardly bring a future wife to a party, then kill her. Also, he'd never have agreed to allow True to come along if he were planning something. The girl's dance partner had said he'd killed his first wife without witnesses. If there were no witnesses, how'd everyone know he was a killer? There were lots of reasons besides murder that folks die, even young ones.

Watching Austin, Jennie hated him suddenly for standing there looking like he was waiting for her mind to kick in. "Maybe you're right," she offered. "I don't understand you, so how could I hope to second-guess a killer?"

"He's not a killer." Austin moved closer, jealous of the way the moonlight touched her face. "I heard the same story about Barkley and did some checking. There was no proof outside of her family's gossip to indicate Colton did anything wrong. Sheriff Morris said as near as he can find out, Barkley's never so much as cut a neighbor's fence to move cattle. He follows every law around these parts, so Morris thinks it's unlikely he killed his wife."

Austin fought the urge to touch her. All covered in calico, she looked almost like a little girl ready for her first dance, not hard and proper as she did in her uniform. "Just because a man doesn't want to talk about the way his wife died doesn't mean he's a murderer." Austin lowered his voice. "Did you ask Delta if he'd mistreated her in any way during the two weeks she's been with him?"

"Of course I did." Jennie spoke before she saw the trap. "I mean, I asked Mary Elizabeth."

Austin smiled. "I know what you mean." He stood six inches away from her, listening to her lie, and still the need to touch her was so strong he couldn't remember his own name.

Emerald eyes flashed in the moonlight. "Then you think she's safe all alone out on that ranch?"

"As safe as you are here with me."

Suddenly the cold room seemed summer warm. Jennie couldn't lower her gaze. His eyes were golden brown with fire. His lips opened slightly, as though he fought the urge to kiss her. His hands, chained with self-discipline, shoved deep into the pockets of his pants. Every muscle in his body looked wire-tight, fighting for control.

She wanted to know if the night he'd kissed her had been as wonderful as she remembered. She wanted to have him touch her once more. The need to feel his arms around her, to believe he could care for her, was an ache within Jennie that quaked through her body, shaking her heart from hiding. She'd longed for such a man all her life, and now he stood a breath away, fighting to keep from moving closer. What did it matter if he thought she lied, as long as he held her.

"Am I safe with you?" she whispered, suddenly feeling as though the world had slowed in time and her heart would forever gauge its beats in the before and after of this moment.

"Yes," he returned in a low voice hoarse with desire. "I told you once I could never care for a woman who wasn't honest. I never go back on my word." His hungry eyes screamed that he spoke a lie. "Nothing has changed."

She slowly began closing the distance between them. The very air seemed reluctant to separate them. "Nothing?" she echoed. "Not even in your dreams."

As he shoved his fingers deeper into his pockets, his hands threatened to rip the fabric. Bitter words brushed against her cheek. "You seem to have the same trouble between truth and lies as you do between telling right from left."

His face was a battle of feelings. She could smell the hint of whiskey on his breath and feel the warmth of his body so near. Mustering all her courage, she moved closer. "What I feel now has nothing to do with right or left, truth or lie."

"I could never care for a woman who placed no value on honesty." His words were the only barrier between them, for he made no move to step away.

A smile trickled across Jennie's lips. She didn't have to argue with him. He was doing a grand job of fighting with himself.

"You could never care for me?" She leaned so close he felt her words against the hollow of his throat. The hour was late and she was tired of fighting. Even if she had to lie to herself, she wanted to believe he cared— if only for this night. She wanted to feel she was alive for at least a moment before her family found her and convinced her of the nothingness of her life.

"No." He tried to swallow. "Never."

"And you're not attracted to me?"

"No."

"You don't come to the Harvey House to see me?"

"No." The fresh smell of her was making his thoughts cloud more than the half bottle of whiskey he'd drunk earlier. He could almost taste the cinnamon blended in her hair and the night air fresh against her cheeks.

"And you didn't come to the dance to see me?" A hint of doubt filtered through her words.

"Correct." He raised his head slightly, knowing that if he looked into her eyes, he'd be lost. Even now he could feel her bare breasts pressed against his chest, though they were both still clothed.

"You weren't thinking of kissing me when we were on the porch tonight?"

"No!" He forced the word out as though he meant it.

"And you're never going to change or bend?" He could hear the doubt in her words. The self-assured woman he'd met was starting to crumble. She'd been bold to ask, but his response had chipped away at her confidence.

"Never." He couldn't allow her to draw him with her beauty. He had to stand by rules without bending. He'd always lived by the rules he'd made up for himself. He wouldn't have been alive if he'd questioned or changed.

"Never!" he repeated, trying to make himself believe his words.

"I thought . . . I thought . . ." She couldn't finish. She'd humiliated herself enough. How could she have believed he wanted to hold her as dearly as she did him? He must have had other reasons for coming to the Harvey House, for asking her to remain on the porch, for looking at her all evening. Each day she'd turned and saw him sitting in her section, she'd thought he was there because of her. Could there have been another purpose to his pestering?

Austin stared at her trembling bottom lip, the sight ripping him apart as no number of words could have.

"I must've been wrong," she whispered.

"You must have been," he added, but his voice was no longer harsh.

Turning suddenly, Jennie bolted toward the door. She wanted to get as far away from Austin McCormick as she could. All the daydreams she'd had, all the memories, were no more real than the pictures in her mind when she read one of her books. He didn't care for her. Just because he kissed her with passion didn't mean she mattered to him.

Tears bubbled in her eyes as she ran blindly toward the door.

"Jennie!" Austin shouted.

She didn't look back. She couldn't endure the laughter in his eyes or the pity at her having made a fool of herself. If she'd known more about men, maybe she wouldn't have fallen so easily into believing he could care for her.

"No," she mumbled, feeling that everything her family ever said had been right. She'd lose, if not her way, then her heart, if she wasn't very careful.

"Jennie!" he yelled again as she fought with the door latch.

Before she could turn the lock, he grabbed her arm and twirled her around to face him. The force of his movements slammed her into his chest. "Jennie, what did you think?"

"Let go of me!" she shouted. "You've made it plain how you feel."

"Have I?" He drew her against him with one arm, forcing her face up with long fingers. "Did you think you could lie to me, turn me away again and again, then come to me on your terms?"

How could she explain to him that she hadn't been around enough men to know? How could she tell him about a lie that was the only thing keeping Delta alive? "I only meant to come here and tell you about Barkley. I didn't mean to bother you."

Austin's stare was granite, but his grip became a caress. "Bother me! You haunt every hour of my day and night. The sight of you sets a fire in my gut that I can't drink enough whiskey to put out. Do you have any idea how you turn my insides out, exposing my heart with each lie you tell?"

"Maybe I tell no lies!" She flushed war-paint red. "You've no proof."

"Maybe I don't want you!" he answered as his lips came down on hers, hard and demanding.

There was nothing soft and loving about his kiss. He wanted to purge himself, burn the longing for her from

him with a fire he knew would explode the moment she
was in his arms. He wanted to taste her, drink in the
smell of her until he drowned in the nearness of her,
then maybe her memory would allow him some peace.

But she didn't fight. She didn't shove him from her
and scream, giving him reason to hate both her and
himself. She wrapped her arms around his neck and
answered his longing with a cry as great.

He knew he was bruising her lips with his kiss, but
he couldn't stop. He'd watched her every day for weeks.
She moved so properly in her black uniform and starched
apron. But one rainy night he'd felt the softness beneath
her clothes. Once he'd dreamed of holding her in passion. Now all he could think about was touching her. He
had to turn away before she saw the need in his eyes.

Running his fingers into the thickness of her hair, he
pulled her head back. "I don't want you!" He forced the
lie out one more time, as if he could make it true.

Her eyes were dark with desire and liquid with unshed
tears. Her life unraveled when she held to him. No one,
including her family, had ever wanted her. She'd been
an extra puzzle piece on a board where everyone else
had a place. But not here, not with him.

Austin's voice was low, echoing from his very soul.
"I don't want you, but I need you. Before I met you, I
didn't know that just going a few hours without seeing
a woman could drive me mad. Every time I walk into the
Harvey House and see you, my arms ache so desperately
to hold you I think everyone in the room must see me
shaking with longing for you."

Jennie blinked away the tears. She couldn't believe
he was saying such words to her, not her, not the Jennie
everyone passed by. "I thought you didn't care," she
whispered.

"I don't care," he answered. "I don't seem to care about anything except holding you."

She lightly brushed her lips against his. "I know how you feel. I've watched your light from my window and almost crossed the darkness every night. But I was afraid you'd turn me away."

"If I were you, I'd be more afraid that I'll never let you go."

Rubbing her cheek against his stubbly chin, she answered, "That fear never entered my mind."

His arms tightened around her, pulling her heart against his. His mouth covered hers, proving his point. The kiss was long and complete, blanketing over two lives filled with years of loneliness.

"Don't leave tonight, Jennie," he whispered as they stopped to breathe. "Let me hold you till first light. God, how I need to hold you!"

Jennie's hands moved slowly beneath the folds of his shirt. She could feel his heart pounding as she slid her fingers over the light scattering of hair across his chest.

"And tomorrow?" she whispered. Her hands spread over his warm skin.

"Tonight there is no tomorrow." His mouth claimed hers once more, this time with a tender yearning, a lifetime of longing.

Jennie closed her mind to tomorrow. She knew he'd never love her if she didn't tell him the truth, but for a moment his need for her was enough. For the rest of her life she might live alone, but this night she'd feel a man in her arms. A man made of flesh and blood, not wishes and romance.

His lips left her mouth as he trailed desire's fire down her throat. "You taste so good," he whispered, pulling her collar open. "Nothing will ever satisfy me again after I've had the taste of you in my mouth."

Jennie didn't move as he pulled the buttons of her blouse open. With each one, he brushed his mouth over the exposed flesh. His touch warmed her skin and spread heat over her. Deep within her she felt desire shatter through a shell of fear and give birth to passion's longing. A longing only he could satisfy.

His hands fumbled with the lace of her camisole, and she smiled. Raising his head, he looked into her eyes. He'd not take what she wasn't offering, and she was so still, he wasn't sure her desire matched his own. "Jennie?" he whispered. "Do you want me to touch you?"

She nodded slightly, and for the first time since he'd met her, a smile warmed her eyes.

Gently he lifted her off the floor and carried her to his bed. When he sat her on the edge, he knelt beside her.

She hesitated, holding him away with hands so gentle her fingers were almost a caress. "I'm not . . ."

"It doesn't matter." He didn't want to hear the number of men she'd been with. "All that matters is now, tonight."

He saw a hint of fear in her eyes and cursed the other men who'd bedded her. Kissing her tenderly, he whispered, "Don't be afraid of me. I could never hurt you."

Green eyes studied him. Slowly, she raised her hand and brushed the hair from his eyes. "I'm not afraid of you." Planting light kisses along his jaw, she smiled, thinking tomorrow would be time enough to talk. Tonight was made for feeling, and all she wanted to feel right now was him in her arms.

His kiss deepened. He brushed his knuckle over the swell of her breast above her camisole.

When she didn't answer, he pulled the ribbon, freeing the lace undergarment. As the fabric fell open, he couldn't resist the taste of her.

Her breasts were full and rounded. He lowered his mouth slowly. The pleasure of her made his nerves feel as if they'd been loaded with dynamite and the fuse burned only inches away.

"Lean back," he whispered, shoving the clothes off her shoulders and out of his way.

She stretched and rested her head on his pillow.

"Close your eyes," he urged as he sat beside her and pulled the clothes from her.

She lay still, loving the adventure of this man.

He moved his hands over her body, feather-light at first, then molding her flesh with passion, stroking the velvet of her skin with fire; loving the way she moved to his touch, as though wanting all parts to be stroked at once.

When she raised her arms to pull him beside her, he pushed her gently away. "No," he requested. "I want to touch you."

As his fingers blanketed her, she moved in a dance where they were perfectly matched. Here the music played in their minds and they never missed a step. She didn't open her eyes, but cried out softly with joy as he circled her breasts and slid his large palm along her abdomen.

"You're perfection," he whispered. "I've lain awake every night since I first kissed you, wondering what it would be like to touch like this."

She raised her arms once more and pulled him to her mouth. His lips were hot with need. She'd longed for a man to touch her with loving strokes and couldn't believe this man, this honest, powerful man, needed her as dearly as she needed him.

Their kiss deepened, as they both knew it must. He lowered his body beside her, gently pushing the hard wall of his chest against her softness.

Suddenly she shoved him back and rose above him. For a blink there was a question in his eyes, and he seemed to think she might yet leave him, but then she smiled.

"Jennie," he whispered, trying to pull her near.

She laughed and shook her head, sending a cloud of ebony circling over her bare shoulders and tumbling to her waist.

"Lie still," she ordered.

Austin opened his mouth to argue, but she silenced him with a playful kiss. "I'll touch you," she whispered against his lips, "the way you've touched me, or I'll get up and leave right now."

He chuckled. "You'd make quite a sight walking back to the hotel with nothing but your hair to keep you warm."

"Would you arrest me?" Her fingers gently moved along his rib cage.

"That I would," he groaned in sweet agony, "and lock you in one of the front cells until morning."

"And would you come get me at dawn?"

"No." Austin laughed when she shoved his clothes aside. "I'd unlock the door and let myself out while you slept. Maybe I'd let you out after breakfast."

He bit at his bottom lip, unable to speak of the pleasure he felt while her fingers moved over his body, touching, teasing, caressing. "Don't be afraid," she echoed his words from earlier. "I could never hurt you."

Austin knotted the blanket below him with his fists. He fought to keep from reaching for her. Her touch was a sweet torture he'd have gladly died from before trying to stop her.

"Just close your eyes and relax." She whispered words against his ear. Her hands stroked paradise across his body.

All control within him snapped. He reached for her and rolled, pulling her beneath him.

Suddenly there was no more need for words. When his body touched hers full-length, she felt a completeness she'd missed all her life. As she'd known it would be, his body was hard where she was soft, demanding where she yielded, rough where she was most tender. The touch of his skin against hers drove her mad with pleasure.

She took his lead, touching him where he touched her. Her fingers clawed into his back, longing to pull him closer, until she could no longer tell where his pleasure and hers separated.

His touch grew rough with desire and his kisses hard with need. He'd meant to be gentle, waltzing her into passion's dance slowly, but she'd have none of it.

She hurried him when he would have gone slower, driving him mad with her demands to touch and kiss and feel and taste. They'd both waited too long to feel the warmth of great passion; there could be no stopping, no halfway.

When he entered her, he heard her cry softly at the same time his heart exploded in delight. For one blink in time he thought he might have hurt her, but desire flooded all reason from his mind as she moved beneath him.

Her body welcomed him where her words had not, telling him of her longing, demanding a passion he'd never known himself capable of giving.

Crying out as all her dreams exploded into reality, she rode the wave of pleasure back to earth in his embrace.

Austin rolled beside her, holding her more tightly than he'd ever held anything in his life.

"Jennie, Jennie," he whispered over and over. He rocked her to sleep in the private world of his arms.

Chapter
Nineteen

*L*ong after Jennie fell asleep cuddled against him, Austin lay awake staring into the night and thinking. Her nearness drugged him with a pleasure he'd thought would always be denied. He could feel the soft tips of her breasts against his side and the gentle tickle of her breath near his throat.

In the shadows life seemed a dream, and dreams real. He pulled a blanket over them both, wishing the wool could block out the world as it did the cold.

He knew it was almost dawn and he should wake her, but he didn't want to return to the world just yet. Reason told him he could never care for a woman who lied so easily, but his heart screamed it was too late; he already did. Now, with the passion spent, it was time to think of how little he had to offer a woman like her. A bushelful of worrying when he didn't come home and a bucket of outlaw's threats to end his life at the first opportunity didn't seem such fine gifts to set on her porch when he came calling.

All he'd ever known was life with a Colt at his side. It was too late to change now even if he wanted to. No matter how much he cared for a woman, he could never lay his guns aside and take up farming like he'd seen a few other lawmen try. Jennie was the type of woman who'd want her man's feet beneath the table every night for dinner, and he was the type of man who never seemed to leave a footprint in the same dirt twice.

Austin kissed her forehead lightly. She'd managed to touch a part of him no one else had ever reached. "I'll never love you," he whispered as she slept. "When Pete died I swore I'd never love another human as long as I lived."

His memory traveled back to a battlefield long ago. Bodies were littered everywhere on land he never knew the name of, and the rebel flag lay soaked with mud, blood and rain. His brother, Pete, was cold in his arms, but he couldn't let go. Austin held Pete all night, listening to the fighting around him . . . praying a bullet would hit him and take away the grief. Pete had sworn he wouldn't die, just like their mother had, but he lied. They'd joined the war as boys, but the war hadn't given Pete a chance to become a man.

As he remembered how a sergeant had pulled Pete from his arms and shoved a rifle in his hands, Austin flinched at Jennie's side. "Fight! Damn it, fight!" the man had yelled, and Austin had been fighting ever since.

Except for last night, he thought, pulling Jennie close. When he'd seen her bottom lip tremble, he'd laid down his weapons and surrendered. Then she'd kissed him, and all the promises he'd made to himself had been forgotten.

He wished he could make her understand. Even if she hadn't lied, there wasn't enough of him left to give anyone. His body might not have died on that battlefield, but his heart had.

"Morning," Jennie whispered, stretching beside him.

All thought of ever leaving her vanished as he felt her move. Her softness gently washed over all the scars on his body and soul, making him feel like he'd just woken up from a year's sleep. "Morning," he answered, wondering how she could feel so wonderful. He'd touched her completely only a short time ago, but he felt like he couldn't wait to discover her every curve all over again.

She rested her chin on his chest. "It'll be light soon. I need to get back before Mrs. Gray catches me out. I can just imagine how she'd react if she knew I spent the night with you."

"Probably not much different than you'd react if you knew she spent the night with Spider Morris."

Jennie laughed. "She didn't!"

"Maybe Spider figures she's been a widow long enough," Austin guessed.

"I can't see them together." Jennie shook her head, making curls tickle his chest. "Not Mrs. Gray."

"Speaking of seeing," Austin slowly moved his hands down her body, "I wish there was enough light for me to see you."

"No." She shook her curls again. "I'll be gone by sunup."

Austin's arm tightened around her. He knew she was right, but he didn't want to let her go. "Jennie, there's so much we need to talk about."

She placed her fingers over his lips. "Not now," she whispered. "For now, just let me remember. I've never had anything happen worth remembering until I met you."

She hugged him tightly and was silent for a long time before she whispered, "My parents were always afraid I'd turn the wrong direction and never make it home, so they'd tie red ribbons along the road to show me the way. I'd see the ribbon and know I was nearing home." She moved her fingers over his chest. "I feel that way with you. I'm not sure where we're going, but I think we're finally moving in the right direction."

A hundred thoughts came to his mind, but Austin didn't say a word as his hand lightly brushed over her body.

She stood and searched for her clothes in the shadowy darkness. He remained silent. Before she covered the beauty of her body, he memorized each line of her form. A smile slowly spread across his face. He couldn't remember ever watching a woman dress. He'd always been the one leaving.

When she began fastening the buttons, she finally turned to him for help. Silently she held up her hair and faced the windows. Austin stood and slid on his pants before accepting the challenge.

He performed the task as slowly as he thought she'd allow, then leaned forward and gently kissed her on the back of her neck. "Jennie," he whispered, knowingly breaking the silence she'd asked for, but wanting to say her name once more.

Turning her to face him, Austin slowly lowered his lips to hers, wanting to taste her once more before they parted. But the sound of horses thundering past shattered the predawn silence and pulled him back to reality.

"They're traveling fast, too fast," he mumbled as he held her to him a moment longer. It sounded like they were headed straight for the office door.

"Stay here!" Austin yelled. He grabbed his gunbelt and ran toward the shouting outside.

He lifted his rifle from a resting place in the office without breaking stride. Flinging the door wide, he stepped back to look before running onto the porch.

A team of horses, lathered and snorting for breath, pulled to a halt at his door. Austin struck a match and lit the lantern hanging from one of the porch poles. When he looked up, he couldn't believe the sight in the wagon. True sat on the bench, eyes wide with fear and hands bleeding from trying to hold the reins tightly.

"Marshal!" True cried. "Marshal, you've got to help us!"

As he rounded the wagon, Austin strapped his gunbelt around his waist.

"They shot at us from all directions!" True was sobbing so hard the marshal could barely understand the child's words. "There must have been a hundred of them, maybe two hundred."

"Who?" Austin looked around, making sure the wagon hadn't been followed.

"I don't know," True answered. "I was asleep in the back, but I think we were about halfway to Colton's ranch, and all at once I heard gunfire. Colton fired back into the blackness as he ordered us to keep down. When shots came again, he was hit hard."

Austin pulled the covers from the back bed. There, cuddled as close as she could to the bench sat Delta, wearing her green dress and cape. Colton's head rested on her skirts as if in sleep, but he looked more dead than alive.

"Is he breathing?" Austin placed his hand on Colton's throat and felt a weak pulse still beating. Blood was splattered everywhere across his clothes.

Delta gently brushed Colton's black hair off his bloody forehead. "It's all my fault," she mumbled. "The bullet was meant for me."

The woman must be in shock, Austin thought. She wasn't making any sense.

He quickly lifted Colton from her arms. "We'll look at whose fault it is after we get this man some medical help."

Delta and True followed him into the office. "He's been gut-shot!" Delta cried. "I couldn't make him stop bleeding."

Jennie ran from the back room. She was within a step of Delta when the tiny blonde's blue eyes rolled up. With Jennie cradling her, the two women slid to the floor together. "It's all right," she whispered to Delta as if the words could somehow make it true. "Everything's all right now; you're here. You're safe."

Austin carried Colton into the first cell and placed him on one of two bunks. A crimson puddle of blood darkened his white shirt from just above the belt line to his shoulder. He also had a cut across his forehead just below his hairline that looked like it might have happened when he fell from the wagon.

Pulling clothes away from the wound, Austin glanced at True. "Can you help, son?"

"Yes, sir," True answered, hiding tiny bloody hands from sight.

"Good, 'cause I need you now." Austin didn't like the size of Colton's wound. Whoever had shot at the man meant to kill him. "Go tell the doc I need him fast, then go over to Spider Morris's house and tell him what happened."

"Yes, sir," True said while already running to follow orders.

Austin spread a blanket over the wounded man and turned to Jennie. "How's Delta?"

For once Jennie didn't bother to defend her lie. "I don't think she's hurt. She just fainted."

Austin lifted Delta and carried her to the other bunk inside the cell. "I think it would be best if I ran over to the Harvey House and got Audrey." The look on his face told Jennie he didn't give Colton much hope. "She'll probably do as much good as the doc."

Jennie nodded. For a breath's length they stood, staring at each other, wishing there was time to say goodbye. Wishing their night together hadn't ended so quickly. Both wishing there were no lies between them.

Without a word Austin disappeared into the back room to finish dressing.

DELTA WOKE, THINKING for a moment she'd had a nightmare. Then the memory of the night before focused. When they'd left the dance, she'd been feeling dizzy and had feared she might have to ask Colton to stop alongside the road if her stomach didn't settle. Too much punch and dancing, she'd decided.

But her queasiness calmed as they traveled along the midnight dark road, avoiding holes as best they could. True was asleep in the wagon bed. Colton remained silent as always, but he put his arm around her for warmth and she leaned into him. The shadows moved like an old man needing slumber, fanning Delta to sleep with a cool breath.

From somewhere up ahead gunfire flashed in the blackness like ground lightning. Delta came full awake, staring into the night that seemed even blacker after the flashes of light. Colton reached for his rifle and swung her over the bench to safety before he stopped the horses.

"Stay down," he ordered. "No matter what happens, stay down!"

When True appeared at his back, Colton shoved the reins into his tiny hands and whispered, "Hold on tight, boy, no matter how much it hurts. If you lose control of the horses with the next round of fire, we're all dead."

Colton stepped down, away from the wagon, making as much noise as he could. He raised his rifle and fired one shot into the night.

Delta screamed, suddenly aware of what he was doing. Any future shots from the highwaymen would be pointed toward him and away from her and True. Bright light flashed from another round he issued, marking him for the attacker.

An answer came before her scream died in the air. Colton took the bullet straight on, as though he'd been bracing himself for it for years. Then he crumpled without a sound.

Delta jumped from the wagon and felt in the darkness for his body. "Colton?" she cried as her hands moved along him.

No answer.

"Colton!" Panic hit Delta so hard she shook from the blow. She pulled at his arm while her ears ached with waiting to hear the unseen killer fire again.

Silence. Only silence. Whoever was out there seemed in no hurry to kill her.

Delta moved her fingers over Colton's clothes until she felt the warmth of his blood gushing out an opening at his waist. Frantically, she pushed against the wound, trying to stop the flow.

True tied the reins around the brake and climbed down. "We got to get out of here, miss."

"Not without him," Delta answered. She couldn't just leave Colton to die in the roadway.

"But it ain't gonna take whoever shot Colton long to figure out we're here. Our only chance is to try and make it to town by sunup."

"Leave me," Colton whispered between clenched teeth. "Leave me. I've been a dead man for years."

Delta felt him go limp in her embrace and knew the pain had finally won over his consciousness. She also knew the boy was right. They had to move quickly. "Help me lift him."

Together they managed to get Colton in the wagon. Delta climbed in with him and whispered to True, "Can you drive a team?"

"You bet." True moved around to the front wheel. "Don't look all that hard. Henry explained it all to me the other day."

True threaded the leather through his tiny fingers as Colton had done and slapped the horses into action.

Delta forced out all thought except holding on to Colton, until she saw the outline of town at daybreak. He hadn't moved, and she'd kept her hand over his wound, pushing as hard as she could against the steady flow of blood oozing out. But the crimson banner of death spread.

Finally, she'd known she was safe when she saw Jennie. The horror of the night slid away, and the dizziness she'd felt after the dance returned with a mighty vengeance at having been set aside because of her fears. Without warning, the world floated away, and she watched consciousness fade first to gray, then to black.

When Delta opened her eyes, she wasn't sure how much time had passed, but the dizziness had lessened. She took in her surroundings: the dusty cell, the sheriff's office beyond, morning shining through the open door as though the sunshine could warm away all the darkness. Colton quietly slept in a bunk four feet from her. Jennie was shoving logs into an old stove while the smell of coffee drifted across the room.

Without caring that she was ruining her dress, Delta crawled out of her bunk and knelt on the floor beside Colton. She placed her arm protectively over his shoulder. "I'm sorry," she whispered as she pulled the derringer he'd given her from between the folds of her skirts. "The shooting was all my fault." She could almost see her stepbrother hiding in the shadows waiting for them. He'd probably shot Colton just to get him out of the way. Delta was sure Ward planned to kill her more slowly.

Resting her head on his shoulder, Delta couldn't stop the tears. "I'm so sorry," she cried.

Colton's hand covered her hair. "No." His voice was so weak Delta wasn't sure she heard it.

"What?" She turned and stared at his ghost-white face.

Colton stroked her curls with his fingers. "It's not your fault, Mary Elizabeth. I've a number of men who want me dead."

Pain won another battle as Colton's eyes closed.

Delta held his hand as tightly as she could. "Don't worry," she whispered. "I won't leave you." He was the only man she'd ever admired in her life. In the two weeks she'd been with him, she'd known what it was like not to be afraid for the first time in her memory.

"Promise you won't die and leave me."

Colton was too far into his battle to answer, but Audrey took up the challenge. "He's not going to die." The tall redhead set down her sewing basket that doubled as her medical bag. "Not if I have anything to do with it."

True stood behind Audrey, close as a noonday shadow. "The doc's out of town delivering a baby but Sheriff Morris will be here in a minute."

Audrey looked down at Colton, then smiled at Delta. "Does he really treat you good, honey?"

The question was too honest to be answered any other way but directly. "Yes. He's been good to me. In the two weeks I've been with him, he's never said an unkind word." In fact he'd said very few words at all.

"Well, then, I'd best go to work, 'cause he's too handsome a man to die." As she worked, Audrey continued talking. "Let the bushwackers kill off a few of those no-accounts a poxed pig wouldn't breed with and leave the good-looking men alone."

Delta wiped tears from her cheeks and smiled. With Audrey around, it was hard to believe everything wouldn't be all right.

Audrey smiled back. "That's better. Even death can't ride in a buckboard full of smiles."

The redheaded woman yelled orders so fast at True and Jennie, the little jail seemed like a crowded train station. Delta helped when she could and steadfastly refused to leave Colton's side. Austin and Sheriff Morris appeared, wanting to ask Colton questions.

But Audrey shooed them out of the cell. "We'll worry about saving this man's life first, before you two try to figure out who used him for target practice."

Both lawmen moved reluctantly to the porch. "I'd rather step in a nest of rattlers with one bullet in my

gun than argue with that woman." Spider shook his
head. "I sure hopes she marries Wiley. With her fire
and his strength they oughta have some fine younguns
populating this country in no time."

Austin agreed as he stepped off the porch. "I'll ride
out to the site where they were attacked and see if I can
find out anything."

Spider Morris pulled up a chair in the morning sunlight to wait out the day's events. "I'll keep my eyes on
things around town."

Within a few minutes Austin had ridden out and Spider's eyes were half-lowered in sleep. Forcing himself
alert, he pulled out his pipe and was about to light
it when he heard someone crying very softly. For a
moment he just listened, placing the sound, then he
moved around the corner of the jail to the alley.

A tiny ball of rags looked like it had blown up in the
corner between two buildings.

"True?" Morris moved closer. "Is that you crying?"

True looked up with eyes burning in anger. White
streaks washed down dirty cheeks. "I ain't cryin'!"

Spider drew out a knife and began cleaning his pipe.
"Course you weren't. Everyone knows nobody but sissy
girls cry."

"I ain't no sissy!" True's body straightened.

Only one bushy eyebrow showed Morris's surprise.
What True hadn't said told far more than what *she* had
said. Morris moved a little closer. "But you are a girl,
aren't you?"

True shoved a tear from her face. "Maybe I am. I
don't see that it's none of your concern. I ain't breaking
no law if I'm a girl or a boy, am I?"

Spider shrugged as if he didn't care one way or the
other and leaned against the side of the building. "Boy

or girl, what you did last night was a mighty brave thing. I don't know many pint-sized younguns who could have driven a team as well as you did."

"A fellow has to do what needs doing sometimes, no matter how much it hurts."

"Or a girl," Spider added and noticed True didn't argue. He looked down at the hands she'd hidden in her armpits. "Driving a team can be hard on even a man's hands."

"They don't hurt much," True lied. "I've been hurt more and never even cried one tear."

Spider acted as though his pipe were the only thing that really interested him. "Why don't you go inside and let Jennie or Audrey take a look at those cuts?"

True shook her head. "I ain't gonna bother them. They're trying to keep Colton alive. And I want him to live powerful much." She sniffed. "They don't need me whining about a few little scrapes. I can take care of it myself."

Morris nodded. "I reckon you can. You probably already know to wash the cuts real good with lye soap and then rub alum root into the wound."

True looked at him closely. "Course I do. I ain't no half-wit kid."

"I got some alum in my bottom desk drawer if you're thinking of doctoring yourself. It's amazing how much better you'll feel once you've cleaned the wound and put some salve on it."

The sheriff pulled a twist of taffy from his vest pocket. "Oh, *son*, before you go to washing those cuts, you might want to put a chew of this in your mouth. It'll give you something to bite down on when the doctoring hurts."

Taking the candy, True added, "I might could use some of this. Not that I can't take a little hurting without making a fuss, but I do like taffy."

True stood slowly. "I reckon I might as well get to it." As she walked past the sheriff, she looked at him closely. "You ain't gonna tell anyone you think I'm a girl, are you, 'cause I didn't tell you if'n I was or not?"

Spider stared up at the sky for a long moment. "Tell you what, I won't tell a soul if you'll tell me who your parents are."

True's mouth opened, then stopped as if weighing the price of the truth. "Would you stop pestering me if I told you Jennie Munday was my mother?"

"I might," Spider watched her closely. "And your father?"

"Austin McCormick, of course."

Spider fought the urge to laugh outright. "Of course," he added to the bold lie, but a tiny seed of doubt tumbled across his mind and planted an idea.

Chapter
Twenty

*A*ustin rode along the crude road leading to Colton Barkley's property. He watched for signs where the wagon had turned around. There he knew he'd find any clues to Colton's shooting.

As he tried to force himself to concentrate on the tracks, Austin's mind kept drifting back to before dawn, when Jennie came to his bed. He wished he could somehow freeze memory and bottle it so that he could take out each moment and live it fully once again.

Jennie would become a memory, just like all other people he'd met, but she'd always have a special place. In her arms he'd felt at peace. He had a feeling that in the years to come he'd return to her in his dreams, reliving their night together until the pages of his memory were shredded with wear.

Barkley's shooting was the start of the trouble, and Austin knew he might never have the time to spend another night alone with her. But he'd had one night, and that was more than he'd thought existed.

The tracks in the road suddenly changed, and he realized he'd reached the place where Colton had been shot. Dismounting, Austin read the markings as easily as a conductor reads a timetable. Colton's blood. Deep cuts where the wagon had been turned sharply. Two horses, heavy with riders, following the tracks back toward town.

The wind seemed to shift slightly, and Austin felt that familiar sense warning him. He brushed his fingers over the handle of his Colt and studied the rock formation to the left of the road.

Whoever had ambushed Colton was long gone by now, but Austin could still feel something, or someone, near.

Instinct pushed him into action. He raised his gun and pointed straight toward the pile of boulders. "Game's up!" he yelled. "Come out with your hands flying."

Silence followed, but Austin didn't move. If he were wrong and no one hid behind the rocks, then he'd made a fool of himself to an empty house.

"Don't shoot!" someone yelled in a voice too high to be a man's and too low to be a woman's. "I'm not armed."

Austin pointed toward where the voice was coming from and waited. Slowly a youth unfolded from the rocks. He was taller than most men but about half the width. His clothes hung on him like old Glory on a wet flagpole. As he moved over the uneven ground, his arms and legs seemed cursed with a few extra joints, making him look like a string puppet.

"I ain't doin' nothing wrong." The boy never removed his stare from Austin's gun. "Honest, Marshal. I was just scouting around. Mr. Barkley didn't come home

last night, so my pa told me to ride out this mornin'
and look for him. I come upon the blood in the road,
and a blind Comanche could have figured out somethin'
bad must have happened."

"Why'd you hide in the rocks?" Austin replaced his
Colt.

"I heard you coming, and for all I knew you was one
of the bushwackers coming back."

Austin studied the boy carefully. He was fifteen, maybe sixteen, and judging from his dark skin and black
eyes, half or more of his ancestors were Indian. "Step
on out here and tell me your name."

Six feet of nervousness headed toward Austin.
"Name's Lincoln Raine, but folks call me Link. My
pa's foreman at Mr. Barkley's place."

Offering his hand, Austin said, "Pleased to meet you,
Mr. Raine." What the boy lacked in maturity of voice,
he more than made up for in his firm handshake. Austin
continued. "Your pa was right to worry. Colton Barkley
was shot last night. They brought him into town about
sunup."

Link's Adam's apple bobbed. "Is he dead?" The voice
was low, and tears threatened to bubble over his eyelids,
reminding Austin of Link's youth.

"No. At least not when I left," Austin said honestly.
"You find anything in those rocks that might be of
help?"

Blinking hard, Lincoln Raine squared his shoulders.
"Only this, sir. I found this shell on the ground without
any dust on it, so I guess it was dropped less than a
day ago. Judging from the bootprints beyond the rocks,
there were two men hiding back there. A heavy stepper,
down on his luck. One print showed a hole worn through
leather. The other must have been a smaller, nervous

type. Ever'where he stood he left a hundred markings in one spot, like he was constantly moving."

Austin studied the boy as closely as he looked at the shell. Whoever had taught him to track had done so with great knowledge.

"Want to ride along with me back toward town?"

The boy smiled. "Pa'd have my hide if I came back with more questions than answers." He didn't say another word but disappeared behind the rocks to fetch his horse. Austin turned the shell over in his hand as he waited.

When Link reappeared, they rode back toward town on either side of the road, both knowing what signs to look for without bothering to ask.

An hour into the ride Austin found what he was looking for. One set of tracks led off to the left while the other continued to follow the wagon.

Link jumped down from his horse and studied the road. He didn't say the obvious, and for that Austin was grateful. He just looked up at the marshal and asked, "Which one you want me to follow?"

Shoving his hat back, Austin stared at the winter sun already warming to noon. "We're not more than a mile from town. Why don't you ride in with me and check on Barkley? Then I'll buy you lunch before I send you out to follow this trail."

Link smiled at the mention of food. "I appreciate the offer, but I don't take handouts."

"I wasn't offering a handout," Austin answered. "I was offering a job. I could use some help, and the meal comes with the responsibility of helping me find these men."

"In that case, I accept." Link didn't try to hide his excitement.

Ten minutes later, when Austin and the youth rode into town, the streets looked like Saturday night just after a town meeting. Folks were everywhere. Austin avoided any conversation with a few quick waves and stepped into Sheriff Morris's office. As his eyes adjusted to the sudden change in lighting, Austin took in the room. Sheets were draped over the cell they'd put Barkley in, and several tables had been moved in and covered with Harvey House linen. One tabletop, just outside the jail cell, was covered with supplies, while another several feet away was set with china. The air was rich and humid with coffee and water, both boiling on the stove.

"Whoa!" Link whistled as he passed Austin. "This is some office."

Audrey stepped out from behind the curtain covering the cell. "About time you got back." She planted her hands on her hips and stared at Austin with the intensity of a schoolmarm counting heads after lunch. "We could have used your help around here. That no-account doctor of yours still hasn't shown up. I had to dig the bullet out myself, and it took everyone of us including True to hold Colton down."

"First, he isn't my doctor. And second, is Barkley still alive?" Austin jerked off his gloves and tossed them on the only surface not covered in white—Morris's desk.

Nodding slowly, Audrey silently told Austin she thought it only a matter of time. "Mary Elizabeth is with him. We've got enough whiskey down him so that he's resting. I sent Jennie back to the hotel to bring lunch."

Austin couldn't help but smile. No matter what else fell apart in this world, the Harvey Girls would serve lunch on time. Somehow their determination put an order to life.

Austin put his hand on Link's shoulder as he addressed

Audrey. "This is one of Barkley's men. You think it would be all right for him to see his boss?"

Audrey lifted the curtain. "Only a moment, please," she whispered as if the sudden lifting of the sheet made it possible for those in the sick room now to hear. "He's very weak."

Link removed his hat and raked his fingers through his coal-black hair. He moved into the makeshift hospital room, then paused.

Placing her arm around the youth, Audrey asked, "You all right?"

Nodding, Link stammered, "I ain't never seen him like this. He's so pale and still. Usually he's walkin' double-time and expectin' us all to keep up."

"He lost a great deal of blood." Audrey looked back at the marshal. "Seems to be a liquid used to water this wild land. I've seen my share since I've been here." She moved away, allowing the boy some time.

Austin poured her a cup of coffee as she joined him. "Thanks for your help," he said as he offered her the cup. "I'm not sure what this town would do without your nursing."

Audrey leaned against the sheriff's desk. "Maybe it's me. Maybe I just attract trouble. If there's anyone bleeding within a hundred miles, they manage to stumble into my arms."

He couldn't help but laugh. "I've thought that about myself for a long time. Felt like I carried trouble in my saddlebags."

Lowering her voice, Audrey added, "Speaking of trouble, Jennie didn't come home last night, and I have a pretty good idea where she was."

Austin's face remained stone. He wasn't about to lie or dishonor Jennie by telling the truth.

"I'm not saying another word, but this." She moved to within an inch of his nose. "If anyone hurts Jennie, it'll be his blood next we see."

Austin almost kissed the tall beauty. Jennie was lucky to have such a grand friend. That farmer Wiley had best marry her and get started raising a few dozen children before Audrey decided to move on to another career.

"Marshal?" Link's voice came from behind them.

"Yes?" Austin raised his coffee cup in salute to Audrey before turning to Link.

"I can't get Miss Mary Elizabeth to leave Mr. Barkley's side even for a bite to eat. I was wondering if it'd be all right if I fixed her a plate when the food got here. She don't look like she's got any more blood in her than he does. They're a matched set of ghosts."

"Sure. A little food might be just what she needs." Austin moved to his back room. "I'll wash up and join you in a minute."

When he stepped into his tiny back quarters, he shut the door behind him and closed his eyes. He could still feel Jennie's presence in the room. The warm, fresh smell of her was lazy in the air.

Slowly, not wanting to disturb a memory, Austin moved to his bed. The sheets remained crumpled from where he'd held her in his arms all night. He could still see the two dents in the pillow where their heads had rested.

As his eyes traveled the length of the bed, his memory drifted in shadows remembering the way she'd fit so solidly against him, as though they'd been molded for each other.

A tiny spot on the cotton pulled him from his day-dream. *Blood!*

He lifted the sheet in his fist and looked around.

Nothing had been disturbed since he'd left. No one had been in the room.

The blood could mean only one thing. He'd taken Jennie's virginity. But that couldn't be possible. She was True's mother. How could she have lived well into her twenties without another lover when she'd come so easily into his arms? No woman loved with such passion her first time.

She hadn't protested. She hadn't manipulated. She'd come into his arms like a woman taking a lover, not a virgin learning of life.

He tried to remember what she'd told him. Had she said that it was her first time? Had she told him things he hadn't taken the time to believe?

Austin wadded the sheet into a ball and tossed it in the corner. He had to talk to her. For once he had to know the truth.

WHEN AUSTIN STEPPED from the back room, Jennie smiled up at him as she served a large helping of roast to Link. "Did you find out any news?"

For a moment he didn't know what she was talking about. Surely she didn't want him to mention the spot of blood in front of everyone in the room.

Link saved him from answering. "Only a few tracks, miss."

Spider Morris pinched a bite of roast off the platter when he thought Jennie wasn't looking. "We haven't got any proof it was Buck Lawton and his men, but have you seen what's going on outside?" He pointed toward the door with the stolen meat.

Austin's gaze followed the sheriff's. Several wagons filled with supplies and families were moving down the main street. "What's up?"

"Everyone's decided it must be the outlaw gang, and they're all leaving. It's amazing how in one day everyone decided he's got a relative in some nearby town he needs to visit for a few days." Spider scratched his whiskers. "Those that can't think of anywhere to go are over at Salty's place drinking away their troubles."

"But if it is Buck, won't they even stay here and stay sober to protect their homes?" Austin asked, knowing the answer as well as Spider did.

"Nope. That's what they claim we're here for."

"Well, none of us at the Harvey House are leaving," Audrey mumbled between bites. "Town folks or no, the trains will still be coming in and there will still be people to feed. Besides, I have a theory about running from trouble. It has a way of following you, so you might as well face it on home ground."

Spider began unloading rifles from the rack behind his desk.

"I thought you didn't believe in shooting outlaws." Austin watched the old sheriff.

"These aren't for shooting, son," Spider said. "I plan to put them in a few windows so if the Lawton gang does hit town, they'll think I have extra backup."

"You think they'll come here first?"

"If they know Barkley's still alive, they'll come here first. For some reason Lawton has singled him out as the first one to die."

Before Austin could ask why, shots rang out from far down the street. Women screamed and horses bolted. Austin and Morris were across the room and onto the porch before the air stilled. Link was only a step behind, still holding his soup spoon in his hand.

Chapter
Twenty-one

When she heard the round of gunfire, Delta raised the derringer Colton had given her.

Colton's fingers tightened around her other hand. "Hand me my guns," he ordered in a voice weak with pain.

"No," Delta whispered back. "I'll protect you. I can shoot. You're in no shape to hold a weapon, much less aim one."

A smile crossed his pale face. "Thanks for the diagnosis, but I want you to leave. This isn't your fight."

Delta knew she could no longer keep her lie from him. The poor man was very likely dying because of her, and he didn't even know why. "Correction. It's not your fight," she whispered. "When I came here, I was running from my stepbrother. He must have followed me and decided to murder you before he killed me."

"Don't try to make me believe some story, Mary Elizabeth. You're a poor liar. Give me the gun and get out of here while there's still time. The man who shot me last night would like nothing better than to shoot you, too."

"I'm not leaving you to die because of me." Delta didn't believe him. Why would anyone want to kill him? The man who attacked them had to have been her stepbrother.

"You have to get somewhere safe. You're still not strong from the wreck two weeks ago."

"No!"

Colton shook his head slightly. "I know you have no family, so there is no use in trying to make up a story."

"Mary Elizabeth had no family. I have more than I want."

Colton closed his eyes. She wasn't sure if it was because of what she'd told him or due to the pain. How would this strong, quiet man react to having been used? Delta didn't want even to guess, but she couldn't take her gaze from his face. She'd never seen a man so strong-minded. Even weak and near death he was determined to send her to safety and fight alone, as she guessed he had all his life.

Another round of gunfire rattled the air like thunder. Slowly, with determination in his black eyes, he looked at her. "It's you who doesn't understand," he said above the noise outside. "The man who shot me last night is an outlaw named Buck Lawton who'll stop at nothing to see me dead."

"But why?" Delta couldn't imagine anyone hating Colton so completely.

"Because," Colton clenched his teeth. "Because I killed the woman he loved."

A cry escaped her lips before she could stop it. She couldn't bring herself to believe any man would do such a thing. "Are you sure? Maybe it was an accident. Maybe he blames you unjustly. Maybe you only hurt her or thought she was dead."

"No." Colton's eyes were even darker and colder than before. "She was dead. I buried her the next morning. She was my wife."

The air suddenly left the room. Delta pulled her hand from his grip, dropped the gun and ran. She didn't want to believe what he'd just told her. How could a man kill his own wife? Somehow she'd found a man even more evil than her stepfather.

As she rushed from the cell, she collided with Sheriff Morris. The old man managed to hold onto his rifle while she spun him around. "Steady, girl." Spider held her tightly for a moment, until they both had their footing.

"Colton just told me . . ." Delta couldn't bring herself to repeat the horror she'd just heard.

The old sheriff didn't seem the least alarmed. "Easy now. I reckon Colton told you whatever he thought he had to to get you to let go of his hand and get to safety."

"But . . ."

"But whatever it was he said to hurt your feelings, you can patch up later. Right now you'd better get in the back with the other women because all hell's fixing to break out."

"All hell's fixing to break out in this office if you think you're shoving us in the back room!" Audrey lifted two rifles and handed one to Jennie. "Can you use this?"

"I can learn." Jennie stared at Austin, leaving no doubt that she did not consider the subject of her staying up for discussion.

Another round of gunfire sounded from the street, along with Link's shout. They all took a step toward the door as the boy bounded in. "There's not any trouble. The gunfire was just Amos from north of town. Doc just delivered twins to him and his wife!"

Everyone in the room lowered their guns a few inches and took a breath.

"Then the trouble's over," Audrey said. "Maybe the town folks will settle down."

Spider Morris nodded his agreement but didn't move to replace the rifles. "It wasn't Amos who shot Colton on the road last night, so I'd say the trouble's not over, but at least this scare might help the town's folks to come to their senses and stop running like frightened groundhogs at the sound of thunder."

"Maybe." Austin didn't sound hopeful.

Spider cradled his rifle and moved through the door. "I think I'll go have a word with the new father and try convincing him to buy a round of drinks while leaving his gun in my custody." The old man glanced at Austin. "You stayin' here?"

The question was casual, but Austin understood the importance of words not said. "I'm staying right here with Colton until we have some idea who shot him."

Jennie set down the rifle without looking at Austin. "Mrs. Gray told me that the jail is no place for the likes of a fine gentleman like Colton Barkley. She said if he's able to be moved, we can get a room ready for him at the Harvey House." She looked from Austin to Delta. "What do you think?"

Both glanced around the room. With the building's two entrances and windows all around, the jail would be almost impossible to guard if someone attacked it. Austin remembered seeing several private dining rooms downstairs at the Harvey House with no windows at all.

"We'll move him as soon as Audrey gives the word," Austin decided. "Tell Mrs. Gray to make him up a room downstairs."

Jennie gathered up dishes in a large basket. "I'll go tell her."

She didn't wait for a reply, but hurried from the office. As she walked back to the Harvey House, she didn't notice the weight on her arm. All she could think about was the way Austin had looked at her when he'd returned from the back room.

Every moment except the few when they'd thought they might be under attack, Austin had stared at her like he expected her to run at him and try to scratch his eyes out. Had he really thought she'd be angry with him about last night, when it had been she who'd gone to him?

Jennie was so deep in thought, she didn't notice the man sitting on the steps of the hotel until she was within six feet of him.

She was almost at the bottom step when he stood and drew her attention. At first glance he seemed like someone she knew but couldn't place. Average height, barrel-chested, hairless.

"You Jennie Munday?" he shouted in a tone void of all manners.

Jennie hesitated, recalling the night she'd spent almost in this very spot looking for such a man. The night of the wreck. The night she'd carried a gun in her pocket and had been ready to shoot on sight. But she didn't have a gun now.

Carefully she weighed her options. She could run for the back door and probably get away. She could scream. Surely someone inside would hear her and come running. Why had she packed Delta's pocket pistol away with the rest of her things?

"I may be," she answered, the only sign of nervousness her death grip on the basket. "Who are you?" She asked the question even though she already knew the answer.

The man shoved his large chest out farther and replied, "I'm Ward Hall, and I'm thinking you're the woman I've been waiting to see."

"What do you want?" Jennie could feel her teeth starting to rattle.

"I've been following my dear lost sister for over three weeks now. Stopped at near every town along the tracks. I know she got off somewhere. Finally found a fellow who remembered seeing a little woman in a wine-red coat getting on the train leaving Kansas City bound for Florence."

"I don't think I've seen such a coat. Maybe she moved on further down the line." Jennie tried to sound convincing.

"No, miss, she stopped here."

Jennie forced down a swallow. "What was her name?"

The huge man took a step down and answered, "Delta Criswell, but I think she registered here at the Harvey House as Delta Smith."

Jennie looked at her feet as the man took another step. "If you're Jennie Munday or Audrey Gates, my sister was your roommate when she first came here. I saw it on the hotel employee count."

She finally looked up. "Did Mrs. Gray tell you that?"

The man smiled, showing most of his yellowed teeth. "She didn't. Thought she'd put me in my place by telling me no in her high and mighty manner. But I outsmarted her. I waited until she got called away and looked for myself. I ain't no fool. I went to school long enough to learn to read."

Relaxing some, Jennie knew that once she told Delta's lie, this horrible man would go away. "I don't know a Delta Criswell, but I did meet a Delta Smith. She was injured in the train robbery that happened the day we got to Florence. She was very ill but lived a week before she died."

The huge man jerked back as though she'd struck him with her words. "Dead! She couldn't be dead!"

Jennie took the opportunity to move past him. "I'm sorry, but if Delta Smith is your sister, we buried her over two weeks ago. I could get someone to show you the grave if you like."

"That can't be!" He stormed at her as if he'd been wronged personally by her announcement. "I saw her here, myself, last night at the dance. She was dancing and walking in the dark with some tall gentleman like she was a lady and not soiled trash."

Jennie stood her ground even when he leaned close enough to her to sour the air with his breath. "There was no Delta Smith, or Criswell, at the dance last night."

"I should know what my own sister looks like!"

She took a step back. "I remember Delta Smith saying she had no kin. No brothers or sisters."

Ward swore and spit in the flower bed beside the porch. "Well, maybe I ain't no blood kin. But my pa married her ma, or at least he was planning on it. We was just one happy family before Delta run off in the night."

Jennie knew he was lying, but she couldn't tell him so without giving too much away. It was better if he didn't know how well she knew Delta's problem. "If you're the only kin she had, we packed her belongings away in a small trunk hoping we'd have some word from family."

Ward's whole hairless face lit up. "Well, why didn't you say so?" He tried to hide his delight. "Not that I'm not real sorry to hear about my dear sister, but if you have her things, at least I can take them home to her mother as a comfort during her loss."

If it hadn't been for the greed in his eyes, Ward would have almost looked as if he cared about Delta and her mother. But Jennie could see his hands opening and closing in anticipation of the trunk.

Jennie didn't want to allow the man back into the hotel, but she had to move him off the porch before Audrey brought Colton over. She might convince him he didn't see his sister the night of the dance, but if Delta came walking up the steps in daylight, the lie might be harder to get him to swallow. Jennie had to get him away from the front of the hotel and fast.

"I understand your concern," she lied. "If you'll just step into Mrs. Gray's office, I'll go get Delta's belongings."

Ward took a step, then stopped. "I caused such a ruckus," he glanced at Jennie, "in my grief and worry of course, that I'm not sure I'm welcome back in the Harvey House."

Jennie knew he must have made quite a fool of himself if Mrs. Gray had given up handling him and had him pitched out. She also knew there might be one too many questions if she tried to explain why she was talking to him. Mrs. Gray might even mention how much Delta and Mary Elizabeth looked alike. She needed a plan.

Using her best "welcome to church" smile, she looked down at Ward from the top step. "I understand your problem, Mr. Hall, and I'm willing to help in your time of grief. I didn't know Delta very well, but I'm sure she would want her family to have her belongings."

Ward seemed to relax a little, as if he thought himself skilled enough to have suckered her into believing his lie.

Jennie pointed toward the walk leading around the hotel. "I tell you what. If you'll wait out back near the barn, I'll bring down the trunk as soon as I finish my shift. Then you won't have to face Mrs. Gray again or even walk past the front of the hotel. You can just head on down to the station and wait for the first train back toward Kansas City."

She could almost see Ward's mouth watering at the thought of finally getting what he'd spent three weeks looking for. She knew he figured the deed would be among Delta's belongings, and she didn't want to be around when he found out it wasn't. "But if I do this, you have to promise to take the trunk back home to Delta's mother without opening it. A mother should be the first one to touch her departed daughter's things."

Ward frowned, but like a child caught in higher logic, he didn't have the faculties to argue.

"Promise?" Jennie knew he'd never make it back home without looking, but at least he might get out of her sight. He could hardly come yelling about something missing if she made him promise not to open the trunk until he got home.

"All right, I swear." He folded his arms across his huge chest, trying to act like it didn't matter. "There ain't nothing among her things I'd care about."

"Wait around back then, and I'll be down just as soon as I can."

He moved off along the path, then turned back. "You're sure all her things are in the trunk? There won't be nothing missing?"

"Everything Delta kept in our room will be there," Jennie answered truthfully as she hurried inside. She couldn't wait to wash up and hopefully rid herself of the ugliness of Ward Hall.

Ten minutes later True helped her pull the chest from beneath Audrey's bed.

"You sure this is her brother?" True had heard most of the conversation on the porch but didn't like the idea of Jennie handing over Delta's things to the man. "That man's so low-down not even the maggots would have a banquet if he died."

"He's her brother all right. If I'd have seen him the night of the train wreck, I would have killed him to keep him from finding Delta. Now all I have to do to get rid of him is give him this trunk. Then he'll go away and never bother her again."

"But he'll know the deed ain't in it." True looked as if she could see trouble coming from a mile-high window.

"Hopefully he will wait at least until he's a few miles out of town before he opens the chest. Then maybe he'll just think Delta destroyed the deed."

True played with the latch on the trunk. "Where's the key to this lock? Maybe we could bolt it and throw away the key."

Jennie shook her head. "I thought of that, but it's just some old trunk a passenger left here and there was no key for the lock."

True pulled a stick of taffy from a coat pocket and crammed it in an already full mouth before Jennie noticed. "I best go down with you to meet this Ward.

I wouldn't want you going alone. He don't look like the kind of man I'd want to even talk to without there being a crowd around."

"No." Jennie lifted the small trunk. "You stay here. I don't want that man even seeing you."

True opened the door for her. "All right. But I don't like this."

As Jennie passed with the trunk, True pulled the taffy out and shoved it deep into the hole by the latch, knowing that unless someone opened the trunk within a very short time, the taffy would harden. "Take your time going down the stairs."

Chapter
Twenty-two

Delta rode on the wagon bench with Audrey toward the Harvey House. The sunny morning had turned cold, and low clouds rumbled, promising rain. Austin walked several feet ahead of the wagon with his rifle over his shoulder. His gait was casual, but his gaze constantly shifted from one side of the road to the other.

"Audrey," Delta whispered in a voice too soft to draw Austin's attention, "do you think if a man was dying, he'd tell the truth?"

Audrey glanced back at Colton. Though he rested quietly, the bandage she'd wrapped around him was already covered with blood. Delta didn't look in much better health than her intended. "Are you all right?" Audrey asked.

Delta waved away her concern. "I'm fine. I just got sick last night from all the dancing. My stomach feels like it twirled once too often, but it'll settle down now the excitement's over." She looked back at Colton and lowered her voice even more. "About dying men and the truth?"

Audrey shrugged. "I don't know about that. I figure most good men tell the truth even on their deathbeds, and those in the habit of lying will do so even with their last breath.

"As for Colton, after the whopper we told him, I figure he's got a right to one or two fibs," she continued as she carefully maneuvered the wagon. "One time while I was nursing an old lady when I was in training, she told me some really bad things about what she'd done in her life. I asked my teacher about it, and she said a nurse never remembers what a patient says when the patient has fever. Even the nicest folks can get ornery as devils when they're hurting."

Delta nodded, making up her mind to take Audrey's advice. Colton Barkley couldn't have killed his wife and have both Sheriff Morris and Mrs. Gray think so highly of him. She'd act like she'd never heard him say such a thing.

Austin helped the women get Colton into a downstairs private dining room that had been converted into a bedroom. He didn't see how the man was still alive. His blood loss seemed enough to fill a bucket. The sight of the bloody bandages made Delta have to step from the room. When she returned, her face was ghost-white, but she steadfastly refused to leave Colton's side.

Within a few minutes Audrey had done all she knew to do, relying on Delta's gentle touch to help as much as any doctor's skill.

After he'd drunk a cup of coffee at the counter, Austin's concern for Jennie's whereabouts turned to worry. Something was wrong, or she would have been

there to meet the wagon. At the very least she would
have ducked out of her duties long enough to see about
Colton.

Looking around, Austin searched the dining room and
the hotel lobby. He didn't have to wait for the uniformed
girls to face him. Judging from their movements, he
knew none of them could be Jennie. She had a formal
grace about her, fluidity in the way she did simple little
things. The polished, crowded room seemed void of
beauty without her presence.

He thought of storming through the kitchen in his
search, but that was off-limits to all but employees; so
he went out the front door and headed around the path
to the back of the hotel. She had to be somewhere.

As he rounded the corner, he noticed a man lurking in
the darkness along the side of the barn. Austin slowed,
choosing to remain in the shadows himself. With one
glance he knew the stranger was the same one True had
complained about hanging around the livery.

Jennie stepped from the back of the hotel, carrying
a small trunk. She walked slowly to the barn entrance.
Austin noticed that the stranger stared at her, but made
no move from the shadows to help her carry the trunk.

When she reached the barn door, her back was to
Austin. He moved closer without being noticed.

"I was about to give you up," the stranger said in a
voice layered with impatience. "I'm sure my mother will
want to see these things." His tone mocked any honesty
in his words.

As she handed the trunk over to the man, Jennie
didn't smile. "Remember," she ordered, "don't open it
until you're home."

The man almost jerked the trunk from her hands. "I'll
remember." He shoved it into a bag and roped his load

over his shoulder. "When I get home, I best find all my sister took when she left home, 'cause anyone, man or woman, who steals from me or mine will pay dearly." His dirty hands knotted around the rope. "Good day to you, miss."

Jennie didn't even bother to wave good-bye as she lifted her skirt slightly and turned back toward the hotel. She was glad to be rid of the man who called himself Delta's brother. The underlying threat hadn't missed her. Jennie had a feeling she'd be seeing him again.

Ward Hall swore suddenly and increased his pace down the road. She glanced first at his back, then at the hotel, where she couldn't mistake the tall man coming toward her. Somehow she wasn't surprised Ward Hall would want nothing of a lawman.

Austin was still ten feet from her, and she could already see he was angry. It was obvious his only interest was in Jennie. "You all right?" he shouted loud enough for Ward to hear.

Jennie didn't move. She couldn't tell if he was angry with her or with Ward.

At five feet away, Austin repeated his words more softly.

"Yes." She tried to hide her fears. Maybe the man would never return. Maybe Austin just didn't like seeing such a man hanging around town. "I just had to give Delta Smith's belongings to her brother."

Austin raised an eyebrow. What he saw in her emerald depths was something besides grief. Her whole body seemed to be shaking with more than the chill of the north wind.

He gently removed his coat and placed it over her shoulders as he had once before. "Walk with me, Jennie?"

Without answering him directly, she fell into step beside him. Only this time, instead of moving along the path toward the depot, where Ward had gone, Austin led her across the pastures behind the barn. The earth was dried with winter, making Jennie feel suddenly cold deep inside. The land had been grazed down to almost level with the road.

They walked as close to each other as they could without touching. His arm lifted twice, but he hesitated before reaching for her.

Austin didn't know how to begin to say all that he needed to say to her. When they were several feet away from the back of the barn, he reached down and took her hand.

"Cold?" he asked.

"No," she answered, suddenly fearing what he was about to tell her. The night before had been heaven to her, but what if it hadn't been so for him? What if he'd come out back to tell her good-bye?

Suddenly she wanted to talk of anything except last night. "Did you move Colton yet?"

"Yes," Austin answered, as she had, with a single word.

"Is he better?"

Letting out a long breath, Austin said, "He's dying. I've seen it before. Men don't lose as much blood as he's lost and live. I've noticed Audrey change the bandage again and again so he doesn't appear as bad as he is. But my guess is he won't live the night."

Jennie's hand tightened in his as Austin continued. "That boy Link is extremely loyal to his boss. I finally got the kid to leave the room, but he took up squatter's rights in the hallway outside Colton's door. He told me Colton has no family to notify."

Jennie's voice was soft and slow, as if she were thinking her words through as she spoke. "Maybe, if he's held in such high esteem by his men, he's not as bad as I first thought."

"Maybe not." Austin smiled, remembering the reason Jennie had come to his office last night. "Maybe every man deserves a chance."

She uttered a slight hum of agreement, and they continued walking, both caring little about any destination.

Clearing his throat, Austin searched for the right words, but they wouldn't come. Finally he asked, more to break the silence than for information, "Are you sure that was Delta's kin?"

"Yes," Jennie answered. "He only came for her belongings."

Austin stared at the endless sky rippled in clouds. "Want to tell me the truth about Delta?"

Jennie's fingers stiffened in his hand, and he wished he hadn't asked. He no longer cared if she lied about Delta. What difference did it make to anyone? Did she think he was going to do something about their lie? In a few weeks he'd probably be back in Texas, and Colton Barkley would be cold in his grave. So what did the lie matter? Why couldn't she end this farce between them?

He couldn't help but hold Jennie's hand tighter as he realized that even though the lie didn't matter any longer, the fact that she'd lied to him did. If she'd just tell him the truth, he'd forgive her anything. But he couldn't forgive her continuing to lie to him.

Jennie didn't look up at him when she spoke. "Delta Smith died the morning after the train wreck. I walked behind the casket and watched it being lowered myself."

He wanted to remind her of all the facts. Mary Elizabeth had been the one so badly hurt, not Delta.

He'd seen them both, and bandages or not, he knew the two apart. He needed to tell her how True once had called Mary Elizabeth Delta. How in the middle of the trouble this morning she hadn't questioned him when he'd called Delta by name. He wanted to call Jennie a liar to her face, but he couldn't.

When the sun melted completely into the horizon, Jennie crossed her arms over herself, pulling his coat tighter around her. She seemed to feel the cold more than most people. Maybe she felt everything more than most.

He let out a long sigh. "We'd better get back. It'll be dark in a few minutes."

She nodded and waited for him to move.

Austin didn't want to go back to where others could hear, but he knew they couldn't stand in a field forever. Though they walked almost touching each other, he could tell they were moving miles apart. The end was coming; he'd felt it this morning. Soon all the feelings he now had for her would pass into memory.

They were to the corner of the barn before he asked, "Why didn't you tell me you were a virgin?"

"Did it matter?" Her question was matter-of-fact, without any emotion.

Austin shook his head. "I'm not sure I could have stopped even if I'd known. Maybe you did tell me, but I didn't believe you."

"Are you sorry you touched me?" Her voice was so low he wasn't sure she'd asked the question.

"No." He suddenly pulled her against the blackness behind the barn. His hands gripped her shoulders hard as he leaned close so that his words were only an inch from her ear. "Of all the things I've ever done in my life, touching you is one I'll never be sorry for."

He'd meant to talk to her and leave without weaving his life and her lies together any further, but her nearness infected him with a fever he wasn't sure he'd ever recover from. Even now she looked up with those eyes that promised more than he'd ever be able to accept.

"Jennie," he whispered as he pulled her close. "Why can't you trust me with the truth? Why won't you believe that I'd never hurt you if you trusted me?"

She didn't want to answer. She wanted to feel his hands warm her once more. Her mouth opened slightly as she raised her lips to his. Hers were yielding, his firm. Yet when they touched, passion burned through them both like a wildfire out of control.

Their kiss was long and complete, making him forget all the promises he'd made to himself about not touching her again. She was heaven in his embrace. Touching her was like being struck by lightning on a clear night; there was nothing he could do but feel his need for her burn all the way through him.

Raising her arms around his neck, Jennie leaned her body's full length into his, loving the way he met her gift with a warm wall of strength. She could feel his heart pounding against her breasts, and his arms were loving bands around her.

"Jennie," he whispered against her ear as his mouth moved along her throat, lightly tasting her skin. His large hands spread wide across her back, molding her against him. "Answer me, Jennie," he said as the last ounce of logic gave over to pure pleasure in his mind.

She cupped his face and gently forced his lips to hers, wanting to taste passion once more before she had to lie to him again. How could she ever tell him that it wasn't her lie to tell? That she had to protect Delta?

His mouth was hot with need as his kiss reached her very soul with longing. Jennie closed her eyes and pretended there was no world but Austin's arms. He was more wonderful than she'd ever dreamed a man could be. He made her feel a passion she hadn't even known existed in this world.

"You folks gonna kiss all night?" True stepped from the corner of the barn.

Jennie jerked backward so violently she would have fallen if Austin hadn't caught her.

"I've been waiting, but a fellow can only wait so long on folks doing something as silly as lip touching."

Austin laughed and grabbed True by the shoulder. "Someday you'll do the same thing, son."

True struggled to break free. "I don't think so. It seems like something I could do without in this lifetime. Unless of course my partner had a wad of taffy already soft and was waiting to share."

"True!" Jennie tried to sound stern, but she couldn't contain her giggle. "Little boys shouldn't talk of such things as kissing. Or spy on folks."

"Well, if I don't watch, how am I going to learn so I can someday practice like the marshal seems to think I will?" True's question was direct.

"Good point." Austin took Jennie's hand as they stepped into the light of the barn. "Why don't you wait until you're a tad older and I'll tell you all about it?"

"Thanks." True made sure she was several steps ahead of them before she continued. "But I think I'll ask Audrey instead. When her and Wiley kissed, she let out a hoot and told him he was a better kisser than the boys in seven counties back home. I figure that kind of woman can give me some advice."

"Does Audrey know you eavesdropped on her and Wiley?" Jennie looked at the child she'd grown to love.

"Nope." True danced in front of them. "Folks don't take too kindly if you interrupt them while they're spoonin'."

"Then why'd you—"

True didn't allow Austin to finish. "I bothered you because Audrey told me to come get you fast."

"Colton?" Jennie breathed in the word.

"Is he already dead, son?" Austin doubled his speed and pulled Jennie toward the house.

"Worse than that, sir." True ran to keep up. "He's gone and asked Del— Mary Elizabeth to marry him tonight."

"No!" Jennie and Austin both said at once.

True jumped up on the porch. "Yes, ma'am. Seems he wants to leave a widow."

JENNIE WAS THE first to reach Colton's room. Link blocked the door like a self-appointed border guard. The boy's eyes were tired. He'd aged a step further into manhood during this day of waiting for death.

Colton didn't look any better than he had at the jail, except someone had pulled a clean shirt over his unharmed shoulder and the shadow of a dark beard framed his chin.

Before Jennie could ask any questions, Spider Morris hurried into the room, with the undertaker plowing the same row just a step behind. Since the town had no official minister, the choice for a preacher was usually between these two men. Most of the time when a minister was needed, one or both of them would already be on hand anyway.

"Barkley?" Spider moved slowly toward the bed, figuring his job would soon be passed to his companion.

The undertaker looked as if he were studying Colton's body for the size of the box.

Colton glanced up, his eyes as black as buried death. "Sheriff, sorry to have to ask you to hurry, but I don't know how much time I've got."

"I understand, son." Morris sounded more like a priest than a lawman. "What can I do for you?"

"I want you to marry Mary Elizabeth and me."

"But—"

"I'm not sure I have the strength for much discussion. I've talked to her, and she agrees to become my wife tonight." He closed his eyes, allowing the pain to win a battle. "We've made a pact. She'll inherit half my ranch if she'll marry me."

Delta looked up at the others and, with her voice shaking, finished his terms. "The other half will be divided up between the employees. The land I get will contain the grave of Colton's first wife. I've promised to never sell it. When Colton dies, I'll bury him next to his wife then be free to marry and live wherever I like."

Before anyone could stop her, Delta darted from the room. She ran up the stairs and vanished through the panel behind the watershed before anyone but Jennie could catch her. Jennie slipped behind the water container and slid along the narrow tunnel until she touched Delta.

The small woman was curled into a ball, softly crying. "I can't go through with it. I'm not strong enough."

"Then why did you agree?" Jennie whispered as she slid her arm around Delta.

"He's dying," Delta answered. "He said he had no relatives and he doesn't want to die alone."

"He doesn't know who you really are, does he?"

"I don't think he cares." Delta wiped her eyes on the now filthy green dress she'd been wearing for over twenty-four hours. "I've been called trash all my life, but I don't want to even think about what folks will call me if I marry a man on his deathbed."

"It doesn't matter what folks think." Jennie couldn't believe she had spoken against what she'd been taught all her life. "You've got to do what you believe to be right."

"If Colton dies and I don't marry him, I'll be alone with nowhere to go. At least this way I'd have a home."

Jennie could feel trouble riding double toward them. "You don't have to worry about your stepbrother finding you. I talked to him today, and he's on the train back home by now. I convinced him you were dead. I even gave him the trunk."

"I don't care about him anymore," Delta answered. "I know what I have to do. I have no choice but to marry Colton."

"No, you have a choice." Jennie had always thought people married because they wanted to spend their lives together, not because they wanted someone to come to their funeral. "You can leave. Even if Colton dies, we can find the money somewhere for a train ticket."

"The only option I have is to marry." Delta's cry was soft but marinated in sorrow. "Audrey told me this afternoon why I've been sick these past few weeks. I think I guessed it but didn't want to face the truth; I'm going to have a baby."

"No!" Jennie now knew trouble had just stampeded into their lives.

Delta raised her head, pulling together her last bit of pride. "I knew it was bound to happen sometime with Ward forcing me every time he got drunk. Now I could never go back. He'd take the baby as his and raise it to be like him and his father. I could never stand by and allow that to happen. Unlike my mother, I'm going to plan for my child. If Colton lives, I'll go back someday and claim my family land for my baby and kill all the Halls if I have to."

"And if he dies?" Jennie asked.

"Then my child will have Colton's land. Either way he'll never be homeless trash."

Jennie pulled Delta close and held her while she cried. Delta seemed to be crying for the life she'd had and the future one she was about to give up by marrying a man who didn't want a wife as dearly as he wanted a widow.

Chapter
Twenty-three

Dearly beloved." Spider cleared his throat. "We are gathered here together—"

"Cut out all the extra, Sheriff," Audrey ordered, "or the groom may not live through the ceremony."

Spider nodded and jumped to the only part he knew to be vital. "Do you Colton Barkley take this woman to be your wife?"

Colton didn't smile but stared at the sheriff with dark, determined eyes. He'd insisted on being at least raised to a sitting position for his own wedding. "I do," he said in his low voice that seemed to always rumble with anger.

"And so does she, Sheriff, so get on with it," Audrey added. Patience was a trait only slightly visited in Audrey's tour of virtues.

Spider agreed once more to hurry. "Then I pronounce you man and wife."

"And I witness it," the undertaker added. "So when the judge makes it by here next month, we'll swear it was all legal."

Jennie looked around. Now that the wedding was over, everyone in the room seemed to be just standing by waiting for the groom to die so they could console the widow. Audrey, Link and True had been watching him all afternoon. Now Spider and the undertaker everyone called Mr. Hatcher looked determined to join the group. Jennie couldn't stand the sight. Maybe Austin had been right to disappear before the wedding started. "I think everyone should leave." When no one but True and Link moved, she added, "Now!" in a voice sounding more like Audrey's than her own. More meekly she continued, "We should give the bride and groom some time alone."

Spider and Mr. Hatcher followed True and Link out. Jennie heard the undertaker ask Spider if he thought they should just wait downstairs, for in his words, "it can't be long."

Audrey stood at the door with her hand raised toward the man's back when Jennie rushed to his aide. "He doesn't mean anything. It's just his job." Jennie knew Audrey wouldn't understand, but she'd grown up with her father discussing what the widow might donate at the mourners' dinner.

Audrey looked every inch a redheaded warrior. "Well, he may be waiting on himself if he doesn't watch his manners. I don't like the idea of everyone thinking Colton's going to die. I figured out about half an hour ago that any man strong enough to face marriage on his deathbed just might surprise everyone and live."

Glancing back at the newlyweds, Jennie noticed Delta gently lowering him back into the covers. Jennie didn't want to eavesdrop, but she couldn't help but pause, listening to them whisper.

"Thanks for marrying me," Colton said in a voice that sounded hoarse. "I didn't think you would after what I told you this morning over at the jail. And to tell the truth, I wouldn't have blamed you."

Delta lightly brushed the midnight hair from his forehead. "I know you were saying whatever you thought you must to get me to safety."

Colton slowly shook his head. "No," he started.

Delta continued to brush back his hair. She'd discovered she enjoyed doing the little gesture, and he didn't seem to mind. "It doesn't matter what happened before we met," she said. "All that matters is now. I promise I'll stay with you for as long as you want me to."

"And if I die?"

She looked down. "Then I'll carry out our bargain."

Colton reached up and took her hand. "Why? When you arrived, I'd already heard Lawton was on his way, and I knew I'd be the first one he wanted between his sights. I figured the best thing for me to do was stay away from you until our month was over, then hand you a ticket. But you didn't seem to notice. You settled into winning the hearts of all my staff and even bringing True to stay with us like you thought my ranch could be a real home." His voice sounded very tired. "Now you marry me without knowing anything about me."

"But you know nothing of me either." She looked down, afraid to face him. "Maybe if you did, it would be you who didn't want to marry me."

"I knew all I needed to know when you told me you wanted to take care of True just because the kid needed someone. I figured a woman with that big a heart might someday learn to care for me."

Delta lowered her head and cried softly against his pillow. "Would you care for a child who wasn't yours?" she whispered between sobs. "One without a father who needed love to have a chance to grow up and be somebody?"

"I would," he answered, "if I had the opportunity."

Jennie's eyes were so filled with tears, she couldn't see to leave the room. When she glanced at Audrey, Jennie found her in much the same predicament.

As she closed the door, Audrey announced, "That man's gonna live if I have to fight the grim reaper myself for his soul. I don't care if he stuffed his first wife down a dry well, he's going to make a damn good husband to Delta if he pulls through this."

Smiling away her tears, Jennie added, "I'll go down and tell Mr. Hatcher we won't be needing him tonight."

AUSTIN COULDN'T FORCE himself to stay for the wedding. He'd heard some insane reasons for marrying, but to insure where you were going to be laid to rest hit the top of the list.

The night had turned cold, but he didn't notice. He walked the streets of Florence, wishing he were back in Texas. Things always seemed simpler there. He was more at home among the longhorns and the sagebrush. A person didn't feel as lonely, maybe because the land itself was lonely.

"Want me to walk with you, Marshal?" True fell into step as Austin turned the corner of the depot. "I saw you from the window of the hotel when you passed and figured I'd tag along just in case you got into trouble."

Austin couldn't help but smile. "Where's that sidekick of yours—Henry?"

True shrugged. "I figure his was one of the families

who left. The town's quieter than a whorehouse on Sunday morning."

Laughing, Austin wondered where True had lived before here. Now that he knew Jennie couldn't be the child's mother, he wanted, like everyone else it seemed, to keep an eye on True.

"You ever kill a man?" True asked before Austin had time to finish laughing.

Austin nodded. "When I had to."

True's huge eyes danced with excitement. "I got a little time for you to tell me about it."

The marshal shook his head. "There's nothing worth telling about watching a man die."

"Still, you must be awful brave. I'll bet you're about the bravest man who ever rode across the West."

"No, son," Austin answered. "I was just doing my job."

True looked disappointed.

"But you've got a grand turn for words," Austin added. "Maybe you'll grow up to be a writer."

The child laughed. "I can't even read yet. Jennie makes me try every time she gets her hands on me, but she keeps changing the words she wants me to learn. I was thinking I'd be a marshal like you and not ever have to worry about nothing but keeping my guns clean. I'd kill so many outlaws they'd name a cemetery after me, True's Cemetery."

"Who knows?" Austin couldn't imagine the child ever being anything but wild and free.

They returned to the hotel after circling the depot. Austin lifted True up on the porch. "It's a little cold. Why don't you turn in, son?"

Giving his suggestion some thought, True yawned. "You sure you don't need me to help?"

"Not tonight, but you can tell Link I need to see him at first light in the morning."

True saluted and vanished.

Austin smiled, knowing Link would have True for a shadow when he appeared in the morning. The marshal leaned against the porch railing and pulled out a cigar. It had been a long day and seemed like a million years since he'd held Jennie in the predawn light.

As though his thoughts took shape, she stepped onto the porch. Her eyes looked tired even in the moonlight, but she still held herself as straight and tall as ever.

"Evening," she whispered as she moved a foot away from him. For a few minutes they both seemed happy just to be in each other's presence.

Finally she faced him. "We need to talk."

Austin could hear the rapids coming. He fought the urge to yell "White water" and jump off the porch before she could go any further.

"I've thought all day about last night. What happened between us was—"

"Beautiful," Austin finished her sentence. "Magic. Wonderful."

"Unreal," Jennie answered. "I've always thought I wouldn't allow a man to touch me unless I was sure he loved me." She waited, as if giving Austin the chance to reply.

But he couldn't answer. He'd never said the words. Maybe he did care for her more than he'd ever cared for a woman, but to love her would be opening himself up to be hurt again. He'd loved his mother. He'd loved his brother. They were dead. He wasn't sure he could survive another love in his life. Why couldn't she be like the few other women he'd found comfort with?

Why couldn't he just walk away from her before either of them was hurt?

Tossing the unused cigar away, Austin shoved his hands into his pockets. "Love's something for poets and romantics." Suddenly, for no good reason at all, he wanted her to feel as uncomfortable as he did. "Now, honesty is a trait worth looking for. If a man and woman can be honest with one another, then they've something to build on."

Jennie's eyes shone with tears. "I think we have nothing more to say to one another, Marshal McCormick."

"No," Austin agreed and watched her leave. When he'd heard the door close, he added, "Except that I'll miss you every day for the rest of my life."

Only the wind and a small child listening at the window above heard his statement.

Chapter
Twenty-four

I don't understand. By all rhyme and reason you should be food for the worms by now." Audrey spread another quilt over Colton's bed. "Granny Gates would have made you spit three times in an open grave for the trick you played on death."

"Sorry to let you down," Colton grumbled, "but other than feeling like I swallowed a handful of lead, I'm doing pretty good."

"Oh, I'm not sorry, just surprised. Three days ago I wouldn't have given you a hare's chance in a buffalo stampede, but now I'm beginning to think, thanks to you, my calling is doctoring. I keep changing the bandage expecting to see fresh blood, but you've decided to keep what little you have left."

"Since I'm doing so grand, how about sending up something besides broth?" Colton's words still had an edge to them, as if he were giving an order, not making a request. "A rare steak with a half dozen eggs on the side sounds like a fair follow-up to that bowl of soup you called supper."

Audrey wasn't ruffled by his gruffness. "You'll have nothing but broth until I say you can eat more." She diluted her order with a smile. "Now, get down in those covers. We've got a norther blowing in that promises snow before nightfall, and, even with the quilts, I doubt you've got enough blood to keep you warm. If you survive the night, I'll give some thought to oatmeal in the morning."

Colton closed his eyes and growled at her suggestion. In truth he'd felt chilled all day as the temperature had been dropping. He knew it was more thanks to his blood loss than the weather, but he'd fight it alone. The girls here had enough to keep them busy without having to worry about one gut-shot rancher feeling cold.

As Audrey said good night and left the room, he heard his wife enter and take her seat by his bed. He hadn't been too ill to notice she ate little more than broth. Even that seemed to make her sick from time to time. He tried to remember the color of her eyes, but couldn't. In all honesty he'd never looked at her closely before he'd been shot, denying himself a passing pleasure so that he wouldn't miss her when he sent her away.

He'd been a fool to ask a woman to travel all the way to Kansas in hopes of marrying him. What did he have to offer her but widowhood? If the bullet hadn't found him three days ago, it would have before the year was out.

"Colton?" Delta whispered. "Are you awake?"

He slowly opened his eyes and stared at her. Sky blue, he thought. How could he have forgotten that her eyes were sky blue? Just as she had the nights before, she'd left the room to change into a cotton gown and robe. He had no idea why she changed. She spent the night, as she spent the days, sitting in the chair between him and the window.

She looked so fragile, like a sudden gust might blow her away. But he'd seen her inner strength these past few days. Like a true wife, she'd been there whenever needed. She made decisions quickly yet never said a harsh word, even though he knew she had to be exhausted. He looked at her closely for the first time, remembering how she'd cried when she thought they were alone and he was asleep. "I'm awake." He tried to force the edge out of his voice. "How are you, Mrs. Barkley?" he asked, even though he knew she wouldn't tell him if she were ill.

Delta smiled shyly. "Fine," she answered. "Or I will be as soon as I warm up. With the sun setting, all warmth seems to have vanished from the world. The house is packed with folks asking for more blankets."

"Are you sorry I haven't died yet and left you a widow?" He knew she hadn't married him out of any love, and he'd already guessed his land wasn't the card that had won her. She had her reasons, just as he had his, and she might tell him if there was enough time shared between them.

"No," she replied. "I'm getting used to having you around. I'd miss you if you died on me now."

"You know, I'd miss you, too," Colton added honestly. He'd decided years ago that he preferred being alone, but he didn't mind her nearness.

The wind rattled against the windows already white with frost. Delta glanced at the open space the curtains didn't cover and hugged herself. She could feel the storm blowing across the country.

"Take the quilt Audrey brought," Colton ordered as

he tried to lift it off his legs. "You'll freeze tonight sitting in that chair."

"No!" Delta jumped to straighten his covers. "I couldn't. You'll need it."

Colton leaned back among the pillows, frustrated that he wasn't strong enough to force her to accept. How could he rest easy in a bed when she was shivering at his side?

Delta tucked the covers around him, her wide blue eyes filled with worry. "Please," she said, "you've got to stay warm." This night promised to be hard on the healthy. "The last thing I want is for you to catch pneumonia."

"I can't lie here with you cold. Leave me. Go find a warm bed among the girls' quarters."

"No." Delta's voice was low, but firm. "I belong here with my husband." She didn't add that she felt safe here even though he was wounded. Delta had no faith in Jennie's belief that Ward was gone. She knew he'd be back for the deed or to make sure she was dead and buried.

Colton opened the covers at his side. "Then lay beside me and we'll both be warm."

Fear hit Delta like an icy slap. She'd seen her stepbrother make the same gesture, and she'd been beaten when she hadn't joined him. Backing against the wall, she raised her hands as if to ward off another blow. "No!" she cried, trying to push herself into the very wall.

Colton took one look at her face and would have given all he owned to be able to take back the words. He'd only voiced an option, but in his usual way his words had come out too harsh. She stared down at him with a terror unlike any he'd ever seen.

"Mary Elizabeth?" he questioned, hating himself for having frightened her so. "It was only a suggestion for warmth, nothing more. Mary Elizabeth!" He realized she wasn't hearing him. "Mary!" Even the sound of her own name didn't shake her.

He leaned back against the pillows, wishing he had the strength to stand and pull her back to reality, but knowing that if he touched her now, he'd probably only frighten her more. "Mary, don't be afraid." He rubbed his forehead in frustration.

Slowly, she forced a mask across her face and lowered her fists to her side. "Yes," she said, seeming to pull away, even though her body remained stone still.

Colton raised his hand slowly, as one might to a wild, frightened animal. "I don't know what crossed your mind just now, but I assure you I would not hurt you in any way even if I had the strength."

Delta nodded, as if forcing herself to listen. "Thank you for the offer, but I'm really not that cold."

"You act as though I asked something improper. I don't think it's all that unusual for a man and wife to sleep in the same bed."

"No," Delta reasoned.

Colton relaxed back, wishing he wasn't so tired. "If I live, I had thought we'd be married in every way; but if you don't wish it, I'll not press the point. I have no illusion of you marrying me for love. There'll be no physical side to our marriage if you wish." He had to make her believe he would never hurt her. He felt as if he'd just slapped an angel.

He could see her body relax a fraction from a fear she must have been fretting over since the wedding. "Thank you," she answered. "I don't think I could live if . . ."

"Then I won't touch you!" He didn't want her to have to describe what she obviously found so ugly. "You'll be my wife in name only if that's what you want." Colton couldn't bear to see the pain returning to her face. He wondered if something terrible had happened in her past or if it was him she found so distasteful. "I swear I'll never touch you. You still have my gun. You can shoot me—if you can find a place left undamaged to aim at."

Delta smiled, remembering their first day together and how he'd handed her the weapon.

"That's better." Colton had never wanted to hold a woman so much in his life, but he didn't make a move. "Now, will you make me a promise?"

"Yes," Delta answered. "If I can."

"Will you promise to crawl beneath the covers if you get cold? I swear I'll not attack you, and sharing the bed seems our only option."

She nodded, realizing he wasn't even strong enough to pull on his own shirt; he could hardly overpower her.

Colton closed his eyes, wishing he knew more about this beautiful creature who was his wife. Wishing he'd live long enough to convince her he wasn't going to harm her.

An hour later, as the storm raged outside, Colton felt the covers move on the far side of the bed. Delta slipped beneath the blankets without touching him. After several minutes he felt the warmth of her beside him and relaxed. As his breathing returned to normal, her hand slid across the sheet and touched his arm. Her fingers rested lightly just above his elbow.

He didn't move, or cover her hand with his own as he longed to. He kept his promise. He fell asleep for the first time in years with a wife beside him and a reason to wake up in the morning.

JENNIE HELPED THE late crew wash up because she was restless. Snow already covered the ground, convincing those passengers who'd arrived on the afternoon train to spend the night and take a look at the weather come morning.

As she put the serving dishes up along the top shelves, she couldn't get Austin's last words from her mind. They'd only known each other a little while. How she wished she could go back and change everything they'd said from the beginning. How she wished she could tell him the truth.

The back door to the kitchen blew open, sending freezing winds whirling around the room, rattling hanging pots with enough noise to make the entire hotel seem as if it shivered.

"Close the door!" one of the cooks yelled while the other raised her apron to protect against the blast.

"Sorry," a railroad employee answered as he fought the door closed. "It's a hell of a night. Freeze the—" He glanced up at the women in time to stop his remark from embarrassing both himself and them. "Freeze . . . the winter corn off its stocks," he finished, smiling proudly that he'd thought of something decent to say.

Jennie moved to find a cup. Most of the railroad employees had learned where the back door was and that there was always coffee on as long as the light burned. "I hope you're planning on staying here tonight."

"You guessed it, honey." The railroad man smiled, showing teeth that looked like a piano keyboard, with every third one or so solid black. "I thought I'd come up here rather than sleep down at the depot; but I'm not getting out in this again until the wind dies down, even if I have to sleep on the floor."

One cook poked the other and smiled with pride. "He'd have to look hard to find a cleaner or warmer place to bed down."

The railroad worker agreed with a nod. "Everyone's looking for warmth tonight. Everyone except that little ragamuffin kid who hangs around here. I saw him down at the barn over an hour ago. He said there were too many people in this place, and he was making him a pallet on the hay."

Jennie turned around. "Was the child named True?"

The worker shrugged. "Didn't tell me his name. But he's the one who came in about the same time all you new girls arrived a few weeks ago. I've seen him around but never paid much notice."

She didn't wait. Running up the back stairs, she checked her room. True had taken to sleeping under one of the beds, but he wasn't there. She checked all the dark, warm corners the child had discovered in the past few weeks, but nothing. True wasn't in the hotel.

Audrey rolled over and pushed her nightcap from her eyes. "Time to get up?" she asked with a yawn.

"No," Jennie whispered. "I was only looking for True. Go back to sleep. I'll make sure the boy is sleeping warm and try not to wake you again."

Audrey rolled over without argument. Four A.M. came very early for a pastry cook and part-time doctor.

As she moved back down the stairs, Jennie's worry for True grew. She'd always thought the child wise for one so young, but if True were sleeping in the barn, there might be a death come morning.

Jennie grabbed Delta's stained jade-colored cape from the hook by the door. She wrapped the soiled garment around her and headed out toward the barn.

As she stepped from the porch, the icy wind hit her full blast. Snow blew around her so thick she could barely make out the outline of the barn. Pulling the cape's hood over her face, she marched on, determined in her mission. She had to save True.

She turned once, twice, glancing back toward the hotel. Even though the wind whirled around, seeming to come from all directions at once, she thought she heard someone running across the frozen ground behind her. She could see nothing but a white, blinding blur, making the blackness beyond even darker.

Her fingers were almost too cold to move as she reached the small barn door to the side of the big opening. Everything seemed out of place. Jennie couldn't remember ever seeing the barn doors closed and barred. Even when it had rained, the workers had left one door slightly ajar in case they had to house another wagon. But anyone would be a fool to be out tonight.

Glancing back once more, she still couldn't shake the feeling someone was walking in her footprints even before the wind had a chance to erase them.

Forcing panic down her throat, she pulled the door open and stepped inside. The sudden stillness pressed against her chilled skin, heavy with the smell of damp hay.

"True?" Jennie whispered as she moved into the dim light. Four lanterns flickered from poles in the center of the barn. Stalls, filled with horses, surrounded her. Each horse had a full manger of oats and a blanket over his back. The thought occurred to her that folks around here paid more attention to their animals than they did to a child.

"True?" She took another step. Without the wind,

the freezing air drifted silently around her, chilling her slowly.

Something moved in the shadows. Jennie jumped to one side, silencing a scream with her fist. The shadow moved again closer, materializing from blackness.

For a moment she couldn't relax, even when the shadow turned into a gray-and-black cat. Her mind registered the animal, but her heart wouldn't stop pounding and her legs still ached to run. The huge cat stretched in front of her and moved away.

"True?" Jennie's voice was unsteady. She forced herself to relax her fingers. She couldn't go around screaming at shadows. She'd frighten the poor little child to death.

As Jennie looked around the barn for True's sleeping form, the little door she'd come through popped open, allowing wind to enter. The animals along the barn walls stomped and neighed noisily, complaining about her lack of sense in allowing the door to reopen.

Moving back into the shadows, she faced the snow so that she could close the door more securely this time. A strange smell of sour whiskey and unwashed flesh blended with the fresh, icy smell of snow. She pulled her cape lower against the wind and ignored the foreign odor.

As her hand reached for the latch, someone's fingers closed around her arm, biting into her skin like cold iron— huge, fleshy fingers strong enough to snap the bone if she fought.

Jennie's blood seemed to leave her body at once. She opened her mouth to scream as the hand jerked her sideways into the darkness beside the door. A large palm slapped across her mouth even before she could fill her lungs with enough air to make a sound. She fought for breath, but the hand shoved even harder against her, splitting her lip and blending blood in with the taste of dirt and whiskey.

"Make a sound and I'll gut you right here, missy," a low voice hissed against the side of her face. She felt the cold blade of a knife sliding along her throat, taking the top layers of skin as it moved.

The jingle of a bridle sounded from the other side of the barn. Male voices reached the dark corner where Jennie struggled. Even though they were too far away to make out individual words, hope glimmered for an instant as she realized she wasn't alone.

The man holding her heard them also and swore to himself in a drunken slur. With one mighty push, her attacker shoved her from him. Her back hit the rough barn wall. He grabbed her shoulder with the hand that held his knife, as if to steady her. When Jennie looked toward his beefy fingers trying to hold her shoulder and the knife, his other fist slammed into the side of her face.

For a moment she felt no pain, only the sudden jerk of her head in reply. Then lightning exploded across her brain and burned an instant before shattering into total darkness. Another blow replaced the first, then another, then another, piling pain upon pain until her mind could accept no more.

As her body crumpled helplessly, Jennie's last sense was of the cape being wrapped tightly around her, cocooning her in velvet blackness.

"Got you now, Delta," the attacker laughed as he lifted her to his shoulder. "And you'll wish you were dead and buried in that grave with your name on it before I'm finished with you tonight."

Chapter
Twenty-five

*Y*ou're not going with me, son, so you might as well stop following me." Austin's voice echoed off the inside walls of the barn.

"But, Marshal," True ran to keep up with Austin, "I'm the one who told you Jennie was kidnapped. If it weren't for me, she'd have been miles away before anyone missed her."

Austin jammed his rifle into its sheath and crammed an extra box of shells into his saddlebags. "I haven't got time to argue, True. You stay here and keep your eyes open for more trouble. I'll be back before dawn."

"You'll be dead before sunrise if you go out in this blizzard." Spider Morris entered the barn, shaking snow off him as he moved.

Swearing beneath his breath, Austin knew the old man was probably right. But he couldn't just stand around and let some stranger take Jennie without doing something.

"Besides," Spider moved nearer, "whoever took her will hole up to wait out the storm. He's not going anywhere until the weather clears a bit. Our best chance is to check out every house in town and wait till morning."

Austin didn't want to think about what a man who was capable of kidnapping might do to Jennie while waiting. "You check town; I'm going!"

Spider shook his head. "Well, if you're determined to head out tonight, you might want to think a minute before you go off half-cocked. My guess is there's only a couple of places he could have made it to in this snow. There's an old abandoned farmhouse a few miles north of here, but the road's so grown over you'd never find it in this snow."

"And the other place?"

"If a fellow knew where to look, he could find a cluster of caves just past the bend of the tracks heading toward Kansas City. It's not far, but no one would hear a woman scream from there. Not in this storm. Problem is unless you know where the caves are, you'll walk right past them."

True pushed past Spider and planted feet toe-to-toe with Austin. "I know where the caves are; Henry showed me. I could find them with my eyes closed. And I know what the kidnapper looks like. He's the same fellow who took Delta's trunk."

Austin pulled his fingers into leather gloves. "Tell me where to look, kid."

"No. I ain't goin' to do it." Tiny fists braced on slim hips, followed by a look that meant to fight both men if need be. "I'm the reason she's kidnapped. She came out to the barn looking for me. I'm going to the caves with or without you. Only difference will be that when

I get there, I'll be alone if you keep trying to tell me what to do."

Austin squatted down to True's level. "Son," he tried to make his voice calm, "this storm is no place for you to be wandering around."

"I've slept out in worse and survived. Last winter I would have considered this a warm night compared to some I was out in." True didn't budge. "You'll never find her without me."

"I've got Sheriff Morris," Austin countered.

"Don't count on me." Morris shook his head. "I haven't been out to those caves in years. They're something only the younguns around here play in. I probably couldn't find them on a clear day."

"Well, hell, I'm not taking a child!" Austin tried to sound determined. What kind of lawman takes a kid on a hunt? He'd be laughed out of Texas if this story traveled south.

"Well, hell," True answered. "I don't see as you have much choice. Besides I care about Jennie just as much as you do."

Spider could see the stubbornness reflected between the two and figured they had to be kin, whether Austin admitted it or not. "We've no time to argue," the old sheriff said as he pulled off his gloves and handed them to True. "Take my gloves and coat, True. You'll be as warm as need be. If True really knows the way to the caves, you two should be back in an hour."

Already weighted down with layers of wool, True pulled on the sheriff's coat and gloves, looking like a ball of rags and worn leather. Spider's waist-length coat hung to the child's knees. "Time's a-wasting, Marshal."

The last thing Austin wanted to do was take a kid along with him to look for Jennie, but he had no choice.

He grabbed the back of True's coat and lifted the orphan onto his saddle.

Spider handed Austin a lantern. "Best as I can remember, there ain't but three caves, so it won't take you long. Follow the tracks until True tells you to turn off." The old man looked very tired. "And head back in an hour, no matter what. I don't want to have to look for your bodies come morning."

Austin climbed up behind True. "We'll be back with Jennie, if she's out there." He pulled his hat low and motioned for Spider to open the door. When the icy wind hit them like a blast, Austin leaned forward instinctively, protecting True as much as he could.

JENNIE THOUGHT SHE was in a nightmare as the world came back into focus. Her body was so cold she had no feeling in her hands and feet, and the side of her face ached. The world was so black inside the wrappings of her cape, she wasn't sure if her eyes were open or closed.

Trying to move slightly, she felt a rope binding her. One loop cut into her throat, then the rope ran along her back, circled her waist, and continued to below her hips, where it bound her legs together. The taste of dirty cloth filled her mouth from the gag that twisted into the corners of her lips.

The sudden crash of a bottle made her stop wiggling. She could hear someone moving around only a few feet from her. The steps seemed heavy and slow. Since she couldn't feel the wind, she guessed she must be inside, but without the smell of animals, it couldn't be the barn.

A flicker of light blurred its way through the material covering her face. Another flicker. She smelled the warmth of a fire even before she felt it.

"There." The sound of a man's voice came closer to Jennie. "Now the fire's going, it's time we had a little talk."

A huge, beefy hand slid along the cape covering her. "There seems more to you, girl, than I've felt before. Maybe you grew a little now that you've been eating regular." His hand stopped over her breast, trying to feel her through the layers of clothing.

Jennie jerked, rolling away. The cluttered floor slowed her progress, but she moved blindly, trying to get as far from the voice as she could. With a sudden, violent tug on the rope, the man pulled her back. "Well, now, you're awake!" he shouted. "Wouldn't be no fun feeling you when you couldn't let me know how much you like it." She tried to twist away, but he held the rope tightly.

"When you gonna learn, girl, that you belong to me? Pa gave you to me last year and said I could do whatever I wanted with you. Most time you're more trouble than you're worth, running from me, but tonight we're gonna have a fine time."

Evil laughter distorted his voice. "I ain't never taken you when I didn't have to worry about making too much noise and waking Pa up." He howled like a wild animal. "This is gonna be a long night. I'm gonna let you scream until you can't scream no longer. I heard if a woman does that one time, she ain't likely to do much yelling again no matter what a fellow does to her. I've been planning this time ever since you ran away. There's a lot I can do to you that I ain't done before. Then come morning, you're gonna tell me what you did with that deed."

He grabbed the rope binding her throat and yanked it hard toward him. "You be still when I want you, girl," he ordered. Without caring that he was choking her, he tugged at the rope. "That's better!" he yelled when she finally stopped trying to pull away.

"Easy now, Delta." His words were slurred with whiskey. "I've drunk too much to fight you untied, so we'll have to leave you bound till you settle down. If you cause me any trouble, I'll beat you until you can't stand up, then I'll untie you and we'll dance awhile."

He laughed when she reacted to his words. "You got sense enough to be good and afraid of what I'll do. In that way you ain't as dumb as your ma. Pa will probably have to beat her the night before we put her in the ground. But it don't have to be that way. Once you learn how, you'll treat me real nice. I won't have to hit you but ever' once in a while, just so you don't forget." He snorted in delight and pulled the rope, making her hooded head move up and down as if in a nod.

"Like that, do you?" He relaxed his hold on the rope as he guzzled more whiskey. "Before I'm through, you'll be begging me to let you stay with me. If you ever leave me again, you'll be going in a box to the cemetery. Remember that, girl," he threatened.

Jennie wanted to throw up. She'd never known such evil existed in the world. Her heart pounded so wildly she thought it might explode. She forced herself not to move as she listened to him drinking and mumbling to himself.

"You're learning," he yelled after a long silence. "You wait there nice-like until I finish this bottle, then we'll have a look at you."

While she heard him swallow several times, she tried to figure out where she was. The voice had to be that of Delta's stepbrother, Ward. Somehow he'd come back, and he thought she was Delta. At first Jennie found that idea ridiculous, though she had been wearing Delta's cape and the barn had been very dark. Was he drunk enough to mistake her for a petite blonde?

Ward pulled on the rope around her neck. "Ain't you ever gonna ask about your ma?" When she didn't even try to answer through the gag, he dropped the rope, letting her head fall backward against the floor. "Your ma was mighty upset when you left. She kept walking around, calling you like you'd just been hiding somewhere around the house. Finally Pa had to shut her up. She hasn't said nothing ever since."

Jennie moved, fighting to get farther away.

"Now, stop that!" he yelled, suddenly angry. "Or I'll take the whip to you."

Jennie froze, guessing he'd take great pleasure in whipping a woman.

His hands grabbed the material of the cape. "I should have broke you back home and saved myself this trouble now. Ain't never had a woman to ride ever' time I wanted to. When I get you back home, I'll want you waiting in my bed ever' night." He laughed, as though he thought his plan brilliant.

When his fingers pulled at the cape, he swore at the ropes binding her. "This damn cape is getting in my way. Roll over on your belly." She could hear him moving around, throwing another log on the fire, tossing the bottle against a far corner.

Because she didn't move onto her stomach as he'd ordered, Ward kicked her so hard it seemed as if her entire body left the ground at once. "I ain't in no mood to not have you mind, girl." He yanked at the rope. "You got anything to say about that?"

As all the air was suddenly cut off, Jennie fought to keep from blacking out. Even through the layers of material, the rope was sawing into her flesh.

"I didn't think so." He dropped the rope and let her head hit the floor once more. "You're learning fast. Now, roll over."

Jennie did as ordered. She could feel blood dripping from her nose and forehead, and she couldn't seem to get enough air into her lungs. The side of her face throbbed in pain, and she was sure blood was matting the hair on the back of her head.

Jennie tried to breathe as she heard him moving above her. Suddenly, without warning, she felt a knife slide between the rope and her throat. She wasn't sure whether to pray that his hand would be steady enough to cut the rope without cutting her, or to pray he slipped and ended this nightmare once and for all.

When the rope suddenly slackened, Ward jerked the cape and her body rolled free. "I figure you've had enough beating to remember your place."

She pulled at the gag in her mouth as she stared at the remains of a cabin around her. Any hope she'd had that she was in a place near help vanished, for she'd never seen this one-room shack. From the layers of dirt on everything, she figured that neither had anyone else in years.

"What the hell!" Ward yelled and stepped back. "You ain't Delta!"

As she blinked away pain, all Jennie could say was "I told you. Delta is dead."

"No, she ain't!" Ward stormed toward Jennie. "I seen her wearing this very cape four nights ago. She thought she could leave, but I seen that Harvey House schedule on the wall back home and knew she'd be at one of the houses. The man in Kansas City told me Florence was the only place hiring, so I waited around till I saw her. You and her cooked somethin' up to keep me from getting my land."

Jennie knelt and pulled the rope from around her feet. His talk was giving her time to clear her mind. "Your land? I thought the land belonged to Delta and her mother. Not you."

He raised his hand to strike her, but she was faster. Jennie darted across the room and looked around for something to use as a weapon. The only way this man would ever touch her again was if she were dead.

Ward scrubbed his face with his hand, trying to sober up. He could handle a beaten Delta, but he wasn't so sure about this woman. From the look of her, she could claw his eyes out and scramble them for breakfast.

"I ain't arguing with no woman!" Ward yelled. "If you know about the land, then you know where the deed is."

Storming like a raging, blind bull, he moved toward her. He was within three foot of her before he saw the stock of an old rifle in her hand. As Ward took another step, she raised the wood and swung.

The dried timber splintered against the side of his face. Blood from a hundred tiny cuts streaked across his hairless head and cheek. As another blow struck him, Ward screamed in pain.

He swung blindly, storming around the room, out of control.

Seeing her chance, Jennie was out the door before he could wipe the blood from his eyes.

"Oh no you don't!" Ward yelled and ran after her. "You ain't leaving here alive!"

Jennie knew she'd have no chance if she left the cabin. She had no idea which way to walk to find help, and if she didn't reach warmth fast in this weather, she'd freeze to death. Her only hope was to stay near the house or barn.

Staggering outside, she crumpled into a ball amid the clutter on the dilapidated porch. It was a gamble. If Ward hesitated at all, he'd see her. But he didn't. He ran into the blizzard shouting what he planned to do with her if she didn't stop.

She waited until his voice was several feet away, then moved in the blackness along the side of the house until she reached a barn. It looked like a dozen snowflakes might destroy it, but she could hear a horse. Ward hadn't taken the time to properly put away his mount, and the poor animal was still saddled.

Talking softly to the animal, Jennie felt for the reins. Since Ward had come into town on the train, there was a good chance that this horse belonged to either the Harvey House stables or the livery in town. As she climbed into the saddle, Jennie just prayed the horse had a better sense of direction than she did.

"Take me home," she whispered as she tied the reins to her hands. "Please take me home."

She kicked the animal into action and lowered her head. The wind seemed to cut into her dress, but she'd risk freezing to death before she'd go back into the cabin for the cape.

As the horse moved through the night, she could hear Ward scream somewhere in the distance, but Jennie didn't turn around. His voice grew farther and farther away. Tears streaked her face for the first time since she'd been kidnapped. She was safe from him. Now all she had to do was reach shelter before she froze to death.

Closing her eyes, Jennie pictured herself back home riding to town, always looking for the few red ribbons her family tied to tell her which fork in the road to take. Only now there were no more ribbons, and even if there had been, she couldn't have seen them in the storm. Tonight there seemed no direction for her except away from Ward.

Chapter
Twenty-six

Marshal! Marshal!"

"Yes, True?"

"I gotta stop."

"What? Out here in the middle of nowhere? Why?" Austin tried to see through the blinding snow. They'd only turned off the tracks twenty feet before. Surely the cave couldn't be so close to the train tracks.

Before he could react, True threw one leg over the saddle horn and slid off Austin's horse. "I'll be right back. But like Henry says, 'A fellow's got to do what he's got to do.' "

Austin swore. He'd never been around children much, but stopping in the middle of a manhunt didn't make any sense. "What's the problem?" Austin yelled.

"I forgot to go before we left town!" True yelled from somewhere in the blizzard. "And it ain't easy with all these clothes on."

Austin couldn't believe what was happening. He was

standing in the center of a storm trying to find a cave, the location of which only a child knew, in time to save Jennie. And . . . and his guide had to stop and go to the privy.

"All right," True yelled. "You can help me back on the horse now."

He reached down and lifted True into the saddle with one hand. "How much farther?"

"Straight ahead. I'll tell you when we get so close we have to go on foot."

True's judgment proved to be correct. Within a few minutes Austin followed the child into the first cave. It was so well hidden by trees and rocks the marshal wasn't sure he could have found it on a bright day much less in the middle of a storm.

There was no sign anyone had been in the cave since the snow started. A foot of drifted snow protected the entrance with not so much as rabbit tracks across the powder.

They moved to the next cave, then the last.

True ran to the back of the shallow rock room calling Jennie's name. Austin stood at the entrance slowly swinging the lantern back and forth. He didn't need to go any farther. The only footprints were True's.

"She's not here!" True gulped back a sob.

"Looks that way." Austin knew how the child felt; he was disappointed also. He'd like to get his hand on any man who thought he could just walk up to the Harvey House and steal one of the girls. There wouldn't be much left of him to take to trial.

"We have to find her." True looked up at the marshal for reassurance.

Austin wished he believed in himself half as much as True believed in him. "We'll start again come morning.

There's nothing else we can do tonight."

True kicked at the snow then slowly followed Austin out of the cave. As they walked toward the horse, a tiny hand slipped into Austin's gloved palm.

He hugged the child tightly as he lifted True up onto the saddle. "It's all right, son. We'll find her." He acted as though he didn't see huge tears rolling onto True's dirty cheeks.

Wanting the words to be fact, he repeated, "We'll find her. Maybe the sheriff turned up something in town." Maybe?

They rode back toward the Harvey House. True mumbled, "We're going to get that bad guy and pull him apart limb by limb and dry him out in the sun till he's raisin done, then use his bones for firewood. And if he ain't dead yet, we're going to shoot him twice in the heart and once in the foot and cut his head open with an axe and use his brains as—"

"True," Austin scolded. "That's enough."

"I ain't finished with my plan yet."

"But don't you think you're getting a little bloody?"

"Oh, all right," True agreed. "We'll tie him up and drain him like I saw them do a hog once. After all his blood drips out then we'll—"

"That's enough." Austin almost wanted to play the game with True. Thoughts of what he planned to do to the man heated his blood and staved off the bitter cold. But he needed to be thinking about catching the bastard first.

As they neared the lights of the hotel, True yelled, "Look, Marshal, the light's on in Jennie and Audrey's room!"

Austin looked up. "Doesn't Audrey get up about this time?"

"Not for hours yet." Hope wouldn't die in True's voice. "Jennie must be back. Maybe she killed the bad guy and left his body somewhere in the snow. We'll find him come morning stiffer than a week-dead cow."

"Maybe." The marshal set the child down on the porch. "You go up and check with Audrey. I'll take care of my horse."

True disappeared instantly, but Austin took his time riding to the barn. He didn't like coming back empty-handed. If he'd been out by himself, he'd have tried to find that abandoned farmhouse, but he couldn't risk True's life.

When Austin opened the barn door, he was surprised at the activity going on inside. Several of the hands were already up and dressed. They were working with an animal that looked very near frozen to death.

The Texan dismounted and pulled his saddle off his horse. "Everything all right?" he asked in passing as he grabbed a handful of straw and rubbed his animal down.

"Maybe it will be. We about lost one of our best mounts. A fellow stole him earlier tonight and we figured he was gone for good, but one of the women just rode him in a half hour ago. She was almost frozen in the saddle. Didn't even have on a coat. We had to pry her hands loose from the reins."

Austin stopped moving. He could only think of one woman who never seemed to have a coat and who might be out in this storm. "Jennie?"

The hand nodded. "Yes, sir, I think that was what I heard someone call her. We wrapped her in all the blankets we had and carried her up to the house."

Handing the reins of his horse over to the man, Austin ran toward the Harvey House. He didn't bother to speak as he stormed through the kitchen and started up the stairs.

"Marshal!" True yelled from the top of the steps. "She's back."

Unaware of the commotion he caused walking the dorm wing of the house, the Texan followed True to Jennie's room. When he opened the door to her room, Audrey blocked his path.

The tall redhead took one look at the marshal and raised her hands to stop him. "Now, hold on there, Austin. I know you're worried, but I can't have you bear-hugging her. She's so frozen she's liable to shatter like an icicle."

Austin fought the urge to shove Audrey aside. The woman had given up nursing and taken to bossing. "Get out of my way." He tried to hold his voice to a low roar.

"All right, but be careful. The feeling's coming back to her arms and legs, and even the slightest touch is going to hurt her."

He forced himself to move slowly. He walked to where Jennie was sitting up in bed all wrapped in quilts. Her black hair was wet and shiny and her face ghost pale.

"Jennie?" he whispered without touching her.

"I made it back," she mumbled through swollen lips. "I believed I was dead when I reached the lights. I couldn't feel the cold anymore. I couldn't even climb down from the horse."

She'd thought the ride endless but had stayed in the saddle even when a layer of ice formed over her. Now she looked up at the man she'd wished for every step of the way home. "I hoped you'd be waiting when I got back."

Looking more closely at her face, he noticed several

bruises, and her lip was cut on one side. Blood caked along her hairline and another spot near the crown of her head. She'd been through more tonight than just the storm. "What happened?" he asked as he knelt on one knee by the bed.

Jennie allowed a single tear to escape. "I went to the barn to see about True. A man must have followed me, for I remember feeling him near even before I saw him. He hit me on the head, and I woke up in an old run-down house somewhere. He . . ." Jennie couldn't say the words.

He didn't need or want to hear the details. Austin could see in her eyes that the man had hurt Jennie, and his mind was already planning ways he'd kill the kidnapper. Suddenly True's plans looked mild compared to what he had in mind.

Austin rested his hand lightly on Jennie's shoulder. "Do you know where he is now? Did he follow you back?"

Jennie pulled away from his touch and shook her head. "I don't know. It seemed like I rode a long way. When I left, I could hear him yelling for me to come back or he'd kill me. But I don't think he followed me. I took the only horse."

Audrey opened her mouth to order Austin to stop his questions, but the marshal raised his hand to stall her. He needed answers.

"Do you know his name or have any idea why he kidnapped you?" Austin knew a few men in this world didn't need any reason.

Jennie shook her head slowly. "I think he thought I was someone else."

"What did he look like?"

She closed her eyes trying to remember details. "Broad-chested, not much taller than me. I hit him across the face to get away. I don't remember what he looked like, only the blood running down his cheek. The things he said to me . . ."

"Marshal!" Audrey couldn't remain silent. "That's enough for now."

"I have to ask questions," Austin snapped, "if I'm going to find this man."

He touched Jennie once more, and again she pulled away. "Jennie, please, tell me anything that will help us catch him."

Jennie fought back more tears. "I don't know who he was." She wasn't sure why she lied, and she was too tired to answer any more questions. If she told the marshal who the man was, he'd have all kinds of questions about Delta. All Jennie wanted in the world was to pull the covers over her head and sleep.

"He must have said something to tell you who he was," Austin pleaded, guessing she was lying.

Unable to look at him, Jennie stared at the flower patterns on the quilt covering her. Now, if she told the truth, it might end Delta's marriage to Colton. With a baby on the way, Delta needed a home more than ever. If Ward ever showed his face around here again, she'd kill him herself.

"I must insist," Audrey said to Austin. "You have to leave."

Austin reached for Jennie again, but she rolled out of his reach. She hadn't trusted him with the truth before, and now she didn't trust his touch. Austin swore he'd find this man who hurt her and make him pay for every tear Jennie cried. If True was right about the man looking like the brother who came after Delta's belongings, he shouldn't be too hard to find.

* * *

DELTA LEANED AGAINST the door to Jennie's room and listened. Her tears fell silently as she shared Jennie's pain. There was no doubt in Delta's mind who had kidnapped her friend. She'd guessed the truth when she noticed her cape missing from the hall.

She had to stop this before someone else got hurt. She wasn't sure Ward had shot Colton, but there was no doubt he'd hurt Jennie. The truth had to come out, and Delta was the only one who could release Jennie and Audrey from their promise. She had to stop Ward. But before she told Austin, Delta knew she owed the truth to Colton.

Moving silently back to their room, Delta crawled beneath the covers once more. In an hour it would be light enough to dress and talk to the marshal.

"Colton?" Delta whispered as her hand touched her husband's arm. "How are you feeling?"

He moved slightly. "Stronger," he answered in a voice that told her he hadn't been asleep. "Where have you been?"

"Upstairs. Outside Jennie and Audrey's room," Delta answered. "There's something I must tell you."

"You no longer want to be my wife?" Colton questioned. Before she could answer, he added, "I've been expecting it every hour I've stayed alive. I know you agreed to marry a dying man. Staying with a living one is another story. I'll try not to stop you even if I am able."

"Oh, no," Delta cried. "I'll be your wife for as long as you want me."

"Forever sounds reasonable to me." He said the words slowly, as if he could soften his tone with lack of speed. She had no reason to be loyal to him, but she was.

Delta lightly brushed his arm and moved an inch closer. He might be a hard man, but his words were so direct she always found strength in them. "I must tell you about my past. Then you may not want me to stay."

"Tomorrow."

"No." Delta couldn't wait any longer. Enough had happened because of her lie. "Tonight."

"It won't change my mind," Colton answered, his dark eyes watching her in the shadows as she continued to touch him. Her small hand moved across his bandaged waist as if she were smoothing out all pain beneath her touch.

Delta drew courage from her husband as she said, "There's a man following me. He's my stepbrother, and he hurt me the night I ran away from home. He plans to kill me and anyone who gets in his way."

"Are you afraid?" Colton's voice was low.

"No. Not for myself," Delta answered as her hand moved up to brush the dark hair from his eyes. "Not when I'm with you. I'd never felt safe with anyone until I met you."

Colton captured her hand and pressed it against his chest. "No one will ever hurt you again." He said the words like an oath. "I may have no love left in me to give, but I promise you protection."

She relaxed against him. She could live without love in her life as long as she was safe. "I promise I'll never lie to you again. I should have told you about him from the first, but I didn't think he'd ever find me."

"Then we'll both start from right now," he answered. "No more lies or half truths between us, Mary Elizabeth."

"My name's Delta," she whispered, closing her eyes so that she couldn't see his reaction.

To her surprise he laughed softly. "I wondered what it was. Delta. How beautiful. It fits you somehow."

"You knew I wasn't Mary Elizabeth?" Delta raised herself up in the bed so that she could see his face more clearly.

"The minute you spoke," Colton laughed at the shock on her face. "Mary Elizabeth was Irish, she'd only been in the States a few months when she answered my ad. Almost every one of her letters told of how she hoped I'd be able to understand her."

"But you took me to the ranch. You let me think you believed me."

"I couldn't very well call you a liar in front of everyone in town; and by the time I'd thought of what to say, you'd intrigued me. I wanted to see what game you were playing."

"I'd meant to only stay the month and take the ticket you'd offered Mary Elizabeth," Delta answered honestly. "I'd hoped to earn my way working for you all month."

"I guessed as much, and before the dance, I'd decided it would probably be best to let you leave and never tell you I knew you weren't Mary Elizabeth."

"And after the dance?"

Colton let out a long breath and was silent for so long she wasn't sure he would answer. "You touched me." He looked at her, his black eyes reflecting the firelight. "I was starting to believe I'd been given another chance. I thought maybe my life could know some peace. I could have a woman at my side who wasn't afraid to touch me."

"What woman would be afraid of you?" Delta asked, trying to appear brave but remembering how she'd first felt when she'd met him.

"Every woman in the state," he answered. "But not you. I thought I might be able to walk the streets of town with a woman by my side and live a life like any other. But the shot ended that. When I thought I was dying, I wanted to know someone would bury me. Now that I may live awhile, I'm not sure what would be fair to you. I was thinking before you came in that I could send you away. Anywhere you like."

"I want to go back to the ranch with you."

Colton shook his head slowly. "Impossible. It's too dangerous. I know you think your stepbrother shot me, but I think it was more than likely one of Buck Lawton's men. Next time he might miss and kill you. I can't take that chance."

Delta cuddled a bit closer. "We both seem to have folks wanting us dead. Let me stay on the ranch."

"No."

"But I feel safe." Delta looked up at her husband. The first light of dawn had turned the shadows from black to smoky gray. His features were as hard and unyielding as ever, but she'd learned his heart was not. "Please, let me stay with you."

"I can't," he whispered, closing his eyes as though in pain as she brushed his whiskery chin with her fingers. "You're no part of this feud. It started long before you were my wife."

"I'm not leaving." She smiled, knowing she'd win when he reacted to her touch. Her fingers lightly touched his face, exploring, caressing. "Tell me to stop." He was a man starved of all human touch for years.

"No," he whispered as her fingers crossed his lips.

"Tell me you don't want me by your side."

"I can't," he answered. "It's been so long since anyone wanted to be with me. I'd like you to stay forever, but I have nothing to give. All the caring in me died the night my wife was buried."

She knew any man who could react as if her slightest touch were a treasure couldn't be as heartless as Colton believed himself to be.

"You didn't kill her, did you?" Delta had to ask even though she was afraid of the answer.

"I might as well have." Colton's body stiffened slightly. "She wanted to leave me, but she was carrying my child. I tracked her and her lover down before they could escape. I dragged her back against her will. I locked her in our bedroom and told her I'd not allow her to leave with my baby."

He was silent for a long time, and Delta knew he was telling the whole truth for the first time. "She took a mixture of poisons to cause her to lose the baby. It worked; my son was born dead only hours later. But the bleeding never stopped, and she died cursing me with her last breath. Swearing her lover would come for her and kill me."

"You buried her without telling anyone the truth?"

"How can a man tell his neighbors that his wife preferred to die rather than live with him? I threw her bags into the coffin and wrapped my little son in a blanket I cut from the black coat she'd been wearing. I placed him in her arms, but even in death she didn't seem to want him. The hardest thing I ever did was lower the coffin lid and leave him with her. I wanted to hold him so badly. I needed to hear him cry. I needed to know that I hadn't killed him. But I had, just as surely as if I'd shot them both. If I'd have let her go, they might have lived. All the softness went out of me that night. All that was kind in me was buried with her."

He was silent for a long time. His face looked as hard as ever, but Delta could almost hear the tears he cried deep inside him, where no one else would ever see. When she touched his hand, he didn't react and she realized this strong man was more afraid of her than she was of him.

She lifted his hand and placed it on her abdomen. Spreading his hand over her nightgown, she whispered, "I carry a child no father wants. Would you accept him?"

Colton's long, slender fingers spread across the cotton in a caress. "Whose child is it?"

"Mine," she answered. "I'll not give the baby up, even if it means I have to go away and you divorce me. The baby has no father, but he'll have a mother."

His hand rested on her. He didn't have to ask to know that she'd gotten pregnant from an attack. He'd seen the fear in her eyes when he'd told her to get in bed. "I'd never hurt you, Delta," he swore. "You've no reason to ever be afraid of me."

"I'm not," she answered. "I'd like to stay as your wife."

A light came into his eyes that she had thought she'd never see. "Stay with me," he said. "Both of you."

Without thinking of how he might react, Delta rolled toward him and kissed him gently on the cheek. "Thank you," she whispered. "Thank you for wanting us both."

Cupping her chin hesitantly, slowly, very slowly, he lowered his mouth to her lips. The kiss was light, tender against her mouth. "Thank you, Delta, my wife."

He rolled back on the pillow and relaxed with his arm pulling her close to his side.

Delta smiled as she touched her lips where he'd kissed

her. He might think he had no love to give, but she'd bet
Colton Barkley had a great deal. For the first time in her
life she felt wanted. He had given her a home and her
baby his name, and she'd given him her heart.

Chapter
Twenty-seven

*A*ustin McCormick combed the countryside for three days looking for any trace of the man who'd kidnapped Jennie. He found the old farmhouse with Delta's jade cape partially burned in the fireplace, but no barrel-chested man. As the days passed, all signs of the storm disappeared except the coldness left around Jennie's heart.

Every time Austin tried to see her, one of the others waylaid him. Delta asked him to come to Colton's room the day after the kidnapping. Without tears she held her husband's hand and told Austin the truth about who she believed kidnapped Jennie. She confessed to trading places with Mary Elizabeth, but Austin figured if this fact didn't bother Colton Barkley, it wasn't anyone else's concern. A name on a grave in this country weathered away faster than a cowboy's memory of home on a Saturday night in Dodge. Besides, from what she'd told of Ward, Austin couldn't blame her for hiding.

When Delta left the room, Austin and Colton talked about who they considered the true threat to folks in these parts—Buck Lawton. Spider Morris had heard word that he was holing up not more than thirty miles from town, waiting for his chance to strike. The tracks Link followed the day of Colton's shooting had turned into many, lending credence to the belief a gang was watching the town.

Austin felt like he had two rattlers within striking distance and only one bullet in his gun. No matter which way he turned, he left the path open for attack. The Texan was willing to bet Lawton's reason for not moving into town had something to do with Colton, but the pieces didn't fit together.

He worked from dawn to long after dark, always on edge. Any moment trouble might stampede in without warning.

Almost a week after the storm he caught himself arguing with his own shadow as he made rounds. What bothered him more than any outlaws was the fact Jennie wouldn't even see him. He'd reasoned that she might be afraid he'd confront her with lying. But, hell, they'd both known she was doing that long before Ward Hall came along. Or maybe she'd had such a bad time that night, the sight of any man bothered her. Austin didn't like to think about that being the case.

"Gun shy," he mumbled as he stepped into the only lighted place in town after dark, Salty's place.

Moses looked up from cleaning the tables with a rag dirtier than most floors and smiled. "Evenin', Marshal, want a drink before you call it a night?"

Austin nodded. "Only one." He'd need to be stone sober when trouble hit.

"You bet." Moses hurried across the empty room and poured a shot of whiskey. "Did I hear you say gun shy when you walked in?"

Downing the drink, Austin said, "I guess I was thinking out loud about how some folks get so afraid of something, they don't go on with their lives."

Moses appeared to understand, but Austin guessed it was a charade he'd developed for business reasons and to hide the vacant space beneath his bowler hat.

"You know, Marshal, I knew a man once who almost got scalped by Indians when he first came west back in '52. Ever'time he'd get within a hundred feet of an Indian, he'd start sweatin' and shaking and fearing he was dying."

Interested, Austin leaned closer. "How'd he get over it?"

"Changed his attitude and that's a fact." Moses spit a brown string of tobacco within three inches of the spittoon. "Married a Quaker widow who outweighed most buffalo I've seen. She already had a wagon load of the ugliest brats this side of the Mississippi. From what I hear, she never tired of reminding him how much less of a man he was than her first husband. Now ever'time he sees an Indian, he don't sweat or shake at all, just smiles and prays it's time to meet the maker."

Austin couldn't hide the smile that tickled across his face. "Thanks for the drink and the company, Moses, but I'd better be heading back."

Moses bobbed his head in agreement and picked up a broom he used mostly for swatting wasps in the summer. He leaned on the stick for support. "Good night, Marshal."

When Austin stepped out the door, a small shadow

fell into place just behind him. "Evening, True," Austin said without turning around.

"Henry said I'd find you here."

"I thought Henry left town with his folks," Austin said.

"Oh, he did, but like most of the town folks, he came back 'cause he was afraid he'd miss something. I think he figured I would have all the fun."

True's voice lowered. "Henry thinks you might be drinking too much, but I told him it weren't none of our business long as you were able to shoot straight."

Austin slowed his steps to match True's. "Tell Henry next time you see him, since you seem to be the only one who does see him, that he'd best mind his own business."

"Oh, I do tell him that, but he is just downright nosy sometimes. Like take tonight. I was thinking of finding you early and helping you make rounds, but Henry wanted to stay at the hotel and hear what everyone was talking about."

True waited until Austin asked, "And what was everyone talking about?" He wasn't really all that interested, but True's coloring of everything never failed to entertain him.

"They were all discussing whether or not Colton and Delta should go back to the ranch. Finally Colton storms in a voice loud enough to wake a few dead people that he doesn't care what they all say, he's taking his wife and going home. I think all the women mothering him at the Harvey House are getting to him."

Austin turned and faced True. "A man's got a right to do what he thinks is best for his family."

"Yeah, but that ain't all. Next, Delta invites Jennie to come and recover."

"Colton allowed this?" Austin knew Colton had sense enough to object. With Buck's gang hiding out somewhere between town and Colton's ranch, the trip would be risky at best.

"He started to object, but Delta put her hand on his arm and he turned to mush right before my eyes. Some men's brains seem to rattle loose from all sense and fall plum out of their heads when a woman touches them. I never thought it would happen to a strong man like Mr. Barkley."

"You've a great deal to learn." Austin smiled and turned toward the Harvey House. If Colton planned to leave, the marshal needed to know what time.

True shrugged. "He told Audrey he'd send Link after half his men to ride in with them, and the ranch house will have guards day and night."

"I imagine Audrey had a few objections."

"She started to, but that big farmer, Wiley, interrupted us about that time, and her brains fell out, too. I swear it must be some kind of brain-rotten plague going around town. I hope I don't catch it."

"You will." Austin laughed. "When you're older."

"I don't think so. The minute I noticed my mind starting to slip, I'd hightail it to Alaska or somewhere. I'd rather freeze to death than make a fool of myself over something Jennie's books call love."

"Jennie's books?"

"Yeah, they're something. Delta's all the time making me read them. I'm getting where I know enough words that sometimes a string of them make sense. Jennie loves that stuff about heroes and villains out in a place called the Wild West."

Austin looked at the lights of the Harvey House. "You mean those dime novels where the good guy always saves the heroine from the bad guy?"

"Yeah," True answered, running up ahead toward the house. "Hope Audrey had enough brains left to leave me a slice of apple pie out on the stove before she went walking with Wiley."

"The good guy saves the girl," Austin whispered to himself. "Damn!" That's just what he hadn't done. Maybe Jennie couldn't look at him because he'd let her down when she really needed him. He not only hadn't rescued her, he'd killed her belief in him as a hero.

Austin realized that even though he doubted there were any more heroes, he had to make Jennie believe in them once more.

Chapter
Twenty-eight

Jennie watched for signs of trouble. She kept telling herself she was safe as they moved along the road to Colton's ranch. Both the driver and Colton carried rifles over their laps, and ten men road alongside the buggy and supply wagon. Even Austin and Link scouted ahead. Yet she couldn't seem to stop shaking.

By the time the small party reached the ranch, Jennie was exhausted from waiting for trouble to strike. The day loomed dark and gloomy like her mood, and she wished she'd stayed behind at the Harvey House.

Colton's place was huge, with barns and corrals surrounding the ranch house and looking more like a small fort than a home. The rancher's strength seemed to grow as he rode onto his own land.

As he slowly climbed from the buggy, several men stopped their work to welcome him. His wave was short, but his smile genuine. "Now, don't make a fuss over

me!" he shouted. "I'm mending. To tell the truth the
bullet was worth it when you think that I was able to
talk a woman into marrying me. Some of you met her
as Mary Elizabeth, but I've decided to call her by her
nickname, Delta."

Delta smiled with pride at the consideration he gave
her.

"I'm not going to try and tell you folks there may not
be more trouble," Colton continued. "Any of you who
feel you need to can move to town until this trouble is
over, with no hard feelings on my part."

The men glanced at one another. If Colton Barkley
was willing to bring his wife to the ranch, they didn't
plan to leave.

A man who looked so much like Lincoln Raine he
could only have been his father walked to Colton's side
and silently paid his respects by tipping his hat first at
Delta then toward Colton.

"Work goes as usual, Sam." Colton didn't waste time
with small talk. "But double the guard along the fence
lines. Also, have men riding the ridge every two hours."

Jennie followed their gaze and saw a jagged ridge
running along the top of the breaks about a hundred
feet north of the buildings. A man on that point could
see for miles.

Austin stepped to the other side of Colton, agreeing
with the rancher's plans after being introduced to the
foreman.

Colton's voice suddenly lowered. Jennie barely heard
him whisper, "Get me inside while I can still walk."

Link's father and Austin put their arms beneath
Colton's coat and walked him into the ranch house.
No one but Jennie noticed that Colton's feet dragged
through the dirt the last few feet.

The rest of the day was a maze of activity for Jennie. She helped Delta tend to Colton, who didn't even bother to complain when they put him in bed and brought a tray for lunch. He ate only a few bites before falling asleep with his spoon still in hand.

Delta carefully slid the spoon away. "Tough guy," she whispered to Jennie.

"He's made of strong stuff to live through the shot he took. I only wish I were as brave."

Delta touched her shoulder. "You are. I think of you as a courageous and true friend."

Jennie laughed. "I only wish I were. I know I'm safe, and Ward can't hurt us with all these people around, but I still can't sleep at night. I lay there thinking of him waiting just outside the window."

"I know," Delta agreed. "That's why I always carry a gun in my pocket." She pulled out the derringer Colton had given her. "If I ever see him again, I think I'll shoot first and say hello second."

Jennie smiled. "Sounds like a good plan to me, but I can't see myself carrying a gun. The night I kept one in my pocket while helping with the train wreck victims, I kept thinking about what if the thing went off by accident and shot off a few of my toes."

Delta fought to keep her laughter quiet. "That would end you dancing at the next ball."

Jennie shook her head. "Who knows? It might help. I can just see the farmers fighting over who gets to dance with Jennie-three-toes next."

Both girls were still giggling when the door opened.

Sam looked apologetic for interrupting. "Sorry, ladies, but there's trouble over on the north pasture. Someone's cut the wire."

"Please don't wake him unless it's necessary." Delta

ushered Sam back out the door and onto the porch, where the marshal and several men waited.

"I figure I know what he'd say." Sam finally found his voice. "Take some men and get it fixed."

"Then do it." Delta's tone told the men her worry was with her husband's health and not cattle.

"Yes, ma'am." Sam stepped off the porch, yelling for the men to be ready to ride in ten minutes.

"You going with them?" Delta asked as she turned to the marshal.

"No," Austin answered. "I thought I'd saddle up and ride around the place. Spider seemed sure Lawton would strike here first, so if it's no bother, I think I'll hang around a few days."

"No bother." Delta smiled. "I know Colton was relieved to hear you were riding out with us. I'll have a room ready for you, and supper's at sunset."

"I'll be back," Austin answered as he turned and followed the men toward the main barn. He wanted to be back for supper not so much because of the food, but because he hoped to see Jennie. She couldn't go on acting like she could see right through him, or he'd go mad.

His efforts proved wasted, for when they sat down to dinner, Jennie was missing. She'd told Delta she was tired and needed to retire early, but Colton figured her absence had more to do with Austin.

Because Colton sent the cook with a chuck wagon out to his men on the north pasture about mid-afternoon, Delta cooked and served the meal. Unless the weather turned bad, the ranch hands would stay on the range until the job was done, rather than waste half the daylight riding to and from the job.

Colton insisted on sitting at the table. He hid his pain

well from all but Delta. As she sat beside him, he talked of his work as if Delta understood every detail.

Austin ate the meal, trying to ask Colton enough questions about Buck Lawton to figure out why the man hated Barkley so much. But Colton was no help. Austin guessed Barkley had never been a man of many words; and regarding anything about the outlaw, he seemed to have been struck deaf. Delta was also of no help. Every time Austin figured he had the conversation headed in the direction he wanted, she changed the subject.

Finally Austin excused himself and went for a walk. As he'd expected, he hadn't gotten more than twenty feet when True fell into step. "Evening, son." Austin smiled. "Haven't seen you around much today."

"I rode out in the supply wagon. Since then I've been scouting out the place. It don't do to let too many folks know you're around before you find a few places to disappear into."

"Have any supper?"

"Sure, over at the bunkhouse. Link even told me I could sleep on the top bunk, but I think I'll take the room across from Colton and Delta. She said I could have it as mine for as long as I wanted. Imagine that, a place just for me."

"Imagine that," Austin echoed, knowing how unbelievable that must be to a child like True.

"There's gonna be big trouble, ain't there, Marshal?" True lowered her voice slightly.

"I'm afraid so, son."

"And all because of a woman," True added.

Austin stopped in his tracks flabbergasted that True could find something out when he couldn't. "What woman . . . Delta?"

"No." True giggled. "Delta didn't start this hatred

between Mr. Barkley and that outlaw. Mr. Barkley's first wife did. Seems she wanted to run away with Buck Lawton when he got through with his business, which was robbin' trains."

Austin looked doubtful. He'd known True too long not to question the honesty of anything the child said. "True, are you sure about this?"

"Sure as I'm living. If I tell you what else I know, will you promise to keep me with you if trouble starts? I care about the women, but if there's going to be shooting, I'd rather be behind you."

"Tell me what you know."

"Promise."

"I promise," Austin answered.

True smiled like a gambler who'd just found himself in a front-row seat for the state prize fight. "There ain't all that much to tell. Mrs. Barkley, the first one of course, ran off planning to meet Buck Lawton." As if to verify the story True added, "I heard the hands talking at the bunkhouse during supper."

The Texan slowly started walking as he waited for True to continue.

"Well, Mr. Barkley got real mad when he seen she was gone, and he hightailed it out after her. One man said it wasn't three hours later when he brought her back. Talk was he locked her in her room, and come dawn he was out at the barn building a coffin."

"Do they think Colton killed her?" Austin couldn't believe he was asking the child's opinion.

"No. One fellow said something about how she probably took her own life. Another said that the ride and all might have hurt her somehow 'cause she was pregnant."

"Didn't they ask?"

"No." True's eyes sparkled as imagination found a

plot. "Maybe Colton is a witch. I heard tell witches can be men with black hair and gypsy eyes. Henry says you can't kill a witch by shootin' them in the gut, neither. Maybe Colton put a curse on his wife and killed her that way, then poured frogs' blood or something in the men's food so they wouldn't ask no questions. That's why to this day they're still sitting around trying to guess how she died."

"True!" Austin fought down a laugh. "Stick to the facts."

"How do you know I ain't telling the facts? He buried her out there beneath those three crooked elms. I'll bet they make a witch's cross in moonlight. I might just hang around till the next full moon and see if a ghost walks over the grave. Spirits do, you know, if they're killed by a curse. I know that for a fact."

"We'll see." Austin laughed. If he saw Colton's first wife walk over her own grave, he'd arrest the man himself.

As they circled back toward the house, True pulled on the marshal's sleeve. "Don't forget your promise. If trouble comes, I'll find you, but you have to let me stay with you."

Austin tousled True's hair. "I wouldn't want you any- where else but with me, partner."

"Good, 'cause trouble's coming. I can smell it in the air," True said, using one of Spider Morris's favorite sayings. "Just before supper a ranch hand came in asking if some men could help him come morning round up horses that broke loose."

"That doesn't mean trouble."

"It does when things like that come in threes. First the fence is cut on the north pasture, then the horses break loose."

"And the third?"

True hesitated. "Delta told me I was gonna have to take a bath tomorrow come hell or high water."

Austin tried to hide his smile. "I see what you mean. You'd best stick close."

True saluted and vanished into the night as Austin stepped onto the back porch. He'd left through the front, but he figured if he went back this way, he'd at least pass Jennie's door.

The house was laid out in a square, with a private, unkept garden in the center. The main rooms—parlor, dining room and study—were along the front. The kitchen, washroom and sewing room were on the left, where most of the day shade from the cliffs kept the rooms cool. Colton's rooms were on the right of the house, facing the sunrise. The last section of the square had been cut into four bedrooms designed for company who weren't staying long or children. The two rooms along each wall were small with a dressing area to divide them.

Though across the hall from Jennie, Austin's room might as well have been across the county. He walked down the hall wishing he had the nerve to knock on her door. But she'd given him no indication that she'd welcome such an advance.

Everyone in the house had either gone home or retired. Austin decided he'd just look in on Jennie and make sure she was sleeping peacefully. He had reached for her doorknob when he realized he might frighten her. After a moment of hesitation he moved down the hall to the bedroom next to hers.

Austin passed silently through the empty bedroom, following a light shining from the dressing area.

As he slowly pushed the door open a few inches, he

froze at the sight before him. Jennie was sitting in a copper tub of water. Several candles lit the room to a yellow glow. Steam from the water made the air seem thick enough to grasp. Her ebony hair was piled high, and her skin glowed in the soft light.

For a moment Austin just watched. He couldn't remember ever seeing anything so beautiful in his life. An artist could have never captured the beauty of her slender neck and back as soapy water trickled over her flesh.

While he watched, she stood. Without bothering with a towel, she took the few steps to the stack of hot bricks banking coals designed to keep water hot and the room warm. She lifted a large kettle of steaming water and poured it into her bath.

He slowly moved his gaze along her slender lines. He'd touched her in the darkness and known that she would be beautiful, but nothing as grand as the wonder standing before him.

Climbing back into the tub, she reached for the lye soap and Austin caught sight of her face. Tears streamed down her cheeks. He watched in horror as she dipped the harsh soap into the water and roughly scrubbed her body. The smell of the lye filled the thick air. She dipped the bar again and again into the water and rubbed the soap across her tender skin.

Austin looked more closely. Her skin didn't just glow with the warmth of the candlelight, it had been reddened by the soap as well. All along her body, bruises darkened just beneath the skin. Her eyes were puffy and red from more than a few minutes' tears.

Finally she stood, and Austin took a breath, thankful she'd stopped bathing. But she only moved to the small stove and gathered more steaming water. She took a moment to add cold water to the kettles for later.

He watched the same scene he'd once thought so lovely, now with a bitter ache twisting through him. Again
she poured the steaming water over her skin. Again she
scrubbed with the harsh soap as though she were washing her very soul. Again she cried.

"Jennie," he whispered, feeling in his heart every
stroke made over her flesh. "Jennie, stop!"

She looked up, for a moment not believing she'd heard
her name.

Austin appeared from behind the door. "What are you
doing?" His words were kind as he took the soap from
her hand.

"I can't get clean," she cried. "I can't get clean."

Austin didn't care if he got wet. He didn't care if he
woke the whole house. He pulled her from the tub and
lifted the kettle in one hand.

The water tested warm as he poured it first on his
hand and then over her skin. Up close he could see how
raw her flesh was from the bathing. Judging from the
amount of lye soap in her bathwater, she'd been here
quite awhile.

Jennie didn't move as he washed the soap off her.
She only stared at him with huge eyes.

Grabbing a towel from the shelf, Austin wrapped it
around her. "Stay here," he ordered as he stormed across
the hall and grabbed a bottle of lotion someone had left
in his bedroom.

When he returned, Jennie hadn't moved, but she was
shivering. He carried her into her bedroom and jerked
one of the quilts from her bed. Before putting it over
her shoulders he rubbed the lotion on her back and
arms. With the blanket resting over her, his large hands
quickly moved up and down her body spreading lotion.
He knew if he didn't do something quick, her skin would

be so dry in places it would be cracked and bleeding by morning. All pleasure of touching her was forgotten in his haste.

"There," he said as he wrapped the quilt tightly around her. "That'll help."

She stared at him with tear-filled eyes. Feeling as though she'd reached the bottom pit of her world, she realized that somehow he'd found her.

"Jennie," he whispered. "Everything's all right, Jennie. No one is going to hurt you."

"Promise you'll come if I need you," she whispered. "Promise."

"I promise," he answered as he held her. "I'll watch over you for as long as you need me."

She cried softly against his shoulder. "I can't get clean." How could she tell him that no matter how hard she scrubbed she could still feel the touch of Ward's hands clawing at her body?

"You're clean, Jennie." Austin's words interrupted her thoughts. "I'm here if you need me."

As she forced her grief into a darkened closet of her mind, Jennie realized she'd lived through the attack and must go on with her life. "I'm afraid," she whispered, remembering her family, who'd always said she couldn't survive alone. "More afraid than I've ever been."

Austin swore in frustration. He was never any good at talking. Fighting was much more to his liking. But how could he fight a memory of what she'd gone through? How could he fight past pain?

He looked at her, so beautiful all wrapped in a quilt, with her hair clinging around her face in damp, soft curls. What could he say to her that would make her feel better?

"Jennie," he whispered, but she didn't look at him.

Slowly he lifted her in his arms and walked over to the room's only chair, a rocker. He sat down with her and rocked back and forth. Where was the strong fighter he'd met on the train, the compassionate woman who'd stayed up all night helping during the train wreck, the warrior who'd been willing to lie to him forever to save her friend?

As he rocked, her body slowly relaxed in his arms. He pulled her close against his chest. "Come back to me, Jennie," he said over and over, like a prayer.

After a long while her arm slid up around his neck and her head rested on his shoulder. But when he said her name, she didn't answer. She needed time to think and heal, but she couldn't deny the tender way he held her, making her feel cherished for the first time in her life.

Long afterward she fell asleep wishing he could reach her . . . wondering if he'd be able to help even if he did. Maybe he'd done all he needed to do. He'd held her.

Chapter
Twenty-nine

*J*ennie awoke long past dawn. The pale light of day ambled lazily into the room as though only planning a temporary visit. When Jennie moved, the quilt tumbled around her, mingling with the memory of Austin coming to her bath the night before.

Crossing to the window, she remembered how he hadn't tried to kiss her or make love, yet all his actions had silently whispered of loving. He'd rocked her in his warm arms until she felt safe, with all the pain of the attack melting from her mind. She'd thought of telling him how much he meant to her, but the days without sleep had finally overtaken all reason, and she'd slumbered so soundly she hadn't even felt him lift her into bed.

Now, looking at the gray, brooding sky, she wished she'd told him how she felt. He'd sailed like a dream lover through her fears and brought her to rest on tranquil shores. The night had been a passing, a healing, that she'd needed.

Jennie scrambled into one of her two dresses that weren't uniforms. She hadn't worn her calico since the dance, but the cotton still felt soft against her skin, and the layers of petticoats brushed warm over her legs. Combing her hair, Jennie let it hang free, for within she felt a new freedom building.

When she looked in the mirror, she liked the person looking back. Not the dress and hair, but the eyes. She'd had her days of feeling sorry for herself and wishing she could run back home, but now was a time to realize she was a survivor. She wasn't some mousy, homely sister who'd always need others to make decisions for her. She'd faced evil and won.

Squaring her shoulders, Jennie opened the door, ready to face the world.

But the world didn't seem ready for her. The house was quiet. She walked from room to room expecting to find Delta or Colton and a few of his men behind every door she opened. But the already drab house seemed even more so without the sound of voices. Even Austin's room looked like it hadn't been occupied all night.

Finally, Jennie pulled on a light shawl and went out onto the long front porch that ran the length of the house. The breeze was cold, encouraging her to stay close to the house and out of its path. The only sound she heard was the creaking whine of the porch swing as it twisted like an old man in the lazy wind. Bubbling blue-gray clouds hung so low they almost touched the roof of the barn. A whistling sound whispered of a storm brewing in the sky far above her.

The yard was empty. No ranch hands moved between buildings. No idle talkers on the front porch of the bunkhouse. No men in the corral. Everyone had vanished, leaving Jennie alone.

Refusing to allow panic to overtake her, Jennie fought down a scream. What if everyone were busy somewhere and they all heard her yell like a frightened child in a corn patch only one row away from his mother?

She moved slowly along the length of the porch, knowing the dark calico of her dress blended with the shadows. There was a simple answer to the silence. She'd wait until someone returned. Only in a nightmare could an entire ranch population disappear without a trace.

Looking toward the barn, Jennie felt panic dance along her spine. Barn doors were never closed and bolted during working hours, yet this one looked like it was blockaded against a storm. She could feel trouble blending in the breeze even before she saw the lone barrel of a rifle poking out the loft window.

Her first thought was that Ward had found them, but that was impossible. There had to have been more than twenty men around the place when they arrived. All of them couldn't have vanished because of a lone gunman.

She paced the length of the porch. Reason told her to remain in the shadows until she knew whose hand was on the trigger of the one rifle; fear told her to scream for help and hope it arrived before a bullet.

When she reached the swing at one end of the long porch, she turned, risking another look at the rifle. Maybe it had been left there some time ago. Maybe there was no man in the blackness beyond the loft opening. But maybes were no protection to stand behind if firing started.

"Miss," someone whispered from behind her. "Miss,

stay back close to the house!"

Jennie recognized Link's voice. "Lincoln? Is that you?"
Relief filled her. She was no longer alone. "What's
wrong?"

"I don't know, but something is," he whispered back.
"Move real slow to the door and slip inside. I'll go
around back and meet you in the entry hall. Take your
time. You don't want that rifle to swing this direction."

Jennie followed his instructions. Whoever held the
rifle pointed his aim away from the house, toward the
road, so there was a good chance he hadn't noticed her.

Slipping inside, Jennie bolted the door. The house
appeared even darker than before; only now the heavy fur-
nishings and plain walls seemed stark and unwelcoming.
Colton had built the house to stand as a fortress with
waist-high windows and thick walls. Today the windows
seemed even smaller and the walls felt as though they
were closing in.

Link almost ran into her in the shadows.

"Where is everyone?" She grabbed Link by the arm,
panic tightening her grip.

"Most of the hands are either on the north pasture or
trying to round up the horses someone set loose. I was
supposed to go with them this morning, but with the
cook gone, Pa told me I needed to stay and clean up.
He figured I ain't much of a cook, but I could haul wood
and water for you and Mrs. Delta."

Link's thin body jerked with nervousness, reminding
Jennie of a willow facing a full gale. "After Colton and
Mrs. Delta decided to take a morning nap, I curled up
on the cot in the supply room and fell asleep. When I
woke up, I looked out the window. Two strangers were
dragging one of the hands into the barn. I watched them
from the corner of the house until they disappeared

inside. I was headed in to check on Mr. Barkley when I noticed you walking right into a trap."

Before Jennie could ask more questions, they heard several horses approaching fast. Jennie moved to the parlor window, with Link a half step behind.

Two strangers ran from the barn. "How'd it go?" one yelled to the leader of the riders.

"Just as expected," the rider answered. "We won't be seeing any of Barkley's men before nightfall."

"Good. We've got everyone around here tied up except Barkley and his wife. He's too shot up to give us any trouble. Wanta go in with us to get them?"

One of the men on horseback grunted. "I don't much like the idea of killing her, too. Buck's feud is with Barkley, not his wife."

The head rider climbed from his saddle. "If you got any objections, J. D., maybe you'd best take it up with the boss. He's got his reasons; and with the money he promised, I can drink my conscience clean."

Link moved to the other window in the parlor. "We've got to do something."

"Are you armed?" Jennie whispered.

"No," Link answered. "But we can lock them out. Every window in this place has got shutters that bolt from the inside."

"But they'll see us."

"Then we'll have to act fast. I bolted the back of the house earlier. Except for your bedroom and where Mr. and Mrs. Barkley are, the place is closed up."

Jennie looked at the window before her. She'd have to shove up the glass and reach way out to pull the shutter in. They'd never be able to close all six windows running along the front of the house without being shot. The men were not thirty feet from the porch.

A question arched Link's eyebrow. "Do we give it a try or give up?"

Jennie glanced at the men. They were a gutter lot, scraped from the charred bottom of humanity. Everyone of them looked as if he would kill her and Link without blinking.

"We give it a try," she answered. "When I say now, we both move at once. Then maybe they'll only have time to shoot one of us."

"Great plan." Link's smile didn't hide his fear. "Wish I had a better one."

Jennie slowly slid the glass up into its casing. As she opened her mouth to say "Now," something darted across the space between the corral and the barn.

One of the men saw it also. "Damn," he yelled and started running toward the corral. "It's that kid. He was the hardest to catch and now he's got untied."

The men on horseback climbed down, laughing. "Can't keep up with one that size, Red. You'll be facing hell when Lawton gets here."

The other men hooted and yelled as if they were watching a horse race.

"Now," Jennie whispered as she leaned from the window and pulled the first set of shutters closed. Link did the same.

They ran to the dining room. As Jennie pulled the second set shut, she noticed that the men had moved toward the barn and were taking bets on how long it would take Red to catch True. There was no doubt in her mind who the child was, and she almost felt sorry for Red for wasting his time. True could outrun a jackrabbit on hot sand.

As she and Link shoved the locks on the third set, Jennie took a deep breath for the first time in several minutes. "We're safe," she whispered.

"Mr. Barkley's room!" Link answered, breaking into a dead run down the hall.

Jennie was right behind him when he opened the bedroom door. Colton slept quietly atop the covers with only a lap quilt for warmth. He was fully dressed except for his boots. Delta sat beside the bed, unaware of any trouble.

"What's wrong?" she asked the moment she saw their faces.

"Trouble!" Link yelled. "Bolt the windows!"

Colton jerked full awake, gripping his abdomen in pain as he paid for his fast action. "What?"

Delta's hand moved to his shoulder as Jennie and Link crossed the room and took care of the windows. "We're not sure what's happened or where everyone is," Link said, "but some men were headed toward the porch planning to kill you."

In fear, Delta's face drained of all blood, but Colton didn't even look surprised.

"Impossible," he answered. "I've men on guard. We would have heard shots."

Looking ill at ease in arguing with his boss, Link glanced at Jennie for help.

"There's a man with a rifle up in the barn loft. We saw seven, maybe eight others, and none of them were your men." Jennie looked straight at Colton. "They're here to kill you and Delta."

Colton nodded and gripped Delta's hand resting on his shoulder. "Link, there's a rifle in my study and a Colt in the middle drawer."

"Yes, sir," Link responded and vanished.

"Delta." His words softened as he looked at his frightened wife. "My gunbelt's in the wardrobe. Get it and load both guns."

He looked at Jennie. "Can you shoot?"

Jennie shook her head. "No." She silently promised the Almighty that if she got out of this alive, learning to shoot would be her first priority.

Delta returned. "I can use a gun."

"So can I," Link answered as he ran back into the room. "Whatever we do, we'd better do fast. I looked out the front and saw three more strangers ride in."

Colton took a deep breath and pushed himself to the edge of the bed. "Did one of them have a scar streaked across his cheek?"

"I didn't notice," Link answered. "You want me to go back and check?"

"No. It doesn't matter. I know he's here." With a grunt of pain, Colton reached beneath the bed and pulled out a tray loaded with rifles and boxes of bullets.

"There's only two doors they can come through. Link, you and the women stay in the back watching the kitchen door. You'll be safer there. There's slits in the shutters, so shoot at anything that comes within ten feet of the back door. I'll take the front."

Delta started to object, but Colton added, "With the solid door, I can handle the front alone, but I have to know my back is safe. I'm banking my life on no one getting past you and Link." He handed Jennie one of his Colts and a box of shells. "We'll consider this your first lesson in how to shoot. Can you load this?"

Jennie nodded as she fumbled with the weapon, dropping several bullets on the bed as she tried to load.

Colton looked at his wife and whispered, "Lawton might come in both directions at once, so make sure you've got plenty of rounds. Turn the kitchen table over. It'll protect you if they storm the back door." He took a breath and fought back the hurting in his gut. "I don't know how many there are, so stay in the kitchen no matter what you hear from the front."

Delta looked as if she might argue, but she knew there was no time. Colton's orders continued in his cold rapid-fire manner. "Take Link and go get ready. Jennie will help me get in position in the front hallway, then join you."

Delta, her arms filled with rifles, stopped in the doorway to their bedroom and turned back to her husband. "No matter what happens," she whispered, "I'll never regret marrying you."

Colton stood slowly. "And, madam, whether we live through this or not, I'll never stop loving you."

Delta almost ran from the room, but not before Jennie saw the tears tumbling from her eyes.

"You've made her very happy." Jennie smiled at this hard man called Barkley. Without another word she handed him the Colt she'd loaded.

"I hope I haven't just sentenced her to death by making her my wife."

Jennie went to his side and allowed him to lean on her as they moved to the front hallway. "The other reason I wanted her in the back," he whispered between clenched teeth, "is I didn't want her to see me shot. If I'm lucky, they'll kill me and leave her be."

The first pounding sounded just as Jennie pulled a chair up for Colton to sit in so he could face the front door. She had no time to think of his words. They both froze until the pounding stopped.

"We've got a few more minutes until they figure how to break in. There's no use my hiding behind something. I could never get up and down to fire. Bring the rest of the guns in, and I'll show you how to load them."

Jennie ran back to his bedroom for the rifles. She could hear Colton checking the weapons as she returned. His cold manner didn't change as he showed her how to load each weapon. He was as hard as ever, looking as though he'd been steeling himself for this moment for years.

"When they come," he ordered, "run for the back. Don't look back at me. Keep a pistol in your hand just in case they kill me. You'll have six shots to hit anyone chasing you." He rammed his fingers into his vest pocket and handed her a small two-shot derringer matching the one he'd given his wife. "When they take us, keep this in your pocket. If they kill me first, I won't be able to help Delta. If they follow you to the back, don't let them take her alive."

Jennie accepted the small weapon. "Are you saying I should shoot her?"

Colton nodded once, his dark eyes dead serious. "If you're her friend, you won't allow them to hurt her."

"I can't." Jennie couldn't believe he'd ask such a thing of her.

"I've heard of these men. Most of them escaped with Lawton from prison. If you care anything about Delta, you'll not let her suffer."

Before Jennie could answer, rounds popped in rapid succession from the back of the house. Within a minute, something heavy slammed into the front door, rattling the front wall with its force.

Jennie curled behind Colton's chair and prayed every prayer she could ever remember hearing. "Austin," she whispered. "Please help us!"

The heavy slam sounded again, echoed by the cry of wood being split. Colton raised his guns. "Run, Jennie!" he ordered as he cocked the weapons.

Chapter
Thirty

*T*rue ran the length of the corral and darted under the gate. The man called Red swore as he had to stop to unlatch the opening.

By the time he'd finished, True was across the open space and hiding behind the bunkhouse. The child slid into a gap between the pier and beams forming the floor of the building and crawled to where the porch had been added. Safe! No grown man could crawl between the spaces only large enough for a cat to deliver a litter in.

But safety wasn't True's goal. Getting away and finding help had to come first.

The outlaws' plans had dribbled out of Red's mouth while he'd tied the men in the barn. He told all about how they'd snuck up the dried creek bed last night and captured the men one by one. Thanks to the low clouds, the guards on the cliff above were useless. He'd bragged that Buck Lawton might let all the ranch hands watch him kill first Delta, then Colton.

True wrapped a bandanna over the rope burns that had cut into the scabs left from a week ago. No sound punctuated the pain, for there was no time for tears.

Crawling to the end of the porch, True saw Red run around the bunkhouse, his gun ready like he was chasing something as worthless as a rat.

When he disappeared around the corner, True rolled free of the building and within a blink was crawling through tall grass toward the creek bed. If these bad men could get to the ranch this way, she could escape the same way.

Reaching the hard ground of the dried creek bed, True stood and ran. The wind pushed her along as though she weighed no more than a winter leaf. She'd been the only one awake when the marshal left long before dawn. He'd said he couldn't sleep and wanted to circle the place. True had ridden with him before and knew he started and ended his circle along the creek bed. She just hoped she was running in the right direction. He could be anywhere for miles, and Lawton's men might have already overpowered him. His body might be all that was left of him.

True shoved the prospect of Austin being hurt from her mind. Her marshal would never let them catch him unaware. He was alive. She'd just have to find him before everyone else died.

Sweat and tears were starting to blind her when True turned the bend in the ghost stream's path and saw the marshal. He'd unsaddled his horse and built a fire for coffee, obviously planning a morning of solitude.

"Marshal!" she shouted and ran full-speed into his arms.

"Easy now, True." Austin wiped the hair from the child's face. "You're running like the Devil himself has got you by the tail."

"There's trouble!" True fought for air. "Men at the ranch. They have everyone tied up in the barn except for Colton and Delta."

"What about Jennie?" Austin stood and threw the saddle blanket over his horse.

True leaned forward to breathe. "I don't think they even know about her, and I haven't seen Link in a while."

Austin swung up his saddle as if it were no heavier than the blanket. "You stay here and don't come near the ranch even if you hear shooting. You'll be safe and warm enough with the fire."

"Don't leave me here!" True fought back tears. "You promised if there was trouble I could stay with you."

Kneeling down, Austin put his arm around the child. "You'll be safer here, son."

"No!" True cried. "I won't stay. Not again."

"Again?"

"My momma told me there was trouble and I should stay behind. But she never came back for me. I waited all winter and she never came back!"

Austin kicked out the fire. "How long ago was this?"

"Two winters ago. I tell folks she died, but she left with a man who had been telling her over and over how much he hated kids. They used to make me wait outside when he visited, and sometimes I waited all night."

Austin climbed into the saddle. "Are you telling me the truth?"

"I reckon," True answered, lifting a bleeding hand to him. "If I was or not, you'd still keep your promise."

Austin pulled True onto the horse. The child had more grit than any ten men he knew. "I'll take you, but you have to swear to me you'll do what I tell you."

"I swear on my mother's grave." True hugged Austin tightly, pressing tearstained cheeks against his coat. "That is if she's dead."

Gunfire rang in the distance, and Austin kicked his horse into action.

Chapter
Thirty-one

*P*ounding hammered against the door again and again while shots rang out continuously from the back of the house. Delta and Link must have been firing at anyone trying to come near the back door.

Colton remained still, saving his energy for when needed. "Run!" he ordered Jennie again. "Get back to Delta before they break in."

Jennie gripped the Colt in her hand and ran toward the kitchen. Delta and Link might need her help. There were only two ways into the house, and she had to do her share in protecting one.

Two ways in! Jennie suddenly felt her blood freeze like a shallow pond. There was another way into the house! Her bedroom window. Link had said he hadn't locked it.

Without hesitation, Jennie bolted toward the hallway to her bedroom. She had to close the last window. From her room an outlaw could sneak in and shoot them all in the back.

As she opened her bedroom door, a man was already halfway inside. He'd shattered the glass without her even hearing it above all the other noise.

When the outlaw looked up, Jennie raised her gun, closed her eyes and fired. The revolver jerked in her hand as the bullet blasted out. She heard a crash shattering into the broken glass on her bedroom floor.

When she opened her eyes, the man was lying in a pool of his own blood, but another man was only a step behind him. One long leg already reached over the sill and into her room.

Jennie raised her gun again and closed her eyes. As she pulled the trigger, she heard Austin shout, *"No!"*

This time the jerk of the gun vaulted right into her heart. She opened her eyes in time to see Austin fall through the window onto the dead man. Her heart shattered into a million splinters as she realized whom she'd killed with her second bullet.

Jennie opened her mouth to scream, but a hand from behind gripped her mouth and pulled violently backward. With more force than necessary, the attacker jerked the gun from her fingers and dragged her toward the now open front doorway.

The outlaw didn't have to hold her so tightly; she'd lost all fight within her. She'd killed Austin. The one man she'd ever love was dead because of her. Nothing these men could do could hurt her any more than she was hurting now. The memory of Austin's strong arms blended with the sight of him lying facedown in blood.

The man holding Jennie shoved her to the floor in front of Colton's chair. When she looked up, Colton's black eyes were still filled with fight even though he no longer had a gun in his hand. His dark gaze erupted with hate as he watched the outlaws before him.

"So." A man with a thin red scar cut along his cheek paced in front of Colton. "We finally meet again."

"Get it over with, Buck. Kill me." Colton's voice was as hard as ever, daring the outlaw to finish what he'd started. "I'm not afraid to die."

"Oh, no." Lawton laughed. "I'm not going to kill you just yet. Remember the last time we met? You pulled your wife from me. I can still hear her screaming. She must have known you'd kill her. Now I plan to return the act."

"Buck!" someone yelled from the kitchen. "What you want me to do with this woman and boy we found guarding the back door? They're both wounded."

"Throw them in the barn with the others. We'll set fire to every building before we leave. I want nothing on this land remaining but Rachel's gravestone."

Lawton grabbed a handful of Jennie's hair. "She's real pretty. Not as pretty as Rachel, but I guessed you might have trouble finding another woman willing to marry you after what you did to the first one."

Colton didn't defend himself. He knew it would be useless, for Lawton's hatred had been simmering for six years. "My wife isn't here," he said simply. "If you kill this woman, you'll be killing her needlessly."

"Of course, I'd expect you to say any lie." With a fistful of hair, Buck Lawton pulled Jennie to her knees. "I didn't get a good look at her the other night by the road. One of my men fired too soon. I was real worried you'd die before I had the pleasure of killing you."

Lawton twisted Jennie's face upward. "How about I cut her open like you did Rachel? That's how you killed her, isn't it? You told her she couldn't leave with your son, so you cut him out of her and let her bleed to death."

Colton shook his head.

"Don't try to deny it. I figured it all out for myself. Too bad for me the baby died, too, or I would have had the fun of letting you watch him be butchered today also. Or was it a girl, Barkley, that you wanted so badly you dragged your wife from my arms?"

Colton didn't answer. Lawton's patience was at an end. He shoved Jennie to another man behind him. "Take them outside. I want enough light for him to see me kill her slowly. You'll go to hell with her screams in your ears."

Lawton gripped her chin between his fingers and twisted her face to him. "You are Mrs. Barkley, aren't you?"

Jennie knew she could deny she was Colton's wife, but she doubted the outlaw would believe her. And if he did, he'd only go to the barn, get Delta, and kill her instead.

Jerking free of his hold, Jennie stood tall. "I'll not deny it." She almost spit the words at Lawton. If she were to die, then so be it. She'd not put Delta through any more, and she'd not beg and cry for her own life before these scum. What did it matter anyway if she lived? She deserved to die for killing Austin. He'd come to save her just like a hero in her books, and she'd shot him.

Two men held Colton up between them and dragged him from the house to the center of the yard. The wound along his abdomen had reopened and was bleeding once more. His blood left a trail, but he didn't make a sound. They pulled his head back so that he was forced to watch what was happening.

"Do you hate me so much," Colton asked, "that you'd kill an innocent woman?"

Lawton brushed his gun barrel across Jennie's stomach. "Is that what you think this is all about? You're a fool, Barkley. I wanted Rachel, but there are other women in this world. I'm going to kill the second Mrs. Barkley to pay you back, but whether I do it fast or slow depends on you."

Colton's eyes darkened from stormy anger to black hate. "What's your price?"

"You act as though you don't know." Lawton moved closer to Colton's face. "We've played this game long enough. You know what I came for. You took it from me when you took your wife. What I've waited to collect for six years." A touch of insanity blended in his laughter. "The money from the train robbery is my price. Rachel left with the bag in her hand. Maybe she valued it more than me. Maybe she knew I'd come after it, if not her. Since I can't have her back, I'll take the money we collected off the train."

"I know nothing of the money."

"The hell you don't!" Lawton screamed. "You'll remember where the money is or we're going to kill this lady of yours real slow and painful. We'll make her scream so loud, Rachel will hear it from her grave, and I'm willing to bet your memory'll return."

The man holding Jennie had released all but her arm. He was pacing in one spot, and she remembered him as the one called J. D., who'd objected to the killing of a woman. She'd shown no sign of resisting, so he'd thought his job easy. His eyes glassed over with greed when he heard about the bag of money Colton had.

Barely moving her arm, Jennie slid her hand into her pocket and felt the cool steel of the derringer.

As she pulled the gun free from the calico, one decision flickered through her mind. Did she turn the gun on herself or Lawton?

"I'll explain someday," she whispered in prayer. A heartbeat later she swung the gun toward Lawton and fired both rounds straight into his chest.

He looked at her with total shock, then crumpled in the dirt like a straw doll. The men holding Colton dropped him and ran to Lawton.

Jennie hurried to Colton's side and put his arm around her shoulder. Using all her energy, she pulled him into a sitting position before glancing back at Lawton's gang.

For a moment she saw the outlaws for what they were, a pack of wolves left suddenly without a leader. They were greedy, heartless killers without direction. As they realized Lawton was dead, they turned like a hungry pack toward their prey.

She faced her death as they all lifted their guns. At least she'd stopped Lawton. At least her end would be fast. Closing her eyes, she heard the guns fire and waited for the bullets to rip through her body.

But pain didn't come.

She looked up and watched the men in front of her fall one at a time as gunfire scattered the dirt all around her.

"Help me up!" Colton ordered, hurting her with his grip on her shoulder. "We have to get out of the line of fire."

Jennie pulled him to his feet and half-carried him toward the porch. As she passed the steps, she saw Austin crouched low, with True behind him loading guns as fast as the marshal emptied them.

"You're alive!"

Austin continued to fire, trying to provide a cover for her and Colton.

"Well, he won't be for long if you don't stop bothering a man while he's shooting!" True yelled, then ducked. A bullet shattered the wood along the porch railing. "We ain't got time to visit now!"

Jennie helped Colton up the steps and behind the railing. "Get me my guns!" he ordered.

She scrambled to do as he asked. When she returned, she rolled shoulder to shoulder with Austin, who had stopped to trade guns with True.

"True, you should be inside." Jennie wanted to say so much more, but now was not the time.

"I'm safer here with the marshal."

Austin smiled and winked at the kid. "I know I promised, but I need you to do something real risky. Do you think you could sneak around and cut free some of the others in the barn? We can't hold Lawton's men off for long."

True smiled. "I can handle that easy." The child ran into the house, picking up several of the guns before vanishing toward the back door.

Jennie touched Austin's arm. "I thought you were dead."

"Lucky for me you're not much of a shot." He touched the hole on his sleeve. "Just before I fell, I saw the man behind you and thought it better if he figured I was done for."

"But the blood?" She touched his blood-soaked shirt.

"That's from the first man you shot, who wasn't so lucky."

He pushed the reloaded gun into her hand. "Time to practice your aim. Try to remember who the bad guys are and keep your eyes open. If you can't shoot straight, shoot often. Maybe you'll get lucky and hit something."

Jennie raised the weapon.

Chapter
Thirty-two

Jennie fired until her gun was empty, certain she hadn't shot a thing except the window out of the bunkhouse.

As she reloaded, she glanced at Austin. His aim was sure and true as he fired round after round. He was doing what he did best. The fact that his life was in danger didn't seem to bother him overly.

The outlaws had scattered around the buildings. They'd jump out from hiding and fire a single round without aiming, then return to safety.

Jennie put her hands over her ears. She'd never been around guns much, and the sound of both Colton and Austin firing at once rang in her mind as if someone had installed a huge bell.

Glancing at Colton, she wondered how the man was still moving. The left side of his shirt was covered in blood from his wounds reopening, but his grip on the Colt seemed granite.

Suddenly shouts came from the barn. The huge doors

flew open, and Colton's men stormed out like rescuing cavalry in one of her dime novels. The remaining outlaws surrendered without another shot being fired. As quickly as the storm had started, it stopped, leaving the smell of sulfur and blood clouding the air.

Austin stood and helped Jennie to her feet. "It's over, darling," he announced as he watched Colton's men rounding up the outlaws. "My job here is finally over."

She could still hear the ringing in her ears. Looking out across the dusty yard, she saw Delta running toward the house, her skirts fighting her progress.

"Colton!" she screamed as she passed the hitching post. "Colton!"

Jennie looked at Barkley. He stood despite the pain and smiled as his wife cried his name. Using his hand, he tried to cover the blood on his shirt. When she reached him, she hugged him wildly, crying and laughing at the same time.

"I thought you were hurt," he said questioningly in his rough voice.

"It's nothing." Delta didn't stop hugging him as she raised her arm, bandaged between her elbow and wrist with what looked like a row of cotton lace from her petticoat.

Colton buried his head on her shoulder, and Delta held to him so tightly even death would have been afraid to claim her man.

"Easy." Austin touched Delta's shoulder, making no real effort to pull her back. "You'll squeeze out what little blood's left in him."

Others joined them on the porch. Barkley put his arm around his wife, the Colt still gripped in his fingers. "How many hurt, Sam?" he asked in a voice only slightly softer than usual.

"Link took a bullet in the calf, and another brushed just over his eyebrow. A few of the fellows are carrying him from the barn now. We wanted to make sure it was safe first." The foreman looked around, checking to ensure none of Lawton's men were in the house. He continued. "West was hit in the hand." Sam gave the report without emotion. He'd learned that was the way the boss wanted it. "Mrs. Barkley here has a few flesh wounds that'll need tending. The rest are just black eyes and bruises that'll heal fine."

"Send someone to town to fetch Audrey," Colton ordered. "Do what you can until she gets here. I want Link and West brought into the ranch house for care. We may have more men hurt on the range, so saddle up as soon as you can."

"What about the doc?"

"I'll put my money on Audrey." Colton motioned for Austin to lift Delta off his shoulder. "Tell the redhead the stitching she did on me didn't hold in one spot."

"Yes, sir," Sam answered. "I'll send men to check on the lookouts and the others."

"Tell them to get in as soon as they can." Colton tried to straighten. He'd been very lucky to have only lost a little blood. "It'll be raining by sundown." With his last words he almost fell into Sam's arms. The tall foreman lifted his boss and looked at Austin.

"If you've got a few men ready to ride," Austin shoved his guns back into his holster and moved off the porch, "I'll take care of these outlaws. We've got a jail just waiting for the likes of them." He glanced back at Jennie. "I'll be back. We need to talk."

True appeared at Jennie's side, hugging Jennie's skirt as they watched Austin move away and Sam carry Colton into the house. "Were you afraid?" True asked.

"Yes," Jennie whispered.

"Not me," True lied. "I've been in tougher spots than this one and made it through. One time I was in the middle of this gunfight and all I had was a knife."

"True!" Jennie smiled at the child. "Could you finish your tale later over a meal? Right now I need to help Delta."

"You bet," True answered. "Only this is the truth, I reckon."

Jennie nodded. "When you finish the story, we'll talk about a bath."

True tried to pull away, but Jennie grabbed the ragamuffin by the shoulder. "No one as brave as you are needs to be worried about a little water."

"I'm not afraid of nothin'."

"Prove it!" Jennie challenged.

Three hours later, after helping Delta make Colton as comfortable as possible and tending several minor wounds, Jennie dragged the copper tub to the corner of the kitchen, near the stove. Before True finished the meal, Jennie started heating water for the child's bath.

"I ain't stripping in front of everyone," True complained.

"There's no one here but me," Jennie answered as she pulled off the child's coat. "If someone comes in, all I have to do is pull this blanket across and you've got all the privacy needed." She lapped a quilt over a rope she'd strung between a hook on the fireplace and the top of a kitchen window. "But I'm keeping you in the same room with me because I'm not taking any chances of you not scrubbing down to the hide."

Uninterested in True's complaining, Jennie stripped off the first layer of clothes. Most of the dirt came with the garments. Shirt and pants came next, along with shoes that looked like they were three sizes too big for the child.

"Now, pull those long johns off and step into the tub."

True slowly did as told, swearing every step of the way in broken curses. Climbing into the tub, the child covered her eyes waiting for the water to hit.

But Jennie just stood there, the bucket high in her hands looking as if she'd been frozen in mid-chore. True parted her fingers and opened her eyes. "Well!"

"You're a girl!" Jennie whispered.

"Don't make no crime out of it. A fellow can't do nothing about that."

Jennie set the bucket down. "True, you're a girl. All this time we all thought you were a little boy."

"I liked it that way. Folks leave a boy alone, but if they know you're a girl, they think they got a right to see to your raising."

Jennie laughed suddenly. "We've got a little while before Audrey gets through tending Colton. When she has time, are we going to have a surprise for her!"

True groaned as the water hit the top of her head full force. Jennie took to bathing the child as she'd taken to shooting. Full force and deadly.

An hour later not even True's own mother would have recognized the child. Jennie had combed her hair and dressed her in a white shirt. True had refused to wear a dress, so they'd compromised with a pair of Link's long-outgrown pants that were at least clean. Without the layers of clothes she looked so thin Jennie didn't see how she could be more than six or seven at the most.

When Audrey arrived with Austin and Sheriff Morris, True stayed in the kitchen, embarrassed by her new outfit. No matter how many times Jennie told her she was pretty, True didn't change. She'd learned a long time ago that girls couldn't have half the fun as boys. She sat quietly at the table and drank her milk, silently plotting her escape. She'd be on the next train, before Jennie had time to burn her traveling clothes.

Audrey went straight to Colton's room and ordered a bottle of whiskey delivered and shooed everyone out but Delta.

When Austin and Spider entered the kitchen, Morris smiled at True, but Austin paid her little attention. He wasn't in the habit of talking to children, and little girls had always made him nervous. He could usually think of even less to say to them than he could to little boys. True, of course, was the exception; he could talk to that boy all day and still wonder who was learning more by the conversation.

"Want a cup of coffee?" Austin asked Spider as he moved to test the pot resting on the corner of the stove.

"Sure." Spider sat down beside True. "How you doing, kid?"

"Fair," True answered. "I've had better days. The gunfight wasn't so bad, but the bath liked to killed me."

Spider laughed, and Austin sloshed coffee over his hand. He yelled and turned toward the table in disbelief.

"Who are you?" Austin slammed the hot pot down and moved to stand beside the little girl who sounded so much like True.

Spider looked up in disgust at Austin. "How long you going to deny this child, McCormick?" Spider's voice was sharp. "She's about the bravest, cutest little girl I've ever seen."

"Girl!" Austin felt like his brain was full of coffee grounds. "Girl!"

"Oh, stop the farce. You know True is your child, and I think it's pretty low of you and her mother to let the kid run around half-wild."

"Father?" Austin rubbed his hand through his hair. He had to think. Hell, he had to say more than one word at a time. Slowly he looked from True to Spider Morris and said, "I'm her father? I'm True's father?"

Spider got up to get his own cup of coffee. "I know that, son. I've known it for days, but I figured how a man and his woman raise their kid was none of my business."

Austin stared at True, who raised both eyebrows and grinned like an innocent angel. Austin looked back at Spider. "I guess you know who the mother of my child is?" Austin was afraid to guess at this point.

"Of course." Spider handed True half a cup of coffee and smiled as she added half milk. "I think Jennie Munday would have been a great mother. But you never know, when the father of her child ain't willing to give her his name."

Curiosity shoved astonishment aside. "Who told you all this?"

Morris shrugged. "True told me some. The rest I just put together. When you got all the pieces, it ain't hard to figure out the whole picture. Only thing I ain't got figured is why you haven't married Jennie."

Jennie stepped through the door as he finished. All she heard was her name. "What?" She smiled at both lawmen. "Oh, you've discovered my little surprise." She'd hoped to tell them about True first.

Spider turned on her like a first-year lawyer in a murder case. "Are you or are you not the mother of this child, Jennie Munday?"

Jennie glanced at Austin, knowing he could prove she

wasn't. He alone knew she'd been a virgin the night she'd come to his bed.

Austin didn't know what to say. If he told Spider she couldn't be True's mother, he'd be dishonoring their private love. If he didn't tell, he'd have to stand by and let Jennie defend herself.

She looked to him for help, but he remained silent, unsure of what she wanted him to say.

After a long moment she turned to Spider. "I'm no more this child's mother than Austin McCormick is the father."

Spider slapped his hands together and hooted louder than a pack of wild coyotes. "That's what I thought. I'm not as easy to fool as you young people might think."

Jennie threw her hands up in disbelief. "Come on, True. I'm putting you to sleep in a real bed tonight, and don't you dare even think of bedding down in the barn after I got you all cleaned up." She pulled True through the room.

True swore as loud as she could over Spider's laughter.

"And quit that language, son!" Austin yelled. "I mean, young lady." He looked at Spider, but the old man just shook his finger and nodded his head like they were connected with a string and only operated in unison.

Austin glared at Morris. "Hell, I call True son the same way you call me son. I don't mean blood kin."

"Sure you don't." Spider giggled like an old gossip telling a lie.

"You've lost your mind, old man." Austin turned his back to the sheriff. "If I'm True's father, I'm hereby declaring you her grandfather. How do you like that?"

"That's just fine with me, son. Your mother didn't happen to be a black-eyed, fiery miss who lived in El

Paso about the time of your birth, did she?"

"No." Austin fought to keep from smiling. "But I'd like to hear that story sometime."

Spider shrugged. "It was too long ago, and I was too drunk to remember the details even the next day."

Austin couldn't stay mad at the old man. He'd grown to care for him and would miss Spider Morris when he rode out. And he would be riding out in a few days, now that trouble was over. The fact hit him like a punch in his gut. For the first time he didn't want to leave a place three days before he saddled up.

Austin swallowed the scalding coffee and tried not to think about leaving Jennie behind.

Spider grabbed his coat and shouted, "Going hunting! Want to come along?"

"It'll be raining in half an hour," Austin answered. "Whatever you're hunting can wait till morning."

"Not this." Spider opened the back door. "I've waited six years for this." He laid down his rifle and picked up the shovel by the porch.

Austin pulled on his coat and followed without asking any more questions.

THE FOLKS IN the kitchen hadn't heard Colton swear when Audrey cleaned his reopened wound.

"I declare," she said more to herself than him, "if you ain't the orneriest man alive, I'd like to meet him. You should be dead, I figure, but you're still kicking. This time when I say you'd best rest while this heals, you'd better follow orders."

"Sorry to disappoint you about dying," he said between swallows of whiskey. "It ain't from lack of trying."

Audrey took the bottle from his hand and downed a healthy gulp herself. "For medicinal purposes," she added, then handed the bottle back to Colton. "You'd best take a few more swallows."

Colton followed orders as Audrey continued. "Do you think you could stay healthy long enough for me to go over to Chicago and take the test to be a bona fide doctor?"

"You'll be back before my child is born?" Colton looked at Delta and smiled.

"I don't think I'd have to learn much more after all the practice I've had since I've been here. Some days I feel like I do more doctoring than cooking."

"What about the blood?" Delta reminded her.

"It's getting where it doesn't worry me so, after I seen how much a man," she pointed at Colton, "can lose and still keep kicking. Doc in town told me no one around would go to a woman, but I figure between the Harvey House and the Barkley ranch I could keep busy. Mrs. Gray offered to let me still live at the Harvey House. That way if the doctoring is slow, the rolls are good."

"What about Wiley?" Delta smiled, knowing how fond of the farmer Audrey had become.

A sadness crossed the tall redhead's face. "It weren't meant to be. He came by town to tell Spider Morris there was a body of a man out by an old shack next to his place. From what he said the body must be your stepbrother, Ward."

Audrey waited for Delta to react. When she didn't, Audrey continued. "Spider said he'd check on it tomorrow. He thought, if you were able, you'd ride over and identify the body."

Delta nodded slowly and slid her hand into Colton's. "I'll do that, and I'll have him buried along with that part of my life."

"What about the deed?" Audrey asked as she motioned

for Colton to take another drink.

"I'll mail it back to my mother. She can do whatever she likes with the land. I want no part of it." Delta forced a smile back on her face as she watched Audrey thread a needle. "You didn't finish telling me about Wiley."

Audrey examined the small place where her stitches hadn't held. "Wiley wasn't too happy about my heading for Chicago. I told him if he wanted me to stay, he'd best be making a declaration 'cause I was for getting on with my life." Audrey ignored Colton's groan of pain as she stitched. "The big oaf just stood there and told me his declaration was he was going to Texas."

"To Texas?" both Delta and Colton said at once.

Audrey nodded. "Said he had money to buy a ranch down there, and maybe by the time I become a doctor, he'll have the place started."

"Did you make any plans?" Delta asked.

"No." Audrey raised her head slightly. "He wouldn't talk of nothing but this ranch, and I'm not promising to wait for a man who talks more of land than love."

"I'm sorry," Delta whispered.

Audrey raised her head proudly. "Way I figure it is my Granny Gates may have been right. I heard her say once that trying to keep a man from going to Texas once he sets his mind to it is like trying to talk a body into floating upstream. I may have only *thought* Wiley was man enough for me."

Delta looked into Colton's bottomless black eyes. He was man enough for her, she thought. Man enough to be the father of all her children. Of course she wouldn't tell him that until he was well.

Chapter
Thirty-three

*R*ain poured in endless sheets against the windows of the ranch. Jennie stared out into the blackness wondering where Austin had gone. He'd hurried out of the house behind Spider Morris without a word to her or anyone else. Maybe she'd gone too far in letting folks believe he was True's father, but she hadn't started the rumor.

Everyone in the house had turned in for the night, but Jennie couldn't bring herself to go to her room. She wanted to talk with Austin. He'd said his job was through. Was that his way of saying good-bye? She pulled a chair into the warm corner beside the kitchen stove. The constant patter of the rain slowly washed away all the violence of the day, and she relaxed.

Back home it would be time to think of spring and the future. For the first time in her life she was afraid to plan, for she had no idea what awaited. She'd gone from a life of sameness to a life of change and wasn't sure which was heaven and which hell.

The kitchen door rattled suddenly, making every muscle inside Jennie tense. Spider Morris and Austin clambered in looking like two huge mud monsters.

"It was there!" Spider yelled as he tossed his hat on the floor with a plop. "Just like I told you it would be."

Austin flung a mud-covered carpetbag on the clean kitchen table. "Yeah, it was there, but I'm not sure I would have dug up a grave to get it."

Spider tried to smear the mud off his face with an even muddier hand. "I didn't bother the coffin. I wouldn't have done that without asking Barkley, even if this is official business. The bags were laying right on top of it like I thought they'd be."

Jennie could hold her curiosity no longer. "What bags? What grave?"

Austin turned, noticing her for the first time. "Jennie," he whispered, as if her name answered some prayer. She'd never seen a man so muddy, or so handsome. He had the boyish smile of an adventurer, while his wet clothes plastered against his lean, hard frame reminded her he was solid man.

Spider glanced at Austin as if deciding the marshal must be slow witted. "Evening, Jennie. Sorry to have to leave without telling anyone, but I had a stroke of genius while True was telling me everything that happened this afternoon. I figured if Lawton came all this way for the robbery money, it must still be here on the ranch. But where?" His smile reached from ear to ear. "I heard one of Barkley's men say once that Colton buried his wife in her traveling dress and even threw her bags into the grave."

"You found the robbery money?" Jennie put the puzzle together.

"Darn right I did." Spider smiled. "Now only question is who does it belong to? The gamblers around that table on the train were either killed or they're long gone by now. And since the railroad don't have any claim to the money, I guess that just leaves me."

Pulling off his coat and draping it over one of the kitchen chairs, Austin shook his head. "Every man who had anything to do with the train that day or the capture will lay claim to this money. Enough people have died for this gambling money. It would have been better to leave it buried with Rachel Barkley."

Spider twisted the leather strap. The rotting latch fell off in his hands. "I can think of a few things I'd do with this much stash. Quit sheriffing and go down to Mexico, where I could stay drunk the rest of my life on warm tequila and warmer women." He closed his eyes and allowed himself a moment to mentally picture his fantasy before continuing. "We'll fight over it later. Right now let's take a look."

Turning the bag over, Morris dumped the contents onto the table. Several gold twenty-dollar pieces rolled off, but the bulk of the loot hit the wood with a plop. Molded, decaying currency tumbled like a fallen hope before the old man.

Spider stared at the smelly pile of molding dreams without blinking.

Jennie lifted a handful of the wealth turned to rubble. "It's worthless," she whispered.

"It was never worth the trouble it caused," Austin agreed.

Spider Morris lightly brushed the decaying money and sighed. "There goes my dream of a feisty retirement.

Good-bye fiery tequila and hot-blooded women."

"I'm sorry." Jennie looked up into his disappointed face.

Spider scratched the stubble across his chin. "Now I'll have to marry some hardworking, bossy widow and stay sober the rest of my life."

"You'll live years longer." Austin patted him on the back.

"That's what I'm afraid of," Spider answered as he picked up his hat and moved to the door. "Night, folks. I'm sleeping in the bunkhouse."

As Spider closed the door behind him, Austin laughed. "He'll never talk Mrs. Gray into marrying him, but he'll be happier trying than flirting with trouble in Mexico."

Jennie suddenly felt like the room was closing in around her. She looked down at her hands and tried to think of something to say to the man who'd held her so tenderly last night and saved her life only hours later. She wasn't sure she could say good-bye to him. Maybe it would be better if he just left without a word. There was nothing to keep him in a small town like Florence, and his work didn't lend itself to hauling a wife around with his saddlebags.

Austin lifted the copper bath. "I think I'd best wash off some of this mud." He watched her with a look that seemed to say there were a thousand things he needed to tell her but he didn't know where to begin.

"I'll check on True," Jennie answered, wishing she could break down the wall that had formed between them since the gunfight was over. They both knew he'd be leaving, but somehow putting it into words seemed impossible.

JENNIE KISSED TRUE gently on the forehead and covered

her. She was sleeping like an angel, with Audrey beside her. The redhead was still fully dressed, in case Colton needed more doctoring during the night. Audrey, after several tries, had found her career if not her love. Who knows, Jennie thought, maybe Wiley would be waiting for her in Texas when she finished schooling. Audrey was a woman worth waiting for, and Jennie had a feeling Wiley would realize that fact in time.

Jennie left their door open and walked across the house to the hallway where her room was located. As Jennie passed Austin's door, she heard the sound of water splashing. The door was slightly ajar. Curiosity pulled her into his room. She almost tripped over his muddy boots as she reached the door leading to a little dressing area.

He might think his job was over and he was Texas bound, but she wanted to see him one more time. She had to hold him and tell him that now she knew heroes were real and not only in her books.

As she pushed the door open, she saw him sitting in the copper tub. Steam thickened the air as she watched him stand. He poured a bucket of water over his head and thin streams ran down his body, twisting slightly over the bulge of each muscle.

Without making a sound, she stared at him. His hair was brown with water and pulled back away from his face, making his jawline seem even stronger. As her eyes slowly moved over his body, she saw the scars from a lifetime of being a warrior. She wished she'd have time to ask him the story of each wound.

He moved suddenly, slinging water with a jerk of his head. His chest was ribbed tight down to his flat stomach. His powerful thigh blocked her view of his manhood as he reached for a towel.

Wrapping the white cloth around his waist, he turned to her. "Are you going to stand there staring all night?" he asked without changing the expression on his face, silently telling her he'd known she was there all along.

"I'm sorry." Jennie backed away. "I didn't mean to eavesdrop."

Before she could reach the door of his bedroom, Austin caught her arm and pulled her against his still-damp chest. "Don't ever be sorry for being near me," he said as he held her. "I've been waiting since the day I met you on the train to have my say with you."

"But not now." Jennie tried to pull away. She didn't want to fight when she knew they only had a few hours left before he rode toward home. She pushed past him.

Austin followed her to the door and closed it before she could escape. He captured her with his arms on either side of her bracing the door.

"Now." He stood so close she could feel the warmth of his body, but his arms didn't hold her. She could smell the soap and water warming on his skin and longed to dry all the places he'd missed. Talking to him was not what she had in mind.

When she didn't protest, he began. "First, in the matter of you always lying."

"I never lie," Jennie answered quickly, wishing she could taste his clean skin.

"Hell, woman, if lies were buttons, it would take you half a day to dress." His words softened in laughter, and his autumn eyes already darkened with desire.

Jennie saw no use in defending herself. In truth she was having trouble even remembering what he said with him standing so close. A single drop of water trailed its way down the center of his chest, and she fought the urge to follow its progress with her finger.

"Take today, when Lawton asked if you were Mrs. Barkley, you lied, knowing he planned to kill Colton's wife."

Jennie opened her mouth to protest, but he silenced her with a single finger on her lip. "I know why you did it, but it was a lie." His finger remained against her lips, caressing now. "Which brings me to the second problem you have. This willingness to die for others. Hell, woman, you're a walking sacrifice looking for an altar."

Jennie giggled as his fingers moved to her throat after tickling their way across her ear.

"You've got to put yourself first, Jennie. Now and again it has to be what's good for Jennie. What Jennie wants."

She smiled, knowing exactly what she wanted. She wanted this man before her for a night or a lifetime. Without hesitation she raised her hand and pulled the towel from around his waist.

"Now, wait a minute," Austin objected, without moving away from her or trying to stop her hands as they teased along the sides of his body. "I'm not finished talking to you yet."

"I'm finished listening," Jennie whispered as she raised her mouth to his.

The moment her lips touched his, he couldn't have remembered enough words to form a sentence. He pulled her against him and kissed her as he'd longed to do from the moment she'd tried to shoot him that morning. She'd shown him a bravery he'd thought no woman and very few men would ever have. Brave enough to face anything. Brave enough to die.

His hand slid down her back and lifted her in his arms. He carried her slowly to his bed, not breaking the kiss as he lowered her onto the covers.

"I love you," he whispered against her mouth as he pulled the clothing from her. "I've loved you since the day I met you on the train and you stood up to me." He'd never said the words before, but they seemed as natural as breathing now with her.

She pulled him down against her. "Then love me," she answered. "Love me tonight like there is no tomorrow. For you are and will always be my only love."

His strong fingers trailed slowly down her body, loving every curve. When a moment later his lips followed his fingers, she cried out softly in pleasure.

He wanted to move slowly, to make their time together last forever. But her body drove him insane with desire.

This time there was no hesitation when he entered her, no pain. She knew she was welcoming home the only man she'd ever love, and if he only stayed a night, she'd still love him for a lifetime.

They moved together in a passion born of caring. He took her to a height she hadn't known existed and brought her down cradled in satisfaction. She'd found what she came west to find—adventure, excitement and a reason for living. A man worth the loving.

THE NEXT MORNING Jennie awoke to an empty bed. She felt the place where Austin had slept, but the sheets were already cold. She slowly stood and picked up her robe. As silently as possible she crossed the hall and dressed in her own room.

Ten minutes later when she entered the kitchen, she had to fight to hide her disappointment that Austin wasn't in the room.

"Mornin'," True said between bites. "You ready to go?"

"Go?" Jennie looked from True to Spider.

Spider glanced down at his plate. "Marshal left before sunup. He said he wanted to get back to the prisoners in town. It don't seem practical to leave them with Moses too long."

"Oh." Jennie wanted to scream that he hadn't said good-bye. Or maybe he had last night. In his way.

"As soon as you're ready, I'll take you back to the Harvey House. True wants to ride along, but she's already told me she's planning on riding back later to check on Colton."

"How is he?" Jennie felt bad. She'd been so wrapped up in her own life, she'd forgotten Colton.

Spider smiled. "He's fine. Couldn't have a better nurse than Delta, and that Audrey can work wonders."

Jennie felt out of place. Suddenly she didn't belong again, the only person at a dance without a partner, and she didn't know what to do or say.

True offered her the answer. "We best hurry. I'll bet Mrs. Gray is having a time with all her girls running out on the Harvey House. She's lost about half a dozen to marriage this month already. I swear it's worse than some plague. They've probably got Henry serving meals."

"I'll be ready in a few minutes," Jennie answered as she hurried back to her room to pack. It was happening all over again. She was just an extra, not really belonging anywhere. At least she could get back to the Harvey House, where she'd always be needed.

Spider had the wagon loaded by the time she finished packing. Jennie hugged Delta good-bye, trying to smile. The sheriff, Jennie and True drove off, with every man on the place stopping to wave.

Jennie forced her head high as she rode silently along

the muddy road. She'd learned a great deal about herself. She was a survivor, and with or without Austin she'd make it. At least she'd had last night to warm her dreams for the rest of her life.

When they turned the first bend toward town, she noticed a red ribbon tied to a tree beside the road. Within a few hundred yards she saw another. Then another.

"How strange." Jennie looked at Spider, who didn't seem to see them. "My family used to tie ribbons to fence posts back home so I could find my way. I wonder if there's another person in this country who can't tell direction any better than I can?"

They passed another ribbon before Spider answered. "I doubt it. Far as I know everyone in these parts knows north from south. Otherwise they'd have been smart enough to stay back east."

Jennie watched as another ribbon came into view. "But they couldn't be for me."

"Well, they ain't for me," True chimed in from the back of the wagon. "I was born knowing directions. I could follow a map even before I could walk."

Jennie remained silent as they passed ribbon after ribbon until they were within sight of the Harvey House. There a red ribbon was tied around the door handle.

"Can't think of anyone else it could be for but you." Spider smiled as he helped her down from the wagon.

Jennie lifted the long streamer and followed it into the house. As she entered the dining room, the first thing she saw was that all the tables had been pulled back. The employees stood lining the walls, and at the end of the line was Austin.

He walked slowly toward her, smiling as though he were witnessing a dream taking form. His dream.

"I hoped you'd find your way." He held his hand out to her. "I'd hate for you to miss our wedding."

Jennie looked around at all the smiling faces. "But . . ." She couldn't believe he'd done all this for her.

He raised her left hand and slid a gold band on her third finger. "This ring will never come off, so you'll always know you're cherished."

Jennie stared at the single band of gold. "But . . ." He couldn't be doing this. Not Austin McCormick.

"Now, don't waste time." Mrs. Gray stepped forward. "If you're agreeing to marry this man, you'd best answer. We have to have these tables back in working order by the lunchtime train."

"Are you sure?" Jennie looked up into his smiling face.

"No," he answered honestly. "I just know that I can't live without you. I love you more than I thought a man could ever love a woman. I'm not sure about you being able to live with me. I don't know if I can change, but I know I'll never stop loving you."

Jennie closed her left hand around his. "There's nothing about you I'd change."

Austin smiled and fought the urge to grab her and kiss her in front of all these people. With great control he leaned near and brushed her cheek with his lips. "Plus, I feel my child's parents should be married. Don't you?"

Jennie glanced at True standing beside Spider. Dirt already creased across her nose, but her blue eyes were dancing with excitement. "Of course," Jennie replied.

Austin offered his arm. "Will you join me?"

She closed her fingers over his arm. "It's bound to be an adventure."

"That I promise," Austin answered as he closed his hand over hers.

They walked toward Spider Morris. Jennie felt as if her heart might explode. She'd found a place where she belonged. Not a state or a town, but in Austin's heart, and there she'd always be needed, cherished and loved.